Gerry Barton was born spent a number of years about Asia and England before studying anthropology and East Asian history and politics at the University of Auckland, New Zealand, leaving in 1979 with a Masters degree in archaeology. During 1980-81 he studied cultural conservation in Italy and Canada and afterwards worked as an art restorer of tribal art in New Zealand, publishing numerous articles on the subject. He is the author of *Once There Was an Empire: The Travel Diaries and Paintings of Cranleigh Barton, 1912–1937*.

Gerry Barton currently lives in West Germany with his wife and three children.

SELANGOR

Gerry Barton

CORGI BOOKS

SELANGOR

A CORGI BOOK   0 552 13560 7

First publication in Great Britain

PRINTING HISTORY
Corgi edition published 1989

Copyright © Gerry Barton 1989

This book is set in 10/11 pt Sabon

Corgi Books are published by Transworld Publishers Ltd.,
61–63 Uxbridge Road, Ealing, London W5 5SA,
in Australia by Transworld Publishers (Australia) Pty. Ltd.,
15–23 Helles Avenue, Moorebank, NSW 2170, and in New
Zealand by Transworld Publishers (N.Z.) Ltd., Cnr. Moselle
and Waipareira Avenues, Henderson, Auckland.

Made and printed in Great Britain by
BPCC Hazell Books Ltd
Member of BPCC Ltd
Aylesbury, Bucks, England

To Sabine and to Jacqui, whose enthusiasm
for the story helped me complete this book.

Prologue

10 March 1952

The Lockheed Lodestar winged northward seven thousand feet above the tropical bush-clad coastal hills of Queensland. It was the rainy season and the airliner had flown in and out of several squalls and dodged a number of dark billowing anvil cumulus formations during its flight to Cairns from Townsville. This leg of the journey was its last for the day, the flight having originated in Sydney, hopping its way up the Australian eastern seaboard to a scheduled arrival at its Cairns destination a long ten hours later.

A Lodestar of Australian Pacific Airways flew this route once a week. North on Tuesdays and south with the same aircraft on Fridays, the twin-finned airliner's time being used in the turn-around period on short haul, mainly cargo trips, around the far north. For this dual purpose the passenger seats were light and easily removed to make room for cargo if necessary.

Unaware of these finer design points, Kenneth Clouston squirmed and stretched in an attempt to ease the painful spots that regions of his cramped anatomy had acquired from the thinly padded seat during the long flight. He was one of the few remaining passengers of the full complement of fourteen who had boarded in Sydney. Some had left the aircraft in Newcastle, others in Armidale, Brisbane, Bundaberg, or Townsville. At the early stops the craft had filled each time, but after Brisbane, the airliner had departed half empty and half of these again alighted in Townsville.

Kenneth Clouston was not especially aware of the comings and goings of his fellow passengers. This annual

trip to meet the managers of the sugar cane farms con-
tracted to Dalgeish Holdings Ltd in north Queensland
was one he had still not got used to, even though he
had been doing it for the best part of a decade. Having
left Sydney at 8.00 a.m. he had spent the first hours
in looking at the agenda of the meeting, re-reading the
correspondence relating to specific problems that had
developed since the last trip, and scanning the Dalgeish
Regional Manager's speech which Kenneth was to deliver
by proxy at the opening address at tomorrow's meeting.

By midday, the incessant roar of the engines had dead-
ened his hearing and at mid afternoon he abandoned
the attempt to distract himself with an Agatha Christie
paperback and slipped into a restless slumber, broken by
landings and unexpected lurches as the airliner pulled its
way into the increasingly unpredictable air of the tropical
north.

Only half awake, his thoughts now thoroughly numbed
by the engine noise, he glanced out of the window at his
left shoulder. A change of pitch indicated that the aircraft
was descending and, below, between patches of cotton-
wool cloud, he could see the forest. Directly before and
above him reared banks of cumulus clouds. In the evening light Kenneth's torpid mind associated freely with the
view. At one moment the cumulus stacks resembled the
ramparts of huge fantastic castles, back-lit by the setting
sun; at another, surrealistic mountains riven with preci-
pices and overhanging cliffs created by updraughts, their
peaks tugged by the high altitude winds into long streamers to the south-west. From the darker canyons deep in
the cloudspace, lightning sporadically cracked down the
clefts. The tropical evening thunderstorms were perform-
ing their daily show.

The airliner slowly converged on the nearest of the
electrical storms, gradually descending as it did so. The
gently sloped foothills with their forest cover became
closer and moved under and away at an accelerated pace.
Details began to separate out and Kenneth's attention
casually registered a small flock of crested cockatoos in

the highest branches of a camphor laurel ahead. The birds started up in a quick movement of white flapping wings in startled reaction to the approaching aeroplane and fled across the forest canopy.

We're low, must be approaching Cairns, he thought. Rain began streaking the window, although the cloud precipitating it was out of Kenneth's line of vision. The view remained, the cumulus mountains now towering to his left. Framed by his window, three more white cockatoos winged across the land below, their evening communion also broken by the racketing engines powering through the gathering dusk. A flash of lightning exploded in the sky next to the airliner, blinding its passengers momentarily. Shocked by its abruptness, no one beyond the cockpit discerned the drop in air speed and the sagging of the craft's trajectory. Travelling at 200 feet a second, the Lodestar clipped the highest tree and, moments later, was a fragmented hulk at the end of a long narrow scar of broken and scorched vegetation. The wreckage of the starboard wing and engine, suspended in a shattered eucalypt, marked the point of immediate contact with terra firma. Further along the port wing and tail with its twin fins somehow still intact indicated the area of total impact, empty seats and wreckage making an awful path through casuarinas and pandanus to the rest of the fuselage, which had continued its forward momentum a few seconds longer.

The event which ended the earthly existence of Kenneth Clouston and six other souls had been brief. The diminishing peal of thunder had been eclipsed by the sound of torn metal and breaking trees, followed instantaneously by the explosion of the three-quarter-empty fuel tanks. These sounds quickly died away – a loud, ugly din out of all proportion to the brevity of its existence. Silence fell upon the new glade and its deceased occupants. Within five minutes, crested cockatoos were again in the tree tops nearby, their whiteness stark in the darkening evening as they caught the last rays of the sun stabbing through gaps in the clouds. The thunder from the towering clouds overhead rumbled repeatedly and falling light rains swept the forest.

13 February 1953

Maeve Clouston, hearing the front gate slam, looked up from her gardening activities. From the shade of frangipani she could see her daughter wheeling her bicycle up the path towards the house.

'How was the first day?' she called.

'Hello. Great. It should be a good year.' Maeve's daughter Leila lifted a string bag containing a folder and some books from the cane basket strapped to the handlebars, letting the bicycle fall to the lawn, and walked over to her mother.

'Yes, in retrospect, it was worth last year's grind to be able to do this year's papers. God it's hot isn't it?'

'It's this sort of weather that keeps me in Sydney. I never tire of the warmth and sunshine.' Looking up, Maeve focused on the creamy petals of the frangipani and the tree's elegant ribbed leaves. 'Or, for that matter, the plants that grow here. Can you smell the frangipani?'

The scent permeated the part of the garden where the two women sat. From their vantage point at the upper end of the sloping lawn in front of their home, Leila and Maeve could see, beyond the laurel hedge and the silky oaks spaced along the street, the red tile roofs of the nearest houses. The green foliage broke the orange and red geometry into a view that was genteelly rustic. Between the roofs and leaves, a few patches of the blue water of Sydney harbour sparkled in the mid-afternoon light.

Maeve had bought this house in Cremorne after Kenneth had died. The sale of the larger home in Crow's Nest, coupled with Kenneth's life insurance, had allowed her to move to a small house in an area of the city that suited her mood and temperament better – now that she was without a partner –

than the neighbourhood where they had grown together as a family.

Maeve had a comfortable income as manager of a small fashionable women's clothing shop. Her day was organized in a way that left her free from 2.00 in the afternoon. Leila was a student at Sydney University, majoring in archaeology. A minority discipline at any time, Leila formed an even more diminutive minority by being one of the few females to study the subject.

The similarity in looks between the two women had always amused Kenneth who on occasion would facetiously remark that all Leila had inherited from the Clouston gene pool was dark hair and the family's intelligence. Maeve was forty-eight years old, Leila twenty-two. They were both about five foot three, and Leila now had the womanly shape her mother had possessed in her own youth — well-proportioned, with a becoming softness to the lines of her figure. She had also inherited her mother's looks. Both had an easy open smile set in square countenances which suggested they had found a modicum of happiness and an inner understanding of the complexities of life. The women's moods always showed first in their eyes and it was the eyes that usually captured people's attention first. Maeve's brown and Leila's grey, both reflecting common sense and good-natured humour.

Maeve's fair hair was cut to a longer style than many women of her age would wear and while she retained the physical attractiveness of a younger woman, she had a dress sensed that befitted her and ensured that she would never have been dismissed as mutton dressed as lamb, but seen as a woman with taste and dignity. Leila wore her hair long and falling over her shoulders. Today she was wearing a summer frock and sandals, standard variations of the limited wardrobe she needed for the long Sydney summer.

'Have you started work already?' asked her mother, pointing to the string bag containing four or five books.

'Well, after enrolling, I went along to Professor Manson who is giving this paper on Far Eastern and Australian archaeology,' replied Leila. 'He's nice. He's about the same age as Professor Dilly whom I moaned on about all last year. He's easy to feel comfortable with. None of the condescension and pontificating Dilly always comes out with to put us in our place. I ended up spending about half an hour with Professor Manson and it was fascinating talking to him. I'm so excited I am already thinking of planning next year's dissertation around a project which he can supervise. God, when I think of some of the stuffy lecturers I've endured, Professor Manson is a breath of fresh air.'

'Apart from the fact that you've got a lecturer who seems human what's so interesting about this subject he teaches?' Maeve was enjoying her daughter's company and enthusiasm for university and asked the question more to keep her bubbling on beneath the frangipani, than in any burning desire to learn about Australian archaeology.

'You don't hear much about Australia in the archaeology course,' Leila replied. 'It's usually about British and Middle East digs and their finds. And about Egypt; the pharaohs and all that. It's interesting but it's not here. There's been a few excavations in Australia and they're talking about the Aborigines having lived here for thousands and thousands of years. Longer than the things I've been learning about such as Ur and the Valley of the Kings, Stonehenge or Mycenae. I'd like to know more about Australia. One of the things that really interests me is how the Aborigines came here originally and that's the other part of the course Professor Manson is giving. He has done a lot of work in Malaya, Sarawak, and the Dutch East Indies and he thinks they came through all those islands and places.'

Leila nudged the books with her bare foot.

'These are about the only books on the subject. Professor Manson gave me a list of texts he thought were a useful introduction to the topic and I nipped over to the library before coming home and got the ones they had. There's also some articles in journals apparently, but I'll read that stuff later on when the course is well under way.'

'Malaya is such a mysterious place,' mused Maeve, lying back and again focusing on the sight and scent of the frangipani. 'I love the sound for a start, Maa-lay-ah.'

'You and Dad lived there didn't you?' Leila said off-handedly, knowing as she asked the question that the subject was one that she had rarely heard being spoken of among family and friends and was therefore off limits for some unknown reason. Such secretiveness had only made her more curious over the years.

'Yes.' There was a silence for several seconds.

'Actually you were nearly born there,' Maeve went on. 'Or rather, you could have been born there but your father got his job in Sydney when I was four months pregnant and we settled here a couple of months before you arrived.'

Maeve looked at her wrist watch.

'Time I made a move.' She stood up and smoothed down her skirt. Looking at nothing in particular in the middle distance beyond her daughter's upturned head she said, 'I haven't thought much about our life in Malaya since you were a little girl. We left and that was that. The three years I had there were the most exciting and the most upsetting of my life. Kenneth and I found it easier never to talk about those years, more for his sake than mine, but also for the peace of our home. Once I had you I thought less of Malaya, and those years, as life progressed, became a very short time.' She walked across the grass to the path and disappeared around the side of the house.

Leila reached down to her bag of books and pulled out the nearest at hand, *Ethnology and Archaeology of the Malay Peninsula*, by I.H.N. Evans. It had a dusty and faded binding which nevertheless was almost pristine. It probably hadn't been borrowed for twenty years. Flicking to the chapters on archaeology she began to read: 'The ancient monuments of Pengkalan Kempas, Linggi, Negri Sembilan . . .'

13

That evening it was Maeve who brought up the subject of Malaya again.

'There's no reason not to talk about Malaya now that Kenneth is dead. I've been thinking about the place ever since this afternoon and it's lovely to go back to those memories. It was an extraordinary time for someone like me to go through – a young bride in a new country. Why, I can even tell you something about Malayan archaeology because my closest friend there ran a dig near where Kenneth and I lived.

'Let's have a cocktail and I'll tell you about Malaya. After purposely putting the subject out of my mind for twenty years, I think it can stand an airing. Anyway, even before Kenneth was killed, I could see that the day would eventually come when you would want to know more of your family history.'

Leila put aside I.H.N. Evans and asked, 'I don't even know when you went there or how.'

'It was in 1927. I was twenty-two. Good grief, the same age as you. What a coincidence! I knew Kenneth for two months before marrying him and we sailed to Malaya the day we got married.'

'And how did Dad get there?'

'Oh he had been there since just after the Great War.'

Chapter 1

The tropical night was paling with the coming day as Kenneth Clouston climbed a companionway to the boat deck of the P & O steamer *China*. The young man leaned against the teak railing, and with eyes shining at the novelty of the occasion, breathed deeply to drink in the early morning air. He was slender and looked a little taller than his actual five foot ten inches because of his slight build. His brown hair was cut short and neatly groomed with a parting several inches above his left ear. He had a long face with, if not arrestingly handsome features, ones pleasing enough to make him look a nice sort of a chap. Wide-spaced grey eyes under wispy brows, an almost aquiline nose and a small, well-chiselled mouth suggested a quiet personality. As he stood at the ship's rail, back straight and shoulders set, watching the sunrise, he appeared the typical example of a young British colonial about to carve himself a career in British Malaya. His unassertive middle-class London accent, however, betrayed a certain anxiety and a lack of confidence, a human hesitancy a true colonial would never have betrayed.

The *China* moved slowly along the channel towards its anchorage off George Town, the capital of Penang, Straits Settlements. Kenneth from his solitary vantage point scanned the expansive view of sea and land. As dawn swept across the scene, the sky resembled an inverted celadon bowl – a wash of pale green – which became more and more transparent as the minutes passed. To the east as Kenneth watched the spectacle of the awakening morning, the last green tints faded into a pearl

translucency, shifting imperceptibly into the palest of
rose hues as the steamer plied through the flat sea towards
its mooring. The hills of Kedah stood in sharp silhouette
against the now rose-tinted sky. From this coast a breeze
assailed Kenneth with smells and scents that confirmed
all the romantic notions he had entertained about his
destination. Heavy, almost sickly-sweet aromas redolent
of wet jungle, and dry, hard, industrial smoky smells –
both underpinned with a pungency of salt and mud of
the mangrove fringe to the coast – filled the air, their
origins evading Kenneth's sight in the blue mist which
hid the mainland lying far below the sharply delineated
meeting point of summit ridges and sky.

The liner slowed. Kenneth turned his back on the new
dawn and walked across to the starboard railing to look
at Penang. Directly opposite, about a mile across the still
water, was the city. Kenneth could see an esplanade lining
the shore. At its western end stood a grand-looking, two
storeyed edifice in white stone, its colonnaded ground
floor and arched windows denoting some official function
of imperial importance. It faced an established park which
stretched for some distance along the foreshore before
merging with a group of buildings dominated by a lofty
flag staff on a point of land. Through the trees Kenneth
could just make out the city proper.

The *China* rounded the point and entered the shipping
road off Penang. The great ship moved carefully through
a fleet of stationary freighters and smaller packets towards
its appointed mooring.

Lit by the rising sun, the scene about him looked almost
imitation, so hard-edged and clean-cut seemed the man-
made elements of the scene in the early morning light.
The first rays of the sun illuminated the primary colours
to an intensity out of all proportion to their real value.
Patches of red rust seared the black starboard side of a
Japanese tramp steamer, its flag of a red circle within a
white rectangle flying almost luminously against the oil
green of the water. Kenneth watched the bow waves from
the *China* quietly collide against the tramp's scabrous hull

as the steamer sidled past. A coastal packet steamer of the Straits Steamship Company shone among its less salubrious neighbours. Completely white, its cabin and broad bridge above a clean hull reflected the early light brilliantly. About four hundred yards away Kenneth could see another passenger liner, its black hull divided into two slices by a narrow white stripe running from bow to stern. Above its complicated buff-coloured superstructure towered two black funnels with wisps of dark smoke drifting from them. Although too distant to make out a name on its side, Kenneth recognized the distinctive livery of another P & O liner, perhaps about to take its leave along the sea route Kenneth had just crossed himself these past five weeks.

Between the anchored steamers swam small lighters, barges, tongkangs, and sampans, foreign-shaped to Kenneth's eye. High in the stern and robust amidships, they multiplied in their hundreds across the harbour as the sun rose above the peninsula hills, some laden with great bales wrapped in hessian, others with coal and forty-four-gallon drums, some seemingly empty.

The backdrop to this burgeoning activity was Penang Island with George Town as its gateway. High jungle-clad hills dominated the view but in one place their verdant paramountcy gave way to the cultivated environs of the colonial city. Here was to be the starting point for his career as a rubber plantation manager for the firm of Dalgeish McElroy Ltd. George Town, or Penang as it was universally called, was the oldest British settlement in the Colony of the Straits Settlements.

Kenneth's attention was pulled to the quay of formal architecture that welcomed every visitor to George Town. A number of wharves and jetties projected out into the sea, all busy with tiny figures loading and unloading the miscellaneous vessels tied alongside. Near the point with the flagstaff, which the *China* had by now rounded, was a large block of buildings of a government nature marking the northern end of the impressive frontage. Next to it, running along the bustling quay towards the south, were two-and three-storey banking and commercial head offices. Midway, a tall clock tower broke the regular line of orange-tile roofing as it soared twice as high as anything else along the waterfront. The vista exuded an air of established prosperity, with the columns, cornices and Palladian-proportioned windows of the fine stone Victorian architecture sharply profiled as the rising sun illuminated them with its oblique early morning rays.

The *China* shuddered to a halt and hawsers were flung overboard to tether the steamer to its buoys. Here at last! thought Kenneth, his insides aflutter with excitement and nervousness. He continued to stand at the railing gazing at all the activity as the Immigration and Customs officials embarked up the lowered companionway from a little steam launch which had just pulled alongside. The day was heating up rapidly and Kenneth was soon forced to seek out the shade cast by a lifeboat in order to continue to soak up the ambience of the scene before him. Eventually the public address system announced that all disembarking passengers should make their way to the companionways on the starboard side in readiness to be ferried to the island. Kenneth joined the throng and, at 10.00 on a Monday morning, found himself stepping ashore at Victoria Pier.

Kenneth strode along the pier to the quay. His instructions, as given to him before he left London, were to go to the head office of Dalgeish McElroy. He took his wallet from his jacket pocket and checked a small paste-board card that was in the card sleeve: 60 Beach Road, was printed under the firm's letterhead and coat of arms. Pencilled in underneath was, 'between Church and Bishop Streets'.

After the relative peace and quiet of shipboard life, Penang was intimidating. The quay was a mass of oriental humanity busily going about their day. Rickshaws pulled by near-naked, wiry men criss-crossed the entrance of the pier, double-decker trams rocked noisily along their tracks in the centre of the road; carts of produce, bales and drums were lugged slowly to and from the jostling mass of craft moored against the seawall; between them all rushed men on bicycles, the shrill bells on their handlebars tinkling ineffectively at the more cumbersome vehicles in their path. Wheels creaked, men shouted, trams rang bells, and, to add to general din, the great clock three hundred yards down the quay clanged out the quarter hour.

Where is Beach Road? wondered Kenneth. A sign hinged to a lamp post told him that the chaos before him was on Weld Quay. Looking around he saw a newspaper stand. Approaching it, he asked the seller for directions.

'Straight down there,' said the vendor, a man of indeterminate race, pointing to a street directly opposite the pier. 'Where do you want to go? Beach Road very long street.' Kenneth told him. 'Ah well, turn left at the end of street. That take you to corner of Bishop and Beach Streets.'

Kenneth thanked the man and in less than ten minutes found himself in front of his employer's brass plate. He mounted the short flight of marble stairs, pushed open the heavy mahogany door with its leadlight window and found himself in the cavernous interior of Dalgeish McElroy Ltd. The dark-timbered office was refreshingly cool after the heat of the streets. Large ceiling fans slowly turned overhead and the office had an atmosphere of industrious efficiency.

Kenneth introduced himself to a young man behind the chest-high counter and he was taken past a collection of ledger desks to an office where he was presented to the Assistant Manager, a Mr Edwards. Edwards was an angular, tall man, with a cadaverous face. He looked, thought Kenneth, a dry stick. He was right.

'Sit down Clouston,' said Mr Edwards in a toneless school teacher's voice. 'Mellows,' he addressed the clerk who had brought Kenneth to his door, 'tell Sweeny to come here.'

'Young fellow,' he began, 'our plans are that you will become an assistant manager on one of our rubber planta-tions in the Federated Malay States. As to where, I don't

19

know yet. Before you go into the field you will work here, in this office, for ten weeks. Company policy is to train its young recruits into understanding some of the business side of rubber production before they disappear into Malaya to grow the stuff. We've found it helps planters to do their job better when they learn where their part of the business fits in with our agents and offices. Also, you will have Tamil language lessons three hours daily. You're no good to the company if you can't speak the lingo of the employees under your responsibility. There's a proficiency exam before you leave Penang and another in six months' time. The company is willing to show some flexibility in assessing the results of the first exam. The second one, however, determines whether you stay with Dalgeish McElroy or seek employment elsewhere. You'll commence the language lessons tomorrow at 2.30, after lunch. Half of the ledger clerks you passed on your way to my office are learning, so stick with them.' He looked over Kenneth's shoulder. 'Enter Sweeny, enter,' he said impatiently. 'Sweeney this is Clouston, our newest assistant, just off the steamer from Home. I want you to get him organised out at the hostel and kitted up so that he can start work as of tomorrow. That will be all,' he said, dismissing them both and making a show of returning to the perusal of some papers on the desk before him.

Outside Mr Edwards' office, the young clerk turned to Kenneth and extended his hand. 'I'm Terence Sweeny, old man. Welcome to Penang. Your timely arrival has given me the rest of the day off. At least sort of. I enjoy a stroll about the city while everyone else toils on.' He looked about the large office with its clerks bent over their work. 'I'll introduce you to this lot tomorrow morning. Let's get you looking the part of an expatriate and get you settled in. Come on.'

Terence grabbed his sola topee off the hat rack by the entrance and led Kenneth out into Beach Road. The street was nearly as busy as Weld Quay had been. The two young men walked up the footpath towards what must be a distant square, for the centre of the road at that point was dominated by a large clock tower with an onion-like dome top. They got nowhere near it however, as, only a couple of minutes' walk from Dalgeish McElroy's, Terence turned into a large men's outfitters on the corner of Bishop Street – Whiteway, Laidlaw and Company. They were the biggest stockists of virtually every dress requirement the Englishman in the East would need, long-wearing work-day suits, boots for all occasions, jodhpurs for polo players, evening formal wear, clerical garb for missionaries on their way to China, hats, cummerbunds, spats and shooting sticks; it was all here in this bastion of empire-builders' requisites.

Terence helped Kenneth open an account. An hour later they emerged with Kenneth several hundred Straits dollars in debt but with a wardrobe of clothes that would last him years. Terence had arranged for the new kit to be delivered to the company hostel Kenneth would be staying at while in Penang. They themselves would walk there in order for Kenneth to get a feel for the city.

They headed down Bishop Street towards a church and a distant backdrop of hills.

'The chummery is about a mile away, just off Argyll Road. The tram goes nearby but today we'll leg it,' said Terence.

'Chummery?' asked Kenneth. 'What's the chummery?'

'The hostel, old boy. Very pukkah India, the name, isn't it? Chummery means bachelor quarters I suppose. Dalgeish McElroy have two for their junior and transient staff. That way they can keep an eye on any high-jinks one of us might get up to. But above and beyond that it's convenient for all of us to be able to share a cook and servants. I live at Argyll Street. You'll make the complement up to six.'

They passed the church with its fine porticoed entrance of four paired columns and squat tower and steeple. In front of it stood a small circular pavilion of classical Roman proportions. Large mahogany trees shaded the lawn about it.

21

'St George's, old boy,' said Terence airily waving a hand towards the building. 'We muster there every Sunday for early-morning service, whether you like it or not. Church-goer are you?'

'Not really,' replied Kenneth.

'Well, out here us English are expected to go to church and not to be seen as letting the side down. One does what one is expected to do, and to buck the system is to ask for more trouble than it's worth,' Terence explained.

They turned up a busy thoroughfare. Chulia Street.

'This will take us through to Argyll Street,' said Terence. 'All this neck of the woods is Indian. Different parts of Penang have concentrations of different races. Over there a few streets away,' he gestured to the south-west, 'is the Moslem area, ahead of us is the Chinese area, and Koreans and Japanese tend to hang around Cintra Road. You'll soon get to know the various places. It's a lot of fun shopping and wandering in the different areas.'

Chulia Street fascinated Kenneth. Either side were the shops, typical as Kenneth was now beginning to appreciate, with their upper floors built over the footpath so that the pedestrian way was permanently sheltered. These footpaths, he was discovering, were not always the easiest to negotiate. Produce and workers, such as sewing machinists, spilled out from their tiny shop frontages on to the footpath and Kenneth and Terence often had to wend their way in single file in order to proceed. There were scribes writing letters for illiterates, food and tea vendors, spice merchants, tailors surrounded by bolts of textiles, saucepan makers, furniture makers and bicycle repair shops. The intermingling odours accompanying the mixture of sights added to the exotic impression of the busy street. The variety of shops amazed Kenneth, and he began to feel that life in the East was going to be interesting in all sorts of unexpected ways.

From Chulia Street they crossed Penang Road and entered Argyll Street, a tree-lined leafy road that was increasingly residential in character as the two young men walked along it.

'Here we are,' said Terence and he turned into a gravel driveway. The chummery was a two-storeyed building, each floor having a broad sheltered verandah running the whole width of the building. Terence led the way up some mossy steps into the cool, dark entrance hall. He pointed out the various rooms either side – 'Lounge, dining room, bathroom down there, study in here' – as he walked towards the staircase leading to the floor above.

'Up here to the sleeping quarters.'

Kenneth's room for the next six weeks was at the south end of the building and was entered from the verandah.

'New bods always get this room,' said Terence. 'This end of the building cops the sun more than any other part and this room gets to heat up more than others because of it. It's all right though, you'll survive.'

The room looked spacious and airy with its large window of louvres flooding it with filtered light from the shady verandah. Its spaciousness was actually exaggerated by the lack of furniture occupying the room – a bed, a side table, a chest of drawers, and a squat gentleman's wardrobe – but to Kenneth's eye, by now accustomed to the cramped cabin he had shared for five weeks with another young man on the *China*, his Penang quarters looked very inviting.

'It will do me fine,' he said, mopping the sweat from his forehead with a large handkerchief. 'My word it is hot, isn't it?'

Terence pulled a watch from his white linen jacket.

'Nearly twelve o'clock. Near enough to luncheon. I could get Bindi to rustle up something for us here.' Bindi was the chummery cook. 'But I tell you what. Let's nip around to the local watering hole for a few beers and a curry. It's just around the corner and you look like you could do with a drink.'

They left the chummery and walked back down to the crossroads, this time turning left to head up Penang Road. A minute or two later and they were outside the Australia Hotel. It was a building of character. Its lower floor sheltered behind a curving line of squared columns

23

which, linked together by arches which followed round the hotel, supported the upper floor which extended right to the street frontage. This consisted of a uniform line of large shuttered windows behind which were the guest accommodations. The roof, low-pitched with wide eaves, was of the orange-red terra-cotta tiles that seemed to be on every building in the city. The double-door entrance was on the corner and within was a tiled floor with a dozen or so wooden tables, each with a number of straight-backed chairs. Half of these were occupied by drinkers and diners. Terence and Kenneth took a table near the overhead fan.

'Two bottles of Tiger beer, Ah Lee,' ordered Terence when a Chinese waiter appeared. To Kenneth he enquired, 'Eat fish? Yes? Okay, and fish curry for us too, Ah Lee.'

The beer was cold and refreshing, and the food good. Kenneth discovered he was ravenous and cleaned up the meal with gusto. Terence noticed and commented.

'It's not too bad, eh? I suppose me and some or other of the chaps are in here three or four times a week. Being so close to home, it's a bit of a temptation at times and now and then I make a resolution to call in less frequently. Bloody hopeless though. A beer in good company makes you forget the heat. Talking of which, how about buying a round before we go back to the chummery?'

'Certainly, but look, I only have pound notes on me. I meant to change some in town but forgot,' replied Kenneth.

'No problem, old chap. I can give you some change right now. I'll take you to a bank when they re-open this afternoon, everything closes at lunch for a couple of hours.'

Kenneth bought two bottles of beer and, as they consumed them, Terence told him about the routine of the working week and what it was like living in Penang.

It was an existence he quickly grew to enjoy. The crowd at the chummery were used to incorporating new lodgers rapidly into their social life. There were always one or two like Kenneth, young men passing through on their way to postings outside of Penang, and consequently the usual reserve associated with British social intercourse had long been dispensed with in order to have a good time while the opportunity prevailed.

In the main the young men at Dalgeish McElroy Ltd were much like Kenneth. They had usually come from modest, middle-class backgrounds, had an education broad enough to make them suitable for an office job and enough ambition and sense of adventure to apply for one in the colonies. But their aspirations ceased at this point. Although Kenneth and his new friends wouldn't realize it, or in fact even have cared if someone had taken the time to point it out to them, the decision each of them had separately made when joining Dalgeish McElroy curbed the heights of seniority any of them could attain in this or any other business firm. Terence, if he were diligent, might rise to be an assistant to the crusty Mr Edwards; Kenneth could in due course be a plantation manager but never of a top-rung estate because of his lack of education in the specifics of tropical horticulture. The more single-minded of his contemporaries were studying precisely this, either back at Kew in England or at the Botanical Gardens in Singapore, even as Kenneth happily became part of the young bachelor group in Penang.

Learning the rudiments of the rubber business wasn't too arduous. Most mornings were spent at the head office in Beach Road being taught the basic paperwork which was generated by the latex shipments Dalgeish McElroy exported from the colony. The routine did on occasion extend to visits to the company's go-downs, or storage warehouses, to learn to judge the various gradings of rubber latex, and the rights and wrongs of packaging and storage. Their go-downs were at the far end of Weld Quay and Kenneth enjoyed the visits, partly to get away from the office, and partly for the glimpses of Malay life the trips offered. At this part of the town, the city began to give away to native kampongs or villages and floating communities of boat people – folk who avoided the bustle of the town in preference to their quieter life among the coconut palms and mangrove littoral. Of all the mysteries he had encountered since he had arrived in Penang, the unobtrusive Malays seemed the most inscrutable.

The afternoons were, as Mr Edwards had said, devoted to learning the Tamil language he would need on whatever plantation to which he was dispatched. *Strang's Essential Tamil Primer* was a difficult book to concentrate on after a decent lunch, but Kenneth proved a conscientious enough pupil of Dr Bose Ramachandran, the small, bespectacled language teacher used by Dalgeish McElroy, to save him from being the class fool. There were no natural students of the language in the group while Kenneth was in Penang and so, in varying degrees, they all found it a hard grind to master the basics. As the week approached for the preliminary test, Kenneth usually spent breakfast with his dog-eared Primer propped up against the large enamel teapot at the table, trying to memorize declining verbs he was supposed to have learnt a night or two before. Despite the frequent intention to do otherwise, Kenneth spent most of his evenings out with the lads among whom he lived.

The imperial city provided a feast of fun for young men with money in their pockets. Small as their salaries were, the Straits dollars could go a long way when spent in the less salubrious areas of Penang. By and large they avoided the centre of British social life in the Colony, the Eastern and Oriental Hotel, for their interests lay entirely in getting value for money in their entertainment. A drink was a drink, and if it could be purchased for a fifth of the price at the Australia Hotel then, as far as they were concerned, only a fool would try and insinuate himself into the Palm Court Bar at the Eastern and Oriental to pay an outrageous price for it. On top of that there was the dubious pleasure of having to consume it in the company of mems, their stern-faced public service husbands, and coy daughters. To the lads of the chummery, an evening was far better spent getting primed at reasonable expense at the Australia, followed by a foray into night life provided by any one of the different quarters in the city.

In the final week of his ten weeks cadetship at the office

on Beach Road, his experience of Penang social life was to be extended by a visit to Swatow Lane. It was traditional for the Argyll Street chummery to indulge any of their number who were due to leave Penang to an evening at a particular cabaret in the Chinese quarter. The establishment in Swatow Lane was a sailors' dive, known from Gibraltar to Hong Kong for its transvestites, curious floor shows, and for the bizarre ways the waitresses delivered bottles to patron's tables and collected their tips. Kenneth had heard about the place before being in Penang a fortnight. It was legendary, not only in the British and merchant navies, but also with European expatriates. Not to have been to Swatow Lane, if one had lived in Penang for any but the briefest of times, was tantamount to denying that one was a red-blooded Briton. Kenneth, actually, was not very keen about visiting the place. He had only limited experience about the seamier side of life and what he had heard about this particular bar made him apprehensive. It wasn't just the sex that was touted and sold there that put him off, but also its reputation for brawls and fights between the seamen who nightly flocked to the place. However, as none of his friends suggested going as the weeks passed, he put Swatow Lane out of his mind. Until his last Friday in Penang.

On the day before, Mr Edwards had asked Kenneth to come to his office after the language class was over for the day.

'Sit down, Clouston,' he said when Kenneth punctually arrived at 5.30. 'You've passed your Tamil Proficiency Test.' Kenneth inwardly heaved a sigh of relief. He knew he had lagged on the homework side of things and had been none too confident about the result because of it. 'Not brilliantly I might add,' went on Edwards dryly, 'but well enough to get you into the field.' He looked down at an open manila folder before him. 'The company is posting you to Selangor. To Kuala Tanah Estate near the Kemudi River in the south-coast region of the state. You'll be the junior of three assistant managers resident there. The manager is Mr McGregor Reynolds. Mr Cartwright, the travel officer, will make the requisite bookings for your journey. From memory, the next sailing south is this Sunday. See him first thing tomorrow morning will you?'

Back at Argyll Street, Kenneth told Terence and the others about his imminent departure.

'To the Kemudi River, eh,' commented Terence. 'Could have been worse. You could have been one of the poor devils that have got to go to the new estates over in Kelantan. A fate worse than death, being dispatched over there.'

'I don't know anything about this part of Malaya,' said Kenneth. 'All the files I've been involved with have been on Perak Estates. Does anyone know where the Kemudi River is, or, for that matter, anything about Kuala Tanah Estate?'

'The Kemudi is a big river near the Negri Sembilan border with Selangor. It meanders across the coastal plain for about eighty miles before winding into the Highlands,' said Terence. 'I've actually been up it once on a Straits Steamer that took me from Singapore to Penang a few years back. There's a port a couple of hours inland. Can't remember what it's called, but it's your typical wharf and collection of corrugated-iron sheds. These small places all look the same.'

'It's small then is it?' asked Kenneth.

'That part of Selangor is pretty much backwoods, old man,' chimed in another cadet. 'It's well south of Kuala Lumpur, the capital, and away from the railway line too. Kuala Tanah is one of the lowland plantations. Swamps, mosquitos, crocodiles, and disease kept the rubber companies away from the region until about twenty years ago, so everything is pretty unformed and a bit isolated. From what I've heard, it's a productive estate. It's only had the one manager and he and some of the others in the area have been conscientious in dealing with the problems of disease.'

'Well, it doesn't sound too awful,' said Kenneth. 'I apparently leave first thing next week.'

'Aha!' cried Terence, looking at the others. 'Time to call

28

a meeting of the Argyll Street entertainment committee. Shall we all meet at the Australia Hotel in an hour's time to discuss the farewelling of our esteemed colleague?'

There was a general murmur of agreement. The upshot of the resulting meeting, apart from a splitting headache from drinking too much, was that Kenneth was to be taken to Swatow Lane the very next evening for a final fling. Saturday night would be a more respectable evening of drinks at the Penang Swimming Club.

The bar at Swatow Lane was crowded by the time the Argyll Street party had wended their way from the Australia Hotel to the heart of the Chinese quarter. Men from a score of different nations jostled each other for space in the three large areas which made up the night spot.

The lights were few and dim except for the bar and stage locations. The noise, deafening as only a babble of languages could be, washed back and forth across the room. A haze of tobacco smoke suffused what illumination there was into greenish haze. As the six young Englishmen entered they passed a barely conscious Korean seaman being carried out by his mates, blood oozing from a wound along his right eyebrow and from a squashed nose. At this sight Kenneth felt Swatow Lane wasn't his sort of neighbourhood. However, as his companions were bent on spending the evening here, there was no way he would be able to extract himself from the group without looking silly. Grin and bear it, he thought to himself.

Terence spoke to the host, a slick-haired Armenian in a tuxedo. The man palmed a bank note discreetly passed to him by Terence and led them to a table near the stage, occupied by a group of oriental women. A word from the man and the ladies moved to the bar, leaving the table to Kenneth and his friends.

'Right chaps, on with the show! What will everyone have, a beer all round?' asked Terence, who seemed quite at home. Out of the smoky gloom came a waitress. To Kenneth's amazement and discomfiture, she was naked except for high-heeled shoes and a French naval cap with its red pompom upon her head. She held a tin tray in one hand. He had never seen a naked woman before and despite every effort to appear casual, he gawked at her standing a mere three feet away taking Terence's order. She was utterly indifferent to the stares from around the table. The young men were, in fact, behaving like gentlemen in comparison to much of the rabble who frequented Swatow Lane and the shadows of bruising on her bottom and breasts were indications of how some of the patrons responded to her appearance. She disappeared back into the noise and darkness and Kenneth's gaze followed her wiggling behind until she was out of his line of sight. Looking about he discovered other waitresses groomed to the same level of undress as their own, taking orders and fetching drinks.

Terence caught his eye and laughed.

'Now you see why Swatow Lane is the last binge before you leave for the lonely life of a planter. Take it in, take a gink at every bottom and every pair of knockers that pass us by, old man, for you aren't going to see many in the foreseeable future over in Selangor. Get an eyeful while you can.'

They drank whisky and Tiger beer chasers with a vengeance and the night quickly became a cheerful blur, alternating between raucous good humour and earnest advice. Much of the latter was directed to Kenneth in preparation for his new job. He listened with the attentiveness of the drunk, his brow furrowed with concentration as his befuddled brain tried to take in the ramblings of his equally inebriated friends. But, inevitably, his attention would eventually be torn away from the table as yet another waitress walked by, all breasts, rouged nipples and bottom to his obsessive gaze.

The dance floor ebbed and flowed as tangos, *paso dobles* and ragtime were mechanically cranked out by the listless band. The ladies who had occupied the table before the arrival of the young Englishmen turned out to be taxi dancers. Other partners of patrons were obviously not ladies at all. Masculine faces, softened with make-up and extravagant wigs, and angular bodies rounded out with padding failed to disguise the more manly of the transvestites enjoying the attention of their man. These creatures, like the naked waitresses, were completely beyond Kenneth's experience in the ways of the world. He inspected them with some curiosity, unable to come to any conclusion as to his feelings about them. He had a further insight into their demi-world a short time later. In the lavatory he blundered into a booth he mistakenly assumed was vacant. A heavily made-up individual, but a male undoubtedly despite the high-necked brocade dress he was wearing, was on his knees in the act of fellatio with a strongly built sailor in a British uniform. Kenneth stood transfixed, suddenly at a loss as to which way to turn to escape the scene he had no wish to know about. The transvestite opened his eyes and focused up at Kenneth. As the flustered Kenneth retreated, the young man gave him a slow wink with a long eyelash heavy with mascara. Kenneth, speechless, closed the door and fled. The evening was, however, to become even more explicit.

'What's up, old man?' ask one of the party when Kenneth returned to the table. 'You're looking a bit green about the gills. Feel all right?'

'Oh yes, need a drink I suppose, what,' joked Kenneth feebly. He hadn't realised the significance of his words. Like a fairy-tale peasant who is granted three wishes by a bottled genie, but never really intends that every 'I wish that' counts as a genuine wish, Kenneth had, without meaning to, conjured up a pair of brown-tipped breasts and broad hips in front of him. A voice beyond the swelling bosom inquired, 'What would you like to order?'

Kenneth looked blearily at the navel in the centre of the soft belly before his face and said, 'Whiskies all round please,' and was vaguely relieved when the apparition departed.

'You know,' he said to the party at large, 'there's just so much naked flesh a man can take in one evening.'

'Ha,' cried someone. 'You say that now, but let's hear it

31

in a year's time. Good lord, you'll be grateful to have one of those queers in your arms after three years of staring at rubber trees.'

Kenneth thought of what he had just witnessed in the lavatory and, taking the joke seriously, shook his head from side to side.

'Nooo, I don't think so, I really don't.'

A red spotlight was suddenly switched on. The babble hushed as the patrons turned their attention away from their drinking companions towards the stage where the light was playing. Two men carried a settee-like piece of furniture, but without a back or arms, to centre stage. They were followed by a naked Chinese woman, young and well proportioned, who proceeded to give a show of sexual athletics, firstly with a beer bottle, then with three shaven-headed, well-endowed men who materialised out of the surrounding half-light, and finally with a donkey which was cajoled into a state of arousal by one of the waitresses. Kenneth was successively shocked, amazed and appalled by the performance which ended with a shower of coins and bank notes wrapped round dollar pieces being flung at the girl as the donkey was led off-stage.

The assault on his sensibilities, plus the amount of alcohol he had consumed and the cigarettes smoked, was taking its effect on Kenneth.

'Terence, old bean, I need some fresh air. Let's call it a night. I'm going to throw up if I stay here much longer.'

A much too bright-eyed Terence inspected him.

'Look chaps, Clouston's nearly under the table. What shall we do with him?' A muffled conference took place in mock secrecy away from Kenneth's side of the table. 'An excellent plan, Charles. Such a treatment should completely revitalise him. Kenneth, we are leaving this den of iniquity. Leave a tip for the waitress, would you?'

The group shambled to the exit. Hooting and shouting, they made their way to the street and there allowed Kenneth time to clear away some of the fug his senses were enveloped in.

'Come on, we're on our way,' said one of the group, slapping Kenneth on the shoulders.

'Home, I hope,' muttered Kenneth.

'No fear, we're off to Chan Lu's for the main course of the evening.'

Kenneth hadn't the faintest idea what they were talking about. A few minutes later, he did.

'Clouston,' called Terence, when the gang staggered to a stop outside a decorative doorway which had joss sticks burning in a miniature shrine above it, 'this is a shout from the Argyll Street Social Club. Before you venture forth from the fleshpots of Penang into the monastic life of a rubber planter, we want you to appreciate what you are leaving behind. Please enter these portals and partake of its offerings.'

Good-naturedly Kenneth pushed open the door. To his horror, the foyer beyond contained a scatter of half-naked young women lounging around in cane chairs, quite obviously waiting for clients. The place was a brothel. He tried to back out but the lads pushed him forward and before he knew what had happened, he was alone in a bedroom with one of the girls. The bravado he had managed to maintain at the club in Swatow Lane had depended on the presence of his friends. Alone, his confidence completely evaporated and all he could think of in his whisky-dulled state was how to get out – and promptly. The girl, however, wanted her fee which would only be paid for services rendered. She pushed him on to the bed and deftly removed his trousers and began to fondle him. For Kenneth there was no sense of the erotic; there had altogether been too much exposed flesh and thrusting genitalia that evening for him to rise to the occasion. In an alcoholic swoon, donkeys, jiggling breasts, men dressed as women, tattooed arms embracing nude bottoms and sailors fighting, all swirled into a nightmarish vision. His senses completely befuddled, this girl biting his belly while pulling on his flaccid member, joined the maddening medley in his brain rather than, as was her and his friends' intentions, stirring his libido into action.

33

He wanted to be away from here and back at the haven of Argyll Street. Forgetting he had no trousers on, he staggered to his feet and lurched to the bedroom door, flung it open and headed for the stairs. He vaguely remembered climbing from the foyer. A great hoot went up as he reached where his companions were waiting.

'Hey, Kenneth, what about your pants?' yelled one.

'Looking for more action, eh. One not enough?'

He looked about the room, nonplussed at the laughing, grinning and giggling men and women surrounding him. Stupefied, he was at a complete loss as to how to behave in these bewildering circumstances. Suddenly he felt horribly sick. He made a dash for the door and threw up in the deep drainage ditch between the footpath and the street. Just as his friends caught up with him, falling over themselves in the hilarity of the moment, Kenneth slowly rolled into the ditch himself, and the night passed into oblivion.

Chapter 2

Maeve Stephenson's attention was beginning to wander from the subject at hand. The sixteen-year-old schoolgirl glanced out of the classroom windows to see if she could spot the blackbird which was giving voice so gloriously not far away.

It was a beautiful early summer's day in May. The old oak tree just in view was a mass of soft green in its new foliage and the sky beyond a cerulean blue with puffs of white clouds floating across its vault. A quintessentially English day, but as Maeve continued to let the blackbird's song enchant her, her thoughts slipped to visions of far more foreign climes than the one that had started her reverie.

Maeve was a pupil in one of the more senior classes at Ealing Dean Grammar School. Twenty classmates sat about her in neat rows, each paired behind battered and initial-scratched desks which had seen at least a generation of pupils pass through the school since the furniture had been first installed. Maeve shared her desk in this particular class – history – with her friend Alexa Cubbins. There were only six girls in the room, female friends of earlier days had left over the recent years for education was by no means regarded as essential for children, especially girls, once they had reached fourteen or fifteen years old. Maeve enjoyed school and was grateful her father had allowed her to continue.

At sixteen she was an attractive young woman, although the serge tunic dress and blazer of the school uniform did its best to keep her looking like a girl. The white blouse with its neatly knotted school tie at her

throat camouflaged her mature bust and thick grey coloured stockings minimized the shapeliness of her ankles
and calves. The deliberate dowdiness of the uniform
however could not diminish the prettiness of her face.
She had a frank friendly countenance which was always
alight with an enthusiasm for fresh ideas and experiences;
her brown expressive eyes sparkled with keen intellect.

A shaking of a clump of oak leaves at the top of the
tree indicated where the unseen blackbird was hopping
amongst the twigs. The movement caught Maeve's attention. What a beautiful day, she thought to herself. Summer
at last! Again her thoughts drifted away.

The lesson today was about the establishment of British rule in India. Maeve particularly enjoyed studying
history but the romance conjured up in the first fifteen
minutes of the lesson had been more than enough to
set her daydreaming about the topic. Clive of India; the
Viceroy of Ouida; Calcutta with its Georgian architecture and parasoled ladies in their carriages; bejewelled
Indian princes; red-jacketed, sabre-wearing English officers astride Arabian mounts; tiger skins on marble floors:
Maeve's imagination flitted among the visions she created
from the historical outlines the teacher had described. She
had never understood the complaints some of her fellow
pupils came out with when it came to history, namely that
the subject was as dry as dust and of no use to anyone.
On the contrary, to her the events deemed important by
historians were populated by the most fascinating people
she knew, and the places of action enthralling by way of
their strange and exotic locations. English history was
interesting in its own right too but Maeve much preferred
the topics which took place in such wonderful-sounding
localities as Macassar, Hispaniola or Delhi.

'Maeve.' A voice broke into her thoughts. 'Maeve, I'd
appreciate your attention along with the others if you
don't mind.' It was Mr Lewis, the teacher. At the same
time she received a furtive dig in the ribs from Alexa's
right elbow which helped jolt her back into the Ealing
present.

She pretended she had only momentarily been distracted from the lesson and focused her eyes on the blackboard which suddenly was a mass of writing. I must have been miles away, she thought to herself and, glancing about unobtrusively, she discovered her classmates taking the notes down in their exercise books. Hurriedly she picked up her pen and, dipping it in the inkwell, began to copy the stuff too, discovering in the process that Bengal had been left behind and the lesson had shifted to events in Mysore.

When Mr Lewis turned to complete what he was chalking on the board Maeve looked to Alexa's book to see how far behind she was. Her friend scribbled 'dreamer!' on her blotter and turned it so that Maeve could read it. She grinned at Maeve. Maeve scrawled 'it's a good day for it' underneath and, pushing it back to her friend, returned to her note-taking. Writing quickly she caught up with the others in time to listen with complete attention to the last of the lesson.

Mr Lewis was her favourite teacher at the school and a good few of her daydreams of historic exploits in distant tropical colonies had included his presence. It couldn't have been otherwise really, for it was he who had introduced her to the wonderful subject in the first place. He was, Maeve had calculated once, probably in his mid-thirties, and with his interesting face, rangy physique and disarming smile which he bestowed now and then on pupils who did well in his classes, Maeve had decided that he was a fascinating man. Once he had alluded to a life in Kenya before coming to Britain and he walked with a slight limp, the result, rumour had it among his youthful admirers at Ealing Dean Grammar, of a wound inflicted during the war in East Africa in 1916. His lameness only added to his mystery and of the teachers discussed in Maeve's circle of friends, Mr Lewis was unanimously accepted as one of the nicest. Certainly he enjoyed teaching and, because of her particular interest in his subject, Maeve felt a bit proprietorial towards him. He had a knack of fleshing out the great events of the

British Empire with amusing anecdotes which made the famous participants seem human rather than embalmed in the legends of their times.

Yes, Maeve thought to herself, an adventure in a tropical part of the Empire was what she was cut out for, somewhere heady with spices and palms and heat. Preferably with Mr Lewis as her husband. She watched him as he did a sketch map of India on the blackboard and decorated it with some directional arrows and circles which denoted British advances into the subcontinent. His curly hair was falling over his forehead as he scribbled a few names and the earnest expression on his face added to his glamour in Maeve's eyes. Just the sort to make a go of it in Zanzibar or somewhere else equally remote where she must live one of these days once she had grown up and left London.

A bell clanged in the distance and, with an instruction from Mr Lewis, the class packed up and noisily left the room. History was the last lesson of the morning so Maeve and Alexa grabbed their cases from the corridor and wandered out into the school grounds to have their lunch.

'You looked a hundred miles away in history,' said Alexa as they headed for a bench in the sunshine. 'You were lucky Mr Lewis didn't say more to you. Towards the end of the lesson he was giving you some looks; what were you thinking of?'

'Travel. Journeys to somewhere totally foreign,' replied Maeve. 'I couldn't help it. Today is so lovely. Doesn't it make you want to get up and go somewhere completely unlike London? Especially when Mr Lewis is talking about such marvellous places.'

'Not desperately,' said Alexa, gnawing a piece of carrot. 'Just a day off school in this weather would do me.'

'Hhmmm, it is great isn't it,' said Maeve, starting in on the sandwiches she had made after breakfast. 'You know, one day I'm going to visit these places we hear about from Mr Lewis. There's so much adventure to be had in the world. I want a share in it.'

Several miles away, in Upper Park Road, Hampstead, the pleasantness of the day was not uppermost in Nick Manconi's mind as he sat over lunch with his parents and a young woman friend.

'Tell Cook the beef was delicious,' said Mrs Manconi to the maid as the girl removed the dinner plates from in front of the diners.

'Yes Ma'am.'

Mrs Manconi put her napkin aside and looked affectionately at the young people seated side by side across the table from her. Her husband, Dr Manconi, sat at the head of the table with Nick to his right and his wife to his left. At the other end was an unused table setting. George, the younger son, had at the last minute decided to lunch elsewhere with a chum from work.

'Now when are you two going to announce your engagement?' she asked with a smile. 'Everyone knows your intentions so a formal declaration is about due.'

'Nick keeps saying he is going to do it, but never gets round to it, do you,' said the girl, reaching out her left hand to clasp Nick's lightly and give it a squeeze.

Elizabeth Buchanan and Nick Manconi had been regarded for years by their parents and friends as a perfect match and the developing friendship had been indulgently watched with everybody anticipating their eventual engagement and wedding with the satisfaction that at least some things in life were fatefully and happily predictable. Nick had got to know Elizabeth because of his schoolboy friendship with her oldest brother Edward. Edward had been a year older than Nick and it was this age difference which had enabled him to enlist in the army in 1918 and end up in Flanders as a second lieutenant before the Great War ceased in November that year. Edward never celebrated the Armistice however. In late September, a mere seven weeks before peace was declared, he and his platoon were blown to pieces by an artillery barrage. His death had devastated his family and friends. Nick, as Edward's best friend, had been drawn into the grief of the Buchanan family, and, in their shared sense of desolation, he and Elizabeth formed a close relationship which didn't slacken as the months passed and they began to accept the loss of Edward.

Nick had gone up to Cambridge to begin his university degree at the end of 1918 and the friendship between him and Elizabeth had continued through the mail. Visits to London soon largely became reserved for Elizabeth, and their pleasure in each other's company was benignly encouraged by both sets of parents. By the end of 1919 all tacitly acknowledged that the pair were made for each other. Enveloped in their remembrance of Edward, Nick and Elizabeth felt the same, and after two years of court-ship, though neither would have seen their friendship in quite that light, they discussed the desirability of getting engaged and married. The proposal was well received. Nick was in his last year at university and mid-1921 would be looking for employment. With an engagement to Elizabeth his parents saw his commitment being a steadying influence towards finding a secure job. By the time he would have begun his climb to promotion within it, the wedding would be due; all in all, they agreed, the timing of the betrothal was perfect.

The trouble was, although these things had been decided all of four or five months ago, Nick had not actually given the go-ahead for the engagement announce-ment. It was for this reason that his mother had asked the question at luncheon.

Nick had not been his usual good-natured self for the last few months. His open, thoughtful-looking face with its deep-set eyes had lost some of its carefree aspect and more and more frequently on his visits home his expres-sion had betrayed some inner restlessness. He hadn't talked of problems however and had remained polite and considerate so, in the end, his family put his quietness down to study pressures. After all, this was his examina-tion year, and three years, study were in the balance.

'I'll get around to it,' he said casually. 'It has been an incredibly busy term.'

'Excuses, excuses,' teased Elizabeth. 'All you have to do

is tell Father to put the announcement in the papers and it's done.'

'Yes, well all right. I'll do something about it,' Nick replied giving her a smile which disguised his real emotions. Inside himself he was feeling sick at heart. His unhappinesss was not connected with his studies at all; on the contrary they had been stimulating and a future using his university qualifications looked to be an interesting one. His anxieties were wholly to do with his relationship with Elizabeth and the expectations both his and her parents had created for them as a married couple. He had known, with ever more awareness as the year passed, that he did not want to marry Elizabeth. At first the procrastinating over the engagement announcement had been to gain time while he explored his feelings about her but now that he was certain he could not make his life with her, any further delaying tactics could not be justified. Today, this afternoon, he must tell her there would be no engagement announcement uniting their names.

After lunch he grabbed his opportunity.

'Beth, it's a beautiful day, let's go for a stroll on the heath.'

They ambled along one of the paths, Elizabeth enjoying the sun, the open space and the sight of some new rabbits making their first tentative explorations with their mother – but Nick felt awful.

'Beth, I've been thinking something over all year. It's about us. I don't want us to announce our engagement. I don't think I can marry anyone just now, let alone my best friend.'

It wasn't, he conceded to himself, the most brilliant start to the discussion, but at least it was honest and sincere and he hoped the discussion to follow would not be too wounding.

'Why?' asked Elizabeth, quickening her pace in an effort to cover her shock.

'I'm not cut out for the life our parents plan for us. I know they all see me settled in the City within four months, pushing a pen for some merchant banker or

41

suchlike, our place in Hampstead halfway between their own homes so that the grandchildren will be handy to them all. A nice family with a nice predictable future.'

'But what's wrong with that?' interrupted Elizabeth. 'I was rather looking forward to it. A good job and a house in Hampstead are what a lot of people would covet.'

'There's nothing wrong with it, it's just not for me. I didn't know this about myself back last year when we became serious. But with our marriage on the cards I've done some soul-searching and have come to realize I want a different sort of life from the one I grew up in. I've watched you carefully too, and see that you are very content here. I'm not certain what I want to do but I do know it will be sufficiently different from life in Hampsted for you to feel you've been misled by me; that is, if I hadn't spoken to you this afternoon. Similarly I wouldn't be the person you thought you were marrying if I compromised my ambitions and made myself conform to our parents' plans.'

Elizabeth said nothing but Nick could see she was fighting back tears, and felt an utter cad at being the cause of her misery.

'University has opened my eyes to a world far bigger and more curious than I could ever have imagined a couple of years ago,' he continued. 'I just have to see it. A small demon seems to have grown within me and it keeps calling me to take the opportunities of the times and get out of England and live.' He spoke earnestly and passionately and Elizabeth could hear in the tone of his voice that he was being desperately honest and, at the same time, also regretful for what he had to say to her. His apologetic words didn't count though. She swung about and angrily began to harangue him.

'How dare you come out with this now! You should have said something earlier. Here am I, thinking I am your fiancée while all along you've been having a self-centred debate in your mind as to whether you are in fact serious about marrying me.' She paused to take a breath. 'I haven't been waiting six months to hear this sort of announcement! I'm not a person to be kept waiting in ignorance as to what's really going on in your head. You should have expressed your doubts back in the New Year. At least I wouldn't now be feeling so unpleasantly shocked if you had.'

'I'm sorry, I'm sorry,' replied Nick. 'How could I have told you earlier? Back then I thought I did want to get engaged. It's been a long and worrying process to get to this decision, Beth. I didn't want to talk about it until I could see the thing clearly.'

'Don't you "Beth" me, you ... you worm!' Tears running down her cheeks Elizabeth turned and walked rapidly away from him. Nick watched her stride off and, after a few moments, dejectedly followed her. The discussion had gone as badly as he had anticipated and now he was uncertain as to what to do. He tagged along some fifty yards behind her until at last she slowed her headlong march and he caught up with her.

'Elizabeth, I'm terribly sorry this had to happen,' he said as he again walked beside her. 'If I thought our engagement would work I would have gone through with it. There's no one else in my life, in case that's what you're wondering. If I was to marry anyone it would be you.'

'Thanks a lot,' she said sarcastically and Nick wretchedly felt that he probably deserved her scorn. She seemed calm again however and they resumed their directionless walk, Nick talking some more about the reasons and motives for his decision.

'What are you going to do after you graduate?' Elizabeth finally asked.

'In terms of a lifetime, I don't know,' he replied. 'For the immediate future however, I'm going to learn to become an airman. I've signed up in the Royal Air Force for pilot officer training. I go in as soon as my exams are over.'

'Your father and mother will have a fit. I'm sure the last profession they'd want you in is flying,' observed Elizabeth.

'I know. I'm not looking forward to telling them. Hang it though, I'm twenty-one and my own man, so apart from disapproving, they can't do much.' He took out his pocket watch to see the time. 'Shall we wander back? I'd better break the news to them before my train leaves this evening.'

They turned and walked side by side across the rough grass towards his parents' home, each lost in their own thoughts.

Chapter 3

Selangor, 1920

The small, tidily appointed coastal steamer of the Straits Steamship Company skirted a pyramidal orange-painted iron frame sprouting from a muddy sea, and swung to port. Ahead, out of sight below the horizon was the Kemudi River, the *Jesselton Star*'s fourth landfall. Despite the lack of topographical references to its existence, the Kemudi was nevertheless a physical fact. Its discharge from the Negri Sembilan highlands of Malaya coloured the sea beyond its debouchment a khaki colour, littered with the debris of its route through jungle, paddy and plantation – floating branches, the remains of atap roofs and walls deemed unrecyclable by the last occupants of the houses they once comprised, and the occasional carcass of snake, monkey or even dog. Its silt load over millennia had raised the sea floor for many miles out from the coast, making the wave patterns short and choppy when one approached the vicinity of the Kemudi's outflow. On this day a breeze from Sumatra was lifting the caps of the waves into steep coffee-coloured peaks through which the steamer cut with slow determination. The heat of the afternoon hammered down from a sky bleached of colour.

Beneath the canvas awning which shaded the deck aft of the second-class cabins and lounge, Kenneth Clouston sheltered from the sun's burning rays. Reclining in a cane chair he looked out over the discoloured water with no great enthusiasm. His white shirt, open at the neck, clung wetly to his back and more so to his armpits. His white duck trousers remained a little less intimate to his skin, thanks to his woollen underwear, the wearing of which was virtually regulation in Malaya. The jacket of the tropical day-suit hung from the back of his chair, somewhat out of shape, the pockets sagging from the weight of their contents. Desultorily fanning himself with his solar topee, Kenneth turned to a companion reclining at his right.

'On the home run now. We'll be at Tangga Gajah in four or five hours.'

'Feeling nervous?' replied his companion, a young man named Charles Attwood who was to disembark later in the voyage at Batu Pahat in Johore.

'To be honest, yes. Reynolds has a reputation as being a difficult fellow to deal with and I've got to do more than that. I've got to work under him, learn the ropes and so forth. Kuala Tanah Estate is a lonely place to be stuck with one of the company's reprobates.' Kenneth sighed. 'Not that any of the other fellows' postings looked much better, us being at the bottom of the pile so to speak.'

It was too hot to talk much and the two young men simply lay back in their chairs and let the sea slip by them. A small pile of old *Illustrated London News* beneath a three-day-old edition of the *Straits Times* lay between them on the deck. Their contents had been listlessly flicked through and dismissed as too enervating to read thoroughly, earlier in the day. A waft of the breeze occasionally ruffled the upper copy's pages, the faint fanning sound momentarily created being one of the rare noises to intrude that afternoon on the rhythmic bass thud of the steamer's engine.

Time passed and, had the young men been looking forward, they would have seen a grey-green line emerge above the brown-coloured sea. Behind it a haze enveloped the distant hills of Malaya, giving the false impression that all that lay before the ship was lowland.

An hour later and the steamer was between the mangrove-covered dunes and islets which formed the mouth of the river. There were neither headlands nor defined river banks to indicate that this was a large navigable route inland. The dense mangrove forest ran into the sea from wherever it had managed to establish itself, the

46

sole criterion for the expansionist plants' viability being that the oozing mud sustaining them be exposed at least briefly at low tide. The *Jesselton Star* had scheduled its arrival at the Kemudi's sandbar within an hour of high tide and consequently the tangled roots and branches of the mangrove forest were under water and only its deep-green foliage was visible above the river chop.

The steamer swung to port as the captain made for the deepest channel sluicing the bar. To combat the increasingly apparent current of the river, the engines quickened their pace and the *Jesselton Star* pushed its way upstream. The channel meandered from one side of the broad river, still sea from its appearance as much as it was fresh water, to the other green margin, and the ship edged its way carefully forward.

At last groups of coconut palms broke the mangrove forest's monopoly on land. The *Jesselton Star* was about 20 miles inland and the tidal estuaries now succumbed to the smooth flow of the river. Well-defined mud banks emerged from the mangrove flats. The numbers of coconut and nipah palms multiplied and then were complemented with groves of bamboo, durian, mango and wild fig trees, interspersed with small villages half built over the river and half into the cleared vegetation. Tiny fleets of canoes, moored to the bamboo stilts supporting the piers and huts of the villages, bobbed in the wash of the *Jesselton Star*.

Low rounded hills occasionally served as a distant backdrop to these cultivated scenes. Soon jungle replaced the domesticated riverbanks, its awesome tangle of greenery being broken sporadically by flimsy jetties which gave ingress into the green depths. A substantial and prosperous village came into view. The ship swung a few degrees to port and again skimmed along the northern bank before swinging around a steep jungle-clad hill which overlooked the village and river. The hill was the first piece of landscape which suggested that land along the river could rise more than six feet above sea level. It rose nearly eight hundred feet above its surroundings and dominated the inward bend the river now took as it flowed for a while from the north. The current had under-cut the flanks of the hill, carving a vertical cliff around the base for several hundred yards. Above the cliff the jungle sloped up to a flattish summit before falling away on all sides to the plains invisible behind the trees lining the river bank.

A Chinese steward in immaculate white cottons and canvas shoes walked on to the deck from the second-class lounge and called, 'Tangga Gajah in thirty minutes, Tangga Gajah in thirty minutes!' He disappeared only to be heard calling the same message a minute later from a lower deck.

'Well, old boy, better pack your kit,' said Charles.

'Might as well. I'll only be a couple of minutes so look, order, on me, a last beer before we tie up,' replied Kenneth, getting to his feet. Picking up the magazines from the deck he turned and went inside to pack his suitcase.

A short time later the two young men looked out over the river port as the *Jesselton Star* closed slowly with its rendezvous with the land. The ship was angling towards a stout wooden wharf which jutted some thirty yards into the river and occupied about forty yards of river bank. Several hundred yards either side of this structure, and at least an equal distance into its hinterland, the jungle had been removed and in its place stood a settlement of about forty buildings comprised entirely, at least at first glance, of unpainted corrugated iron. The most prepossessing of these housed the settlement's post office, marine depart-ment and agent's office for the Straits Steamship Com-pany. The shed with its peeling coat of government issue paint stood at the entrance to the wharf, a sign along its river facing eave proclaiming its location: TANGGA GAJAH, SELANGOR.

Adjacent to the office were a dozen larger and shabbier buildings. These were the godowns where the baled latex from the rubber plantations in the area served by Tangga Gajah was stored ready to be shipped out by the little Straits steamers to George Town or Singapore. The rest of the motley buildings were homes of the Chinese labourers who worked the port and the stores, opium shop and bars that sustained their desolate-looking existence.

As the ship drew alongside the wharf, and hawsers tied it motionless against the silent river current, twilight began to fall on the little community. In anticipation of the coming darkness, a petrol generator was heard to start up with a rapid popping sound and the arc lights suspended on bamboo poles around the wharf perimeter lit up. At first it was still too light for the lamps to matter but night falls quickly in the tropics and by the time the first passengers had disembarked, the intersecting circles of light guided their way across the wharf.

The area milled with people. Chinese labourers in baggy singlets and shorts carried tin trunks, wooden boxes and suitcases belonging to the departing passengers on to the wharf where they were stacked. There, identified by their owners, the loads were picked up again, and humped over to where various forms of wheeled transport stood near the godowns. Complementing the movement and shouting of the coolies, the *Jesselton Star*'s forward crane clanked into life and began hoisting from the cargo hold large crates, pallets of fourty-four gallon fuel drums, and bound bales. Some of the freight was dumped unceremoniously on the north end of the wharf. Other pieces whose stencilled addresses across their sides obviously included different instructions, were manoeuvred by twenty pairs of hands on to flat trolleys and, with many bellowed invocations from the wharf labourers, hauled out of sight into the darkness.

Kenneth watched the scene with mixed feelings. So this is to be part of my home for the foreseeable future, he thought. He was in no hurry to disembark among the present hubbub and waited until the bulk of the seventy-odd passengers for whom Tangga Gajah was their destination had dispersed from the wharf. The heat was still terrific and his clothes felt clammy and heavy from the humidity and sweat. There almost seemed to be not enough air to breathe, so sultry was the evening. Small bubbles of sweat dotted his forehead and the skin below the corners of his eyes, in all a most uncomfortable sensation. Now beside the ship there only remained a couple of groups of Europeans chatting to each other and a group of voluble Chinese welcoming back to their hearts a young couple.

'Goodbye Charles,' he said, putting out his right hand. 'Best of luck in Johore and no doubt I'll be seeing you again.'

The two young men firmly shook hands.

'The best of luck to you also, old man,' replied Charles.

Kenneth ducked through the doorway into the corridor where his cabin was located. Catching the attention of the Chinese porter who had been hovering near the young men for the past five minutes Kenneth pointed to his two leather suitcases and a hat box just inside his berth and made for the wharf. There he found the rest of his belongings. Slipping the man a handful of small coinage, Kenneth stood by them and waited for someone from the estate to meet him. He turned to look at the activity focused on the *Jesselton Star*.

The cacophony of Cantonese was quieter now that the first urgency of unloading the ship had passed and again the petrol motor of the generator could be heard. The yellow illumination from the wharf lamps and the whiter light from the ship's own lights imparted the surrounding darkness with an almost tactile feeling reminiscent of sooty black velvet – an illusion assisted by the warm and humid air enveloping the scene. Stepping back a few paces out of a circle of light, Kenneth could see a sky canopied with a blaze of white stars. A sudden muffled crash of leafy vegetation to his right indicated the presence of flying foxes in the jungle about the little port. Other less identifiable sounds of hooting and snuffling sounded out from the blackness of the settlement's perimeter. Mosquitos began to pay attention to the stationary target Kenneth made. A high pitched incessant buzzing began to impinge on the sounds of the generator and jungle, eventually concentrating near his head where his exposed face presented the best hope of a feed for the pests.

A man detached himself from the last remaining group of Europeans on the wharf and walked towards Kenneth and his pile of luggage.

'You just have to be Kenneth Clouston, there's no one else here for me to meet. I'm Reynolds, the manager of Kuala Tanah Estate.' He held out his hand.

'I'm pleased to meet you, Mr Reynolds,' replied Kenneth.

The man who greeted Kenneth was fiftyish with sandy hair thinning at the forehead and severely barbered above the ears and neck. His countenance had a sharpness to it which, although not unfriendly, nevertheless suggested a hint of incipient impatience beneath its tanned veneer. A clipped military-style moustache decorated his upper lip. Kenneth could see from the manner the man's white cotton suit hung on him that Reynolds was a sportsman and the crushing handshake that gripped his palm and fingers tended to confirm his assessment.

Kenneth decided that Mr Reynolds was a man with whom it could be imperative to stay on the right side. He looked as if he didn't suffer fools gladly.

Actually Kenneth's first impressions had already been, to a certain degree, preconceived, for McGregor Reynolds had a reputation widely spoken of among the planters and agents of Dalgleish McElroy Ltd and Kenneth had heard some of the stories.

Twenty years earlier, Reynolds had been regarded as one of the brightest young cadets the company had recruited. A tearaway, yes, but with a quick mind and able in carrying out his responsibilities; the fact that he was a first-class cricketer had negated his sometimes rather outrageous behaviour at numerous clubs and social occasions in Perak where he was an assistant manager at one of the bigger estates owned by Dalgeish McElroy. However, the long-suffering tolerance of the expatriate community finally snapped when Reynolds, against all prevailing social mores, had blatantly flirted with the daughter of an influential Rajah at a ball celebrating the birthday of Edward VII. The brief silly incident had done nothing for Malay–British relations in a social climate dependent on respect for Malay custom and tradition, and Reynolds was summarily declared persona non grata in the State of Perak. His firm, reluctant to lose a good manager, did not dismiss him, but instead posted him to one of their more remote estates, Kuala Tanah, in southern Selangor. The situation he found himself in, one entirely of his own making, had soured Reynolds over the years. Not welcome in Perak, he was not especially acceptable in social circles in the other Protected Malay States either. Firmly orthodox in their Islamic ways, the Malay aristocracy he once moved among would have nothing to do with him. The British in their turn found it socially expedient to close their own ranks to a man who had let the side down, and Reynolds was forced to curtail his social intercourse to the small community he lived among in this relatively isolated part of Selangor, the neighbouring state of Negri Sembilan and in Malacca – hardly the hub of social gaiety of the Malay Peninsula.

When leave fell due he sometimes departed to the brighter spots of the Straits Settlements to debauch among a wider circle of cronies than planter life in Tangga Gajah permitted, but the pervasive ostracism gradually embittered him. Fifteen years in outstation Selangor had not dimmed the memories of when he had regularly been the toast of the Perak Cricket Club, and of the evenings he had danced with the daughters of a Resident. Over the years those times of high-spirited drinking with kindred souls had become drunken binges in the company of a planter mate or two, likewise morbid about the luck that had passed them by.

'That is all your lot is it?' asked Reynolds, gesturing to the luggage next to Kenneth. 'Take your suitcase now and Johnny will bring the rest on the cart. I've got a shipment to get home too. It will be somewhere around here and Johnny will get it all to Kuala Tanah. Hang on a tick.'

He quickly walked to the wharfage area near the office and looked at the addresses and labels painted on the sides of numerous crates and bales and lumps of machinery. Kenneth heard him call into the darkness, 'Johnny, inge!' and after a few seconds, interval, 'Avasaram!' with some ferocity in his voice.

A thin Tamil leading a buffalo harnessed to a cart appeared from a cluster of similar vehicles and ambled up to where Reynolds was standing and noted by nods of his head which crates were to be loaded into the cart. Reynolds then pointed out Kenneth's pile of belongings to the man and instructed that they too were to be transported to the estate and then he strode back to Kenneth.

'Right, old man, off we go. The car is just over there.'

Kenneth placed his suitcase in the rear of the Ford Model T and hopped in beside the driver's seat. Reynolds swung the crank a few times and the motor burst into life. Red clay caked the wheels and mudguards and streaks of the mud criss-crossed the sides of the car where the spinning tyres had flung it.

'It's been raining more than usual and the road is a quagmire, hence the new colour scheme,' joked Reynolds as he heaved himself behind the wheel. 'The estate is only a couple of miles away, however, so you won't have to put up with much.'

For twenty minutes the car rumbled, bounced and squelched along the heavily rutted road. Kenneth could not discern any of his surroundings, the yellow funnel of light cast by the headlamps rendering everything beyond it an inklike blackness. Occasionally a dull thwack against the rattling windscreen sounded the end of a large moth or insect; the smaller ones simply expired soundlessly in their scores in a tangle of spindly legs and wings flattened against the glass. Several white notice boards were passed, illuminated but the lost against the blackness too quickly for Kenneth to read. He guessed they announced the entrance ways to neighbouring rubber estates to the one they were bound for. Eventually Reynolds spun the wheel to the right and slowed to negotiate a shallow ditch which had its banks widened at this point to allow wheeled transport to cross it. The sign to the left of this track proclaimed – 'Kuala Tanah Rubber Estate' in large black lettering and beneath in smaller words, 'established 1897'.

A minute later the car stopped and Reynolds killed the motor. Kenneth stepped out and looked about him. By sound rather than by vision, he knew they were in a clearing enclosed by trees. The blackness of his surroundings was broken by the yellow light of several kerosene hurricane lanterns softly illuminating the porch of a wooden bungalow. High off the ground on wooden piles, and reached by a broad, long set of stairs, the house looked a welcome haven to the travel-worn young man. A moving light to the right of the bungalow caught his attention. Holding the hurricane lamp was the small, stocky, pyjama-clad figure of a house-boy.

'Good evening Tuan Besar,' called the young servant as he drew near.

'Jimmy, this is the new Tuan Kechil, Mr Clouston,' replied Reynolds and, turning to Kenneth said, 'Jimmy is the house-boy for the assistants' bungalow. He can take you there now and when you've freshened up, come over to my bungalow for a whisky.' He jerked his forearm out and flicked his wrist and Kenneth was surprised to see him refer to a wristwatch. Such timepieces were very new and were regarded back in London as an affectation adopted by men of dubious masculinity. 'It's just gone 9.00 so I won't be turning in for another half hour or so.'

Kenneth followed Jimmy round the side of the bungalow and to another some forty yards beyond. A hanging hurricane lamp lit the front door at the top of the stairs. This was the mess where the three assistants to the estate manager lived. Raised about eight feet off the ground, like the manager's home, to reduce the termite and ant infestations and to better catch cooling breezes, the bungalow comprised three bedrooms opening on to the wide verandah which ran around nearly the whole building; a central lounge which carried through from the front door to the back; and a dining room. The broad spacious verandah with its furled cane blinds served in its own right as a large common room. At the back of the building, at ground level at the foot of the back stairs, was the bathroom and lavatory.

Jimmy showed Kenneth his quarters. His home for the foreseeable future was a square, spacious room which on first impression looked inviting enough. Jimmy had lit the two lamps, one hanging from a rosette of fretwork decoration in the centre of the ceiling and the other a wall fixture near the bed. The room had a warm colouring of faded brown and yellow tints provided by careworn bamboo and matchwood bedroom furniture, light ochre-brown paint finish on the walls, cream-coloured ceiling and bare timber floor. Between the window openings stood a massive iron bedstead canopied with mosquito net hanging from a nail hammered into the ceiling. The bed knobs decorating each end inclined slightly towards each other, indicating that the frame had subsided an inch or two in the middle in a floorwards direction during its long life as a couch for tired owners. It was a bed which had obviously in its earlier days graced a far finer establishment than its present location could aspire to and Kenneth briefly mused how it ended up in this isolated part of the world. The walls were undecorated except for a calendar suspended from a nail near the door leading to the lounge. They were not, however, unmarked. The lime-wash paint in some places was patchily applied, while scuffs, dark smudges and half-erased stains randomly patinated the surface. Within a foot of the ceiling scotia, some nine feet above the floor, was a mark that looked very much like a footprint though goodness knows, wondered Kenneth, how it could be so. The ceiling was crazed with countless hairline cracks caused by the ill-mixed paint film shrinking over the years. A pervasive but not particularly unpleasant smell of mould was discernible. In brief, the room was shabby but homely by British-Malayan standards.

Jimmy quickly showed Kenneth the rest of the bungalow; where to find the lamps, matches, wicks and kerosene, how to operate the plumbing; and then left in order
to bring the luggage round while Kenneth quickly washed
the fatigue of travel from his face and torso.

Ten minutes later, Kenneth knocked at the manager's
front door.

'Come in, old chap,' called Reynolds. 'Have a pew,' he
said, waving to a commodious cane and bamboo chair
opposite to his own. Between them was a low table strewn
with magazines and newspapers and mail. Judging by the
separate piles of opened and unopened envelopes, it must
have arrived on the *Jesselton Star* with Kenneth today.
At his right side, on a small occasional table, was a tall
whisky, pale with soda.

'Beer or a stengah? Both warm of course, the nearest ice
is at the club at Bangi.'

'A stengah, thank you sir.' Kenneth did not particularly
care for the taste of whisky even when diluted with soda.
But ten weeks in Malaya had taught him that a man's
drink was a stengah and there was no way he was going
to begin his new job by appearing to be anything less.

Reynolds rose and went to the drinks cabinet, and
Kenneth glanced about the room. Obviously the manager's bungalow was much the same floor plan as the assistants' mess but there were refinements such as skirting
boards, moulded architraving and more substantial doors,
all indicating that this was more than mere lodgings. The
space was cluttered with teak cabinets, shelves, and a large
chest of drawers around the perimeter, and five expansive
cane chairs occupying half the floor area. The walls were
festooned with animal trophies – sambur deer, wild pig,
seladang, a crocodile and a snarling tiger – an array of
kris, and some framed prints of European landscapes. A
small collection of sporting team photographs, mostly of
cricketers formally grouped, occupied the wall directly
across the room from Kenneth.

Reynolds handed Kenneth his drink and companionably chatted about the running of the estate and of his

expectations concerning Kenneth's part in the scheme of things.

'You'll be in charge of about fifty Tamils working the south-western area of the estate. It's area Number Two and backs up to the creek which makes that boundary of the property. It was brought into production about five years ago and is giving a good return this year so you won't have time on your hands.' He took a pull on his stengah. 'There're two overseers under you for the tappers, and a foreman for the weeders. The other two lads have roughly the same responsibilities. Darke, who has been here the longest, has seniority, and he is in charge of the factory. Learn from him because the day will come when you'll have to manage the place.'

'Muster is at 4.30 and breakfast at 10.00. We have a lie-in from 1.00 to 3.00 in the afternoon and afterwards there's usually a bit of office work, books and that sort of thing. After 4.00, the day is yours. Wednesdays you can finish at 3.00, and Sundays we call it quits at 1.00.'

'Tomorrow at muster I'll introduce you to your senior overseer and he can show you the morning's routine. I'll find you after lie-down and take you over the estate.'

Kenneth took his cue, swallowed what was left of his drink and got to his feet. 'Thank you, sir. I'm going to turn in with the hope of a decent night's sleep, good night.'

Relighting his lamp out on the verandah, Kenneth walked back around to the assistants' mess. The house was in darkness but as he traversed the verandah to his room at the end he heard the bed frame of one of his new colleagues creak as its occupant turned over. Blagdon or Darke, he wondered. As he reached his own door the creaks came again, this time accompanied by stiffled giggling and some low murmurings. Whoever it was, he was not alone, grinned Kenneth to himself as he closed his bedroom door.

A vigorous shaking aroused Kenneth from a sleep of the dead. A figure, backlit by a rhomboid of light from an open doorway, seemed to loom over him, prodding and rocking him with what felt like unnecessary violence. Struggling to engage his mind, he called out, 'All right, all right!' as he groggily recalled where he was.

'Tuan, it's gone four o'clock,' Jimmy informed him, and continued shaking Kenneth's shoulder.

Oh Lord, muster, Kenneth thought to himself and swung his feet to the floor. Dressing quickly he left the bedroom.

Two young men, about his own age, were standing in the dining room drinking tea from large chipped mugs.

'Ah ha, the new chum no less,' said the first to spot him as Kenneth made his way across the lounge towards them. 'Hello, I'm Ronnie Darke,' extending his hand to shake Kenneth's. 'This is George Blagdon.' The other young man put down his mug and shook hands also.

'Grab yourself a cup of tea while you have time. The crockery is kept over there.' Ronnie pointed to a shabby dresser against the wall.

The tea was, as it is all over the East, already sweetened and had milk added in the pot. Kenneth poured a cup of the caramel-coloured fluid into a mug bearing the inscription 'Federated Malay State Railways'.

'Cow of a time to start work, but you'll get used to it. George took two weeks to lose Penang time and adjust to estate life, and you haven't looked back since, eh Blagdon?'

George Blagdon gave a doleful look as part response to the observation and said, 'Haven't looked back at Penang either. Remember those bright lights, old man,' he continued, looking back at Kenneth. 'You're not going to see them for years now you are here at Kuala Tanah.'

With the social introductions complete the three sipped their tea in silence. In a few minutes they would have to make their way to the coolie lines for muster so no one sat down.

'Better get going,' murmured George, looking at his pocket watch, and headed for the door. Ronnie and Kenneth followed.

The day turned out to be one long, seemingly endless plod through the rubber estate. It began in darkness but as the night receded and a grey half-light replaced it, Kenneth could at last see the plantation. The rubber trees presented a sombre picture. Row after row of grey trunks, with hammer marks of contrasting ochre spotting them, arched upward to a scruffy foliage of grey-green. They were spaced about thirty feet apart and, pruned of all limbs below a fifteen-foot line, looked like a neglected farm producing second-rate telegraph poles for the Public Works Department. Every trunk was banded for five feet above the ground with scores of parallel striations — scars from the tapping process. At the lowest point of the pattern a cup was fixed to the tree to collect the bleeding latex.

By 9.30 the heat was fierce. The plantation canopy broke some of the sun's intensity but nevertheless Kenneth could feel pools of sweat spreading under his arms, across his back and in his crotch as they criss-crossed the estate. He felt dehydrated despite the cloying damp air, and his feet had swollen tight in his boots. The right-angled geometry of the estate plan began to disorientate him increasingly: the seemingly endless ninety-degree turns down one path should have, in his mind, brought him and his guide back to some recognizable starting point; instead always it was yet more tree trunks merging in the middle distance into a confused mass of greys and greens.

'Talk about not seeing the wood for the trees,' muttered Kenneth to himself. It was very much a surprise therefore when they broke into a clearing on the far side of which was the bungalow he had left earlier. His guide told him it was breakfast time and he would meet him back at this spot at 10.45 and continue the tour.

When Kenneth stepped into the mess Blagdon and Darke were already tucking into substantial bowls of porridge. A place had been set for him at the dining table and Jimmy the houseboy quickly served up the same fare. He was ravenous. Eggs, bacon, sausages and fried bread followed, all cooked by an Indian cook in his unseen kitchen out beyond the mess and carried in by Jimmy. There was no conversation as the young men concentrated on eating and for the first time Kenneth had an opportunity to assess his new colleagues.

Ronnie Darke, Kenneth knew, had been at Kuala Tanah for about six years, thereby making him the most senior, both in age and responsibility, of the three assistants. His appearance belied his surname for he had a fair, clean-shaven complexion and light brown hair. He was thin and his face a little drawn with the beginnings of stress lines appearing down each of his cheeks. Kenneth recognized the signs of malaria and it looked as if Darke was recovering from a recent bout.

George Blagdon, opposite Kenneth, was devouring the last slice of fried bread. His eyes, the whites slightly yellowed, indicated illness of the liver, but his robust build and friendly countenance implied a healthy and outgoing personality. He caught Kenneth's eye and smiled across the table.

Breakfast wound up with more of the strong sweet tea, sipped while Jimmy cleared away the plates.

Ronnie Darke broke the silence. 'After office work, George and I always go over to the club at Salak. It's the closest watering hole and a jolly crowd from the other estates around here usually gather most afternoons and evenings. We've got a bit of a tennis tournament going on, which generally provides fun for players and onlookers. Care to come along?'

'Thank you, I would very much like to meet everyone. As for playing tennis in this heat, well, I'll give it a go. I thought it was hot and sticky enough in George Town, but it's like a furnace here without the sea breeze.' He went on, 'My game of tennis isn't terribly strong at the best of times.'

Ronnie and George exchanged an amused glance and Kenneth guessed that at the Salak Planters' Club the afternoon's lame duck at tennis was expected to buy the other players a round of drinks at the end of play. Obviously

I'm going to make sure my game improves, he thought to himself. Damned if I'm going to be the fountain of free drinks.

In the afternoon Mr Reynolds took him in hand and showed him the office and book-keeping requirements of the estate. Seeing the manager's bungalow in daylight for the first time, Kenneth could appreciate that his boss's interest in horticulture extended beyond rubber trees. The grounds in front of the house were laid out in beds of red, yellow, orange and blue canna lilies, each plot neatly edged and separated by swathes of coarse lawn. The grass alone was remarkable, so difficult was it to produce anything even remotely like English lawn in lowland Malaya. Clouds of purple, red and pale orange bougainvillaea highlighted some of the beds, while full-blown hibiscus blooms, with their languid pistils, and mottled crotons, created a perimeter almost like a hedge. Beneath the front verandah and beside the long front stairs, lurid Livingstone daisies reflected the bright sun. A stand of slender sealing wax palms with their letterbox red trunks, stood at the corner of the building, partially hiding the turn of the road as it continued round the house along to the assistants' mess and beyond. They were complemented at the opposite side of the verandah by a large clump of paddle-leafed strelitzia, their bird of paradise blooms orange and almost iridescent blue in the harsh light.

The effect of the garden was positively therapeutic, the selection of bright and, in the case of the Livingstone daisies, garish blooms, cancelling out Kenneth's mildly depressed state of mind that had been induced hours ago by the monochromatic nature of the plantation.

'What a beautiful garden, sir.'

'Just the ticket isn't it, after a day in there,' replied Reynolds indicating with a gesture of his head the rubber trees beyond. 'A man would go mad without a garden, if you ask me. In fact,' he said thoughtfully, 'many white men have out here. Get a hobby, young fellow, get a garden going, it will keep you on the rails.' And, with that piece of advice, he dismissed Kenneth with a cheerful 'see you later.'

Kenneth walked back to the assistants' mess to find Ronnie Darke and George Blagdon waiting for him.

'You've got ten minutes, old man, and we're away,' called George as Kenneth stamped up the front stairs and into view.

He hurried around the verandah to his room, grabbed a towel and headed for the bath-house. Quickly he had a wash from the large terra-cotta Shanghai jar in the corner of the concrete-floored room out the back of the mess, and with only a sarong about his waist, ran up the back stairs to his room. He dressed to the same informal degree he noticed his new friends had aspired to: white-cotton trousers, open-necked shirts and a well-worn creased jacket.

'I'm ready,' he announced.

'Right oh.'

At the bottom of the steps Darke and Blagdon went in between the long poles which elevated the building and shortly re-emerged pushing a beaten-about BSA motorcycle with sidecar attached. The dented mudguards and petrol tank suggested that the engine would be in an equally woeful condition but, after several hernia-inducing kicks on the starter from Ronnie, the motor roared into life. Kenneth marvelled that a thing could simultaneously vibrate in so many different directions yet still function. Popping and spluttering, the bike appeared to be attempting to shed all its peripheral parts, and Kenneth noted the generous use of wire looped and twisted around various bits and pieces of the mechanism in order to keep them attached to the vehicle.

'George and I share this boneshaker,' said Ronnie. 'It's been owned by various assistants at Kuala Tanah over the years, the system being that each of us has usually bought a share off the departing assistant. Right now George and I own the old girl by default in a way because Percy Knowles, your predecessor, died a couple of weeks ago

62

of blackwater fever. A bad business, but there you are. If you want to use her, a third share is fifty Straits dollars; twenty-five for George and twenty-five for me. We take turns to fill the tank and split any other expenses between owners.'

'Well, I'll have to think about it,' replied Kenneth. Fifty Straits dollars was a lot of money and he wasn't sure that he needed a motorcycle, particularly as he had never driven one.

Ronnie was going to drive it today. George turned to Kenneth.

'You take the flapper bracket,' indicating the passenger saddle behind Ronnie, 'I'll have the sidecar.' The so called sidecar was in fact a wooden deck bolted on to a steel frame, its outrigger wheel partially covered with an obviously home-made plywood mudguard. Most incongruous of all was a battered ancient cane and bamboo armchair lashed to the deck, which gave the vehicle a ridiculous appearance to say the least. George settled himself into the decrepit chair and said in a contrived plummy voice, 'To the club James and be quick about it.'

Ronnie depressed the clutch handle, chonked the gear lever into first and they pulled away from the bungalow. With a stately twenty miles an hour registering on the glassless speedometer, the trio motored across the Selangor landscape to Salak. Where the red laterite road swung near to the Kemudi River, the rubber plantations gave way to paddy fields, brilliant green at this time of the year, with the ripening rice. Water buffalo grazed languidly at the edge of the fields, many of them with burong barau birds standing on their sagging backs. Malayan villages could be seen in the distance across such vistas, small collections of steep-pitched thatched roofs of atap palm shaded by mango and durian trees on the edge of the river.

Several times Ronnie slowed down when lumbering water buffalo, shepherded always by a small boy or two with a stick, shared the road with the motorcycle. The Kuala Tanah vehicle was obviously a familiar sight in the district. At the sound of its approach, in three or four places where houses, a shop or a mosque were close to the road, boys would run out to the roadside and laughingly shout at the white men as the machine trundled by. On occasion, George would regally wave to them as if he were a visiting district officer on an inspection tour. It was impossible to catch much of what was being shouted, but Kenneth knew enough street Malay to recognize 'Mat Salleh! Mat Salleh!' Broadly translated it meant 'Mad White Men! Mad White Men!' He had to laugh inwardly when he visualised how their progress must look when viewed away from the motorcycle, George in that cane chair, what a sight!

Salak was about nine miles from Kuala Tanah and it took the better part of an hour to motor the distance. Kenneth enjoyed the ride, not least for the breeze created by the motorcycle's passage through the still air. Soon Salak appeared, a small cluster of ramshackle shops and buildings built around the intersection of the only two roads in the district. As they turned the corner to head north, Kenneth counted three arak shops, each with a customer or two under their lean-to porches looking distinctly the worse for wear, a Chinese general store, and an Indian curry kitchen. A hundred yards further along, Ronnie throttled back and turned off into a driveway lined with albizia trees. At the end of it was a bungalow which looked from the outside not unlike the assistants' mess back at the estate. It was on a slight rise giving it a low view out to the north and east towards the Negri Sembilan Highlands and was badly in need of a coat of paint. Several other motorcycles were parked outside, a single automobile also, while leaning against trees and tethered in the shade were half a dozen bicycles and four horses. A high wire-netting fence, largely obscured by climbing bougainvillaea, marked the location of the club's tennis court and a regular 'pock pock' sound indicated that a game was in progress.

Cries of bonhomie from the bar greeted Darke and Blagdon as they entered the club. Kenneth was introduced to a group of young men and shouted a stengah by a thin, ginger-haired and freckled fellow, who happened to be buying that particular round of whisky and sodas. The three sat with the group, Kenneth listening with an amiable expression on his face, as gossip and business were raucously discussed. Kenneth was not by nature a very outward-going individual but, from his ten weeks in Penang, he knew that to be part of the crowd was imperative if one was to enjoy life in Malaya. A certain amount of eccentricity was allowed, and in fact encouraged, but individuals breaking with the European colonial mentality were ostracised and lived very lonely existences. He joined in the general laughter when a young man, originally from the Midlands judging by his accent, recited a couple of smutty limericks concerning, respectively, a young maiden from Crewe and a spinster from Clapham. When his turn came, he bought a round of drinks which, he thought ruefully to himself, cost half a day's wages in one go. By sundown, he was regarded by the crowd as a good fellow, one of the lads no less. The whisky made him relax and forget his shyness so that within a couple of hours of his introduction to club life, an outside observer would not have realized that he, alone of the group, was the new chum.

In an alcoholic haze, Kenneth was introduced to the tennis players as they drifted in with the fading of the light. Conversation waxed and waned as young men joined Kenneth's group or called it a night and left for their various plantations. His mood was happy as his conscious and subconscious anxieties slipped away from him: Kuala Tanah was all right; his mess-mates reasonable fellows; the club convivial. He hadn't had high expectations about the job and they had been more than met this day. None of his fears of inadequacy and loneliness, which had been silent, periodic nightmares since leaving England, was going to materialize and he now knew he would enjoy life in the rubber business.

Erratically weaving back to Kuala Tanah on the pillion seat of the motor cycle that night, Kenneth's befuddled mind felt at peace with the world.

Chapter 4

Selangor, 1923

On a late afternoon in February 1923, Kenneth and George Blagdon were motoring along on the old BSA to a friend's place located up the Salak–Bangi road. They had arranged earlier in the week to meet for a few drinks and a couple of games of billiards. The monsoon was nearly over but the daily rains over the past two months had made sections of the road a bog. It was hardly the season for long-distance social calls, but life was so monotonous for the two young men that any chance to give the Salak Club a miss for an evening was to be grabbed at.

George was at the throttle, while Kenneth travelled in the cane chair on the sidecar, more because his weight out there gave the motorcycle stability in the slippery conditions, than for reasons of comfort. The pace of the journey was somewhat erratic. On the dry stretches they kicked along at twenty miles an hour, but every mile or so a muddy patch would force George to cut down to second gear in order to plough through it safely. Now and then pools of water covered the road where it was particularly low-lying. George was negotiating such a puddle when round the curve in the road came a dark-green Vauxhall Prince Henry open-tourer, travelling at great speed. It cut the corner and lined up on the bike, the driver unaware that he was sharing the road. The motorcycle was moving too slowly to do much in the way of evasive action, but George did his best, turning and at the same time accelerating to the left.

Belatedly the driver of the Prince Henry saw them. Swinging his steering wheel to his left, the driver slewed the car into a drift, but with a deft twist he corrected the slide. However, as he fish-tailed away, spraying red mud in plumes behind him, the right back fender nudged the motorcycle. The bike spun in a clockwise direction, engine roaring as George inadvertently wound up the throttle as he hung on desperately, and completed a circle and a half before it stalled.

George was still astride the machine; Kenneth, however, had been flung off almost immediately at the moment of impact, and was lying on his side several yards away. He was smeared from head to foot in red mud, but unharmed. The puddle of sludge they had been attempting to avoid had in fact cushioned his fall.

'Who was that bloody fool? He could have bloody well killed us,' spluttered Kenneth.

'Silly bastard,' added George. 'Only an idiot would drive like that when the roads are in this state. He must have been going at least forty.'

'God, just look at me,' said Kenneth as he got to his feet and squelched towards the motorcycle. 'What a mess! How's the bike?'

As they stood there assessing the damage, a car pulled up behind them. They turned and saw the Prince Henry.

'I'll smash his face in,' said George angrily. 'He's going to get a lesson in driving manners bloody well beaten into him.' Kenneth had never seen him so angry before. Feeling somewhat similarly inclined, but less confident of his prowess as a fighter, Kenneth let George confront the reckless driver of the Vauxhall on his own.

George stalked belligerently towards the car but when he was only a couple of yards away he stopped dead in his tracks. The driver had removed his leather driving cap and goggles and was descending from his seat behind the wheel. It was none other than Rajah Ibrahim u'd-din, the traditional ruler of this part of Selangor.

'You johnnies allright?' called out the Rajah as he walked towards them. Both the young Englishmen had recognized him immediately for he was a well-known sportsman in Selangor. That virtue, plus the fact that he was a member of Selangor royalty, Eton and Oxford-educated, made him one of the Malay social lions among the upper-echelon British administration in Malaya and his photograph had often turned up in the *Straits Times* social and sports pages. In the normal course of events, people of Kenneth's and George's social obscurity would never meet a man of Rajah Ibrahim u'd-din's standing, but today's meeting could hardly be described as a normal introduction.

'Er . . . yes sir,' mumbled George, standing rooted to the spot.

'How about you, old man?' called the Rajah looking in Kenneth's direction. 'No bones broken?'

'I seem to be all right, sir,' Kenneth replied.

The Rajah studied them for a moment.

'I'll tell you what,' he said. 'You young fellows are in a frightful mess and both of you look shaken up. Bit of bad timing, each of us requiring that piece of road just when we did. I'll give you a ride to my place where you can clean up and I'll get you back home. Least I can do in the circumstances. Don't worry about your motorcycle, I'll get a couple of boys from the village up the road to look after it. Come on, hop in the back.'

Kenneth and George were astonished at the invitation but weren't about to disagree with the Rajah's suggestion. They climbed into the back seat of the sleek Vauxhall, Kenneth very conscious of the dripping muddy mess he was creating.

'Thank you, sir,' said George.

The motor car did a U-turn and thundered up the road towards Salak. At the first village the Rajah pulled up and had a quick conversation with a man who had scurried out at the sight of the car stopping.

'Where are you chaps from?' asked the Rajah. George told him and more Malay was exchanged between the headman and the Rajah. 'Right, this man will see that your motorcycle gets taken to your estate. He'll send a bullock cart out for it immediately.'

Off they went. Minutes later the Rajah swung the wheel

and they took off down the road away from Salak and Kuala Tanah estate and towards the coastal town of Batu Laut. It was an almost straight line of road for the twenty miles to the coast, edged with rubber plantations and rice fields and, although not far, as the crow flies, from the estate, a part of Selangor neither Kenneth nor George had visited. Much of the land there was owned by the Rajah and unlike the territory to the south-east of the Kemudi River where Kuala Tanah was, it had not been sold or leased to European planters. The plantations whistling past them on their left were Malayan-owned and run.

Some ten or so miles past the turn-off, they barrelled through the Malay village of Dingkil and, a few minutes later, the Rajah slowed down and turned into a narrow road that ran towards the Kemudi River. They bumped along this for a couple more miles and reached a prosperous-looking kampong of thirty or forty houses. Set slightly away from these was a white-painted European-styled home, the Istana or palace of Rajah Ibrahim. Compared to anything Kenneth and George had seen on the British estates in the region, this house was magnificent. It was very large and made of stone and concrete. Deep bay windows were a feature of the ground floor while above, broad balconies jutted out, each with its own expansive dormer emerging from the sloping orange-tiled roof. Back at ground level, generously proportioned verandahs, shaded with criss-cross latticework and decorated with potted palms and hanging baskets of ferns and cultivated epiphytes, protected the lower rooms from the glare and heat of the equatorial sun. The driveway swept towards the house in a graceful arc and where it passed in front of the broad marble stairs which led up to the balustraded verandah and entrance portico, a carport projected out from the house to provide shelter from rain or sun to anyone alighting.

The Rajah stopped the car at the steps.

'Let's get you johnnies cleaned up,' he said, springing from the Vauxhall. He saw they were hesitant and non-plussed by the surroundings. 'Come on, chop, chop.'

Leading the way up the stairs, he gave instructions to a bevy of servants waiting on the verandah. 'Follow Amin. He will take you to the bathroom. While your suits are being cleaned, wear what he gives you. In an hour you'll look fine again. I'll see you in ten minutes' time in the den.' With that he sauntered into the depths of the house.

'My God, what do you make of all this?' said George to Kenneth. 'Us in the Rajah's palace, who would believe it!'

The two young men were taken to a marble-floored bathroom at the far end of the Istana and, as they bathed behind rattan and bamboo screens from the finest Shanghai jars either of them had ever seen, their muddy clothes were spirited away to the royal laundry. In their place, waiting for them, were left a checkered sarong and a white long-tailed shirt apiece. They dressed and were led by a silent servant along several wide corridors to the den.

'Come in, old chaps,' called the Rajah when he saw them at the entrance. He was standing by a bookcase, browsing through a photograph album. He replaced the volume on the shelf and said, 'How about some iced tea to refresh yourselves?' He spoke to the servant who had brought Kenneth and George from the bathroom and as the man disappeared said, 'We'll have it on the verandah through here.'

The three made their way through french doors and made themselves comfortable on expansive cane chairs just beyond the room. Compared with the temperature outside, the Istana felt wonderfully cool. As Rajah Ibrahim chatted about the accident, the weather, and planting, the two young men began to feel more at ease in their unusual surroundings.

Rajah Ibrahim would have been about ten years older than the two young Englishmen, somewhere around thirty-five, guesssed Kenneth. He was tall for a Malay and, thought Kenneth, beginning to lose his angular sportsman's physique with approaching middle age. In fact he was definitely on the plump side with a pudgy face whose loss of fine bone structure under the smooth flesh was emphasized by the way he pursed his lips in an unconscious mannerism every now and then. His hair was beautifully cut and oiled so that it almost shone. A neatly manicured moustache, shaved to a thin line, decorated his upper lip.

The tea arrived on a silver salver cluttered with glass cups and saucers and plates of sliced fruit and Malayan delicacies. The Rajah dismissed the servant and poured from the cut-glass jug a cup of tea for each of them, ice chinking against the rim of the jug as he did so. The hand that clasped the handle was bejewelled with rings decorating all but one of its fingers. Kenneth looked at the Rajah's left hand and it too flashed with chunky showy jewellery on several fingers. A gold bangle decorated his left wrist.

'How do you young fellows spend your free time?' asked the Rajah.

Kenneth by this time had found his tongue and spoke up.

'At the Salak Club most weekday evenings, sir. We're also at the Bangi Club once or twice a fortnight. It's a bit far for us to go more often and, also, we aren't members. Sometimes we visit a friend on another estate. That's where we were heading this afternoon when we . . . er . . . met. We had a billiard tournament to take part in. Then there's Sundays, and they are usually spent at the bigger estates, like some of the Dunlop ones, where it's easy to get a scratch cricket team together for a match or have a decent sort of a picnic.'

'Do you get a chance to see much of the country?'

'Not really,' replied Kenneth. 'In the two and a half years I've been at Kuala Tanah Estate I've been to Seremban three times – that's as far away as I've got – and a couple of rafting trips on the upper Kemudi, and . . .' he thought for a few seconds, 'some sporting tournaments a bit beyond Bangi. That's it really.'

'You haven't been to Kuala Lumpur?' said the Rajah. 'I thought all roads led to Kuala Lumpur: the Selangor

71

Club, the library and museum, the music theatres. How could you not go there?'

'Being assistant managers, sir, we actually have never been invited to any social functions at the capital. In the European planting world we haven't, how can I put it, we haven't made much of a step on the social ladder yet. Seremban is as high as we've climbed so far. No doubt we'll eventually get to meet some fellows from Kuala Lumpur, but so far we haven't. That's right isn't it, George?'

'Yes,' replied George. 'I've been in Selangor about a year longer than Kenneth, sir, and it seems that, socially, things extend north of Kuala Lumpur rather than south. There's all those big estates, especially up near Perak. Then there's the Cameron Highlands, Ipoh and so forth. From the British point of view, this corner of Selangor is a bit of a backwater. Still it's home for now and we make of it what we can.'

The Rajah laughed. 'So my kingdom is a backwater is it? My father, after all the struggles he fought through to retain Sungei Kemudi, would turn in his grave to hear it described thus.'

George blushed. 'Excuse me, sir, I was only talking about our existence here, I would never dream of implying British planter life represented everything in southern Selangor. I do apologize.'

The Rajah continued to chuckle: the two young men were proving to be a pleasant if simple diversion on this afternoon.

'You mentioned a billiard tournament, are you both keen on the game?'

'Yes,' George replied. 'We play a lot at the Club, though I have to confess I'm not especially good at it. He on the other hand,' he nodded his head towards where Kenneth was sitting, 'is the best player the Salak Club boasts. In fact you're probably as good as anyone over at Bangi as well, aren't you?'

With typical British reticence at anything suggestive of praise, Kenneth dismissed his friend's compliment.

'I wouldn't say that, George, for a start there's Mr Carlisle who is very good.'

'Reggie Carlisle?' interrupted the Rajah. 'He and I have had a few matches in our time. He is good, I agree. Come on, old man, join me in a quick game before my syce runs you back to your estate,' and with that he got to his feet and led the two young men back into his study where the billiard table stood.

The quick game extended into five before the Rajah clipped his cue back into the rack. He had only won a single game, the third one.

'You are good, young fellow. My goodness, it's jolly near unprecedented that I lose so consistently. I shall declare the afternoon one of my off-days to explain it away. You don't by any chance play bridge as well as you do billiards do you?'

Kenneth replied, 'No sir, I really am a most indifferent card player.' Trying hard not to show it on his face, Kenneth was delighted with his billiard performance. He didn't think he'd ever played a better game than he had that afternoon and to have beaten Rajah Ibrahim of Sungei Kemudi four out of five times . . . well! 'Billiards is the only game I really enjoy.'

'You play a jolly good game, well done.' Turning to George who had been playing the role of spectator since afternoon tea, the Rajah said, 'You are right, I also think he is probably better than anyone at Bangi. I've played their better players – like Reggie – over the years in various places and they don't have the eye Kenneth here has. I won't admit he has more of an eye than me though. I spent three years at Oxford perfecting this game.' With that he burst into laughter. 'Come on, time I got you fellows home.'

All things being equal, Kenneth would never have met the Rajah of Sungei Kemudi ever again. However it was only a fortnight later that he received an invitation to visit the Rajah for the pleasure of a game of billiards. Apart from the challenge of a good match, the Rajah had in fact taken a liking to the young Englishman. His youth made him amusing to be around, for most Europeans the Rajah dealt with were at least twice Kenneth's age and endowed with varying degrees of pompous stuffiness, depending on the position they held. Kenneth was closer to his own age and, because he counted for very little socially, was much more himself. Kenneth would be the first to admit he wasn't the life and soul of any party he happened to be at, but he was personable and light-hearted; in a word, likeable, and the Rajah found him refreshing to be around. Kenneth, despite the absence of an upper-class accent, reminded him of his own early twenties as an irresponsible undergraduate at Oxford. And, not least of Kenneth's charms, the Rajah knew, even if Kenneth didn't, that the young Englishman was the best billiards player the Rajah had met in ten years, possibly better than even himself and therefore an excellent opponent.

This first invitation was eventually followed by a second. Before many months had passed, Kenneth had a standing invitation to the Istana every second and fourth Wednesday each month to play billiards. The two players were evenly matched so that the claim as to who was the better man was always in the balance, a fact which turned the acquaintanceship into a good-natured friendship as the months rolled by.

Eventually, towards Christmas 1923, the Rajah said to Kenneth, 'Look old chap, let's knock off the "sir" when we're together. My friends call me Ali, so why don't you.' By his friends, Kenneth knew the Rajah was speaking of the small group of English-educated aristocratic Malays he had been to school with and the old Etonian expatriates working for various Sultans across British Malaya.

'Well . . . certainly,' replied Kenneth, appreciating the enormity of the occasion. He was very flattered to be included among the Rajah's – Ali's – circle of friends and the honour preoccupied him sufficiently for Ali to win the rest of the evening's games.

At the 1923 Christmas Party at the Bangi club, the fourth Kenneth had been to, Kenneth got into conversation with several club members about the Rajah. Sidney Featherston, a manager for Dunlop Ltd, brought the subject up.

'I hear you're in pretty thick with our Rajah, young fellow. How on earth did you meet him?'

Kenneth explained the accident earlier in the year and their mutual fondness for billiards. The question prompted the small group of senior planters he was sitting with to begin discussing the Rajah and his role in local Malay politics, a subject Kenneth knew nothing about.

'I've never really trusted the look of the man myself,' said Mr Featherston. 'I know his leases on land are fair enough, in fact more than fair when compared to His Royal Bloody Highness across the border.' He was referring to the Yang di Pertuan Besar of Negri Sembilan. 'But the rubber and tin taxes are no joke. His labour contracts aren't funny either.' The Rajah controlled all immigrant labour into southern Selangor; how many Tamils could live in the region and how many Chinese could work on the tin fields; and buying his attention was the surest way of guaranteeing a full workforce on the rubber estate or tin mine. Given the mortality rate amongst coolies, labour shortages could sometimes be a problem unless the Rajah authorized the settlement of more indentured labourers.

'What's the new Istana like?' asked another planter. 'Years ago when his father was alive, I went to a Malay shindig at the old palace at Batu Laut where the Abrahim clan have been for years. Huge rambling old place filled with wives and children. I hear the new one is rather grand. Of course, building the place where he did is a poke in the eye for Idris Hussein. He must see the place through the trees every time he steps outside his door.'

'I'm surprised those black bastards haven't murdered one another by now,' said a sour-faced planter by the name of Hawley.

'Give them time,' said Mr Featherston. 'Even if Rajah Ibrahim and Idris Hussein haven't had it out face to face, the families have been popping each other more or less on a regular basis ever since I've been here.'

'And that's a long time,' chimed in two planters simultaneously. The group chuckled at what was obviously an old punchline.

'What is all this about?' asked Kenneth.

'Buy us a round and we will enlighten you,' said Featherston on behalf of the older men. Kenneth beckoned a bearer to the table and ordered stengahs all round.

'Your friend the Rajah may run the show in this part of Selangor but the Ibrahim family are regarded by some of the Malays as johnny-come-latelies. The Idris Hussein clan claim they are the traditional rulers for all this region of the Straits of Malacca and in fact apparently controlled a hell of a lot more of it than Rajah Ibrahim does. That is, until the Portuguese booted them out of the Malacca area in 1422. The Ibrahims, so this story goes, turned up in the 1500s but somehow pulled a fast one that enabled them not only to claim the region as their kingdom by right of conquest, but also through traditional history.' Featherston paused for a gulp of whisky. 'It's very helpful you must understand, if you're a Malayan ruler, to have the correct antecedents, sacred Garuda birds marrying princesses, nephews of Mohammed, inscribed tablets of stone, name in the ancient annals and so on. Otherwise there will always be a more rightful claimant to your kingdom. And that's what has been going on between the Ibrahim and Idris families for about four centuries. Rajah Ibrahim and Idris Hussein are simply carrying on the family traditions.'

'For four hundred years! The Idris haven't been very successful; I'd have thought they would have called it quits ages ago,' snorted Hawley.

'Ah, but they've had their moments,' replied Featherston. 'There were ten years of bloodshed up and down the Kemudi back in the 1870s when a bunch of Idris chiefs finally settled enough of their family differences to take on the Ibrahims in a serious manner. Half of Batu Laut was burned down at one stage and the Rajah forced to take refuge with the Rajah of the Kelang until his armies reorganized. There's a lot at stake after all. Sungei Kemudi pulls in a fair bit of revenue, as we all know to our cost, and up until the 1880s to 1890s the Rajah collected shipping dues from all vessels sailing past Batu Laut. Piracy almost, but profitable nevertheless. Not least either is the prestige and honour that goes with being the Royal Family. If nothing else, it makes piracy and exorbitant taxes respectable.'

Kenneth listened with interest. He had had no way of appreciating the power that Ali had at his fingertips, or the ruthlessness involved in using such power. Ali to him was a billiards friend, or when he spotted the Rajah's photograph in the *Straits Times*, a formally decked-out prince doing the respectable things a member of royalty is supposed to do, such as opening a training centre for Malayan engineering apprentices or being present at the first day of Parliament. That it took murder and intrigue to maintain his position as Rajah came as a surprise to the Englishman.

'I still don't understand,' he said. 'What is it that Rajah Ibrahim has, and Idris Hussein hasn't, that keeps a lot of people loyal to him? From what you are saying, Idris Hussein sounds a pretty powerful individual in his own right. Why didn't the Idris clan become the Royal Family when they kicked the Rajah out of Batu Laut fifty years ago?'

'It's tradition my boy, tradition. From what I can gather, the oldest written records about the history of the kings along the Straits of Malacca mention the Ibrahim family as the local rulers. The Idris are mentioned also, but apparently only as a very powerful family and not the Royal Family. The Idris have always disputed some of the interpretations of the Annals and of course they are open to different interpretations, depending on who is reading them. But, more than that, they claim that older written histories, which mention the Idris as Rajahs, have been destroyed or hidden by the Ibrahims. Could be true. The Annals for this part of the Malay Peninsula only go back four hundred years. Elsewhere along the Straits, they usually date back nearly twice as far, at least 1200 or thereabouts. So, to cut a long story short, the Ibrahims claim to have a divine right to rule and, in the final analysis, this is why, even when their backs are against the wall militarily, such as in the 1870s, the Idris still can't rally enough support to win the day. Pity really, as Idris Hussein is a damn sight more reasonable to deal with than the Rajah when it comes to the business of rubber.'

The other planters around the table agreed.

Even the unpleasant Hawley endorsed the general approval of Idris Hussein.

'As a rule of thumb I don't trust any of the black swine. But Idris is okay. Got a bit of manliness to him, unlike most of the spineless bastards we have to put up with on occasion.' Hawley was typical of the sort of Englishman in Malaya who resented everything about the country. Whatever the topic under discussion, sooner or later either 'black bastards', 'Indian monkeys', or 'slant-eyed swine' – meaning Malays, Tamils or Chinese – would enter the conversation as a root cause to the issue. His bigotry and bile were not solely reserved for them, however. The British administrators were usually described as 'gutless cretins' and the Dutch across the Straits of Malacca in Sumatra, as 'slimy money-grubbers'. There were always a Hawley or two in every club in Malaya and, by and large, their bitter observations and rantings were good-humouredly ignored. The men about the table this evening probably were not even aware of what Hawley was saying, he was to them simply 'going on again'.

'Earlier you said something about the Rajah's Istana. Its location annoying this other fellow or something. What is the story?'

'Well, all of the north side of the Kemudi is either owned by the Rajah Ibrahim or by the Idris. The Rajah also owns most of the south side across to the Negri Sembilan border too, but that land is all leased. The Idris have their home at the village of Bukit Klang which is also the name of that hill on the north bank as you come up the Kemudi on the steamer. You must know it. It's the only thing on the landscape for miles around which warrants the label "hill". The Ibrahims traditionally have their palace on the coast at Batu Laut. They could keep an eye on the Strait and on the mouth of the Kemudi from there, and perhaps just as importantly, it put a lot of miles between them and the Idris. That way the friction between the two families was minimized and each could get on with their own business without having to be continually reminded of the other's existence. It seems to have worked well enough, off and on. Of course, every now and then a particularly stroppy member of one family or the other would cause some trouble, but over all it was a sound compromise.' Featherston went on. 'So what does the present Rajah do? He builds a new Istana on a piece of land right on his boundary with the Idris. That new place is less than half a mile north of Bukit Klang and must be a constant reminder to Idris Hussein as to who is top dog in southern Selangor.'

'It makes Idris hopping mad,' interjected a hitherto silent planter by the name of Newton. 'We were together at the Selangor Club for the polo back in August. I've known Idris Hussein for a few years now – and he regards the Istana as an affront to his authority along that part of the river, and a very deliberate one to boot. He reckons the Ibrahims are going to attempt to push the Idris out of the lower Kemudi, but warned that they will have a fight on their hands before he budges an inch.' He turned to Featherston. 'You are right about the politics. Idris Hussein has told me on occasion that the wrong family rules the region; that the Idris were the Royal Family; and that the necessary credentials to show as such have been long hidden away by the scheming Ibrahims. God knows what is true. But Idris is the better man, that I do know. I mean, what about that business three years ago at Port Swettenham? Shocking.'

He was referring to a local scandal to which no conclusive finish had ever been drawn. Kenneth didn't know what they were talking about.

'What business?' he asked.

The mean-spirited Hawley was happy to enlighten him.

'No mems nearby, eh, so I'll tell you. A young Malay boy – about fifteen wasn't he? – was dumped at the Port Swettenham Infirmary one night back in 1920. Most unusual. Malays don't seek out British hospitals as a rule, but stick to their own doctors. His injury was unusual however. The poor sod had been castrated and needed prompt attention. Well, it turned out upon inspection,' Hawley leered at Kenneth, 'that he had also been well and truly buggered. The swine shagging the boy had almost torn the lad's tackle off in the heat of the moment. It seems that once he understood what he had done he bundled the boy up and dumped him at the hospital gates. The quacks did what they could, patched him up and so forth, but he died of blood poisoning within a week. He was too sick during that time to say anything about who had done it to him. The police, naturally enough, were pretty interested in the pervert responsible.' He laughed coarsely. 'They must have had a list of suspects a mile long, thinking of all those long-fingered, mincing pansies in government service in Kuala Lumpur.'

'Steady on, Hawley,' cautioned Newton quietly. 'You can't go saying that about our colleagues.'

'They're not our colleagues. We're planters in the bloody sticks; they're the pen pushers who run half of Selangor. Call a spade a spade I say. They're a bunch of sodomizing swine even if they have climbed to the top of the monkey tree.'

'You know what I mean,' persisted Newton uncomfortably. 'Damn it, they're British and I don't think a white man would do what was done to that unfortunate lad.' Others around the table muttered agreement.

'Well, in one respect you're right. Suspicion quickly settled on the fat shoulders of our respected Rajah Ibrahim. His car was seen in the vicinity of the Infirmary that night. He and the lad had known each other. There were some other details too, which I can't remember, but the upshot of it all was that no one who knew anything would say so publicly. Consequently, the matter was left to rest. The rumours, nevertheless, were that it was the Rajah who had had the boy that night. I doubt if it's ever troubled him, he's buggered more boys than I've had curry tiffins.'

Kenneth was aghast. He hadn't heard such a story about Ali before, but at the back of his mind knew that the Rajah was prone to fierce passions which Kenneth had chosen to ignore.

Hawley looked at him and said,

'Don't look so anxious, old chap. Rest assured the black bastard is more interested in your billiard balls than what hangs between your legs.'

Kenneth felt himself blush fiercely. He said nothing in return, deciding that any defence towards his friendship with Ali would only invite more teasing and sarcasm.

Featherston returned briefly to the point of the story. 'The Rajah is a shifty character all right. I heard too, that the authorities had identified him as the perpetrator of that crime, but of course it's a brave Administration who would charge one of the Malayan rulers with man-slaughter. Wouldn't be seen as pursuing justice, but rather as meddling in local politics – an attack on the Rajah's integrity and all that. Idris Hussein could have capitalized on the situation very well I imagine.'

The group had forgotten that Kenneth knew the Rajah and, for a few minutes more, chatted on about the man's dealings and reputation. Kenneth ceased to listen. The combination of shock on hearing Hawley's story and the dulling of his senses from four hours of steady drinking, mentally removed him from the circle of half-drunk planters to another evening which had taken place some six weeks earlier.

He and Ali had, as usual, been playing billiards. The day had been incredibly hot and even within the shady coolness of the Istana the air was still and stifling. Another game over, the Rajah called for refreshments to be brought. One of the white-clad servants who had been standing discreetly against the wall of the den, silently exited, only to return minutes later with Malayan canapés and sherbert tea on a silver tray.

'We'll have it through there,' Ali said, pointing to a side drawing room. Within were some cane chaise-longues and a clutter of furniture casually positioned about a parquet floor. Two tiger-skin rugs lay on its polished mahogany surface.

'We can put our feet up. My word, it's the hottest day we've had for a while.'

They sipped their tea in silence as the wide-bladed fan above their heads revolved slowly, stirring the listless air into a more breathable substance.

The Rajah continued speaking.

'Do you miss your stengahs here? I know at the Club they'll all be half cut by now.' He was referring to the lack of alcohol at the Istana. The Koran forbade the drinking of any intoxicants and Ali was a strict enough Muslim to stick to Mohammed's law on the matter.

'No. If anything it's a relief to lay off the booze for a night. Also, it helps the health of my wallet,' said Kenneth, laughing. 'I've spent a fortune pouring whisky into myself and everyone else. No choice though, socially it would be disastrous not to be a good sport when it comes to buying drinks.'

'I'll let you into a secret,' said Ali, putting his cup down as he spoke. 'I do have a small vice myself, which I indulge in occasionally. Opium. Would you care to try it this evening? I feel in the mood myself.'

Kenneth had never smoked the stuff although it was freely available in the tin-mining towns all across Federated Malaya. It wasn't a white man's drug, and in fact, until Ali had brought the subject up, Kenneth had assumed that its use was restricted to within the Chinese community who consumed vast quantities of it. More than half of Selangor's annual revenue was generated by the government taxes on the sale of opium and it was probably the same in the other Malay States.

'I've never tried it and I'm not sure that I care to,' replied Kenneth. His curiosity was aroused however. There was no hurry to get back to Kuala Tanah. Ronnie and George would be over at Salak anyway, meaning that the mess would be empty and boring. 'Oh, why not,' he continued. 'I will.'

'Excellent.' Ali called for a servant and gave him some instructions in Malay. Before long two pipes were brought in and one placed on the occasional table beside each man's chaise-longue. Kenneth looked with interest at his. The pipe was more like a long cigarette holder than a conventional stubby European pipe. It was of ebony, inlaid with ivory, and at one end a tiny brass bowl, capable of holding nothing larger than a garden pea, projected upward. The servant produced a small chased silver casket the size of a match box and, lifting the lid, took out a lump of black, resinous stuff. It was soft enough to break with his fingers.

He placed a small pellet of the substance in the bowl of the pipe and offered it to Kenneth. Kenneth glanced over to Ali where similar preparations were being made by another servant.

'Go ahead, old chap, light up. I've told Amin there to give you just a couple of pipes so there's no chance you'll have too much.' With that Ali lay back and drew on his pipe as the servant held a burning match over the bowl.

Kenneth suppressed his anxiety about the situation and did the same when Amin set a match alight for his pipe. The smoke was surprisingly cool and although somewhat acrid, not unpleasant to taste. He pulled on the pipe at his leisure, Amin patiently refiring the pellet of opium when Kenneth moved the pipe towards his lips. Without being aware of it, he retreated into a world far removed from the room where he lay. He was on the boat which had brought him to Penang three years earlier. The orchestra was playing dance music with crystal-clear clarity and Kenneth stood chatting with George and Ronnie at the edge of the dance floor, each resplendent in black evening clothes and shining patent leather dance pumps.

A beautiful woman approached in a sleek silver evening dress and asked Kenneth to partner her for the Ladies'

Invitation Foxtrot. As one, they glided across the floor, completely rapt in each other, carried along with the music which so enveloped them that they were unaware of anyone else present in the room. What music! A thought occurred to Kenneth: I didn't know George or Ronnie back then, what am I thinking of? And he was back in the Istana again. What amazing stuff, marvelled Kenneth, it was all so real. He looked across to Ali. The Rajah lay back in his cane chair, eyes closed and a smile on his lips. His servant knelt alongside, ready to relight the pipe when asked. Ali looked as if he were miles away.

Kenneth looked away. He was standing on the Terrace of the Crag Hotel up on Penang Hill, stengah in hand and looking out across the town two thousand feet below. Beyond was the crowded waterway of steamers and junks, and beyond them again, the coast of Perak. With only the smallest of surprises, he observed that the blue-grey hills of the Perak Highlands no longer provided the western horizon. In their place soared an enormously high range of snow-clad mountains. Walls of vertical rock riven with ice were separated by the palest blue glaciers emerging from hanging valleys deep within the awesome peaks. Above, so far above that Kenneth had to arch his neck back to look up, were deep snow fields rising to the mountain summits. Lower down there were no alpine meadows or wooded foothills. The mountain range simply burst out of the Perak coastal plain.

Kenneth felt a cool snow-chilled breeze waft over him. This is better than it used to be when there were no mountains over there, he said to himself and breathed in a refreshing lungful of the mountain air. He turned to discover that the Crag Hotel behind him was gone and in its place was the Esplanade at Brighton. Just over there was the Guest House, the Miramar, where he and his parents were lodging for a week's holiday at the beach. Beach? Kenneth turned again and saw the grey English Channel before him. Below, on the pebbly beach, sat his mother and father on striped folding deckchairs. It was hot and the beach was crowded with holidaymakers and daytrippers. He waved to them and caught his mother's attention. Come and have a swim, she called. He made his way through the crowd to the stone stairs down to the beach, but once he had descended, he could no longer see where his parents sat. Everywhere were rows of deckchairs and groups of people. A band played in a cast-iron band rotunda standing, curiously enough, right at the water's edge.

Kenneth opened his eyes. Amin had gone. What weird effects this stuff has, he wondered to himself. He took a sip of sherbert tea from the glass cup standing on the occasional table. How long have I been here? Taking his pocket watch out, he stared in disbelief. Two and a half hours had sped by! Extraordinary! I'd better think about making tracks or I won't be home until midnight. He attempted to stand up, but found he was just too lethargic to do more than raise his body a couple of inches off the chair. I'll go soon, he compromised to himself, settling back.

He looked over to Ali. In the subdued light from a single electric lamp near the door leading to the den, he could see Ali talking softly to his kneeling servant. As he looked he noticed the Rajah's hand slip under the servant's sarong and begin caressing the boy's sex. Was this more dreaming? Kenneth couldn't judge. He continued to view the scene completely dispassionately. It seemed almost in slow motion and possessed the same super-real qualities of the earlier visions. Ali and the boy moved on to a tiger-skin rug next to the chaise-longue. Both disrobed and, with the boy lying on his back, Ali deftly fondled him until the lad ejaculated into the palms of his hands. With eyes closed, Ali spread the boy's seed over his own stiff member and, nudging him to turn over on to his stomach, entered his servant. A hiss of fulfilment escaped from his lips as his belly butted up against the round buttocks of the youth.

Kenneth looked on impassively. He had never been in such a situation before, either as a participant or an observer, but found the event before his eyes only as curious and as interesting as the other visions. Opium was certainly an experience way beyond anything he had ever imagined.

His ponderings about the drug were interrupted by some low cries. Focusing back to the tiger-skin rug, he saw the boy almost bent double, his turbanned head jammed against the neck of the tiger skin, as Ali became more and more vigorous in his drug-enhanced lust, his arms circling the lad's waist in a grip which gave the boy no possibility but to submit to his master. Finally Ali ceased, and, glassy-eyed and spent, lay half over the boy, breathing heavily from the exertion of the last ten minutes. After waiting a little while the servant wriggled away and without a glance towards Kenneth at the other side of the room, dressed hurriedly and left. He did return though, bearing a Kashmir shawl which he laid across the Rajah as a blanket, after which he retired.

In the cold light of day, six weeks ago, Kenneth had decided that what he had witnessed, or imagined (he wasn't sure which was what) under the spell of Ali's opium, didn't alter his friendship with Rajah one jot. That evening had been so bizarre it was easy to push any disquietening elements about it away but nevertheless Kenneth had since felt somewhat uneasy about the relationship. And now, could he really like a man as much as he liked Ali when the Rajah was clearly seen by the white community as a scheming, political manipulator, shady businessman and sexual pervert to boot?

For much of the remainder of the evening's festivities the thought preoccupied Kenneth. About him drunken planters and their mems celebrated Christmas in the usual way by over-indulging in strong alcohol, mild flirting, and gossip. He looked about him: the Bangi Club seemed full of florid-faced men and ladies with long-suffering looks on their carefully made-up stoical faces.

He suddenly felt alienated from them all. To hell with assessing his friendship with Ali on the strength of what he had heard tonight. Would the loathsome Hawley behave any differently had he the power and authority the Rajah wielded? Or Featherston? Or any of them? He took a gulp of his stengah and rejoined the conversation. No good being too thoughtful, he decided, just fit in where you can and, on that note, he made a determined effort to spend the rest of the party as good-naturedly as he could.

Christmas Day, 1923, dawned with heavy rain thundering on the corrugated iron roof of the mess. The air was hot and humid. Kenneth winced at the hangover ripping its way across his brain. Another year almost over. Happy bloody Christmas, he wished himself, and rolling over, attempted to return to sleep.

Chapter 5

'I won't listen to this. I won't, I won't!' cried Maeve as her father berated her in the hallway of the Stephenson house. She was still dressed in her hat and scarf, having entered the house only minutes earlier. 'You've got it all wrong!'

'Don't tell me what's wrong,' he shouted. 'I saw you outside that tearoom in the High Street, a mere half hour ago, carrying on like a floozy with those young men. I couldn't believe my eyes, seeing you in with that crowd, laughing and playing the fool, nearly blocking the footpath with your horseplay. It was a disgraceful display of public ill-manners, and as for that boy who put his arm about you, well! What do you feel people will think about you, eh? My daughter behaving in this way, what will people say? Where on earth was your good sense, doing this, this,' he groped for a word, 'unseemly thing?'

Maeve looked heavenward as if beseeching a higher being to give her patience in this moment of need, but tears glinting in her eyes, about to well over her lower lashes, betrayed how upset she really felt.

'It wasn't like that, Father. You know it wasn't.' She looked back at her father occupying the centre of the hallway.

He stood unmoved in his grey suit with leather elbow patches, clerical collar advertising his profession, a short, plump figure with a round face, red with anger, strands of wispy hair stretched from above his right parting over to his left ear ineffectually disguising a balding head. He was angry, not only because of how he had chosen to interpret Maeve's behaviour in the town, but also because she had the effrontery to contradict him when confronted with his condemnations. As the local vicar, he had become used to having the last word in most issues that involved his inconsequential parish and he expected the same respect for his views in his domestic life. His wife, known to all outside their home, as Mrs Stephenson, and within its walls as 'mother' by both the Reverend Stephenson and Maeve, stood behind him at the kitchen door, tugging an oven cloth fretfully between nervous fingers as she listened to the row. She never contradicted her husband.

Maeve, however, stuck up for herself when she felt her opinions or actions were being misrepresented and because of this, was often regarded by her father as wilful and stubborn. It was unfair of him. Maeve had grown up a high-minded, well-principled young woman. The Reverend Stephenson could probably see his only child's character in this light also if only he would loosen the blinkered approach to life he had increasingly adopted as he grew older. But in truth, he was intimidated by the clever young woman his daughter had grown into and the affection he had once held for her had changed in recent years into a condescension which would degenerate into sarcasm and, if necessary, a hectoring bullying, in order to make him feel she was still a child requiring his constant guidance and approval. Bullying and sarcasm had worked with Mrs Stephenson, but such tactics failed on Maeve. At best, his posturings reduced her to tears of exasperation – but the more regularly he tried this ploy with his daughter, the more her defence of herself became alloyed with a feeling of contempt for her martinet of a father.

Maeve decided to make one last attempt to explain that his fury was mistaken.

'Look, I don't know what you saw in town that has upset you so. I can tell you what was going on. Those of us in the sixth form who wanted to went to the ABC tearooms for a goodbye tea, a break-up tea. Today is the last day of term if you had forgotten. Those people I was with are my classmates. I don't know how you didn't recognize them, as several go to our church. I wouldn't have missed the tea for the world. Some of the class I've known for ages and we're all about to go our separate ways. For all I know I may not see some of them ever again.' The thought made her feel sad and doubly angry at her father's deliberate misunderstanding of what he had witnessed. Any reasonable father, she thought, recognizing the group for what it was, would have come up and said a few words of good luck to the young people. Particularly the vicar, a respected community figure whose job it must be, shaking hands, wishing people well as they ventured into a new stage of life. Oh, he made her cross!

'Where were you? You could have said hello and none of this need have been said.'

'It is none of your business where I happened to be when I observed your party monopolizing the footpath,' he said pompously. 'The fact of the matter is, you were one of a crowd behaving in an unbefitting manner. If I saw that, others would have seen it in that light too. Anyway, you haven't explained away the young man with his arm about you. It's so common, allowing that boy to display affection, or whatever you want to call such behaviour, in public. In my book it's just not done.'

Maeve exploded.

'That's really the limit! You know who that was? That was Edward Drysdale. He and I were the two in the school who got university scholarships. And you know why he ever so briefly had his arm about me? I tell you why. He was offering his condolences because I had to turn it down. Any why?' her tone was now scathing, 'because you made me refuse it. What a joke! The very thing you most object to, you created in the first place.'

She stared at her father fiercely. Mrs Stephenson, who had been the silent witness to the argument so far, turned her back on the pair and returned to the kitchen. The war of words was about to enter a familiar arena and she had heard the resulting argument a dozen times since it had first erupted four weeks earlier. Years of being married to the Reverend Stephenson had left her with no confidence or courage to support her daughter in these instances when it was patently obvious her husband was being unfair. What spirit of independence she had once possessed had long been belaboured into submission to her husband's wishes. She recommenced the dinner preparations while in the background the voices of her family argued back and forth.

'The subject is closed,' commanded the Reverend Stephenson. 'There is nothing further to discuss.'

Unfortunately, he was right. Maeve was one of the few girls in Ealing Dean Grammar School sixth form. It was not a lack of brains that limited the girls in the class to just two among nine boys, but rather the attitude that a grammar school education was wasted on females. In keeping Maeve at school, the Reverend Stephenson was unusual; most girls left as soon as it was legally allowable, but Maeve, obviously bright and strongly motivated towards school work, had been allowed to pursue her studies for a further three years. She had done so well in passing her Matriculation this year that the London County Council had awarded her a grant to encourage her to continue her studies at London University in September. Her father instead was adamant that she should become a school teacher, claiming a lack of funds as the reason. Having Matriculation placed her in a good position for a grammar school job, and to this end he arranged an appointment for her with the London County Education Authority in a week's time.

'I'll never forgive you for this,' shouted Maeve hotheadedly. 'Getting a grant was a chance in a lifetime; I could have taken it. I told you that if it was a matter of the money I would have worked every summer holiday and paid it back as quickly as I could.' The tears were about to flow. 'I'd rather have left school years ago than be in this situation. To have Matric and a grant, and be told I can't continue, it's very unfair.'

'I told you the subject is closed. A university isn't the place for a girl and that's an end to it. I will not discuss it any further.' With that, the Reverend Stephenson turned on his heel and entered the front parlour, well satisfied that his authority had been re-asserted over his domestic domain.

Dinner was, as many before it, a rather tense and joyless repast. The rift between father and daughter over the matter of Maeve's future had inflamed earlier, less traumatic grievances of hers which had been largely forgotten or forgiven. Now, she looked at him out of the corner of her eye as she ate her mother's cooking, and hated him. Intuitively but inarticulately, she knew the real reason for her father's refusal. The family was not wealthy but neither were they impoverished. The late-Victorian home of red brick with ornamental stone facings in which they lived in Mayfield Avenue was owned by the Church – along with two neighbouring houses – and therefore was rent-free to the Reverend Stephenson for as long as he ministered the local Ealing flock. There were no younger brothers or sisters for which she had to step aside in order that they too might have their share of the education a church vicar's salary could support. There was only herself.

No, the real reason was much less noble. The tension between herself and her father had developed and heightened only as it became apparent that she was clever and successful at grammar school. She had realized, only very recently, that her father was threatened by her Matriculation results and, rather than sharing in the reflected pride of having a daughter clever enough to be accepted into London University, felt that it showed him up as a scholarly lightweight in comparison to her accomplishments. Therefore, she was not to go. To prevent her was easy: a tightening of the family purse strings and she would be forced into accepting schoolteaching as the best use towards which she could put her Matriculation.

In coming to this understanding, a distaste towards her father grew within Maeve, like a cancer. Not only was it despicable of him to treat her like this, but when viewed in the wider world context of his calling, it was hypocritical. Each Sunday in church she had listened to her father's sermons about Christian virtues but, when applied to his relationship with his own daughter, his professional commitments were a hollow sham.

However, it was one thing to come to recognize the situation, and another to do something about it.

The interview appointment came and went and shortly afterwards, towards the end of June, Maeve received a brown OHMS letter in the morning mail, informing her that she had been accepted as a teacher at Mill Hill Park Grammar School. In line with the best of her Matriculation results, she would be teaching third-form classes history, geography and English. Mill Hill Park was nearly two miles east across Ealing and Maeve would continue to live with her parents.

The term was not to commence until the beginning of September. Eight weeks of uninterrupted holidays stretched before her and as the late spring became summer, Maeve slowly became reconciled to her fate. Her anger towards her father did not, however, evaporate and, although a sort of truce developed between them, the house in Mayfield Avenue was not a happy one. The summer of 1924 was a mild one and the balmy weather allowed Maeve to stay away from the house for much of each day in the week, her absence helping to minimize confrontations between the vicar and herself. Appreciating that this time between school and work might be one of the last opportunities of enjoying a carefree summer, Maeve made the mot of it. With Alexa Cubbins, who had also passed her Matriculation and was to go on to nursing, Maeve planned her holiday excursions as thoroughly as if she were in a foreign centre of culture, rather than in the city of her birth.

In a way, London in the summer of 1924 was a foreign city. In April King George V had opened the British Empire Exhibition at Wembley. The magnificent pavilions erected by the various dominions and colonies of Great Britain to extol their industrial and cultural achievements and advertise their scenic delights had brought millions to the capital of the Empire. It

was the most lavish exhibition of all time. The Indian
Government had erected a copy of the Taj Mahal; the
Egyptians a replica of the newly discovered tomb of King
Tutankhamen; the South African Government and the
colony of British Guyana had both gone as far as to
each ship a portion of their diamond-bearing lands to
Wembley.

The newspapers had been full of the Exhibition even
before it had opened and Maeve and Alexa made a visit
their first priority. They travelled across to Wembley on
the specially run train serving the Exhibition and, with
anticipation running high, each paid their 1s 6d admis-
sion. The grounds were packed with visitors from every
culture on the planet.

'Everything is bigger than I expected,' exclaimed Alexa
to Maeve. They were standing at the end of the long
narrow pool which extended out from the imitation
Taj Mahal. In every aspect that she could recall from
photographs she had seen of the building at Agra, this
one looked just the same. Near it, equally impressive in
its scale, was a full-size copy of a seventeenth-century
European fortress as it actually stood on the seashore
of West Africa. Its plain, sunburnt-coloured walls rose
above the streets, a square tower at one side giving the
building an impregnable look as stern and functional as
any Norman keep on the English landscape.

'Let's go over there,' continued Alexa, pointing to it.
Maeve referred to the map she had clipped from a newspaper in preparation for the visit.

'It's the Colony of the Gold Coast Pavilion.'

After some ten minutes of pleasurable jostling among
the crowd, they made it to the portal and walked through
into the fortress courtyard.

'Good heavens, there's a whole town in here,' said
Maeve. 'How wonderful.'

Indeed there was. Small wickerwork-walled huts with
insubstantial thatched roofs formed a small village on a
grid pattern of pounded dirt lanes. Among the buildings
traditional handcrafts were being carried out by West

Africans in bright coloured robes. The girls lingered and observed the work with fascination.

'Wouldn't it be marvellous to see the real thing,' exclaimed Maeve. 'To actually walk on the African land and explore to one's heart's content.'

'Maeve,' laughed Alexa. 'You're such an incorrigible romantic! If you ask me, this is a very good second best. It looks authentic enough to pass for the genuine article. What is more it only cost 1s 6d to be here. How would you ever raise the fare for a real passage to the lands of your daydreams?'

'You are quite right,' replied Maeve. 'I haven't a hope of travelling in the foreseeable future. One day I'll marry a colonial official and get to see the world with him. I think it's the only way I'll ever get to leave England. This, however, is a more than satisfactory compromise until he comes along.'

'Perhaps he will have a brother and we can go together,' joked Alexa and they giggled at the thought as they continued to explore the Exhibition.

On the journey back to Ealing, Maeve suggested to her friend, 'What an exciting day, let's come again, Alexa. Perhaps we can stay for the evening next time and see the illuminations as well.'

'Oh, I do agree, let's.'

By the end of the holidays they had been three more times. The stern Reverend Stephenson even let Maeve spend the much-hoped-for evening at the Exhibition on the condition she and Alexa were back in Ealing by 11.30 p.m. It was a liberty Maeve had hardly dared believe would be granted and for a while she lowered her defensive guard towards her father.

On days when either Alexa was otherwise occupied, or they had exhausted their week's allowance, Maeve lay around reading. Sometimes Alexa would come over to Mayfield Avenue and one would read aloud to the other. Mrs Stephenson required little of her daughter's time in assisting in household chores, so the two girls devoured the books they borrowed from the local library.

The weeks could have been ticked off as easily by titles as by dates: *A Rajah's Honour* by Pearl Weymouth; *The Red Lacquer Case* by Patricia Wentworth; *The House of Doom* by Katherine Tynan; *The Broad Highway* by Jeffrey Farnol. This last book, for some inexplicable reason, made the Reverend Stephenson furious when he discovered Maeve reading it.

'I don't want this type of book in the house in future,' he censoriously declared when he observed his daughter quietly finishing the novel in the parlour one wet afternoon. 'I'm extremely surprised the library stocks such romantic drivel. I must have a word with Mr Folkes' – Mr Folkes being the Librarian – 'about the selection available to impressionable girls.'

'Oh Father, don't be silly! I can't think what anyone could object to in Farnol's books,' Maeve replied, with her eyes still on the page. She completed the sentence and looked up. 'I mean to say, have you read one?' Maeve regarded herself as something of an expert on the genre of historical and thriller romances, having read hundreds, and Jeffrey Farnol by no stretch of the imagination could slip into the category of racy and suggestive.

The remark seemed less flippant to her father's ears than Maeve had meant it to be.

'What an impudent suggestion,' he exploded. 'I have the wisdom to know that what you in your youthful innocence see as simply sentimental tales are in fact suggestive in all manner of ways. Of course I wouldn't read this man's outpourings and I don't want to see you reading him again.' The Reverend Stephenson blustered on in the same high moral tone for some minutes more until at last he got a rise from Maeve. The row began and of course behind it was his old intention of asserting himself and Maeve defensively responding to preserve her independence. Quickly the old wound of Maeve's blighted academic ambitions flared up. Each sought refuge in their own entrenched point of view and hurled accusations at the other. The argument was pointless and destructive, and negated much of the peaceful stand-off that had existed within the Mayfield Avenue home for the past six weeks.

'Why don't you leave me alone?' cried Maeve as she finally gave ground and stood up to leave the room. 'I don't know why you had to pick on me to have your argument, it was a quiet pleasant afternoon until you ruined it.' As she got to the door on her way upstairs she turned for a Parthian shot. 'I take that back. You haven't ruined it completely. I'm going to finish this,' and she waved the maligned Jeffrey Farnol novel at him.

The row in fact heralded in a number of equally fatuous arguments in the Stephenson household. In a few weeks Maeve would commence her teaching over at Mill Hill Park. The developing air of excitement enveloping the household, which could have been used positively to enable Maeve to make a successful transition from school pupil to school teacher, was converted into a tense, tight atmosphere by the Reverend Stephenson. Very little Maeve could do was approved by him, yet at the same time, whether he approved or not became increasingly irrelevant as the days passed. Her dresses and suits were inappropriate; her hair unbecoming. He went out of his way to create discord in the small household and it was with great relief to Maeve when the day finally arrived that she was to report to Mill Hill Park Grammar School to have her classes and timetable allocated for the arrival of the pupils the day after next.

Away from the claustrophobic environment of May-field Avenue! From now on life would revolve around teaching – whether she liked it or not – and the Reverend Stephenson's blusterings and posturings become of secondary importance to events in her life.

Chapter 6

Selangor, 1924

1924 was to be a momentous twelve months for Kenneth. The New Year, however, gave no indication that it was to be different from the preceding three and a half years he had spent on Kuala Tanah Estate. Indeed, January that year could have been regarded by the superstitious as an ominous start. It was utterly miserable.

The north-east monsoon was the wettest in living memory. The morning rounds degenerated into a squelching and dismal trudge through glutinous mud and soggy woods. Muster each day was a soaking, steamy affair. The coolie lines and assistants' mess looked squalid as their grounds became morasses of red clay and their unpainted timber walls sprouted strange expanses of variegated moulds and spidery fungi. Scorpions, centipedes and large, but harmless, armoured beetles moved up with the humans to escape the waters filling their usual homes. It rained and rained and when it didn't, which would be once or twice a week, the incessant dripping and pattering of drops off the rubber trees as the plantation shed its load of water into the soil just about drove Kenneth mad. The sounds of rain and post-rain dripping, coupled to the monotones of the grey-green trees and a lowering grey-white sky, were profoundly depressing.

Indoors at the mess, it was nearly as awful. Leather, be it shoes, belts, hatbands or suitcases, turned verdigris-green with mould. The damp, sour smell of decay permeated the whole establishment. Despite the rain, the heat of each day was unabated. Even the evenings lost their dubious quality. The infinitesimal lowering of the temperature, which in normal circumstances brought some relief to the young planters, produced instead a slippery, almost greasy film of condensation over the surfaces of the furniture as the humid, saturated atmosphere shed some of its water. The whole place smelt and felt grubby and fetid. If this wasn't bad enough, mould began to develop on the bodies of the young men. Kenneth found inch-diameter rings of roughened skin turning up on the insides of his arms, behind his knees, on his body, and on his throat – anywhere where there wasn't much hair.

Christ, he thought to himself, this is the bloody limit. But it wasn't. Another variety of fungus produced a painful itch between his toes, the irritation of which, each morning as he plodded about the estate on his duties, put him in a bad temper most days by the time breakfast came around. Blagdon and Darke were similarly blighted, and the mood of the mess was touchy, and not conducive to the usual light-hearted atmosphere that characterized the place. They squabbled over issues such as magazines not returned, clothes left lying about, or noisy slurping of tea at breakfast; things none of them ever bothered about, probably had never even noticed prior to the endless rain.

One Wednesday the rain ceased for long enough for the three young men to decide on a foray to the Salak Club. Their regular routine had been interrupted by the flooding of the road the previous week, and even before that, the journey had been unpredictable. Several times they had set off only to be turned back a couple of miles out by an impassable section of road. They had begun to feel rather cut off from the rest of southern Selangor society. In the expectation that today they would get through, Ronnie decided to take his tennis racquet on the off-chance that the Club court had dried out enough for a game; Kenneth and George were going to settle for a night's drinking.

'Come on, Ronnie,' shouted Kenneth through the house as he and George stood at the top of the verandah stairs waiting for Blagdon to appear. 'We want to get going.'

From the depths of Ronnie's room came a muffled curse in reply. Ronnie walked into view.

99

'Anyone for tennis?'

They stared at him and, when they saw what he was getting at, cracked up with laughter. Ronnie held up his racquet in his right hand. The catgut strings were fuzzy and bright green with mould, and the formerly brown soft leather handle a blotch of mottled green growths. A tennis ball in his left hand was just as green.

'Puts a whole new meaning to the description "lawn tennis" doesn't it?' he said, joining in the laughter. He whacked the ball out into the rubber trees, creating about himself in the action a cloud of fungal spores as mouldy strings made contact with mouldy ball.

'Well, what are you waiting for, boys? Let's go. If nothing else, the airing will do us good. Another week of being cooped up here and we will resemble tennis balls.'

The old BSA was trundled out from under the house. As a barrier against the pervading humidity it had been generously draped with old sacks which had done their job and kept the engine and battery dry. Rubbing the mould off the saddle, Ronnie got astride the machine and after several kicks, and as many curses, revved the thing into life. Kenneth and George piled on and off they went.

They returned at about 9.00. The evening had not fulfilled Kenneth's expectations though he conceded that they had been perhaps too high. The Club was half-empty for, like Kuala Tanah, other rubber estates were also having their communication problems. Much whisky had been consumed and some fun had, but without the whole gang present, the Club had seemed somewhat lonely and lacklustre.

Back at the mess an indifferent mutton curry awaited them. Pravan, the Tamil cook, and his wife had themselves been affected by the oppressive weather, and as the month had progressed, so the quality of their cooking, and its variety of dishes, declined.

'Well, damned if I'm letting the night end like this,' said Ronnie, pushing away a plate of coagulated curry. 'I'm turning in with Lalee.' He stood up and left the room.

This remark made Kenneth feel even more despondent. Lalee was Ronnie's Chinese mistress.

She had been with Ronnie for as long as Kenneth had been at Kuala Tanah. Neither he nor George had much to do with her; she was, in fact, such a shadowy figure to them that they had no cause to enjoy or, conversely, disapprove of her presence. She never sat down and ate with them; it was only rarely that their paths crossed in the mess. This usually happened only if Kenneth or George were laid low with malaria or some other illness which kept them at home during working hours. Lalee never rose with Ronnie at 4.00 a.m., but would sleep on for another three or four hours, gliding silently out of the back door an hour or so before the young men returned for their breakfast. For more than a year Kenneth had no idea even of where she lived. It transpired that there was a much smaller and more modestly furnished bungalow several hundred yards away from the mess and hidden from view by a screen of bougainvillaea and casuarinas. Originally it had been built for European residents, but as the plantation never developed to its proposed acreage, the staff it was supposed to house were never hired. At some point one of the estate managers installed his mistress in it and, in his turn, Ronnie followed suit. Lalee and her mother lived there. If McGregor Reynolds knew, he didn't care.

Lalee's arrivals in the mess were about as invisible as her departures. It seemed to be her, rather than Ronnie, who chose the nights they spent together, and she would often be waiting for Ronnie in his room when the young men returned from the Club or some other social function. Ronnie was discreet about the situation too and never made a show about retiring for the night when it was apparent Lalee was in bed waiting for him.

Consequently, the fact that he alone of the three had a mistress, created no friction between the friends. Even tonight, Kenneth could hardly accuse Ronnie of flaunting his good luck in his face. It was just that Ronnie had something else to preoccupy himself with other than the awful stinking weather. Kenneth and George could think of nothing to do except twiddle their thumbs until it was time for sleep.

The stifling damp continued. Kenneth's mind became more and more obssessed with the problem of how to acquire a mistress himself. It wasn't the first time in the past couple of years that the thought had occurred to him, for Malaya was chronically short of marriagable English-women. However, in the past, some social occasion, sporting match, or invitation from Ali had distracted him from any plan of action he might have come up with. But, with all distractions now curtailed week after week because of the weather, his needs in this direction seemed more urgent than they had ever before been. It wasn't just the sex. Kenneth's libido was generally reduced by alcohol, heat, and sport to a level which could be accommodated by sporadic visits to a house of ill repute in Bangi, and the annual visit to Seremban. No, it was that old ache for a companion as much as for a lover that drove him to thinking about how to get a mistress. So often over the years, as he had walked past Ronnie's room on the way to his own, he had heard his friend and Lalee talking quietly together in the dark as they lay in bed. This sort of intimacy was what he craved for as much as the other.

By the time Sunday evening came round – yet another tempestuous deluge hammering on the roof and thrashing through the leafy branches of the rubber trees – Kenneth decided that he would seek Ronnie's advice on the matter of procuring a mistress. As luck would have it, George retired early to bed that night to nurse a persistent hangover and a throat infection, so Kenneth brought up the subject minutes after he left the living room.

'Something to keep your mind off the weather, eh?' joked Ronnie. 'Well, it shouldn't be too difficult. I tell you what. I'll have a word to Lalee. She is often out and about in town and might know of someone.'

'What would I have to pay her?' asked Kenneth.

'I don't know. Let's see what turns up first. If it is

someone Lalee knows, then the girl will move into the old bungalow with her. That can be taken into consideration for a start. Look, just wait and see and if something eventuates, we'll take it from there.'

Events moved fast from that brief exchange between the two men. The next evening Ronnie called for Kenneth, who was writing a letter in his room, to come and join him on the verandah. Kenneth completed the sentence on the page, capped his pen and ambled out his door. There, much to his surprise, he found not only Ronnie, but also Lalee and a Chinese girl whom he had never seen before. He smiled a hello to Lalee and turned questioningly to Ronnie.

'Kenneth, old chap,' said Ronnie, 'this is a cousin of Lalee's, Jung Hsu is her name. Lalee felt she may fulfil your requirements as talked about last night.'

Even in the subdued light, Kenneth felt the others would see him blushing in embarrassment at the situation. He need not have worried. Jung Hsu kept her eyes cast floorward and Lalee was occupied with swatting a couple of annoying mosquitos with her hand.

Jung Hsu was at least ten inches shorter than Kenneth. In her figure, she was almost plump, with black straight hair descending to her waist in a thick plait. Her round face, with finely arched eyebrows defining a broad forehead, had a shy, pleasant expression and Kenneth's first impression was that she seemed a likeable person. She couldn't have been more than sixteen or seventeen. Like Lalee she was dressed in a short-sleeved cotton dress, and on her feet were sandals.

'What do I do with her?' muttered Kenneth to Ronnie.

'Spend the night with her, old man. See if you get along together.' Ronnie then said to Lalee, 'Show your cousin into Kenneth's room. He'll be along in a minute. Come on, old man, let's have a stengah while you get used to the idea of sharing your bed with someone. Jimmy!' The houseboy scuttled into view and took the order for two stiff whiskies from Ronnie.

Five minutes later, Kenneth returned apprehensively to

his room. Exciting as the prospect of sex was, the situation was almost too calculated even for Kenneth, who had experienced nothing but contrived lovemaking with his visits to brothels over the years.

He found Jung Hsu in his bed, black hair unbraided and spread across the pillow, her shoulders showing above the thin sheet that she wore a white nightgown. Kenneth stripped, wrapped his night sarong about his hips, and ducked under the mosquito net so that he lay beside her.

'Do you speak English?' he asked quietly.

'A little only. My father was houseboy to a big estate in Negri Sembilan. He taught us some,' Jung Hsu replied.

For the first time in Kenneth's experience in sharing a bed with a woman, he wasn't being pressured to get the act of love over and done with as rapidly as possible in order that his place could be occupied by another paying customer. After chatting as well as he could with Jung Hsu and her limited English, she wriggled closer and rested her head on his shoulder and placed an arm on his chest. He was charmed by the simplicity and innocence of her snuggling to him and felt, for the first time, at ease with a woman. He lay there with his arm holding her close and for once enjoyed the sound of the rain hammering on the corrugated iron roof over their heads. Instead of continuing to drive him crazy, the sound of rain and wind beyond the room emphasized the warm sanctuary Jung Hsu had brought to his bed. He lay there happily, musing on the size of the void in his life that had just been filled by the presence of the girl next to him, wondering how he had never realized just how empty his existence had been until she came into it.

They didn't make love, but just continued lying in each other's arms. Kenneth didn't even hazard a guess what he might be offering Jung Hsu by her coming to him. Rescue from starvation; poverty; a terrible home; he didn't know or care to find out. He was simply glad she had come and was determined that she should stay. Listening to her even breathing close to his ear, he drifted off to sleep.

Jung Hsu stayed, as she hoped she might. She moved in with her aunt and Lalee and modelled her life on her cousin's routine of unobtrusive discretion. Kenneth made no unreasonable demands of her, and paid her an acceptable allowance as well as giving her the occasional gift. Living in the bungalow was a huge improvement on the squalid room she and her brothers and sisters had been reduced to living in at Port Dickson since her father had died eighteen months earlier, and she was content with her new circumstances. The hidden bungalow became a friendly place, with Jimmy the mess houseboy becoming a frequent visitor, along with the laundryman and Mr Reynolds' servants. Even the Tamil cook, his wife, and Reynolds' gardener were visitors to the Chinese household.

For Kenneth, the acquisition of Jung Hsu, or Sue as he quickly began calling her, made his life at Kuala Tanah Estate a whole new proposition. Never the most intellectually demanding of men, he found Sue, even with her limited range of English, a real companion. She removed the dead weight of loneliness from him which had been all too frequently endured over the years, particularly those maudlin moods he had been prone to when back in the empty mess half-drunk from yet another evening spent boozing at the Salak Club. Now more often than not, Sue would be waiting for him in bed, idly flicking through a Chinese magazine until he appeared. If she wasn't there, the security of the knowledge that she was only four hundred yards away allowed him to rest easy. Lying side by side on the nights she spent with him, he would tell her of his life as a youth in England, of interesting occasions he had experienced in Selangor, or of the local gossip. She herself contributed little, but the almost one-sided nature of the conversations never troubled Kenneth. The intimacy he had begun to envy Ronnie for, he too now had, and he thoroughly enjoyed it.

Having a companion to share his thoughts with wasn't the only solace Sue brought into Kenneth's life. She had had more experience of men than Kenneth had had of women and she made certain that Kenneth learned of her love-making skills. From that, she instilled in him a wanting which was dependent on her quiet presence at Kuala Tanah. Kenneth, conditioned to drunken gropings or even less, was amazed at the possibilities Sue devised for their love life. She sent him into realms of pleasure he had never before conceived. By example, and by guiding him at times, the girl taught Kenneth to tune in to her particular desires, and Kenneth began to learn that there was far more to lovemaking than what he had hitherto expected. It was an enjoyable, though, as he admitted to himself, sometimes curious education. He had been so innocent, so lacking in experience in some of the ways of the world until meeting Jung Hsu, and he quickly became fond of her. By the end of 1924, Kenneth, if asked, would probably have conceded that love had entered the equation too.

Despite a few misgivings about the friendship with Ali after the Christmas party revelations of Featherston and Hawley concerning the Rajah's lifestyle, Kenneth continued to accept invitations to the Istana to play billiards and partake of the occasional pipe of opium. The first experience with the narcotic had been so pleasantly bizarre, Ali and his servant's antics notwithstanding, that he had had no hesitation when Ali asked him to join him in a pipe or two, in accepting such hospitality. He had probably indulged about three times that year and each time had greatly enjoyed the visions and dreams the drug induced.

It was after one such evening that Kenneth found his circumstances completely overturned.

Ali's syce, or driver, was chauffeuring Kenneth back to the estate in the Prince Henry. It was about midnight and a sickle moon hovered low in an inky sky. Rushing through the darkness along the deserted road, Kenneth revelled in the wind whipping through his hair, cool despite the usual humidity because of the speed they were travelling.

As the motorcar crunched through the dry leaves scattered across the track leading to the mess, Kenneth was surprised to see the manager's house a blaze of lights. In silhouette, he could see about half a dozen men standing together on the verandah near the top of the stairs, seemingly in earnest discussion. He ordered the syce to stop and, dismissing him, walked the fifty yards to Mr Reynolds' bungalow.

'Is there some trouble?' he called from the bottom of the steps. An ashen-faced McGregor Reynolds emerged from behind the hanging baskets of plants suspended from the eave of the verandah.

'Ah, Clouston my boy, at last you're back. Come up.' As Kenneth stepped on to the verandah, his boss continued. 'I've some very grave news, old chap. Prepare yourself for a bit of a shock. Young Blagdon and Darke are dead.'

Dead! How preposterous! thought Kenneth. Why, he had gone to the Club with them on the bike this afternoon. George had been out on the tennis court, and Ronnie propping up the bar when Ali had come to pick him up. What was Mr Reynolds talking about?

'How do you mean, sir?' he asked.

Reynolds took Kenneth's hand in a strong grip and clasped his forearm with his left hand.

'Come with me.' Kenneth followed him past the group of planters standing mutely by. With every passing second Kenneth realized that the situation was serious, that an awful nightmare was unfolding before his eyes which was not going to be interrupted by his awakening. This was real. As he mentally struggled to cope with events, Reynolds pointed to a pair of charpoys against the west wall of the house. The simple rope and timber beds had been borrowed from the servants. On each lay a blanketed body. The faces were uncovered and in the dim light Kenneth recognized the familiar features of Ronnie and George. Asleep, the thought flashed through his mind, they're asleep. But neither moved nor breathed. Panic-stricken, he took a closer look. Apart from the pallor of George's skin, he looked more or less as he always did. A closer glance at Ronnie, however, revealed that there was a caved-in look about the left side of his head above and behind the ear. Then he saw the dried remains of blood which had been mopped up from the ear itself.

'Oh, Christ,' he wheezed. He suddenly had no strength in his limbs. He subsided to the floorboards and rested his back against the wall. 'Oh Jesus Christ, Jesus Christ.'

The minutes passed and he felt no better.

'What happened? I don't understand. George should be all right. He looks like he always does.'

'It happened on the way home from the Club, about three hours ago,' said Mr Reynolds. 'A motor accident, a bloody crash.'

'Where?'

'They hit the concrete fence of the new mosque this side of Salak. There had been a bit of a party at the Club and from all accounts both Blagdon and Darke were in fine form when they left. How they didn't see the mosque I don't know, the damn thing is painted white for God's sake. It looks as if whoever was driving misjudged the curve of the road and they ploughed into the thing at a fair speed. George copped it across the chest; all his ribs are pushed in and his arms broken. Ronnie was found over the fence with his head smashed up against a lump of concrete. There are no braking skidmarks to suggest that whoever was driving tried to stop. Too bloody drunk to know what had hit them, I'd say. Jack Berber found them pretty soon after it happened by the look of things, and they were dead. They didn't feel a thing. I'm sorry, old man. It's a rotten business losing one's friends and two in one go is a tough thing to take.' He walked away leaving Kenneth to his thoughts.

There was none. He felt completely empty. No Ronnie, no George. It cannot be. They were his oldest friends in Selangor. Four years of living, drinking and socializing together, and now, nothing. Kuala Tanah without them was inconceivable; living in the mess without them was inconceivable; what a terrible night it had suddenly become.

How long he sat there, he didn't know, but eventually he pushed himself to his feet and walked back to the stairs.

Some of the visitors were still present and one of them stuck a glass of whisky in his hand.

'Drink up, lad, a couple of whiskies will dull the edge a bit. Come on, knock it back.' Kenneth did as he was told. Someone proposed a quiet raising of glasses to the departed young men and they muttered 'good lads', 'decent chaps too' and similar epitaphs before taking determined swigs of their drinks.

'To Ronnie and George,' said Kenneth, draining his whisky in a single gulp.

By 10 o'clock that morning, Ronnie Darke and George Blagdon were at rest in their graves in the little English cemetery at Bangi. Word was quickly spread to the rubber estates and government offices in the region and there was a good turnout at the funeral. A choleric clergyman delivered the service in the stone Church of England chapel and spoke well of the two young Englishmen, despite the fact neither had been near a church for as long as Kenneth had lived with them, and the vicar couldn't have possibly known them. About them lay other young Englishmen: casualties of the climate and its diseases, of accidents in the course of their duties as surveyors, planters, mining engineers and such-like, or of drunken escapades with fatal conclusions such as Ronnie's and George's demise.

Cowering under the sun, the mourners quickly paid their respects by the graveside and fled to the shadow of their motor cars. Kenneth lingered, sola topee held in his hand, oblivious of the sun beating down on his uncovered head, and watched the graves being filled. Two red humps of crumbly earth soon protruded above the scruffy coarse grass of the cemetery. A Tamil coolie knocked a white cross into the head of each mound, temporary markers until the headstones were cut: George Albert Blagdon 1896–1924 was incised on to the left; Ronald Edward St John Darke 1894–1924 on the right.

A boozy raucous wake was held that evening at the Bangi Club. McGregor Reynolds took Kenneth under his wing and drove him there and back in his old Ford. The young man looked sick and displaced, and many drinks, offered in sympathy for the loss of his two closest friends, were thrust upon him in the course of the evening. When they were back at the estate Mr Reynolds asked him in for a nightcap.

'I'm afraid, despite the tragic circumstances, it's business as usual tomorrow, Kenneth,' he said, using Kenneth's Christian name for the first time in four years. 'I've telephoned Head Office in Penang about it all and they'll arrange for two assistants to be posted here. You have been promoted to senior assistant manager and a letter to that effect will be drafted up and sent to you. You know the ropes, so I know you'll do the job as well as Darke did. I'm sorry your first step-up had to come this way, but to be honest, a colleague popping off is so often the way promotions come one's way out here in Malaya. It's just a bit rough it's a close friend's shoes you are stepping into. But there you have it.'

He put his glass down. 'Time to turn in. Hell of a day, tomorrow can only be better.'

Kenneth rose. 'Goodnight, sir,' and made his way to his quarters. Sue wasn't there. No doubt she was with her cousin Lalee. He collapsed on to the bed fully dressed and slipped into a deep and dreamless sleep.

Chapter 7

Mesopotamia, 1926

It was five o'clock in the afternoon, Baghdad time. Some seventy-five miles north of the ancient city was Samarra, base for Number 72 Squadron of the Royal Air Force. Flying Officer Nick Manconi and Pilot Officer Richard Kirby were preparing to take off. 'A' flight – four De Havilland DH9A two-seater reconnaissance bi-planes – lined up at the edge of the desert which marked the perimeter of the airfield, their propellers inscribing flashing circles in the clear air as the sunlight caught on the tips of the blades. Behind them billowed clouds of brown dust, blown up by the propeller wash. Pilot Officer Kirby gave the thumbs-up sign the three other pilots had been watching for, and wound back the throttle.

With engine roaring, the DH9A trundled off at an ever-increasing pace. As it rolled past a squadron of Sopwith Pups parked outside the low khaki-coloured administration and flight control buildings, Nick Manconi, in the observer's seat behind Kirby, felt the tail of the aircraft rise to the horizontal and, seconds later, they were airborne. The rest of the flight followed and Pilot Officer Kirby circled Samarra until they could take up formation. The scene below was unprepossessing. The airstrip slashed across the stony desert which, from a thousand feet above, looked flatter and smoother than it was in reality.

About the air base were a collection of wood and iron hangars, administration buildings, guard-houses, sheds and Nissen huts, all typical of a British air-force base. The only points of colour diverging from the browns, yellows and ochres of the view were the blue, white and red roundrels on the upper wings of the Sopwiths and the other parked arrangement of fighters – Vickers SE 5As – which were sitting further along the air-strip margin. South, the desert touched the Tigris. Nick could see a ragged fringe of date palms and a smudge of green which marked out its course. A collection of brown squarish shapes up against the green indicated where the town of Samarra lay, indistinct at this time of day because of the lengthening shadows being cast by the palm groves.

The rest of the flight jockeyed alongside Pilot Officer Kirby. Swinging to the north-east, the quartet of De Havillands headed for the purple, shadow-riven Jabal Hamrin Mountains thirty miles in front of their cowlings.

The mountains were Kurdish country, the western frontier of Kurdistan. It was a tribal nation, famous for the defence of its independence from the Arabs to the west of them, the Persians to the east, and from the Turks to the north. Their resistance was legendary, and over the centuries a fighting spirit had become part of the nation's very soul, irrepressible even in times when few outside pressures were being exerted upon it. Now was such a time. With the defeat of the Turks in 1918, Mesopotamian politics had revolved around the control of the oil fields, and the various regional claimants to authority were too busy quarrelling among themselves to take up the old fight with the Kurds. Consequently, since 1919, bands of Kurdish warriors had regularly descended from their mountain fortresses to loot caravans and convoys and attack towns which were suspected of containing wealth useful to them.

Samarra had originally been a forward base in the Mesopotamian campaign of 1916–18, but with the defeat of Turkey, the role of the Royal Air Force changed from that of an attacking nature to one of frontier policing. 'A' flight was one of several that regularly flew the frontier skies reconnoitring mountain passes and paths in order to monitor Kurdish warrior movements. The flights were generally scheduled at early morning and late afternoons, though not regularly enough to make the Kurds feel

112

invulnerable in the midday hours. The timetable had a valuable purpose. At these early and late hours, the raking rays of the rising or setting sun cast a twenty-foot-long shadow from a standing man. Even the smallest boulders stood in high relief during these times and, if the RAF was overhead, it was impossible to move men about without being observed. Goat herders, shepherds and traders had nothing to fear, but the policy had been extremely effective in dissuading armed groups of men from making use of the terrain during daylight hours.

In the early years the reconnaissance flights had been accompanied by Sopwiths or SE 5As which would deal with infiltrators then and there who were heading west. The lesson had been well taught and these days the DH 9As in the sky were enough to deter the movement of bandits down to the lowlands during the daytime. The sound of aero engines signalled that the terrain was unsafe, and the Kurds by and large moved their anarchic activities to less policed regions. Nevertheless, even in 1926, there was still the occasional raid from the mountains and the daily flights were accordingly maintained.

Nick Manconi, back in the observer's cockpit, had a clear view either side of the aeroplane over the surrounding countryside. The job today entailed photographing the trails that led out towards the old entrepot city of Kifri, at the edge of the mountains. The pictures, when developed and printed, would be compared with ones taken earlier and deductions made as to how much traffic was passing over them, and new buildings and such-like identified. The method had sometimes produced good results. Formerly little-used tracks had shown, by the wear and tear on them, that they were suddenly being frequently utilized. As daytime reconnaissance had showed they were empty, the conclusion had to be that they were being used at night and, therefore, for illegal purposes. Army action would then be taken to prevent the practice from continuing.

Nick peered over the port side to the desert below. They

113

were still ten miles from the first of the foothills and the ground was level except for an occasional flat table-top hill casting a wide shadow eastwards. He looked closely at each, searching for something. Many of these mesa, naturally halfway decent forts, had been converted over the millennia into bastions to protect the territory over which they commanded such wide views. In their time, they had been variously used for this single purpose by Assyrians, Persians, Arabs, and Turks.

The less strategic had their heyday when their region, for long-forgotten reasons, became briefly the centre of someone's political destiny, only to crumble and be looted for their bricks when that moment of importance had passed on. Others retained their significance for centuries, alternating in function as the situation required as frontier barracks, imperial fortresses, highway guard posts, and munition dumps. Nick was looking for archaeological remains of such places. For the past two years, really ever since he had been posted as a RAF pilot to Mesopotamia, he had been recording and photographing archaeological sites during the reconnaissance flights. Several other pilots in other parts of the country were doing the same, all inspired by the results of Colonel Beazeley in the last years of the Great War. Beazeley, using aerial photographs taken for military planning against the Turks, had identified over a dozen great buried cities on the Mesopotamian plain.

Extraordinary things had been located thanks to the photographs, and Nick in his turn hoped to contribute something to archaeology using the same method. There was rarely a flight which didn't involve a small deviation or two from the flight path in order for Nick to check out unnaturally straight patterns of shadows across the landscape below. Such patterns were the foundations of ancient forts, caravanserai and cities, virtually indiscernible from the ground, but, given the early morning or late afternoon sun, starkly clear five hundred feet overhead. On further investigation some had proved to be of little interest. But others turned out to be important parts of long-gone empires such as Assurnasipal the Second's or of the great Cyrus.

Nick thought he could see the characteristic rectangular shadows of an architectural feature below on a table-top hill just coming into view from under the right wing. He leaned forward and tapped Kirby on the shoulder with a swagger stick he carried for just this purpose. The pilot turned his head and Nick pointed down, then gave a circling motion with his finger. Richard Kirby gave a thumbs-up sign and dropped the DH 9A out of formation for a circuit over the mesa. No doubt about it. It was a site.

Nick lifted his Newman and Guardia 'Sibyl' camera from the cockpit floor, looped its leather strap around his neck and craned out of the cockpit. Kirby, understanding from practice what Nick required, banked the DH 9A steeply and slowly swung around the hill so that Nick could take his photographs without having to lean too perilously into the slip-stream. When Nick had finished his observation, Kirby straightened out and sped in pursuit of 'A' flight, now some distance ahead.

The reconnaissance was uneventful. The bi-planes fanned out to cover the designated territory for the flight and, thirty minutes later, regrouped at the same co-ordinates to fly back in formation to Samarra. They touched down as the twilight began to settle over the desert. As the men walked away from their aircraft towards their billets some of them arranged to meet in the mess in half an hour's time for a beer. Nick waved an acknowledgement that he would be there too.

He turned up punctually, dressed for dinner, and joined his friends around a bottle-laden table near the centre of the room. There wasn't much talk between them, simply a companionable silence as the airmen browsed through the most recent newspapers from England or flicked through dog-eared copies of *Flight, Aeroplane,* and *Flying,* aviation magazines which were to found in every RAF mess across the British Empire.

The walls of the Officers' Mess were decorated with memorabilia of eight years of combat and duty in Mesopotamia. Pieces of torn aircraft fabric decorated with German crosses or Turkish stars and crescents celebrated victories over the enemy in the Great War of 1914–18, as did several mounted wooden propellers. Sepia-toned photographs of pilots and mechanics standing formally beside their aeroplanes recorded the history of the RAF squadrons which had come and gone from Samarra since 1916. One large frame contained a series of photographs showing a derailed train. Its steam locomotive had been spectacularly wrecked and the pictures commemorated the destruction, carried out as it happened, by bombers and fighters of 72 Squadron back in late 1916 during the campaign to take Kut.

Near it, in another frame, was a picture of a dopey-looking black Labrador wearing a leather flying helmet which had achieved its present status by being the flying mascot belonging to a squadron of Bristol fighters which had been stationed there in 1918. Popular legend declared that the hound died a hero's death, along with its master, in an aerial fracas up near the Armenian border. The walls of photos were reminders of a hundred similar tales which got told, retold and exaggerated over the years as officers came and went.

Nick sipped his beer and glanced through a two-week-old *Times*. Nothing much exciting happening, he thought to himself and turned to the employment advertisements. His five years' tour of duty with the Royal Air Force was due to expire in a couple of months. He had already decided that he wasn't going to re-enlist, being, as he often said to his colleagues, a lot wiser at twenty-six than he was at twenty-one when he joined the RAF. However, there was the problem of what to do for a living once he was back in mufti. Not much here, he thought, running through the columns of job opportunities. School teacher at a private boys' school in Wiltshire? Publicity officer for the Anglo-Persian Oil Company? Police administrator in the Burma Civil Service? God, they all looked dreadful!

His thoughts continued on the same line until interrupted by a pilot opposite, Bill Drysdale.

'Hey, Manconi, you're looking for a job in civvy street, aren't you. This one might appeal.' He handed a folded *Times* to Nick. 'It's near the bottom, under "Government of Sarawak".'

Nick looked at the date; it was a couple of days more recent than the paper he had been perusing; and then searched for the notice. Among the positions for a Public Water Administrator, Public Works Engineer and Harbour Master, Kuching, was Librarian for Rajah Brooke's Library at the Palace in Kuching. Nick read on and with increasing interest noted that the applicant should be university-trained and have a strong interest in history and archaeology. The successful applicant would be expected to contribute to local historical research, as well as maintaining the Rajah's extensive library.

Nick looked over at Bill and joked, 'You're talking about the Harbour Master job, I take it?'

Bill laughed. 'That library job looks your sort of thing doesn't it? A job where you've got to use your brain as well as your wits, I'd say. And you'd be your own boss more or less.'

'Yes, you're right. I'll write away and see what eventuates. Nothing to lose except the price of a stamp. I must say, I don't know much about Sarawak though, apart from the fact that it is in Borneo.'

'And that's more than most people do,' replied Bill. 'It's British, it's in the East, it's not far from Singapore; all in all it could be quite interesting. If I had a university degree like you, and didn't have another fifteen months duty to complete, I'd write away myself.' He took a pull on his beer. 'Just imagine it! Rain-forest, jungle; wet and green. Seems like a vision of paradise viewed from here!'

It could be a half-way decent job, Nick thought to himself. Certainly one out of the ordinary and that appealed to him immediately. The humdrum existence, and he perceived most people's lives to be just that, had always made him anxious, and he had every intention not to have one

117

if it was at all possible to avoid. It was why he signed up for pilot training with the RAF back in 1921. Fresh out of Cambridge University he had been expected by family and friends to go for some aspect of the Civil Service and there forge a safe and remunerative career. In what seemed to them to be the height of sheer perverseness, he ignored these possibilities and instead invited fate to cut short all future prospects by becoming an air-force pilot, risking life and limb continually, or so his outraged father declared, by flying in canvas and wood deathtraps tied together with string. He meant, of course, the aeroplanes which Nick learned to fly.

The RAF had been both good and bad. Nick's postings had sent him to a number of bases in interesting parts of the British-occupied Middle East and the boring times had usually been adequately compensated by flying regularly over the pyramids when he was based at Giza, identifying Crusader castles when on tour in Palestine, or looking for lost cities – which he had been indulging since arriving in Mesopotamia. Dropping Mills bombs on mountain tribesmen and machine-gunning Arab nomads when ordered to had, however, weighed more upon his conscience as his years of service had passed. He had grown to understand more of the underlying politics which created the unrest he and his fellow pilots were pledged to suppress as airmen of His Majesty's Airforce, and had found it increasingly difficult to view the running figures which often took to their heels at the appearance overhead of the RAF, as an enemy. Ragged shapes in their blue, brown or stone-grey robes as they dodged for cover, Nick, as the years went by, saw them as all too human; like himself no less, fleeing helter skelter to avoid the bullets and grenades they expected at the next moment. He had decided, about a year ago, that the RAF no longer suited his ambitions for an interesting life.

'This could be what I'm looking for,' he said to Bill. 'Look, I'll just write down the details and you can have back your newspaper.'

He wrote that very night. Four weeks later a letter was on the mailing board for him, its envelope embossed in green 'Sarawak House, The Strand, London WC1'. The reply to his application requested him to make arrangements for an interview for the job of librarian once he had resigned his commission in the RAF and had returned to England. This was only a matter of weeks away and he replied to the letter to this effect.

On a wet September morning, 'a typical early Autumn day in London', his landlady had commented when he left his digs in Chelsea an hour earlier, Nick found himself outside Sarawak House.

Any ambivalence he had had about the job while in Samarra had been forgotten as he had attempted over the last three months to adjust to life as a civilian in London. Old school friends had welcomed him with open arms and his parents assumed he had at last satiated his boyhood dreams of adventure. Everyone thought that he had left the air force to settle down like any young man of his background should. The experience of returning to civilian life had in fact convinced him of the necessity of finding work conducive to his unchanged outlook on life. He couldn't 'settle down' in England, of that he was sure. He squared his shoulders, checked in the brightly polished brass plate advertising Sarawak House that his Collegiate tie was knotted neatly, and entered the imposing building for his interview with the High Commissioner determined that, come what competition, the job was going to be his.

Chapter 8

London, 1927 – Winter

Four o'clock in the afternoon. The fast-fading light, filtering through a thick cloud layer across the wintry city, cast Ealing into a bleak picture of leafless trees and grubby brick-red-coloured buildings. From the slight elevation of Mill Hill Park, Maeve could see the smoke from a thousand household fires hanging leadenly just above the roofs of terraced and semi-detached houses as she hurried down to Gunnersbury Lane to catch a bus home. It was a completely cheerless day, and, unfortunately, one typical of the last five weeks.

It wasn't just the weather. Although it had been remittently damp and cold, the mood of January had been made more sombre by the increasing unemployment situation in the city. One would have to have been blind not to have noticed the hardships of the out-of-work this winter. Men and women door-knocking in search of jobs, a parent and children begging on street corners and the shops; children hopping painfully about in bare feet along the frigid pavements because their fathers couldn't afford to clothe them adequately. One could not but feel depressed and sad when confronted with such daily sights and Ealing, being a middle-class suburb, was spared the worst examples of the poverty appearing across the city.

Maeve's depressed mood was the result of more than just the day. School was rather grim these days. The seasonal round of colds and sniffles was well at home in her classes and lessons were continually punctuated by coughing and sneezing from a dozen pupils. One in particular, an unfortunately gawky-looking boy, had a sniff that made her hair stand on end each time he sounded off. More than anything else it sounded to her like pebbles on a stoney coast being sucked down as a wave receded off the beach – a horrible grating, gravelly noise that would stop her in mid-sentence. Demands that he use his hankerchief revealed that he possessed no such article of dress, and the use of his sleeve only made matters worse. So, oblivious to the revulsion he was creating, the lad sniffed periodically through the classes, driving Maeve to distraction. Influenza had also struck the school and some eight children were off and at home in bed. Luckily it wasn't the virulent strain that had decimated the population eight years earlier and no children were in danger of dying.

Teaching, Maeve had discovered, can be a soul-destroying occupation with the joys few and far between the slogging monotony of the daily routine. By and large the Mill Hill Park children were nice enough, but dealing with thirty to forty of them on a daily basis was an energy-draining business. The occasional bright child was usually offset by a particularly naughty one, while between these opposite ends of the spectrum grouped the mass of the class – reasonably mannered, respectful enough to do their homework and complete their lessons, but not exactly scintillating.

Maeve knew she should be grateful to have such well behaved classes, there were many schools which would be absolutely awful to work in elsewhere in London, but somewhere within her she still harboured expectations of there being more to life than working as a school teacher. She was pondering this as she waited at the bus stop. A fine mist had deposited a veil of dew over her felt overcoat and headscarf. Her breath exhaled in a cloud of vapour and her hands and feet were freezing. Oh, to get home in front of the fire! she thought to herself. Come on bus, what's holding you up?

At last, out of the gloom, a bus emerged. Maeve hopped on board, found herself a seat downstairs, and sat gazing at her reflection in the soot-streaked window at her right until her stop was reached. By the time she was home, twenty minutes later, the sky was dark and the street lamps were on.

'Hello,' she called out as she hung her coat and scarf behind the front door.

'How was school today?' asked her mother as Maeve joined her and the Reverend Stephenson for tea in front of the fire.

'Thanks,' said Maeve, taking the proffered plate with a slice of cinnamon teacake on it, and a cup of tea. 'Oh, the same as ever. Colds galore and none of the children really feeling on top of things. There still isn't enough heating in the classroom you know. Those who had coats kept them on all day; those who didn't shivered. And that Eustace Carlton and his sniff! I swear I'll kill him one day and be able to plead temporary insanity at the time of the deed. You wouldn't believe how irritating it is. Sounds like drains being cleared. He really is a rather revolting boy.'

'Yes dear,' agreed Mrs Stephenson unthinkingly. Maeve feeling the best she had felt all day, with the fire and tea bringing some colour back into her cheeks, looked over to father, who was reading an article in the week's *Illustrated London News*.

'How is the bronchitis, Father?'

'Not too bad considering the weather,' he replied. 'I won't go outside however, until it is less damp. That reminds me, Maeve, will you tell Mr Thompson' – Mr Thompson was the headmaster of Mill Park Hill Grammar School – 'that I won't give my Divinity Lesson tomorrow. I meant to write him a letter to this effect, but it slipped my mind. I'll write one later in the week because I've decided I'm not going to teach again until the worst of winter has passed. My old bones object too strongly on these bad days for me to be out of doors.' The Reverend Stephenson, along with several other Ealing clergymen of various denominations, gave an hour's instruction in divinity each Wednesday, between ten and eleven o'clock, to the junior pupils at Mill Hill Park Grammar School. The content of the lessons oscillated between Bible stories and tales of valour beyond the call of Christian duty out in the mission fields of Africa, China and the South Seas, and were generally well received by the children as a welcome break from the formal lessons of the week.

The years had finally caught up with the Reverend Stephenson. The pompous self-righteous personality his wife had had to live with for thirty-odd years had wilted as the infirmities of old age crept up on him. His often destructive assertiveness had now faded to an ineffectual querulousness within his house, while to his parishioners he had become simply an elderly clergyman who Sunday after Sunday served up sermons that were comforting in their familiarity to nod off to. Some more spritely parishioners had, at times, unkindly wondered aloud that it was extraordinary that the Reverend Stephenson himself didn't fall asleep while delivering them. Over the years he and Maeve had learned to put up with each other more easily than they had when Maeve had been developing from a schoolgirl into a young woman, and the fierce arguments the Reverend once provoked to make some point or another had subsided over the last year. Nevertheless, the damage had been done and Maeve was always guarded when in the company of her father.

Although long resigned to being a teacher, it now and then still rankled that she had been prevented, for no good reason other than her father forbade it, from going to university back in 1924. This was not on her mind this evening. In fact little was, as she stared into the low flames dancing over the surfaces of the heaped coals in the hearth. The cosiness of the parlour after the bleakness of the day beyond the house was like a balm to her deflated spirits and she was content simply to let her mind drift with whatever whims passed through it.

She was pulled back to the present by her mother calling that supper was on the table. She and her father roused themselves from their torpor and went to sit down.

* * *

The rest of the week was much the same. Everyone had a

yellowish-grey cast to their faces as they went about their business in the cold streets, their reddened chilled noses and ears only heightening by contrast their colourless appearance. The numbers of Maeve's pupils ebbed and flowed as colds and 'flu progressed through the school and the children were hard to motivate into doing anything even moderately well. The winters had, in fact, been the same in the preceding two years and it was perhaps the cumulative memory of them, and the fact that she knew there were three similar energy-sapping months ahead before things improved, that so depressed Maeve this January. How was she going to be able to galvanise forty children into some semblance of enthusiasm for school work, Maeve wondered, when she could hardly get up enough enthusiasm herself these days to come to school. It really was asking a lot.

At morning tea she plonked herself down next to Ruby Palmer, her best friend on the staff at Mill Hill Park Grammar.

'Hello Ruby, how are you?'

'Hello. About as bright-looking as everyone else I suspect. Looks like a collection of cadavers here this morning,' Ruby replied, looking about the small groups of teachers chatting together, cups of tea in hand and a couple of biscuits on their saucers. Maeve laughed. Ruby was known for her caustic sense of humour and dry wit – personality traits Maeve enjoyed in her friend for she could liven up dull proceedings with a wry comment and similarly deflate the more bombastic of the staff with a funny aside at just the right moment.

'The effects of Christmas and positive intentions for the New Year have worn off rather too quickly for my liking this term,' she went on. 'I just cannot get on top of things.'

'I know what you mean. I've been feeling the same myself. Too many sick children, too jolly cold; no enthusiasm to do something other than get home as quickly as possible after school and vegetate in front of the fire. I feel fifty-two, not twenty-two. Anyway, change the subject. Have you read any good books lately?'

'I suppose I have,' replied Ruby. 'I've been having a bit of a binge on H.G. Wells.' She went on to describe the plot of the most recently finished one. 'I really would like to get out of the house though. I passed the Hippodrome in High Street yesterday and tonight they are showing some Charlie Chaplin films. *The Gold Rush* is the only one I remember being advertised. Would you be interested in going?'

'Good idea,' replied Maeve. 'I've been too house-bound as well. I've already seen the film, I went last year, but I'd love to go again. What time shall we meet?'

'I'll meet you outside at 7.45, is that all right?'

'Yes, that will give me just enough time to do the washing up and walk over to High Street. I'll look forward to it. The last film I saw there was also one of his. What was it called?' Maeve paused to think, causing her brow to pucker into a faint pattern of thought lines at the effort. At the same time, her right index finger touched her bottom lip in an unconscious gesture of concentration. Although she was unaware of it, it was a rather endearing mannerism. 'Bother – mind like a sieve. I can't recall its title. It's the one where he plays an escaped convict who dresses up in a clergyman's clothes to avoid capture. Oh, it was so funny! There's this bit at the end where he has been recaptured but the sheriff doesn't want to turn him in. He orders Charlie to pick him a bunch of flowers which happen to be growing along the border in Mexico – they are travelling along the border I should add – with the intention that once Charlie has walked across he is no longer under USA laws. Well, Charlie picks the flowers and while he does so, the sheriff gallops off leaving Charlie a free man.' Maeve started giggling. 'Well, Charlie chases after him to give him his flowers and of course runs back into the USA.' She chuckled so loudly that her hand shook and the teacup rattled on its saucer. 'It was so funny.'

Ruby was giggling too. 'I know,' she said. 'I've seen it too. It's called *The Pilgrim*.'

'That's right, so it was.'

'I saw it with another one where Charlie and his family go to the seaside. One disaster after another, I nearly died laughing. He tries to put up a collapsible deckchair and it just goes on and on without him able to get it right,' said Ruby, giggling again. The two teachers' mirth began to draw attention from the other staff. Laughter had been rarely heard in the staff-room since Christmas break-up and other teachers looked with some bemusement at the two young women giggling away, their heads lowered and almost touching in an attempt to suppress their louder sniggers.

'Ruby,' said Maeve when she finally got control over herself, 'what a good idea to go out. It will cheer me up no end. I'm already feeling better at the thought of this evening.' A bell clanged loudly. 'Back to the coal face. Tudor history here I come,' and she got to her feet, put the teacup and saucer on the trolley and headed for the door.

Later in the week, Maeve came home at her usual time to find her mother unusually agitated.

'Your father is poorly, I'm wondering if I should fetch the doctor.'

'Is he in bed?' enquired Maeve as she briskly hung her coat and hat up. 'What seems to be the matter?'

'I'm not sure. He has virtually lost his voice and he has a temperature. I got him to go to bed at lunchtime. He didn't want to – you know your father's stubbornness – but he did eventually and he's just been dozing, off and on, since then. Not his old self at all.'

'What a relief,' muttered Maeve under her breath as she followed her mother up the stairs to her father's bed.

He lay there on his back, breathing fitfully, his bald head with its fringe of white hair pale against the linen pillow-case. Gosh, he looks like an old man, thought Maeve with surprise. She had never noticed before, because always his expression, his posture, everything about him had emanated from his personality rather than from his physical presence. In this new, obviously

126

quite seriously ill condition, his personality had retreated somewhere within him, leaving this old husk to represent him for the duration. She fetched the family doctor from his surgery a couple of streets away in Loveday Road. The Reverend Stephenson had caught the 'flu and was prescribed two weeks in bed and lots of beef tea. To lower his temperature, a red flannel wrap, damp with warm water, was to be applied to his forehead, to be changed each time it became cool to the touch.

Maeve didn't concern herself unduly about her father's temporary bedridden state. A hitherto unknown worry, a direct result of him falling sick, did however preoccupy her. Her parents were old. Maeve was of a late marriage. Her father must have been forty when she was born, her mother in her mid-thirties. For the first time it dawned on her that she had two ageing parents on her hands, and that if some adversity struck one or other of them in the next few years, they might be completely reliant on Maeve to see them through it. The thought troubled Maeve a great deal. She had never seen herself as the spinster daughter who would support her elderly mother and father in their declining years, but suddenly the situation could all too possibly become a reality. The idea appalled her. And her response also shocked her.

She had never pondered her feelings regarding family loyalty before, but with her father seriously ill for the first time that she could remember, such feelings had, at last, to be considered, and a conclusion reached. There was no way she could reconcile herself to such a future. Analysing her feelings, she could locate no emotions of love towards her father, there was hardly even a glimmer of affection; just acceptance that he was someone she had had to make concessions to in order to live in the same house. His autocratic manner towards her from about the age of thirteen had eventually killed the instinctive love Maeve had once directed towards her father and now there was nothing left. Nothing at all, no dislike, pity, nor anger.

Towards her mother she did have feelings of affection and of loyalty. Ironically, some of these were forged by

127

her father's bullying ways – a sort of solidarity in the face of the unfairness he had so frequently directed towards either or both of them. But her mother, she eventally concluded, would not be the problem. In most situations she would be able to look after herself and if a crisis materialized she had two sisters living at Staines whom she had never lost touch with despite her husband not caring particularly for their company.

Without formulating any plans, Maeve realized that to do nothing, to simply stay on at Mayfield Avenue, would inevitably lead to the future she suddenly so clearly wished to avoid. And it was brought home to her even more emphatically the very next day.

Maeve regularly spent Saturday afternoons with her old school friend, Alexa Cubbins, usually catching the tube and going into the city to browse the shops, see a show or simply visit one or other of the art galleries or parks. Today they were going to do the secondhand bookshops in Charing Cross Road, and later, try and get tickets to the late matinee performance of *The Desert Song* at Drury Lane. Punctually at one o'clock, Alexa knocked at the door.

'Hello,' said Maeve, opening it. 'Come in, I'll just get my coat and shoes on and we can go.' She quickly donned her winter outdoor clothes and calling out, 'Bye mother, don't wait up if I'm late home,' she and Alexa set off for Northfields Station to catch the train to London.

'I've got some news I simply can't wait to tell you,' said Alexa when they reached the end of the street. 'Nigel proposed marriage!'

Maeve stopped walking. 'My goodness, I never anticipated this. Tell me, what did you answer?'

'Yes.'

Maeve gave her friend a quick hug. 'I'm very pleased for you! My goodness, Alexa, you and Nigel Leith married, how exciting. When is the wedding?'

'Nigel has set the date for early August. He is getting transferred to Southampton in the middle of the month, so we thought we should do it before he leaves,' she corrected herself – 'we leave – and have a week's honeymoon before we go. You know,' she went on, 'I never thought he'd ask. It was getting obvious something of this nature was on his mind but I think it was only because the company was moving him that he finally asked. A bit of "it's a now or never" sort of thing'.

'I know,' laughed Maeve. 'There were times when we were all out together and I got the distinct impression from Nigel that I should be elsewhere. But he never seemed especially ardent, so I didn't take up his suggestion. And now this.'

'Will you be my bridesmaid?'

'If you hadn't asked I would never have spoken to you again. There's no one more suitable for the position than myself. Of course I will.'

The bookshop excursion was never completed. Elated with Alexa's news, the two of them abandoned Charing Cross Road for the bridal outfitters in Regent Street to look at the wedding fashions for the coming spring and summer. Maeve was delighted at her friend's happiness, but her thoughts were tinged with a sadness she couldn't shake off. First, Alexa's wedding meant that her best friend was moving away from Ealing to set up her own home. But Alexa's change of circumstances also impinged on her preoccupations of the last few days. Here she was, beginning to feel really trapped for the first time in her life by Ealing, teaching and Mayfield Avenue and Alexa was about to take off into a future, no doubt fraught with its own problems, but nevertheless unencumbered with the kind of difficulties Maeve was beginning to perceive in her own life.

It was a preoccupation which persisted and Maeve, over the weeks that followed, analyzed her situation endlessly. Obviously marriage was a way out, but there had to be a suitable husband in the offing and, in Maeve's life, no such person had presented himself. She had a small number of male friends, a couple of teaching colleagues, and a gentleman in the reading circle she was a member of, but no one special. She occasionally went to a show or an outing when asked by one of them, but the friendships had never blossomed in the way Alexa's and Nigel Leith's had. It hadn't mattered to Maeve. Suddenly, though, she had a vague, uneasy feeling that she was missing out and, by missing out, was heading for a situation of which she definitely wanted no part.

It is one thing to identify the position and quite another to deal with it. Maeve didn't know what to do. There didn't seem to be any great urgency to act, but, she felt, things couldn't continue the way they had for much longer. But romance leading to more serious commitment wasn't purchaseable in Ealing High Street or found cluttering up the staff room at Mill Hill Park Grammar School. Alexa had met her Nigel at the tennis club two years ago. Maeve wasn't especially sporty and, although also a member of the club, played less spectacularly than the lithe Alexa. Maeve had often smiled at the sight of the young men in dazzling whites and brilliantined hair, lining up to a have a match with Alexa and the other fashionable girls at the courts. She herself was quite happy having a lemonade in the little sheltered stand, chatting the while with friends and watching the matches, or having a pedestrian game out on the far court which had everything to do with friendly exercise and nothing to do with romantic overtures.

For the first time in her life, she tried to look at herself as an observer might, particularly as a young man might. But what did they like in a girl? One evening after her bath she gazed into the mirror, trying to see what attributes before her had prevented her from attracting some romantic attention from men she felt would be acceptable. Nothing was revealed. She suspected that her lips were too full, her face too square for current fashions, and her hairstyling somewhat ordinary, but although she wouldn't have described herself as beautiful, she liked her own looks well enough. Similarly, her figure seemed all right to her critical inspection. A bit rounder than the fashion pages suggested was *dernier cri,* and buxom too, but well-formed and comely. She got into her nightie and went to bed. Whatever it was that made things change, she couldn't identify it. Such thoughts, she decided, only made her gloomy and, seeking a distraction, she picked up her book from the floor beside the bed and attempted to lose herself in Arnold Bennett's prose.

Chapter 9

Selangor, 1927

Death was a frequent visitor to the rubber plantations
of the Malay Peninsula. In most situations one became
philosophical as yet another colleague or a servant was
consigned to the red soil of Malaya, but every now and
then a loss would hit a man particularly hard. Ronnie's
and George's premature deaths two and a half years ago
had shaken Kenneth badly. In its own way, McGregor
Reynolds' sudden and unexpected demise in March 1927
also affected Kenneth.

The manager, one morning muster, uncharacteristically
failed to appear down at the coolie lines. It didn't
particularly matter as Kenneth, now an experienced senior assistant manager, could give the day's instructions
as easily as Mr Reynolds could. But his non-appearance
surprised Kenneth.

He turned to Ernest Simpson and Bertie Everdon, the
assistant managers who had filled the empty mess after
George and Ronnie had died, and said, 'I'm going to cut
across to Mr Reynolds' house and see what's holding him
up. It's not like the old boy to miss his duties, even when
he is not one hundred per cent well. See you later.'

The lounge light was on, Kenneth could see, as he
approached the front stairs of the manager's bungalow. 'Hello,' he called as he approached the door.
'Mr Reynolds, hello.'

Reynolds sat slumped in a cane chair, head forward,
chin on his chest, his hands resting on his lap. A half-
finished glass of whisky stood on the low table on his
right. On the floor was a crumpled *Country Life* magazine
which had obviously slipped from his grasp and had been

132

left to lie where it fell. The man was morbidly still. He was dead, Kenneth realized at once. He touched his boss's forearm to confirm it. It was cold. Clearly Mr Reynolds had died suddenly and undramatically; he could almost have passed as simply napping in his chair. He must be at least six or seven hours dead, thought Kenneth. He knew Mr Reynolds always had a nightcap before retiring each night, usually between nine and ten o'clock, and from the unfinished drink on the table, he must have passed on without any warning at around that time.

Where's the servant? wondered Kenneth. He walked past the body into the dining room where a light was also on. A teapot lay on its side on the timber floor with its contents draining through the cracks between the boards. Kenneth touched the pool of tea and found it still warm. He knew what must have happened: Jimmy would have discovered his tuan's body when bringing in the morning pot of tea from the kitchen and, like any other superstitious house-boy, instantly fled the scene in fear of a ghost. No doubt he would turn up again after the burial.

Kenneth wasn't surprised at the behaviour, it was common enough. He pulled his pocket watch out and looked at the time – five o'clock. He would have to telephone Dalgeish McElroy in Penang once the office opened at 7.30. In the meantime he could ring the neighbouring estates and leave messages for their managers, all acquaintants or friends of Mr Reynolds, to get over to Kuala Tanah as soon as they could.

The local telephone calls made, he pondered on what to do next. Dawn was coming and the trees about the bungalow were beginning to make a silhouette against the blue-grey sky. A few mynahs began to squawk and, further away, some roosters were heralding in yet another scorching day. It didn't seem right to leave Reynolds alone, so he sat himself in a cane chair at the far end of the room from where he could see the body but at the same time not be confronted with its mortality, and simply waited.

Mr Reynolds appeared diminished and vulnerable in

133

death. The strongly built, loud-voiced man who had met Kenneth on his arrival in Selangor nearly seven years ago was now a grey-haired old man. The fire within, now extinguished, had at times made him a larger-than-life character. Its passing left him looking somewhat boyish and wistful despite his grizzled head of hair, and the deep creases across his cheeks and forehead had smoothed out with the annihilation of the worries, concerns and thoughts which had created them. Seeing him slumped there, surrounded by the souvenirs of a life – mounted trophy heads, sepia-coloured photographs, a shelf of books, bits and pieces of ethnic Malayan arts and crafts, a rack of sporting guns – produced in Kenneth a feeling of despair and desolation. Not much to mark a lifetime, he thought. No family, just a lonely passing in a lonely part of the British Empire. Would this be his lot also? Yet another poor bloody bachelor leaving his meagre belongings to be disposed of by the company agent, his bones lying in the desiccated Bangi cemetery, remembered occasionally by those at the Club who survived him as a 'damn good chap' or 'one of the best' until they too left Malaya one way or another? He ruminated on the theme without being aware of the time. Eventually his thoughts returned to the present. It was time to call Penang.

For once the connections were clear and the operator got through to Dalgeish McElroy quickly. The conversation with the assistant manager of the head office, Mr Edwards, was equally quick. Kenneth would take over the management of the estate for the immediate future. Penang would arrange for the appointment of a new manager as soon as possible. It was as much as Kenneth had expected.

Mr Reynolds was interred with all the respect a man of his reputation would have wanted. The wake at the Bangi Club was protracted and raucous as planters from all over southern Selangor and Negri Sembilan converged to send him off in a fitting manner. It was not particularly difficult for Kenneth to pick up the reins to the running of the estate where Mr Reynolds had dropped them and virtually everyone's work continued as before. For the month after taking over as acting manager, Kenneth continued to live in the assistants' mess, walking over to the manager's bungalow each afternoon and evening to do the paperwork in the office. It became increasingly inconvenient, however, and in the month of May he packed his kit and moved into the spare bedroom in the manager's quarters so that he could do the job more efficiently. Sue moved with him.

The weeks passed and no replacement for Mr Reynolds had yet appeared. The one enquiry Kenneth made to Penang about the matter received an evasive reply in return, informing him that the position was under consideration and that in due course the estate would have a new manager.

In early July another letter arrived from Penang. With no great anticipation Kenneth opened it that evening after tiffin. With growing amazement he read that Penang had decided to offer him the position. Manager at twenty-nine! What an opportunity! Somewhere over the years Mr Reynolds must have written some complimentary sentences about him in his quarterly reports to head office. There were conditions attached to the appointment however:

The Company takes the view that the appointment should be filled by a married man. If you should decide to accept the position of Manager Grade IV on Kuala Tanah Estate, the Company is prepared to advance your gazetted Home leave, due June 1928, by one year in order for you to make adjustments to your personal circumstances.

The letter continued for several patronising sentences more. Kenneth could only smile at the page in wonder. They're telling me to go home and get a wife and return here as manager. What a turn of events! There was no need to procrastinate, it was the chance of a lifetime.

Kenneth promptly replied to Dalgeish McElroy. In contrast to the preceding two months, events moved fast. Within a fortnight a temporary manager was arranged to replace Kenneth during the four months he was to be away. Kenneth hardly had time to meet him. With his luggage next to him he greeted the new man as he disembarked from the Straits Steamship Company ship at Tangga Gajah. They chatted for about an hour, Kenneth giving the man any necessary background he might require for the job, and then the call for boarding passengers went out from the vessel.

'Cheerio, old man,' said the replacement manager, shaking Kenneth's hand, 'and good luck.'

Kenneth wished him likewise and mounted the companionway. An hour later the *Kelantan* swished past Bukit Klang: somewhere in among the trees to the north of the hill was Ali's Istana. Kenneth strained his eyes to discern it but the slanting light of the setting sun turned the landscape into a mottled patchwork of greens and dark shadows. He settled back into a deckchair and watched the passing shore as the coffee-coloured Kemudi carried him away. It was almost seven years since he had travelled the opposite way.

The journey was a night one. The next morning Kenneth rose from his berth as the steamer's cadence slowed to find himself off Singapore. The great imperial city looked imposing in the dawn light, but Kenneth had eyes only for the giant liner, preparing, even as he watched, for departure later that day. The P & O *Moldavia* was Kenneth's boat back home.

Chapter 10

London, 1927 – Summer

The late summer thunderstorm had caught the shoppers and pedestrians by surprise. Earlier, the weather had given no indication that the day could be anything but warm and blue-skied, and Maeve, when she had stepped out to visit the Ealing library after luncheon, had enjoyed the feeling of the sun warming her bare shoulders and head as she ambled across Walpole Park towards the town. It was the second to last week of the school holidays and she had decided to spend these days relaxing with a pile of escapist books. All too soon it would be back to the tensions and stress of teaching and even less than usual did she relish the return to work.

The storm clouds had rolled in across the city while she was immersed in browsing the book stacks, and it was only when she left two hours later with a shopping bag of books under her arm, that she discovered the change. The clouds were almost black-purple in the way only summer thunderclouds can be. I'm not going to make it home on foot, she thought to herself. It didn't matter. The library was a minute's walk to Ealing High Street. From there she could catch the bus down to Pope's Lane and then catch the number 108 which went up Northfield Avenue, right past Mayfield Avenue.

Seconds before Maeve reached the bus shelter outside Boots, the storm broke. Heavy, large raindrops spilled from the sky to atomize audibly on the warm roadway and footpath. It was like an enormous tepid shower and, in the brief moments Maeve was caught in it before reaching the bus shelter her clothes were darkened with sploshes of the rain. The smell of rain-cooled tar-seal wafted about the shelter, and, above a manhole cover in the centre of the road opposite, a thin mist of vaporized water hovered over the hot iron lid for a half a minute until the continuing deluge cooled it. The storm was so unexpected that it was a novelty and Maeve didn't mind being damp. Summer storms never lasted all day and it was likely to be over by the time the bus would be passing Mayfield Avenue.

Three people shared the shelter. No bus was in sight so Maeve sat down on the bench where she had a view up the road and pulled out one of her library books to browse while waiting. Ten minutes passed. Then another ten. Still no bus. Half an hour: the rain continued to fall and no bus had yet passed. At this point a passing pedestrian under a large black umbrella poked his head into the shelter.

'Are you people waiting for a bus or just sheltering from the rain?'

'For the bus,' chorused Maeve and the other three.

'I'm afraid there aren't any this afternoon,' the man replied. 'London Transport drivers are having a stop-work meeting so the buses aren't running until this evening, if they go back to work at all today that is.'

The four would-be bus passengers looked at each other.

'Oh, dear,' said an elderly woman, 'this is really too bad.'

The others said nothing but simply looked at the rain and the wet road with crestfallen faces. The man with the umbrella asked the old lady where she wanted to go.

'Just along to opposite the church,' she replied, waving a hand down the road.

'I'm going that way. If you want to share my umbrella I'll accompany you.' With profuse thanks she accepted his offer and the two of them splashed away.

'Typical, I say.' One of the two remaining people sharing the shelter with Maeve spoke up. 'Those unions are nothing but a bunch of Bolshevik troublemakers. I thought they would have had enough of strikes after last year's fiasco' – he was referring to the abortive General Strike – 'they shouldn't be allowed to get away with it.' The speaker was a tubby middle-aged man in a tweed three-piece suit who, by the faint halo of steam coming off his jacket, had been caught like Maeve in the downpour. The other would be passenger smiled in agreement with these sentiments. This man was younger, about thirty Maeve idly judged, with a spare muscular physique. His hands and face were tanned brown, indicating not only that he had an out-of-doors profession, but also that he usually didn't live in England. No one could get a suntan like that here. Probably on leave from India, Maeve thought to herself.

She pondered him some more. He had a pleasant face though his expression was, she mused, somewhat wistful and lonely as he gazed into the falling rain. Creases ran from the edges of his eyes, a mixture of laugh lines and squinting from bright light she decided, across his cheek bones and the beginnings of a permanent line down each cheek towards his jaw showed as a pale edge against his tan. On his head he wore a trilby with the brim turned up on the left side just perceptibly enough to give him a hint of style. Similarly his light-grey double-breasted lounge suit gave him a certain carefully groomed appearance which was not typical of Ealing High Street in midafternoon. Hence Maeve's scrutiny of him over the top of her book as the rain continued to fall.

The middle-aged man jumped to his feet and hailed a vacant taxi which was just passing. The man whom Maeve had been observing, now the only occupant apart from herself left in the bus shelter, caught her eye and commented, 'Not a bad idea. I think I will do the same, otherwise I'll be here all afternoon.' He paused, obviously considering in his mind what he was about to say next. 'Pardon me if I sound forward, miss, but perhaps we could share a taxi. I was intending to catch the bus to Brentford. Is a taxi in that direction any use to you?'

It was, but Maeve had set out that afternoon with less than a shilling in her purse, enough, more than enough for her bus fare home, but not sufficient to contribute half of a taxi fare to Mayfield Avenue.

'It's very kind of you to suggest it. I'm afraid I'm going

to have to wait until it stops raining however, as I have very little money with me. I really didn't expect the afternoon to turn out like this for a start, and who'd have thought London Transport would hold a strike. I hadn't heard a thing about it.' She laughed when she realized just what she had said. 'That's obvious isn't it? I wouldn't be sitting here waiting for a bus if I had.'

'Forget sharing the fare,' replied the young man. 'If you're more or less on my way, please allow me to offer a lift. I'll have to pay anyway. Really, you could be here for hours otherwise.'

It was a kind offer and Maeve accepted. As they watched for a passing vacant taxi to wave down, Maeve and the man chatted. The light conversation quickly turned to books.

The man pointed to the book Maeve had put aside.

'I see you are interested in Malaya.' The book happened to be Sir Frank Swettenham's *Malay Sketches*.

'Sort of,' replied Maeve. 'Reading about exotic, foreign travels is a passion of mine. It helps me forget that it's Ealing that I live in. I've just been to the library and borrowed a couple of interesting-looking ones.' She rummaged in her shopping bag and pulled out a chunky volume bearing the title *The Golden Cheronese* and passed it over to the man. 'This one looks marvellous. As it was in the same section as that one,' she lifted Swettenham, 'I thought I'd get them both out. It isn't just Malaya I'm interested in; any good book about far-away places draws me in. Do you read a lot too?'

'Hardly ever I'm afraid,' replied the man. 'But these look interesting I must say.' He feathered the pages of the book he was holding. 'Actually, I live in Malaya. I'm home on leave for a couple of months, that's why I'm in London.'

'Good heavens, do you really? How fascinating. It must be exciting living in the East,' said Maeve. 'Tell me about where you live. I'd love to hear about it.'

The man told her a little about life in Malaya. He talked away with increasing animation for about five minutes

140

before interrupting his own conversation. 'Look, a taxi! Hold on.' He jumped to his feet and waved. The driver saw his gesture and pulled up. They clambered in.

'First to this young lady's address, and then on to Brentford please,' instructed the man to the cabbie. As they pulled away he said 'I had better introduce myself. I'm Kenneth Clouston.'

Maeve shook his extended hand and smiled back at him.

'I'm Maeve Stephenson. Do go on with your story. I was really enjoying hearing about Malaya.'

For the five minutes that it took to Mayfield Avenue, Kenneth continued to chat about Selangor and Penang, jungles and rivers, plantations and people. Maeve was enchanted.

The taxi drew to a stop outside the Stephenson home. On an impulse Kenneth asked, 'Miss Stephenson, could I call on you? I've really enjoyed talking to you, the afternoon has turned out much more pleasurable than I could ever have expected. I don't actually know many people in London, having been away so long, so I would very much appreciate your company.'

'Of course. I'd love to hear more of your travels. Are you free tomorrow? Good. Then come for afternoon tea. I'll expect you at three o'clock. Thanks for the lift. Goodbye.'

She ducked out of the taxi and ran for her door. Under the shelter of the porch eaves, she dug in her bag for her front door key, a pretty sight in Kenneth's eye in her summer frock of fashionable coloured stripes with the waist at hip level, and bobbed light auburn hair. She had a nice figure, he also noted; average height, a bit rounder than current London fashions were endorsing but it suited her warm, friendly personality. Her face too had a sunny disposition. She had a beautiful complexion, soft fullish mouth and gracefully arched eyebrows above deep brown eyes. At this precise moment they were knit in concentration as she continued to search for the elusive latch key.

He was glad he had spoken up. It was not characteristic of him to push himself forward in the way he had just done and he could only guess that it was Miss Stephenson's pleasant and unassuming manner that had given him the nerve. Without a doubt, today's chance encounter was the best thing that had happened to him since he had arrived back in England a fortnight ago.

Maeve too was pleased at the outcome of an afternoon's visit to the library. Her announcement that a Mr Clouston was coming to afternoon tea the next day had put her mother into a fluster. Visitors, apart from people calling about church-related matters, were rare at Mayfield Avenue, and Maeve usually arranged to meet her friends elsewhere in more socially congenial places. A young man too. This was unprecedented and Mrs Stephenson reacted accordingly. The Reverend Stephenson displayed no interest in the matter. It was no more than Maeve had expected and so, in no way undeterred, the next morning she baked a cake and some biscuits to be ready in good time for the visit.

Punctually at three, Kenneth rang the doorbell.

'Good afternoon, Miss Stephenson, I hope I'm on time.'

'Perfectly. Do come in,' said Maeve. She took his hat and placed it on the hall hat and umbrella stand and took Kenneth into the living room.

'Mother this is Mr Clouston, who was nice enough to give me a ride home in his taxi during yesterday's storm.'

'How do you do, Mrs Stephenson,' he said, shaking her hand. 'These are for you.' He gallantly extended a bunch of carnations and ladies' bonnets sprinkled with forget-me-nots wrapped in pale pink waxed paper to her. They had, actually, been bought for Maeve, but when he realized that her mother was home, not to have offered the bouquet to the older woman would have been graceless. The mems back in Selangor would have been proud of Kenneth's quick-mindedness at that moment!

Mrs Stephenson was almost overcome. No one had

given her flowers, apart from Maeve, for longer than she cared to remember.

'It's very kind of you, Mr Clouston, they're beautiful. Please take a seat and be comfortable. Maeve, I'll get the tea trolley, you keep your guest company.'

'My father isn't here at the moment. He's a clergyman and he is over at the Old People's Home until later in the afternoon,' Maeve explained. 'He may get back in time to meet you though.'

Conversation quickly drifted back to yesterday's topic – Kenneth's life in Malaya. Telling Maeve about Selangor and the estate, and seeing her interest in all he had to say made Kenneth re-evaluate much of what had happened there. It was an interesting place to live in, he had simply grown to take it for granted. Here in Ealing, the daily sights of the past seven years began to take on a specialness. Buffalos plodding through paddy fields, distant Malay voices shouting to each other from a smoky village, mosques half-hidden behind huge mango trees; such scenes suddenly didn't seem humdrum when described in a parlour in suburban London.

To Maeve it sounded wonderful. Here, first hand, she was hearing about things she had previously only read about in Kipling, and, as of last night, Swettenham. The rather tedious lessons she had to turn out on British Empire geography and history to her third- and fourth-formers suddenly came to life as Kenneth told her about the wide muddy rivers winding their serpentine courses out of the highlands, of the rawness of the tin-mines and so on. In his new-found enthusiasm for Malaya, he skimmed over the heat, disease, boredom and monotony of estate life and chatted on about the exotic and novel. Never before had he had such a receptive audience.

The afternoon flew by as they sipped tea and chatted. It seemed hardly possible but before Kenneth knew it, the mantle clock above the fireplace was showing 4.30 and it was time for him to leave. Maeve saw him to the door.

'I'm so glad you came over. It's been a marvellous afternoon,' said Maeve, handing him his trilby.

143

'Look,' said Kenneth, 'seeing as you have a week's holiday remaining to you, would you like to come into town for the day next week? As you know, I have exactly nothing to do except sightsee and browse the shops. I could think of nothing nicer than if you would help show me around. I haven't been here since 1920 and my bearings as to where everything is are a bit hazy. When it comes down to it they never were much good. I never did move much out of Brentford until I really moved — all the way to Malaya.'

'It's a lovely idea. Make it Monday. Where would you like to start?'

'Give me a suggestion.'

'Let's visit the West End. I love window shopping there and if it's wet or something we can always go to one of the art galleries. Why don't we meet at Charing Cross Station at ten o'clock? Under the main clock at the Strand entrance, you can't miss it.'

'A great idea,' said Kenneth enthusiastically. 'Until Monday then. Goodbye Mrs Stephenson,' he said to Maeve's mother who was hovering at the kitchen doorway. 'Thank you for the afternoon tea. Goodbye Miss Stephenson.'

The Monday excursion into the heart of fashionable London was a great success. Maeve and Kenneth met as arranged and spent the morning strolling along Regent Street to Oxford Street and to as far as Wardour Street, where they stopped in a tea rooms for luncheon. They each felt relaxed and happy in each other's company and enjoyed looking in the windows of the smart shops.

'What shall we do this afternoon, Miss Stephenson?' asked Kenneth as he lit up a cigarette to finish off his meal.

'Are you done with walking?'

'Not at all.'

'Well, look. If we continue the way we're going, in twenty minutes we'll be in Bloomsbury. Let's go there. If you're in the mood, we can visit the British Museum.

I haven't been there for years, it could be fun. Another thing. Why don't you call me Maeve? This morning has been most enjoyable and I find the Miss Stephenson label a bit in the way.'

'So do I,' laughed Kenneth. 'No more Mister Clouston either. It's odd to hear myself called that in London. I instinctively think the person speaking to me is in fact addressing my father, who must be standing over my shoulder. Maeve it is then.'

The Monday spent this way turned out to be only the first of four successive days spent in a similar manner. As they walked back to Charing Cross where Maeve could catch her train to Ealing, they arranged to meet at the same place tomorrow and spend the day at London Zoo. Wednesday was spent at Kew Gardens. Maeve brought a picnic lunch and they met, as arranged, at the main entrance at eleven o'clock.

'You know, I've never been here before,' said Kenneth, 'even though I lived not more than a mile away for the first twenty years of my life.' They were sitting on the bank of the Thames, with Syon House in the middle distance across the river. Behind them was the Lake with its thousands of ducks. 'I simply never thought to cross the river, I suppose.'

For over two hours they had chatted about every subject under the sun. The picnic lunch and the warm day finally slowed their animated conversation and an air of drowsiness and indolence seeped into their mood. Maeve lay back on the rug she had brought along, hands folded back behind her head, looking at the small bundles of clouds scudding across the pale blue sky. High overhead wispy mare's tails were streaking the heavens.

'What a beautiful day. I hardly dare contemplate teaching again next week, it's too much of a contrast to life's more pleasant events'.

Kenneth sat at the edge of the rug, his weight resting on his left arm as he turned to listen to her. He thought to himself: She's lovely. What a good time it has been since I met her. He looked at her discreetly, so as not to catch

145

her attention. They were in a shallow hollow of the river bank which formed a natural sun trap. It was so warm that he had taken off his blazer and she her summer jacket. She lay there in her apple-green cotton zephyr day dress, its low rounded-square neckline showing her pale throat and chest bared to the warm sun.

Kenneth's eyes covertly glanced at the fabric, tight across her breasts, which compressed each one enough to push them a little above the neckline and reveal the start of her cleavage. His line of sight scanned down, taking in her flat stomach, and shapely hips. The pleated skirt of the dress spread out over the rug and was rucked up a little above the knee by her unselfconscious sprawling. She wore grey silk stockings. God, she is lovely, thought Kenneth, shifting his gaze to Syon House across the river to disguise his thoughts.

An ache grew in the pit of his stomach and he realized to his discomfiture that his thoughts about Maeve were arousing him. Time to think of something less provocative! He pulled his pocket watch out to see the time. Three o'clock, perhaps they could move on.

'Why don't we visit the greenhouses, Maeve?' he said, breaking a silence of minutes.

'Hhmmmm. Yes, all right. Goodness, I nearly dropped off, it's so gorgeous lying here. Just give me a few minutes to get used to the idea.'

Maeve had in fact been aware of Kenneth's inspection of her charms and had made one of her own as she had lain there, eyes almost closed. The conclusion of it had been somewhat similar to Kenneth's, and a warm heaviness pervaded her belly and breasts as she continued to lie there in the sun. She glanced at his tanned, sinewed arm not far from her and liked the feeling of strength it projected. She looked at his hand with its long fingers spread to support the weight of his reclining body and imagined those same fingers caressing the areas of her body which were at this moment starting to tingle. Frequently she had entertained such harmless visions when reading a romantic novel but never before had she applied such daydreams to an actual

146

man, especially one right next to her. She was surprised at herself.

'Okay. Just let me pack up the picnic things and we'll go.' She got to her knees and began to put away the remains of the lunch into the basket. Her position provided Kenneth with an even more expansive view of her cleavage as she bent to gather the bits and pieces, and he turned away to adjust himself before getting to his feet. With both of them vaguely disturbed by the forces of attraction kindling within themselves for each other, they strolled off in the direction of the greenhouses.

The Temperate House with its eucalypt collection didn't spark much interest in Kenneth, but the Palm House was quite a different story.

'This is like parts of Malaya,' he exclaimed. 'Just look at that traveller's palm, isn't it extraordinary?' He pointed to a huge fan-shaped tree with giant oblong-leafed fronds which radiated out from a single thick trunk and rose to twenty-five feet towards the glassed vault of the greenhouse. Near it was a group of carmine-stemmed sealing-wax palms just like the clump at Kuala Tanah. It was the jungle river bank of Kemudi in microcosm and he suddenly felt homesick for Selangor – an emotion two months earlier he felt could never exist for him, so sick of the place had he been. Even the artificially high temperature of the greenhouse made him think of Malaya with affection.

'Well now you have an inkling of what Selangor is like,' he added.

'Just how I imagined it,' replied Maeve.

Before they parted at the bus stop outside the main entrance Maeve and Kenneth made plans to spend Thursday visiting the museums in South Kensington. By this time, Kenneth had quietly had enough of art and museum exhibitions. Madame Tussaud's Wax Museum was more his idea of a museum visit, if there had to be one, but for the sake of being with Maeve he had cheerfully tagged along and listened attentively when she spoke about some of the things they saw. When Maeve returned home at teatime, having spent the preceding hours in the Museum of Natural History and, across the road, at the Victoria and Albert, her father cornered her as she poked her head through the open door of the living room to say hello to her mother.

'Maeve, I'd like to have a word with you about this young man you've been seeing so regularly.'

Spare me, she thought to herself. Aloud she said, 'Yes, Father, what do you want to say?' and she sat down opposite him on the settee.

'I think we should meet him. I mean to say, out every day this week with him and I don't know if he is at all suitable for you.'

Nowadays, Maeve thought to herself, he sounds so old-fashioned and out of touch. The querulous tone of his voice had lost its undertones of righteous assertiveness since his bad bout of influenza last winter and the Reverend Stephenson sounded simply crotchety and old these days. What business was it of his whether Kenneth was suitable as an escort or not? thought Maeve, but she didn't voice the question. She also didn't bother to remind him that only a week ago he could have met Kenneth when he called for afternoon tea.

'I'll ask him to dinner tomorrow if you like. That way you'll meet him.'

As far as the Reverend Stephenson was concerned, the original purpose of his enquiry was to provoke an argument with Maeve, not result in the young man coming around. He hemmed and hawed for a bit, but when it was apparent even to him that Maeve was not going to rise to the bait he acquiesced. Kenneth would come to dinner tomorrow evening.

Much to his surprise the dinner was a pleasant occasion. Kenneth agreed with his opinions on every important issue and was amusing enough when he begged to disagree on smaller things. He suspected that he was, in fact, being humoured but it didn't really matter for once. Maeve's young man was polite and respectful and told some very

148

interesting stories about his life in Malaya. Against his better nature, he liked Kenneth enough to allow the atmosphere at dinner to remain convivial.

They very rarely had guests to dinner at Mayfield Avenue and those who did come were usually church councillors or similarly connected. So, in comparison to such occasions, the evening was, in the eyes of Maeve and her mother, a marked success. At one point Maeve quietly watched Kenneth across the table as he listened earnestly, regularly making the right noises of agreement, as the Reverend Stephenson rambled on about missionary work in India which he judged as geographically close enough to Malaya to be of great interest to Kenneth. She thought to herself that he was a nice-looking man. He was so unlike her father. He had a certain diffidence, a shyness which only surfaced now and then, which she found appealing after the blustering and posturing her father had presented to her all her life.

As her mother and Maeve gathered the plates from the table while the men went to the parlour out of the way of the clearing-up procedure, Mrs Stephenson commented on what a gentleman Kenneth was.

'I can't think when last we had such a jolly evening,' she said. 'Do ask him back if you'd like to.'

Maeve had already decided she had every intention of doing exactly that.

The new term commenced the next Monday and Maeve didn't see Kenneth until the following weekend when he came round to accompany her into the West End. They had planned to see one of the season's most popular plays, *The Silent House*, a mystery involving oriental villains and young ladies in distress, which was playing at the Comedy Theatre. Kenneth had bought the tickets during the week so they were guaranteed good seats. Sunday afternoon was also spent together. They had originally intended to go out to Hyde Park to listen to the soap-box orators at Speaker's Corner – always an entertaining place – but the day was overcast, and when Kenneth knocked on the door at midday, his shoulders and trilby were spotted with first raindrops heralding a wet afternoon.

'Shall we risk it?' Maeve said, casting a doubtful eye at the sky. 'If we don't go out we could always stay here. I could do some sewing if you don't mind just chatting. And we can listen to the wireless.'

Kenneth cheerfully agreed. By this time he was smitten with Maeve and it was her company he sought rather than the entertainments they ventured out to as a couple. The afternoon sitting near her in her own house was as agreeable to him as listening and chatting to her as they walked museum galleries or strolled through London's parks. He only had three more weeks in London before he had to catch the P & O liner back to Malaya and he knew that sometime in the next fortnight he would ask her to marry him.

The job stipulation was irrelevant. Dalgeish McElroy could go to hang with their insistence that the manager of Kuala Tanah Estate must be a married man. He wanted Maeve for what she was, and the urgency he felt in summoning up his nerve to ask for her hand was entirely because of his approaching departure to the other side of the world, and not because she provided him with the means for a promotion in Malaya.

When to ask though?

Maeve felt upset as the September days slipped by all too quickly. Kenneth's appearance had been surprisingly opportune. Alexa's wedding and shifting to Southampton in the middle of the school holiday break had left a large hole in Maeve's life. Of all her school-day friends, Alexa had been the only one to have remained close by, and now she too had gone to live elsewhere. Kenneth's unexpected companionship had filled Alexa's place very well and now with his departure approaching, she felt she was losing another friend all too soon after the first.

Another Saturday came around on the calendar. Maeve and Kenneth went dancing at the Palais de Danse at Hammersmith. Billy Cotton was playing, so the evening promised to be a lively occasion. It was, but there was a tension between them that wouldn't go away, no matter how much excitement the music and the dancing crowd generated. Like the sword of Damocles, Kenneth's departure in a fortnight hung over them. Maeve looked even more lovely than usual in Kenneth's eyes, dressed this evening in a pale lilac crêpe de Chine evening dress and a tiara of artificial flowers decorating her hair.

The dance floor, dappled with reflected light from the slowly revolving globe of faceted mirrors suspended from the ceiling and by coloured spots, looked a place of soft, inviting mystery when viewed from the cocktail bar lounge. Down on it, the scene was a mass of swirling and shimmering dancers. After some lively one-steps and a tango, Maeve and Kenneth took a breather from the milling crowd and retired to the balcony. Large windows – french doors really – looked out over the Thames. It was warm enough to step outside on to the balcony proper and take in the evening air. They leaned against the concrete balustrading and looked out to the lights of Fulham twinkling downstream in the distance. Damn it, thought Kenneth, it's now or never.

'Maeve, would you ever consider leaving Ealing?' Before she could answer, he went on. 'What I mean to say, would you consider coming to Malaya? I realize the suggestion is ridiculous,' he stumbled on, unhappy with his choice of words even as he spoke them. Nevertheless, he launched on with his proposal. 'After all, I've only known you five weeks. I've never enjoyed anyone's company half so much as I have yours though, and I can't go on pretending you mean much less to me than you do. And I can't sail off without asking you this.'

Maeve put her hand on top of his, the first time she had touched him other than in the well-mannered handshakes they always exchanged when they met and parted.

'Kenneth,' she asked quietly, 'are you asking me to marry me?'

'Yes. Yes, I am,' he said and swallowed audibly in his nervousness. 'I know it's at awfully short notice, but if I

151

don't ask now I'll be back in Selangor before I know it and forever kicking myself for never having broached the subject.'

'I'm glad you did. Yes, let's get married and I'll sail away to Malaya with you.' Maeve reached her arms up and put them around Kenneth and held him to her. She felt him do the same and pull her tight. She started giggling. 'To sail off to Malaya with one's lover. It sounds like something out of a romantic novel.' In a more serious tone she went on, 'And it sounds wonderful too!'

She could hear Kenneth's heart beating rapidly under his starched evening shirt. Then his hand was at the nape of her neck and his fingers twined in her hair. For a moment she felt his cheek with its faint scratchiness of stubble against hers, before his lips pressed to hers and they kissed.

Neither of them had any idea how long they spent on the balcony. They kissed and cuddled and talked intermittently between embraces. Eventually, Maeve became aware that the band had stopped playing. Perhaps it was suppertime. It wasn't. When they entered the lounge they saw, to their bewilderment, the band packing their instruments and the last of the revellers collecting their coats and hats at the cloakroom counter. Maeve looked at her watch.

'Good grief! It's after two o'clock. I'd better get a move on. Mother will think some misfortune has happened!'

Kenneth retrieved their things from the cloakroom and they caught one of the few taxis still hanging around outside.

'Oh my goodness, what an evening!' said Maeve, resting her head against Kenneth's shoulder as they trundled through the streets of West London, deserted except for the horse-drawn milk carts beginning their rounds. She clasped his hands in hers.

'I'm awfully glad you asked me to marry you. I think it's going to be a wonderful life living in Malaya.'

They had decided that Maeve should break the news to her parents when her father returned from conducting the Morning Matins service at about eleven o'clock. Afterwards, Kenneth would turn up for Sunday lunch to announce his intentions in a more formal manner.

Their plans were greeted with ambivalence by Mrs and Reverend Stephenson. Maeve's mother was weepy when Kenneth arrived shortly after 12.30, but pleased for Maeve's happiness. Her father, on the other hand, put on a display of petulant outrage, claiming that the speed of the courting and subsequent proposal were indecently hasty. People, he warned, would read all sorts of implications into such a hasty union. The brevity of the thing meant that they couldn't marry in a church – these things took weeks to arrange – and that a clergyman's daughter being married out of church was an utter disgrace to her parents and an insult to the sanctity of marriage – to God no less!

Kenneth attempted to explain that he and Maeve appreciated that the situation was less than perfect. That, of course, they would have preferred a more lengthy courtship and to have been married by Reverend Stephenson in the church Maeve had attended all her life. However, the immutable fact was that he had a ship to catch in fifteen days' time. The wedding had to take place before then. Neither of them were prepared to wait until Kenneth again received home leave; it could be another seven years. Another option, that of Maeve coming out in six months' time after having had some time to consider Kenneth's proposal in a calmer, more contemplative moment than the present hectic situation would allow, was equally unacceptable.

Maeve's mind was made up and to her it seemed pointless to postpone the ceremony – they were going to set up home in Malaya and if the start of their marriage had to be one of haste, well, so be it. Kenneth had his own reasons on this score which he wasn't going to voice aloud. He couldn't begin to count the after-dinner stories he had heard over the years at tiffins and at clubs across

Selangor of engaged young ladies coming out on the P &
O to marry their civil service officer, planter or Public
Works Department official, only to be wooed and won en
route by one of the scores of equally eligible bachelors on
board ship. Many an expatriate's hopes had been dashed
by a change of heart in the Red Sea on the part of his true
love coming to meet him: the eagerly awaited welcome
at Singapore or Penang turning to ashes as the expec-
tant groom saw his wife-to-be disembark on the arm of
another man who usually looked somewhat smug with
his good luck. Kenneth was by no means so sure of his
charms that he felt confident that Maeve could survive
such a voyage unpropositioned. She was an attractive
young woman and the voyage out would provide many
opportunities for fun and romance with men often better
placed than he was in Malaya's colonial social hierarchy.
No, stick with her at all cost.

The Reverend Stephenson, ill-tempered as usual, refused to be swayed by these reasons tendered by Maeve and
Kenneth. Under no circumstances would they receive his
blessing unless they took account of his considerations.
The days passed with no change in the old man's attitude. Things were going to have to be done if Maeve was
going to leave with Kenneth on the P & O *Narkunda* on
6 October, a Monday, from Tilbury Docks.

'Father tried to sabotage my life over that university
grant three years ago, he's not going to repeat it,' Maeve
told her mother after school over a cup of tea. 'He is being
completely unreasonable, as per usual, but this time I'm
not budging from my point of view. He's simply never
accepted that I have my own mind, that I'm as capable
as the next person as to what is best for me. Good grief,
I'm twenty-two years old, not thirteen. I'm going, Mother,
and that's that!'

On the last Wednesday of September she handed in
her resignation to the London Education Authority to
take effect the first Friday in October. Normally teachers
were expected to give a minimum of a month's notice,
but Maeve's deadline with the P & O sailing schedule

was recognized as meeting exceptional circumstances and the usual period was waived. Kenneth made arrangements at the Registry Office in Chiswick for the marriage. It was going to be a finely cut last few days. Maeve had the weekend to pack and the earliest day the wedding could be held was in fact the day they were to sail!

The ceremony was to be at eleven o'clock in the morning and the *Narkunda* left at five o'clock in the afternoon. Kenneth also took care of the cabin arrangements, managing, despite the late notice, to have his shared second-class cabin booking altered to a superior second-class suite, which accommodated a couple. As well as the addition of Maeve's fare, the cabin cost more and he was, he smile ruefully to himself at the thought, leaving England completely penniless. Promissory notes against his salary would have to cover on-board expenses.

Maeve had little time to continue the arguments her father attempted to maintain. A birth certificate had to be acquired, followed immediately by an application for a passport; a marriage application had to be filled out; travel luggage and clothes to be purchased; class files completed at school; bank account closed; library card cancelled. The list seemed endless. By her last Saturday in London things were, however, in order. Kenneth was occupied elsewhere and she decided that the weekend would be devoted to getting along with her mother and father – no matter what it took in terms of nervous energy to ensure a peaceful two days. Perhaps, if her father could calm down at this late stage, they could enjoy the wedding on Monday.

By and large it wasn't too bad, but the Reverend Stephenson would not budge on his issue with the Registry Office marriage and refused to come. The understanding was, of course, if he didn't attend, neither would his wife, leaving Maeve family-less among her friends at her own wedding. Mrs Stephenson however surprised her husband by declaring at breakfast on Monday that she was accompanying Maeve to Chiswick. She surprised her daughter too, for Maeve could not remember a single incident in her entire life where her mother had contradicted her father. Her stand had an effect like a bombshell on her husband. He nearly had an apoplectic fit and, speechless and purple with fury, stormed off to his study. Undaunted by such histrionics, Maeve and her mother later on left in a taxi for the Registry Office in good spirits, the Reverend Stephenson immersed in his misery, completely out of their minds.

The crowd of about twenty at the ceremony were virtually all friends of Maeve's. They made a jolly crowd at the reception after Kenneth and Maeve had been declared husband and wife, which was held in the private bar of a nearby hotel. There was no great formality and speeches were limited to a couple of off-the-cuff anecdotes from Maeve's oldest friends. Alexa had come up from Southampton for the occasion and gave the farewell toast. By mid-afternoon it was time to go. Maeve was in tears as friends gave her a final embrace and wished her well.

'Goodbye old thing.'

'Don't forget to write.'

'Send us some postcards along the way. Good luck.'

'Goodbye.'

'Goodbye.'

Alexa, Ruby and two old friends postponed their farewells. On the spur of the moment they had decided to see the young couple off at the docks. Against some half-hearted protests, Mrs Stephenson was coerced into joining them.

There was one final farewell to make. It was not to be. The Reverend Stephenson had anticipated that Maeve, true to her good nature, would try and make her departure a conciliatory one, and had accordingly left the house for the afternoon to prevent it happening.

'I can't believe it. He's gone out!' exclaimed Maeve. 'What a exasperating man. Well!' she sighed. 'If that's the way he wants it, well so be it. Let us go, Kenneth. I'm finished here.' Kenneth and the cab driver carried Maeve's trunk, hatbox and suitcases out and Maeve slammed the door shut to her home of twenty-two years. 'Goodbye Mayfield Avenue!' she said as the taxi turned left into Northfield Avenue on its way to Uxbridge Road.

Tilbury Dock was a swarming mass of visitors seeing their loved ones off to the colonies of India, Ceylon and Malaya. The *Narkunda* cast her stretching, late-afternoon shadow over the crowd and across the flat-roofed terminal building. It was almost cold standing on the quay for a northerly wind was being channelled between the buildings and the liner. High above, standing at the railing, Maeve could see her mother and four friends clumped together, faces turned upwards now and then to call some, alas inaudible, nearly forgotten advice and good wishes, and to smile encouragingly to her. Then only their hats would show as they talked among themselves for a few moments. With departure time approaching many passengers began to throw coloured paper streamers down to their friends and families, tightly rolled wheels, which unravelled a fluttering thread of paper as they careered dockward to be caught. Kenneth produced a handful of the colourful coils from his pocket.

'Always come prepared. Here we go!' and he threw one towards Alexa and the others. It streamed out but fell short into a group of army officers seeing one of their brothers-in-arms off to his posting.

Maeve waved to Alexa to come to the edge of the wharf to a spot directly below herself and Kenneth. When she reached it, Maeve took five of the coloured wheels and trying their loose ends to her wrist, dropped them one by one on top of Alexa. Her friend laughed up her approval and carried the streamers back to Mrs Stephenson and her companions.

It was sailing time. The huge horn of the *Narkunda* blasted out, frightening dozens of seagulls off their perching places in a confused fluttering and flapping, sending them into short, wheeling flights before they regained their composure and once more settled. A not dissimilar response occurred on the wharf below. Handerchiefs came out in their hundreds and hats were lifted to act as perfunctory flags with which to wave goodbye. The lines of streamers gradually lost their sagging curves as a gap of water began to appear between ship and dock. Maeve watched hers grow taut and stretch out to her mother and friends on the land. On an impulse she untied them from her wrist and held them out for a second. They mustn't snap, these last ties she had with mother, friends and England. Better to let them tumble away unbroken ... She unclasped her hand and the red, green and blue crêpe-paper streamers fluttered down on the gusting wind towards the water, twisting and turning into calligraphic loops as they slowly fell. She waved with both arms at her group among the crowd until the ship began to turn and they were obscured by its great bulk.

Chapter 11

To a New Life, 1927

Maeve slowly surfaced from a sound sleep as the early-morning sun rays projected through the porthole to light up her side of the bed. In a raking stripe they crossed her pillow and slanted up the bulkhead behind towards the ceiling. She blinked, and then rolled over languidly to avoid the dazzle in her eyes. On her bare shoulder she could feel their feeble, early-morning warmth. Through her body she could feel the distant thumping from the propeller blades as they sliced through the sea, their vibrations being transmitted along the propeller shafts and from there to reverberate out to every corner of the vessel.

It was a solid, reliable sensation, just audible – or was it just feelings? – and as regular as a heartbeat. Thump-a-thump-a-thump-a-thump-a . . . She opened her eyes to discover Kenneth's shoulder a few inches way from her nose. He was lying on his back, his face angled slightly towards her, mouth ajar as his bare chest rose and fell gently in the rhythm of his slumber. The bed sheet was scrunched up around their waists for the night had been too warm for the blankets now that the *Narkunda* was in the Mediterranean. Maeve reached out her left hand and laid it on Kenneth's chest. With the flat of her palm she softly rubbed his warm skin, brushing and skimming in circular motion the fine hair that grew on his breast. The hair thinned out into a narrow line under his ribs. She followed its growth with her palm, stopping when she could just perceive the ridges of muscle banding his body. She flexed her fingers slightly to feel his lean torso. Flicking the bed sheet up enough to slide her

159

arm under it, she continued the pleasurable sensation of touching.

Kenneth lay naked. His pyjamas had been flung aside, along with Maeve's nightgown, the evening before in their nightly fit of passion but, unlike Maeve, he had not bothered to retrieve his sleeping clothes when about to fall asleep afterwards. Maeve rubbed her palm over his belly, eyes again closed as all her sleepy attention focused on the tactile sensations Kenneth's soft skin against hers generated. He started, as if to wake up; but didn't. Maeve continued to caress him, sometimes making wider circles to run her fingertips through the dense hair at the base of his body, her forearm resting on the ridge of his hip bone as she did so.

What a lovely way to wake up! she thought to herself. Nothing to think about except ourselves, no work or obligations. This was wonderful. She snuggled up to Kenneth, momentarily removing her hand from his belly to hike her nightgown up to under her breasts so that her skin was directly against his side, before sliding her hand back under the sheet to its original position. Sun on her back, Kenneth against her front, Maeve lay there with every part of her absorbed with happiness. Pondering her wonderful circumstances, she dozed off.

She awoke feeling pressed into the mattress. Kenneth lay on top of her, his chin cupped in his hands with his elbows either side of her shoulders, looking down at her with a smile on his lips.

'Hello,' he said, bobbing his head to kiss her quickly on the mouth. Maeve reached up, put her arms about his neck and pulled him down for a more substantial kiss. Mouth against his, his belly pressed against hers, she felt him immediately harden between her legs and his knees wedge in between hers to push them apart. She spread them in order to accommodate him and, still holding his face to her own, became impassioned at the sensation of Kenneth within her, sliding into her again and again with burgeoning urgency until, at last, with a loud sigh, he spent himself deep inside her.

160

They lay there in each other's arms for ages, unmoving. At last Maeve wriggled from under her husband and said, 'A cup of tea and breakfast in bed would be perfect.' She stretched and pulled her nightgown down. 'Why don't you call cabin service, dear. Tea and toast and a boiled egg, that's what I want.'

'Good idea. I can't be bothered dressing yet either.' Kenneth got out of bed and made for the electric bell button near the door.

Maeve laughed. 'If I were you I'd dress just a little, even if it's only for the steward.' He was stark naked and she reached out and gave him a playful tweak under his ribs. 'I think there must be a minimal standard of dress even when it comes to breakfasting in one's own cabin.'

'My dear,' Kenneth replied mock-seriously, 'I thought I always looked my best this way,' and he stuck his nose in the air, at the same time striking a pose of an elegant man-about-town. This he could maintain for only a moment before joining Maeve in a fit of giggles. He leapt on to her and in a laughing tussle which she didn't seriously resist, pulled her nightgown off over her head and began kissing her neck and breasts.

'Oh go away!' she said between being muffled by Kenneth's attention and giggling. 'I want my breakfast, I want my breakfast!' Kenneth concentrated his attention on her nipples. 'Oh, don't, don't Kenneth! Really, breakfast would be super, I'm starving, Kenneth . . .!' She let out a quiet shriek as he drew one of them into his mouth. 'You aren't really a gentleman.'

Kenneth looked up at her, lips still sealed around the tip of her right breast, hands clasped around them both, pushing them into two prominent mounds and rolled his eyes.

Again Maeve cracked up with laughter. 'Oh you're impossible.' She started to wrestle with him, rolling and squirming and destroying the lay of the bed sheets in the process. Before they knew it, they had rolled across the bed and, with a thump, landed on the carpet.

'Heavy seas today,' observed Kenneth, untwining himself from Maeve. Laughing, they both slipped into dressing gowns and this time Kenneth did call the steward for breakfast.

The *Narkunda* was crossing the Mediterranean en route to the Suez Canal. The first two days out of England had passed with Maeve finding her sea legs. Although never ill to the point of being unable to attend meals, or to being restricted to their cabin, it wasn't until the liner was off Portugal that she could admit to feeling completely her old self. Other passengers were less lucky and the lee handrail had its regulars leaning biliously over it. The passengers stared fixedly at the tossing ocean, chalky-green faces rigid in their misery, and occasionally heaved what little they had had in their stomachs over the side.

After leaving Gibraltar, the passengers began to settle down for the long voyage. Maeve and Kenneth formed quite a little group with the others at their table, and with some nearby, and they kept to more or less each other's company, teaming up together when deck games were proposed, and generally making up a congenial crowd. Being the newly-weds of the group made them the butts of many good-natured jokes and Maeve throughly enjoyed shipboard life. She discovered that ocean voyaging is a serious business. Among the passengers, committees were elected, concerts organized and deck games begun.

In quieter moments she and Kenneth, or a new acquaintance if Kenneth was elsewhere, would lie in deckchairs and watch the promenaders. She found it fun to guess people's characters and professions and eventually discovered that the very same process was going on in virtually every passenger's imagination. Everyone soon had nicknames bestowed on them. A peroxided lady, very much to the fore in everything, and consequently disliked by everyone, was christened 'Canary'; 'Garfish' was an elderly spinster with a strong family likeness to her namesake; 'Checkmate' was an enormous man greatly addicted to wearing check-patterned apparel; there was 'Flippit', 'Plum Duff', and 'Winkle' but Maeve never found out what hers was.

Egypt was reached. The journey through the Suez Canal was largely at night and Maeve came up on deck the next day to see the wild and rugged hills hemming in the Red Sea either side of the ship. She had risen early and the day at that hour was soft and grey and the hills shades of blue and heliotrope. Hardly anyone else was up and so in solitude she watched the coast slip by quietly and contemplatively. It was Sunday and after breakfast Sunday Parade was held. The crew first mustered for inspection, the lascar sailors wonderfully arrayed in silk suits, brilliantly embroidered caps and waistcoats, some looking a little self-conscious with the attention they were receiving from the passengers. Then the stewards marched to their places in fresh uniforms. Lastly, the officers assembled and, conducted by the Captain, the church service was commenced. Maeve, cynical of the sentiments of religion because of the Reverend Stephenson's example, was surprised at her own reaction to the service. She found it moving and for once appropriate. Perhaps, she thought to herself, because the Holy Land is just over these stony hills, that's what makes the difference.

The little harbour of Aden on the tip of the Arabian Peninsula was a coaling station for the *Narkunda* and the ship reached there late one evening. It was a beautiful night. Kenneth and Maeve excused themselves from the group enjoying the Arabian Nights Ball below and came up on deck. Lights twinkled on shore and more bobbed about on the harbour as smaller craft than the *Narkunda* went about their night-time preparations. The sky above was a brilliant canopy of stars. The moon had set earlier. There was such a mosaic of white sparkling pinpricks of light that Maeve could make out the jagged outline of the hills surrounding Aden in their light. Above, Orion strode across the sky on an imaginary path above the hills, his hunting hounds Laelaps and the unnamed Canus minor at his heels. Betelgeuse and Sirius burned with a fierce pureness among their lesser companions. Maeve squeezed her husband's arm affectionately.

'I keep forgetting that this is all old hat to you,' she said.

'No it's not,' Kenneth replied. 'There's no comparison between this voyage with you and the one I made four months ago, or the first back in 1920. With you I see these places, these evenings and night skies in a way I could never have before. You know that rowdy crowd monopolizing the bar this evening? Well, I most likely would have been one of them if I hadn't met you. Certainly I was on the other voyages. You drink and drink and make what fun out of it as you can. There's nothing else to do. You've seen how many unattached women there are on board, one for every twenty men more or less.

'Well, it gets you down after a while. Days and days of watching them, you know, the dances and that sort of thing, but at best being only able to say hello and make a bit of small talk before someone whisks her away. Eventually the lads get together and booze it up. Last trip I don't even remember Aden. Must have been half-cut as usual. This time it's so different. I never noticed half what we were sailing past before. And it's all because you're here this time.' He bent and kissed her hair, and, putting an arm around her shoulders, gazed out into the night.

The gaiety of the trip accelerated as the *Narkunda* pointed her bow to the east and steamed towards Bombay. The days were occupied with tournaments in the different deck games; Maeve achieved a brief fame by winning 'chalking the pig's eye', and concerts, dances and card games passed the evenings. The romance of the sea came into its own. The sunrises and sunsets colouring banks of clouds on the horizon, pink, then gold, to glowing red and orange and crimson, then to purple or wonderful shades of brown while the sea became a golden lake with scarcely a ripple. A wonderful peace descended on Maeve as league after league of the Arabian Sea passed placidly under the *Narkunda*'s huge bulk.

One morning at 6.00 a.m. the liner anchored in Bombay

Harbour. With excited anticipation at her first taste of the Orient, Maeve rose early, and with a certain amount of horse-play also managed to coax Kenneth up, in order to get ashore on the first steam launches. To her disappointment, the excursion was cancelled. The Harbour Medical Officers who had come on board with the Customs Department Officials announced that an outbreak of cholera was affecting parts of the city. Nothing serious, they assured the disembarking passengers with homes and postings in India, but basic precautions must be instigated and that meant keeping passengers bound for Ceylon and Malaya on board away from any opportunity of infection. So Bombay remained a tantalizing five hundred yards out of reach for Maeve and Kenneth for the day and evening the *Narkunda* stayed at anchor.

Colombo in Ceylon was different. The liner berthed in the evening and it stayed for two days and nights. Before it departed, Maeve, unable to sleep with the excitement of the things she had seen, wrote to Alexa in the early hours of the morning.

Colombo, 22 October 1927

Dear Alexa,

Colombo is indescribable! It far exceeds my wildest dreams. My first glimpse of Ceylon was most fascinating: a lovely clear starlit night, a warm scented breeze blowing straight from the shore and the tepid waters of the harbour. Then the crowds of natives, swarms of them, the men in skirts, like women with small lithe figures and many with long hair coiled round their heads, often fastened with tortoiseshell combs. In fact it was often difficult to distinguish men from women.

We stepped from the wharf and found ourselves in a wide street with the Grand Oriental Hotel on our right. It seemed some wonderful dream, not at all real, I had simply stepped into some elaborate Eastern stage setting. The bazaars were all brilliantly lighted and we strolled through them, my brain refusing to take in all the wonderful details. Here were laces and silks, here ivories and there jewellery, and everywhere soft-eyed appealing natives beseeching us to buy at the most exorbitant prices. These prices came down with a crash when the salesman realized you were departing. Oh, the joy of bargaining, and I think the natives enjoy it just as much as the travellers. They ask you ten shillings, then by degree it is reduced to eight, to five. Then, in a rash moment you say 'Why, I wouldn't give you more than sixpence for it.' Before you realize what has happened the object is thrust into your hand and sixpence is being demanded. When you get outside you find you should have paid just half, but the fun was worth it. You cannot help thinking that the natives must get everything for nothing.

We had a wonderful ride to the Galle Face Hotel. I was living in some far off romance: the jinrickshaw ran so smoothly and comfortably, in front gleamed the high lights on the lithe brown back of the runner, the soft pad-pad of his feet as the road slipped beneath us, the mystical tinkle of his bell giving warning of our approach. I was glad we had arrived at night. The darkness left so much to the imagination and veiled so much that I could only guess at. Over all was the spell of the East.

Next morning Kenneth and I were ashore again at day-break and began our day with a motor car ride to Mount Lavinia. It is an impossibility to describe the drive adequately. Although it was so early the streets were full of natives, evidently of many different tribes for they varied considerably in colour and in head dress. Many had chalk on their foreheads, betokening a visit to the Temples. They all have such soft brown eyes and the sunniest of smiles with gleaming white teeth. The little children are particularly fascinating and it was hard to resist them as they ran beside us and begged. One sturdy youngster ran with his hand on the car singing breathlessly 'I don't care what becomes of me, Yip-i-yaddy-i-ay.' We laughed and threw him a coin and off he went spinning to the side of the road.

We sat in the shade of the hotel and had our fortunes told by a native and then watched a conjuror perform for us. He did a number of wonderful tricks with little balls and a cap, eggs and chickens etc., keeping up a ceaseless flow of conversation which sounded like a repetition of 'Golly, golly golly'. He also addressed remarks to the snakes, which reared up and hissed. The Mango trick was the most astounding. He raked with his fingers a little mound of the shingle from the path and in it planted a mango, rather like a small potato. This he watered and after many incantations, he lifted the flimsy cloth with which he had covered it and there were two fresh green leaves sprouting from the ground. He repeated the performance and this time we could see the cloth rise and underneath were found a fine head of about twenty long fresh green leaves. He scattered the earth and we could see the leaves were growing from the mango seed which had made little roots. He presented us each with a leaf. The thing was incredible.

Tomorrow we are going for another motor ride and we sail in the afternoon. At last I'm tired so I'll stop here. Gosh, Alexa, who would have thought I'd be seeing Ceylon this time six months ago. Everything is marvellous!

Give my regards to Nigel.

Your loving friend

Maeve

She folded the pages into a thick package, squeezed it into an envelope embossed and coloured with the P & O flag and sealed it. Behind her, Kenneth lay asleep. Maeve slipped into her nightgown and joined him.

The *Narkunda* sailed from Colombo that afternoon. The days on the Bay of Bengal were uneventful but for a mysterious sickness which went right through the ship, making a number of the complement queasy and off colour for several days. However, neither Maeve nor Kenneth were affected. The last day at sea was unusual for the trip. The sun was unable to penetrate a virtually undefinable cloud cover and the sea looked thick and opaque, like oil. It was grey-blue with not a single ripple and it was impossible to make out where the sea ended and the sky began, giving Maeve the impression of moving through space rather than across the ocean. The day was busy spent packing and collecting fellow passengers' addresses and so forth. Time simply flew and before Maeve had appreciated what hour it was, Penang came into view, misty and ephemeral-looking in the sultry haze of the late afternoon.

'Whew, you weren't exaggerating about the heat when you talked about Malaya back in Ealing,' said Maeve, fanning herself with the hat she had bought in Colombo. 'My goodness, it's hot.'

They were sitting in the Palm Court of the Eastern and Oriental Hotel. It was nine in the evening and they were enjoying cocktails with a group of ex-*Narkunda* passengers who were also stopping at the hotel before setting out to their homes across Malaya.

'Old thing, this is nothing, nothing like it can get. Just you wait and see,' said a bluff, tubby police major who had made himself the resident Malaya expert while on the *Narkunda*. By the end of the journey, he was universally regarded as insufferable, but glowering looks, deep sighs of boredom when he spoke, or even outright sarcasm, had not dented his self-importance a bit. He patted her on the arm fondly. 'No my dear Maeve, come the monsoon after Christmas and you'll look back at evenings like this as cool and pleasant, you wait.'

Kenneth resented the attention the major periodically bestowed on Maeve as the pats and squeezes looked not especially paternal to him, but to the contrary, decidedly lecherous. Randy old goat, he thought to himself.

They were to stay in Penang only for a couple of days before they would cross over to Province Wellesley and catch the train to Kuala Lumpur. There Kenneth intended to buy a secondhand motor car and they would drive to Kuala Tanah Estate. While Kenneth was required at the Office in Beach Road, Maeve enjoyed browsing the shops and taking in some of the tourist spots. The place entranced her with all its exotic smells, colours and sounds, and the heat, although enervating, added to its wonderful strangeness. When it became too hot, she would retire to their room at the Eastern and Oriental for a couple of hours, stretching out on the bed in her underwear to cool under the turning ceiling fan. It spun slightly off centre on its long stem from the ceiling rosette and gave out a soft chunka-chunka-chunka sound at each revolution. The rhythm reminded her in her half wakefulness, of the *Narkunda*. What a wonderful five weeks it has been, she thought to herself, absolutely wonderful.

Chapter 12

Selangor, 1928

Living at Kuala Tanah Estate was bitter-sweet for Maeve.
She discovered that there were to be two Malayas to which
to adjust: rubber-estate Malaya with its regimented rows
of trees stretching for miles and miles about her in every
direction with its ordered daily routine; and the Malaya
she had read and listened avidly about when Kenneth had
fired her imagination about the country back in London.
This was the Malaya of jungle, paddy, peepul-shaded
kampongs, cool mountains and sultry, serpentine rivers.
She had imagined the latter would be virtually at the end
of her garden. It wasn't. It was in fact more than a month
after arriving in Selangor before she actually walked in
this Malaya of her daydreams.

The drive from Kuala Lumpur to southern Selangor in
the Model T Ford Kenneth had purchased from a tin
mining engineer about to retire to Scotland had taken
her through a landscape either red raw and ravaged
by tin extraction, or uniform with rubber plantations.
True, when the road skirted near rivers, kampongs were
usually to be seen half hidden on the banks, and paddy
fields popped up now and then. But the predominant
impression was of monotony. Where was the jungle with
its wild array of palms, animals, and rushing, bubbling
streams? she had asked Kenneth as they had a cup of tea
at a roadside shop halfway through the journey. He had
pointed to the east.

'Up there. You can't see them but only twenty miles
away are the hills. It's all jungle, thousands of square miles
of it with hardly more than a couple of roads crossing it.'
Later, he had stopped the Ford on the summit of a hill

the road cut across to let Maeve take in the view. They climbed the red-clay embankment to the right of the parked car in order to see over the roadside scrub. There, right across her line of vision, and separated from her vantage point by square miles of rubber plantation, were the hills. Their distance from her gave them a palpable blue shimmer; something like a heat haze was making them appear to vibrate at a hardly perceptible but rapid rate. It was extraordinary: the very air seemed blue out there. The contrast between the sombre green of the fore and middle ground and the distant jungle-clad hills was startling in its impact. Maeve noticed in the far south of the vista a brighter green line of vegetation threading through the rubber forest.

'What's that?' she asked, pointing it out to Kenneth.

'It's the Kemudi. Those hills are in the state of Negri Sembilan and the Kemudi starts its course up in there. It's a wonderful outing to go to the upper part of the river.' He laughed. 'Don't worry, old thing, you'll see more than enough jungle before too long. We'll go into the hills often, you'll see.'

They slid and scrambled down to the Ford and motored on. The road twisted and began to descend. After a couple of s-bends another view appeared and again Kenneth pulled the motor car over to the verge. Before them was a vast expanse of lowland, most of its topographical features distorted or warped by the heat haze. Maeve could just make out the coastline by a tonal change in the pervading brown-green colours that saturated the scene – the line where the grey-green met a grey-brown marked the Straits of Malacca. Two broad rivers wound their way towards the line. Kenneth pointed to the one to their left.

'The Kemudi again. You're actually looking at the Estate, though there's nothing to show you which bit of green is ours out of everybody else's. Wait a minute.' He stopped speaking and narrowed his eyes, shading them with his hands in order to see the better. 'Yes . . . yes, there it is. Look, near where the river twists out of sight, right out where it's really hazy. If you strain your eyes you'll see a hill rising above everything else. Can you see it?'

With narrowed eyes to filter out some of the glare, Maeve looked in the direction he indicated.

'Yes I can.'

'Well, Kuala Tanah Estate is near there. It's on the other side of the river and more towards us. You're looking right at it.'

'What is the hill?'

'That's Bukit Klang. My friend Ali, whom I told you about, has his Istana very near it. Bukit Klang is the biggest landmark in southern coastal Selangor. As you can see, there's nothing that sticks up as much.'

Maeve looked at the distant hill. From all of twenty miles away it looked like an irregular-shaped pebble on a discoloured piece of green felt, a black lump against a flat backdrop.

'Let's get going, my dear. A few more hours and you'll be at your new home.'

Being an estate manager's wife took some getting used to after a life as a school teacher in Ealing. It was the finding of things to do that was going to make or break her happiness, Maeve realized quickly. Teaching a crowd of children had conditioned her to having not much free time to herself and she had learned to use the time well. Here in Selangor it was the opposite. She had all the free time in the world and the problem was how to fill it in a satisfying way. Even domestic chores were in short supply. Pravan and his wife did all the cooking and washing up (Maeve found she wasn't even expected to make herself a cup of tea, but rather ring for one), three Chinese house servants cleaned, swept, made beds and spirited the dirty laundry away with very few directives from Maeve being required, and Mani, a taciturn middle-aged Tamil, did the garden and lawns. With such a collection of help even the pleasurable task of shopping was denied her. What was the point of visiting the weekly market at Bangi, or the smaller one at Salak, to look at the wonderfully foreign fruits, vegetables, spices and fish, if she couldn't experiment with them

172

back at the house. The cook, Pravan, who had started at Kuala Tanah as a boy cook before 1920 had never before had to accommodate a mistress of the estate. He quite naturally assumed her to be like the late Tuan Reynolds, or the tuan kechils over at the assistant managers' mess, in that she would expect meals to be planned and cooked by himself and his wife. He shopped, he devised the week's menus, and he ran the kitchen, a small lean-to against his tiny shed-like home out behind Maeve's and Kenneth's bungalow.

It was much the same with the gardener. Although McGregor Reynolds had provided the overall vision for the lovely gardens and lawn that graced the bungalow, it was Mani who had selected the appropriate flowers and shrubs for the various beds. The choice had at times been removed by his master if Reynolds had decided they really weren't suitable, but these things aside, the garden was his domain. Maeve decided that this old-established order would have to change if she wasn't to die of boredom. She was patient however, and understood that it would take time for her to pace herself to the life of a mem and learn the social and domestic tempo of the expatriate way of life.

It wasn't just the servants that she found strange. It was also the isolation of Kuala Tanah she was going to have to come to terms with. There were at least a dozen other British women in the neighbourhood of the estate but even the closest of them was a ten-minute drive away and most were further. Maeve didn't drive as did few of the other women so social intercourse was limited, by and large, to occasions when their husbands could drive them. This meant, essentially, club evenings at Bangi and tiffin parties and picnics on Sunday, and perhaps a couple of times a month to an informal get-together at one friend or another's bungalow on a Saturday evening.

All in all, Maeve's weekly routine comprised long days alone at the bungalow unable to involve herself in housework while Kenneth was out and about on the estate. Added to that were breaks between when, as a couple, she and Kenneth would be among other couples who, of course, led the same sort of existence. Having children was the route most of the women took to add meaning to their lives and Maeve thought she too would do the same. However, until that eventuated there were the weeks and months to marshall into something more satisfactory than the life Selangor offered upon her arrival.

She talked about it with Kenneth. He hadn't been aware there was a problem and listened sympathetically.

'Changing Pravan's and Mani's ways will take some doing I'm afraid,' he said as he and Maeve sat around having a cocktail one evening before dinner. He was, through habit, having a stengah while Maeve sipped on a gin pahit. Like Kenneth seven years earlier, she had quickly cottoned on to the rigid social expectations from the 'old hands' that a mem drank gin pahits – if she partook of alcohol, that is – while her husband stuck to whisky.

'I appreciate that, but I'm sure we can convince them that doing less work so that I can do my bit is no slight on their abilities. I don't want to do all the cooking, far from it. But wouldn't it be nice to sit down to a dinner prepared by me two or three times a week? By doing that I'd have an excuse to get out more often. Wander through the market and bazaar over at Salak and Bangi to shop for groceries, things like that. I want to get out and about more often to get to know the countryside.'

'Hang on a minute,' said Kenneth. 'You're going to need a driver and I can't really justify a syce to the company.'

'Not at all,' responded Maeve. 'You're going to teach me to drive. After all Mrs Winston over at Sagil Estate drives her husband's car now and then. So does Margaret Ambury at Panchar. You don't use the Ford for days on end so you wouldn't miss it. Also I could do things like pick up the mail at Tangga Gajah instead of you having to take time off to fit the trip in.'

Kenneth laughed. 'You're way ahead of me with all these plans. I don't know if I go along with women driving motor cars, Mrs Winston and Mrs Ambury not withstanding. But I can see your point. With all the work I'm up to my neck in I hadn't thought what it must be like for you with servants to do everything for you and no one with whom you can share the free time. You're right. I'll give you a first driving lesson tomorrow.' He sipped on his stengah. 'Anything else?'

'Yes, the garden. After the little garden with next to nothing in it back at Mayfield Avenue, you can't imagine how frustrating it is to have this glorious place and not be allowed to touch it. I'm dying to learn about these wonderful shrubs and flowers, maybe extend some of the beds, bring some new ideas into the place perhaps, but I really don't like to cross old Mani. The other day I took a rug out and put it under that big shady tree over on the left, you know, the one with the green fruit all over it . . .'

'Mango,' prompted Kenneth.

'Well, the flower bed near it had had its day and most of the blooms were disintegrating. I decided to tidy it, by taking the dead flowers off the plants. I was working away happily when Mani turned up. Oh, he looked so affronted. It was almost funny, seeing his expression, but I realized he was upset. He told me he had planned to do that bed the next day so he obviously saw my actions as implying that he was neglecting his gardening duties. It's the opposite. He had done such a lovely job of it all that I want to be involved too. I was thinking, perhaps he could prepare a couple more plots but leave them to me to plant how I like. They could go behind the hibiscus hedge so they wouldn't impose on any existing landscaping Mani might have done. What do you think?' She looked at him with a twinkle in her eye. 'Perhaps we could cut down a rubber tree or two to make more room.'

'Very diplomatic I should say,' replied Kenneth, choosing to ignore the suggestion about his trees. 'I'll put it to him. He's a crusty old devil but open to suggestions if put to him in the right way. He was Reynolds' gardener from the outset so he's been developing those beds and planting and pruning for over twenty-five years. Working for a mem is probably something of a shock to his system. He'll probably be secretly flattered by your interest in his handiwork but he won't show it. He's been the same unsmiling Mani from the day I first met him.'

Kenneth was preoccupied with work over the next few days but eventually he found time to begin Maeve's driving lessons. At first they jolted about the estate tracks but when it seemed she had the hang of it, Kenneth proposed that she drive them to the Bangi Club on the following Saturday for the usual tennis games and drinks. She was a good driver, cautious in the little towns and never pushing the motor car more than a comfortable 20–25 mph on the open stretches of road.

Being independent of Kenneth in getting off the estate made such a difference. It enabled her to make friends with other planters' wives whom she had met at the Club but, until she could motor over and see them at their estates, never got to know terribly well. The Club for all its fun tended to condition people's responses to each other in a very set way. One always had to be jolly, be able to chat superficially for hours, be ready for a game of tennis or cards, and rebuff a drunken boor's advances good-naturedly because his wife was probably nearby and watching. Maeve didn't always feel in that sort of a mood and, at times, it was an effort to maintain a gay appearance. This reservation aside, Maeve enjoyed visiting Bangi Club and others further afield. At the end of four months she had been introduced to dozens of couples and was beginning to feel at home. There were some very nice people who went out of their way to make her feel comfortable, realising the huge changes she must be experiencing in uprooting from her life in England and moving to Selangor. The Club introductions led to invitations to parties, picnics, and curry tiffins at estates all about Kuala Tanah and it was on some of these excursions that Maeve visited the jungle she had so anticipated back in Ealing.

The day had been planned one evening at the Club. Four

couples – the Winstons, the Skinners, the Costers, their various children, and Maeve and Kenneth gathered at the Skinners' estate near Bangi at 5.00 one Sunday morning in March and drove in convoy across the rubber-planted plains and into the hills. They followed a red laterite track which led to a proposed hydro scheme which was yet to be built. Surveyors had done their work but the dam was still only a set of drawings on some Public Works Department engineer's desk in Seremban. The river, therefore, although accessible, was untouched. They arrived sometime about mid-morning. Stanley Winston heaved a large wicker hamper out of the back of his Singer Tourer and lugged it over to the river bank where his wife Margaret was spreading out rugs.

'Breakfast one and all!' he called to the others as they too rummaged in their motor cars for contributions to the repast. Kenneth carried a crate of Tiger beer down to the river's edge and immersed it in the rapid current, making sure it was wedged in by a couple of river boulders to prevent it disappearing downstream. He pulled four bottles out and strode over to the party. Spread out over the rug were cold meats, cheeses, salad vegetables, hard-boiled eggs, curried titbits, and a heap of fruit. Maeve was pouring cups of tea from a large brightly decorated Chinese thermos for those who wanted them. The men took the beer. Someone had produced a pile of collapsible chairs and stools and the adults sat around eating while the children, food in hand, went off to explore the river bank.

It was a spectacular setting after the visual diet of rubber trees down on the coastal lowlands. The Kemudi, crystal-clear here, swirled past. Parts of its rushing surface were glassy smooth in the morning sun but where boulders jutted up from its bed the surface bulged and, if the obstacle was substantial enough, broke into a white wave of splashes and leaps. A dozen yards downstream from the picnic party the river's flow was channelled to the far side of the river by a line of large, water-worn granite boulders which lay immovable in the current.

Their sitings created, beyond them, a quiet pool, limpid amid the rushing waters around it. Lotus lilies spread their circular plates of leaves across its stillest corner and the bank was lined with translucent bamboo stems which arched a tracery of green foliage over the water. Upstream the river splashed and cascaded over other natural dams.

As Maeve took the scene in, two iridescent kingfishers flashed across the river and disappeared into the jungle. The air sang with cicadas, invisible but everywhere present in their thousands. Somewhere, not far away, two Argus pheasants were to be heard calling. On either side of the river away from the clearing two-hundred-foot-high trees crowded down the slopes of the hills, the roots of the closest often bare slippery sinews disappearing into the river, their soil and rock matrix eroded away in the aftermath of seasons of monsoons.

Creepers thicker than a man's arm looped and circled through the spaces between trees, some of them forming plaits almost as they strained for support, any support, to help them spread. Ferns and nameless epiphytes clung to every roothold available to them on the boles and branches. And everywhere, the colour green; greens of every tone and shade, the range further complicated by the dappled light that filtered down from the canopy of the jungle high above. Maeve was enchanted.

After a somnolent recovery from the drive up everyone decided that a swim was the order of the day. The boulders forming the pool were taller than a person and one in particular served as an excellent diving platform. As the children paddled and swam on the pebbly little beach, the more adventurous hurled themselves from the boulder with shouts and cries to land with a thunderous splash in the pool. Only Stanley Winston and Willie Skinner could dive with any sort of grace from such a height and consequently were good-naturedly teased by all the others who flopped and crashed in their attempts to emulate the pair.

'This is paradise,' said Maeve after half an hour of fun. She pulled herself into the shallows and lay there with just her head and shoulders out of the pool. Nancy Winston and Antonia Coster lay next to her, Antonia's eighteen-month-old son sitting on his mother's lap kicking at the water and occasionally trying to grasp dead leaves as they floated by.

'Yes, this is one of the good bits about living in Malaya,' replied Antonia. 'I'm sure we women would go completely mad if we were forever stuck on the estate. On those horribly hot sticky days I dream about places like this. Pretend I'm in the jungle and not surrounded by those tedious rubber trees. How are you finding life as a planter's wife these days anyway? Last time we chatted you were looking a bit down.'

'I won't deny it's taken a bit of getting used to,' said Maeve. 'But I've got things to do now and that makes a huge difference. It's the rubber trees that sometimes depress me. They're so monotonous in colour and so evenly spaced. Hardly seems like nature at times.'

'Every wife would say the same,' said Nancy Winston. 'I'm certain it's one thing to work among them and quite another to have to sit and look at the jolly things like we do. I must say you've done well to prise the car out of Kenneth every now and then and learn to drive. It makes a big difference when you have the means to get away from the estate. Even if I don't leave for days at a time, the fact that I can use Stanley's car has removed much of that trapped feeling.' There was a soft splash out in front of them and her husband surfaced from another dive from the boulder. 'He didn't much care for my driving ideas at first but I won him round eventually.'

'Wore him down, more like it,' laughed Antonia who knew the Winstons well. 'Poor dear, he looked positively harassed when you were on to him about driving.'

'That wasn't about the driving, Antonia,' said Nancy. 'You're thinking of the time he was infatuated with that Irish-American floozy on the Dunlop estate near Port Dickson. Silly boy.' She looked over to the rock where Stanley was sunning himself. 'He was so upset when he realized she had been flirting with every other thing in

179

trousers in the neighbourhood as well as himself. That's when he had the long face. My arguments as to my taking up driving might have been forcefully put, but they were reasonable. More than I can say of that woman. What was her name, something like "Beast" as I remember.'

'Beatie,' said Antonia. 'Carol Beatie. She was a bit of a vamp wasn't she. So affected as I recall, saw herself as a cut above the rest of us.' The two women chuckled at the memory of the woman. Antonia went on. 'Her husband was pretty ghastly too.'

'Oh, wasn't he!' enjoined Nancy. 'A tall skinny chap with a deathly smile. Not an ounce of warmth in it, more like a baring of teeth than an indication of friendliness. Come to think of it I haven't seen them for more than a year. Have they left Malaya?'

'I don't think so. I heard a rumour that she'd run off with a Dutchman, a chap in petroleum over in Sumatra, but Mr Beatie hasn't been around either so I don't really know if the story is true.'

Maeve's attention wandered away from the local gossip, fascinating as it was, and again settled on the scene before her. The men had abandoned their diving and jumping and had gone upstream some fifty yards where they were busy constructing something out of bamboo. One of them had produced a bush knife and was slashing lengths of pliable vine into lengths in order to tie the sections of bamboo together. Nearer to her, the older children were throwing stones at a lump of wood balanced on one of the boulders out in the stream, competing with each other as to which of them could knock it off first. She smiled at their shouts of delight as near misses whistled across the river, some to reach the ferny bank on the other side with a faint crash. Others ricocheted off the boulder itself to spin into the river. As yet no one had struck the target.

'Hey kids! Stop throwing stones for a minute will you,' Maeve looked along the bank to see Willie Skinner jogging towards the children waving to get their attention. She looked to where they were all suddenly staring.

Floating past were Kenneth and Nigel, Antonia Coster's husband, balanced precariously on a bamboo raft. Rather ineffectually they tried to guide the craft with bamboo punting poles as the current sped them forward. With mock cries of terror they drifted into swift, shallow rapids on the far side of the river and zoomed past the pool flailing with their poles, half to keep their balance and half to prevent them running into boulders. Their cries diminished as the river swept them round the next bend and out of sight.

'Oh dear, where will they finish up?' said Maeve, getting to her feet and peering after them.

'Don't worry,' said Nancy. 'There's another calm part of the river a couple of hundred yards downstream. They'll pull the raft out there and probably bring it back along the road. Look! There's Willie and Stanley!' A second raft wobbled its course past them with the two men standing on it, feet almost submerged so flimsy was the raft, legs spread far apart to maintain their balance as best as they could as they barrelled down the river.

'Byeee!' they called as they passed the pool and, like the first raft, vanished from view.

It was the start of a great game. Even Maeve was cajolled into having a go with Kenneth at the helm, and the oldest children were taken by their fathers. The afternoon time flew by as if on wings. Maeve was lying in the umbrageous shelter of a small tree with leaves the size of tennis racquets, half asleep, when Kenneth flopped down next to her.

'Time to go, old thing.'

'It can't be!'

'I'm afraid it is. It's going on 4.00 p.m. Come on, let's get our things together.' He stood up and extended an arm to help pull Maeve to her feet.

Within ten minutes everybody was ready to leave. Maeve stood chatting to Nancy Winston as the men topped up the radiators of their vehicles.

'What a glorious day. The thought of returning to the sticky heat of Kuala Tanah after being up here is awful to contemplate. I didn't think I could ever be this cool again.'

'We'll do it again, and soon, seeing as it all went so splendidly,' replied Nancy. 'We know of a couple of other places equally as nice.' She called out to everyone, 'Stanley and I expect you to stop in for a nightcap before heading home, so see you all at our place.' Kenneth did the rounds of the cars, swinging their crank handles one by one as their drivers adjusted their throttle levers, and as they trundled off down the track, started the Ford and followed.

By mid-1928 Maeve could genuinely say she felt at home in Selangor. Inevitably, though, as the months went by, so her relationship with Kenneth began to change. The first bloom of marriage had, of course, to fade as the realities of the new couple's day-to-day life impinged on the romantic notions of those heady first months of being wed. Maeve felt, however, that Kenneth's interest was waning a little too quickly. They made love less often and, frequently these days, Kenneth complained that he was too tired and bothered by work to do much in the evenings. Maeve could appreciate that Kenneth's responsibilities towards the estate did wear him down on occasion but she was vaguely unhappy with his way of dealing with it.

Earlier, they had spent most evenings of the week enjoying each other's companionship, reading sometimes, or often just stretching out in cane chairs on the verandah looking at the night sky while Kenneth told her stories about the people she had met. Once in a while he would take off to see his friend Ali for a game of billiards, leaving Maeve on her own for the evening. This Maeve found perfectly acceptable; after all, this had been Kenneth's home for seven years before she had arrived, and his bachelor friends would continue to make demands on his time. Every wife, she knew, had to share their husband's free time with friends that antedated their marriage.

Maeve however was taken aback one evening in June when Kenneth, after moodily hanging around the verandah for a while, announced that he had been invited for a quick drink at the Salak Club with the assistant managers and would she mind particularly if he went. He hadn't expressed a wish for their company before and she felt vaguely hurt that, after a day's work, he should prefer their companionship to hers. It happened again a week later; then again. His socialising at Salak developed into a routine of one or two nights a week and, for the first time, Maeve felt a twinge that things weren't quite right between them. She decided to nip the little self-doubts in the bud and, one evening when they were having a cocktail on the verandah (Pravan was cooking dinner), she brought up the subject.

'Kenneth.'

'Hmmm, what?' he was gazing vacantly into the distance, mind obviously miles away.

'I've been feeling lately that something has come between us. You don't talk any more. At least not like you used to. Also I'm not sure why you go out to the club so often these days. You used to like the evenings at home. Has something happened?'

He looked at her and smiled. 'Of course not! I hadn't realized that you were feeling left out by my nights spent with the lads. You've always looked content enough with a book on your lap and I had thought it wouldn't have mattered much either way if I popped out for a drink in the evening. I'm not that much for books really, so it seemed the thing to do.' He paused for a moment. 'You can't change the habits of a lifetime in half a year, old thing. The club was almost home, for lack of anything better, for all my time here and I suppose I'd come to miss it more than I had realized. But, anyway, it's only an evening a week, and I don't see that as a big change in the way we rub along.'

'It's often more than that. For the past month it's usually been twice a week. And you've also been over to your friend Ali's a couple of times in that time. I look forward to seeing you each day after work and it's a let-down to have you just for an hour or two before you dash off again. It's not just the club that's bothering me.' She blushed a little. 'You don't seem to care for me as much as you used to either, if you get my meaning.'

'Yes, well,' replied Kenneth diffidently. 'I don't know what to say there, my dear. There's no one else, if that's what you're suggesting. I just don't think about doing it as much as we did in the first months. Honeymoon and all that I suppose. I wouldn't have felt I was neglecting you. It's the heat and all that, I just don't feel the urge the way I did.' He tried to sound light-hearted. 'I thought you would be relieved,' and stretched out a hand to squeeze Maeve's.

'I'm not,' she said. 'Seriously though, Kenneth, something has changed and I want to come to terms with it before it becomes something big. Is it my altering the household routine that's upset things? I know most of the mems do just sit back and let the servants do everything but to do that would bore me witless. I'm afraid some of the planter's wives that I've met are so boring and uninteresting that I get depressed at the mere sight of them. Evenings with them, like that bridge tournament two weeks ago at Bangi, are just devastating to the soul. Four hours of gossip about servant insolence, about who is flirting with whose husband, and about which is the best school to send the children to when it's time to dispatch them Home – it's awful, particularly when I've heard it all before many times.

'Really, for me, I'd be feeling I was missing out on so much if I didn't have my trips to market and to town. It's that sort of thing that makes it so exciting living out here.'

'Look, it's none of that,' interrupted Kenneth. 'I'm all for you getting out and about. As a matter of fact though, I have had a problem on my mind for a couple of months, but it's about business so I wasn't going to talk about it. If you want to hear about it however I'll tell you. I think it's going to affect all of us anyway.'

'Of course I'd like to hear about it,' said Maeve. 'Tell me.'

'Well, it seems that the price has dropped out of rubber. More than seems, it damn well has! At the beginning of the year it was worth 85 cents a pound. Been like that for the last five years. But suddenly the value of the stuff has been on a very slippery downhill slope and doesn't appear to have reached the bottom yet. It's bad, very bad. Everyone is worried. The talk at the club is nothing but rubber prices, rubber prices, and more rubber prices. The last shipment only got 60 cents a pound and I heard that Gilbert Graves' last lot, which only went out a month ago, was almost half as little again.

'I'm not sure what to do about it. If the prices continue to fall I'm going to lay staff off simply because there's going to be no cash to pay their wages. The consequences are too dire to contemplate yet so we're all just hoping things will pick up. There has been a slump in prices before, just when I started here in fact, and a few planters went broke. It wasn't a permanent state of affairs however and things improved by the end of 1921. Perhaps this will be the same. That's my worry, old thing. How to manage the estate when everything's changing so quickly; and for the worse it seems.'

Maeve could understand his preoccupation and was glad he had finally told her about it. When times were good the estate ticked along with its own productive momentum but she could see that, with the low returns on the rubber, the 150-odd coolies and their families would be a great responsibility which could weigh heavily on Kenneth's mind. No wonder he had been taking off to the Salak Club so regularly of late. There he could discuss the situation with planter colleagues similarly worried.

The situation didn't get better. By the end of the year the prices had fallen to 19 cents a pound, so low that it was no longer worth producing the stuff. With the stress and anxiety the slump generated, domestic harmony at Kuala Tanah further deteriorated.

The first really bad news came in October when a letter arrived from Penang directing Kenneth to lay off 80 per cent of his coolies. The receipts from the last couple of shipments of latex were such that Dalgeish McElroy quite simply couldn't continue to pay them. Even if the company could have, what was the point? Their labours in the plantation only produced more near-worthless latex.

The evening before he had to announce the redundancies Kenneth was in a foul temper. Maeve tried to do her best to sympathize for it was a thankless task he had to perform at the next muster. From sundown on Kenneth drank whisky after whisky, growing increasingly morose as the level in the bottle dropped. When Maeve tried to cheer him up, he snapped at her and became abusive and maudlin. That night, for the first time since their wedding a year before, they slept in separate beds. Maeve didn't see him until breakfast the next morning when he stamped in looking sick and miserable.

'Christ! What a day.' He sat down and rested his head on his hands. 'It's a madhouse over in the coolie lines. It was an uproar as soon as I told them, naturally enough, I suppose. What a din! Everyone yelling and shouting, and asking questions, they were impossible to quell until daylight. What the hell is going to become of it all, I don't know. The place is home to most of them so I said they could stay on and scratch a living any way they can. I haven't the heart to boot them off the estate and I'm not sure I could without forcibly dragging them away.'

'Are they all to go?'

'No, there's a skeleton staff to remain. Fifteen men to maintain the estate for when the good times come again.' He snorted sarcastically. 'If they do return, that is. Hell of a job to choose them. In the end I took the fifteen most senior who had families. At the moment everyone is in a state of shock but when the reality of the situation dawns on them I think it's going to be tough on the ones who still have jobs. Everyone who missed out will think it's unfair that another didn't.' He sighed. 'But what was I to do? The instructions are clear: wind down the estate production but maintain minimum standards of caring for the place.'

Maeve sat down next to him and placed a comforting hand on his arm. 'You did what you had to do. After all it's not just our coolies who are losing their jobs, it's workers everywhere. I'm sure there must be some understanding among them that you are not personally to blame.'

'Yes, yes, I suppose you're right,' Kenneth said sourly. 'I'm just not cut out for this sort of thing. I hadn't realized the rubber business could come to this.'

'Look,' said Maeve, sounding determinedly positive, 'Dalgeish's wouldn't have given you the position if they thought you weren't going to be up to it. You've done a good job up to now. Things have changed but there's no reason why you can't too. Up until now they have expected you to run the estate productively, now they want you to run it unproductively. I know you can do it!'

'Managing the estate is one thing. The cuts aren't just out on the plantation you know. I've got to dismiss most of the house staff too and my salary has been cut by two-thirds. As from today I'm to be paid just about what I earned back in 1920 when I started as an assistant. Talking of which, the assistant managers go as of today. I'm instructed to run the place on my own. What a bloody disaster!' Kenneth thumped the table with his fist. 'A bloody hopeless situation.'

'No, it's not!' cried Maeve. 'We can do without servants. I'd prefer it anyway. And we'll make do. I'll start a kitchen garden. We can make all sorts of savings that will allow us to get by. And we have each other. I can help you dear. I know it's tough on you having to bring so much bad news to people. It's not as if you could do it by letter, the way head office have, and I think you've done well to give the coolies their dismissals the way you have. Look, I'm sure if we work together, we'll see the slump through with flying colours.'

Kenneth looked unconvinced. 'It's never been this bad before. I don't know what is going to happen.' He sat there with the food untouched before him. 'I need a drink to deal with this headache. Then I'll tell young Simpson and Everdon they are now no longer employed by Dalgeish. I imagine they have a strong suspicion that their heads are on the block along with most everyone else's.'

'Don't have a drink, Kenneth. Eat something, you'll feel the better for some food in your stomach.'

'I'll have a drink when I bloody well feel like it!' he shouted, suddenly furious. He stormed to his feet and strode off to the lounge where the whisky was kept.

Maeve held her tongue. There was no point in trying to reason with him when he was in such a state. Better to let him calm down on his own accord once he had completed delivering the bad news to the rest of the estate staff. She poured herself a cup of tea, carried it to the verandah and, as she sipped it, stared thoughtfully out to the rubber trees beyond the lawn, pondering the future.

Chapter 13

Selangor, 1929

Six months later, Maeve's life on Kuala Tanah was still clouded with unhappiness. The crash in rubber prices had proved to be a serious one, and there could be no disguising the fact, no matter how cheerful a face one presented to the world, that the planters in Selangor were in economic trouble. By March 1929 a number of Maeve's friends had returned to England, taking their children, in order to maintain a semblance of middle-class life. Their husbands stayed on to manage their estates as best they could from bungalows stripped of all but the barest of essentials. By and large the planter community had managed the drastic change to their circumstances in a fairly civilized manner. Families had clubbed together to make the best of an austere Christmas for their children's sake, and the less hard hit had made more than decent offers for furniture and chattels being sold up by returning friends in order that they could have some cash upon their return to Britain.

In late March there was a big party at the Bangi Club to say farewell to Antonia Coster who was returning to England with her young children in April. The occasion promised to be a glittering one by local standards as people had decided that, as well as being a send-off for Antonia, the evening would serve equally well as a morale booster for those who were to remain. Everyone by now had been deeply affected by the rubber slump and a bit of a cheer-up, a rallying of spirits after the monsoon as much as anything else, was felt by the planter community as being well and truly due. Both Maeve and Kenneth were looking forward to it as they dressed that evening.

'Will the road be very muddy?' called Maeve from the bedroom to Kenneth, shaving in the bathroom. 'I would rather not have to change into my evening clothes at the Club but on the other hand, I don't want to arrive splattered in mud. What was the road like when you went over to the Rajah's the other evening?'

'It'll be all right. The Public Works Department have pulled their finger out for once and workgangs have been filling all the dips and pot holes. Best it's been for years. I think Ali had a word with the Commissioner about the state of the roads and consequently repairs started happening as soon as the rain stopped.'

Maeve selected the most fashionable of her limited wardrobe of formal wear. It was an evening dress with a loose, chemise-shaped bodice with the waist band at hip level. Its neckline was cut extremely low to reveal much of Maeve's bare back, the narrow straps showing her softly contoured shoulders at their best. The knee-length skirt was overlaid with an uneven-hemmed, filmy overskirt which dipped almost to the ankle at the centre back. As she sat on the edge of the bed rolling her silk stockings up her legs Kenneth strode in from the bathroom bare chested. He put on a starched shirt and began fiddling with his studs and wing collar.

'Damn penguin suit,' he muttered to himself as he failed at his initial attempt to flick the collar over and attach it to the front stud. 'Ah, that's better.' With his right thumb he managed to push the stud through the tight starched slits of the collar and lock in the retaining pin before the ends sprang apart again. Quickly he knotted his black tie.

'I'm ready, Maeve. How about you?'

Maeve checked her dress in the long oval mirror on the wardrobe door and, satisfied with what she saw, turned and sat at the dressing table to apply her lipstick.

'Won't be a moment.'

'I'll get the motor ready then. See you downstairs.'

Five minutes later the Model T Ford chugged purposefully along the driveway in the failing twilight, its headlights lighting the earth road as Maeve and Kenneth set out for Bangi.

There was a large and high-spirited crowd at the Club when they arrived an hour later. Dance music from the gramophone competed with sounds of mirth, shrieks of recognition, and shouts of bonhomie as one familiar face after another entered the reception room. Maeve and Kenneth did the rounds, saying hello to those they knew, before settling down at a table with the Winstons and some other estate friends. Talk, naturally enough, soon focused on the problems of expatriate life on a destitute rubber estate. Maeve, Nancy, and the other women discussed what curious culinary delights they had to resort to over the last few months in order to make the household budget stretch. Nancy came up with the best story, that of curried flying fox, the sole bag from a hunting trip by her husband and some other estate managers who had set out one day to put some food on their tables without having to buy it.

'Really, it wasn't too bad,' laughed Nancy. 'Somewhat leathery I'll admit, but there was a certain something in its flavour that was distinctly piquant.'

'My dear,' called over her husband Stanley from the other side of the table where he had been half in conversation with the men of the group. 'The flying fox was awful! You're confusing it with the goat curry we had a few nights later. Altogether a far finer cooking achievement, that goat.'

Everyone laughed, and Stanley went on: 'It was the damnedest thing you know. I was motoring along one afternoon a couple of weeks back, mind on dodging puddles, when this goat hurls itself out of the scrub alongside the road and in front of my motor car. Of course I tried to miss it, but it seems the brute was bent on suicide and I collected it fair and square. Didn't know what to do with its carcass, it was as dead as mutton, but in the end I chucked it in the back and brought it home. It ended up on the table three days running.'

Again everyone chuckled. Animal losses from motor accidents had been unusually high since the rubber slump had affected Selangor. Straying kampong animals were suddenly fair game and probably every man around the table had, at some time or another over the past six months, attempted to sideswipe a goat or two which had been innocently grazing beside the road. If the manoeuvre proved successful the motor car would be hurriedly brought to a halt and the driver would furtively hop out to lug the prize into his vehicle. It was highly illegal, and would be embarrassing to be caught at it, but it was a very effective and opportune way of securing food in these hard-pressed times.

The party around the table ebbed and flowed as people left to mingle with other friends or to dance, while others joined the group. Maeve was asked for a foxtrot by Stanley Winston and then by some other friends of hers and Kenneth's. It was fun being out. When she finally returned to the table there were some new people there.

'Maeve,' said Nancy, 'I'd like to introduce you to some Port Dickson friends of ours. This is Mervin and Carol Beatie.' As she made the introduction she ever so slightly raised her right eyebrow at Maeve, and Maeve remembered Nancy's observations about the pair a year ago.

'Delighted to meet you,' said Maeve first shaking Mervin's damp hand as he distantly acknowledged her, and then Carol's. It too was perfunctory and belied the quick but searching appraisal Carol's eyes gave her. Maeve sat down, conscious of Carol Beatie's inspection and again caught Nancy's eye.

'Stanley is a good dance partner,' she said by way of conversation.

'Yes, not bad. It was with such charms that he got me out here. Oh, if only I had known what awaited me!' joked Nancy. 'He'd even be better if he didn't get half sozzled by midnight; too many stengahs and he loses his sense of rhythm, and not just with dance steps I might add!'

Maeve laughed at Nancy's innuendo. She had to admit too, that Kenneth also suffered from this particular malady after a night at the Club. She looked across at the Beaties. An odd couple she thought. He didn't seem to care for anyone's company but just sat there nursing a whisky and occasionally laughing quietly at things his wife was saying. Watching Carol, Maeve knew why Nancy and the others had made the jokes about her in the way that they had.

At this precise moment she was pretending, in a most transparent way, to be hanging on to every word Kenneth was saying as he chatted on about some boating incident he had been involved with recently. She gave him admiring glances, and occasionally interjected with the most vacuous of comments, delivered in a breathy American voice. She's nowhere near as dim-witted and scatter-brained as she makes out I'm sure, thought Maeve, why does she bother to imply that she is? Maeve decided that she was an unlikeable woman and tried to judge Kenneth's reaction to her. Nancy, she remembered, had said Stanley had been swept off his feet by such attention.

Kenneth however didn't seem to be aware that the little-girl, simpering look was for his benefit, and simply talked on as he would have to anyone at the table. Maeve was glad to see him unreceptive to what she saw as vaguely sexual overtures. No wonder the woman was disliked by so many women who had come across her. Carol Beatie was quite attractive physically with her small, slight figure, severe, bobbed dark hair and regular if unexciting features, and her need to attract other women's husbands seemed a peculiar obsession to Maeve and she wondered why Carol would bother.

Maeve continued to watch her with interest. Kenneth eventually wandered off on some errand and Maeve noticed him ten minutes later, deep in conversation with a group of fellow planters over at the bar. His place was taken by Margaret Ambury and shortly afterwards Henry, her husband, and another man joined them. Margaret introduced the stranger.

'Everyone, this is Nick Manconi. Nick, this is Nancy, Stanley, Maeve, Bertie, Carol and Mervin.'

As Margaret named the individuals around the table Nick leaned over and shook their hands. Carol, Maeve couldn't help but notice, gave him a meaningful glance as he shook hers. Doesn't she ever give up? pondered Maeve. Henry Ambury and Nick Manconi sat down and the various conversations animating the group recommenced.

Margaret started talking to Maeve.

'Nick is staying with us for a couple of weeks. He is an archaeologist and he's going to carry out a dig somewhere in the neighbourhood. Quite an exciting change, isn't it, from rubber, rubber, and more rubber as the chief topic of conversation from breakfast to supper.'

Maeve looked over to the visitor. He was a handsome man. He had dark-brown hair, slightly wavy, which had been cut carefully to make it longer on top and at the back of the head than most men wore it in Malaya, but still retained the close cut at the sides. Where would he find a barber who could cut men's hair so well wondered Maeve. His forehead was broad, giving him, along with wide-spread eyebrows over warm brown eyes, an open, honest appearance. Unlike any of the men present he wore no moustache, and his lips had a friendly line to them. Maeve thought he looked a pleasant and thoughtful gentleman.

'What does an archaeologist do in Malaya, Mr Manconi?' she asked. 'I know what they do in Egypt and the Near East of course but I've never heard about any archaeology being done in Malaya.'

He smiled at her, revealing a set of regular teeth, their symmetry marred only by an upper incisor having a chip off one edge which gave him a slightly roguish air.

'I'm not surprised you haven't heard about us archaeologists. There's only a handful of us in Malaya. Two handfuls if you count the Dutch over in the Dutch East Indies and our discoveries tend to get swamped by more immediate news in the local newspapers. But we have our moments. Like elsewhere in the world we are trying to uncover the past long after it's been lost to the imagination of mankind.'

'What sort of a past does Malaya have? Most of it seems impenetrable jungle and I would guess that all of it was, prior to the rubber plantations clearing a lot of it away. Without having thought about it before, I'd have supposed the place to have been empty of people.'

'You're partly right. The more remote regions were peopleless, but along the navigable rivers and coastal kingdoms, tribes, and communities have been making their traditions for a long, long time. We might be talking thousands of years. Older and older sites keep getting discovered so none of us knows how long the process has been going on.'

'I had no idea there was the possibility of such history around us. How interesting.'

There was a lull in the conversation as people ordered more drinks. Then Margaret asked, 'Where are you digging, Nick? I know you told us back at the estate, but I've forgotten.'

'Over at a place called Bukit Klang.'

'Why that's not far from our estate,' said Maeve. 'It's the local landmark in fact. What is important about the place?'

'I'm not certain yet that it is important,' replied Nick. 'But to find out I have to make a decent investigation of the place. I walked over the accessible parts of it a couple of years ago – you will know just how steep and jungle-clad the hill is – and noticed that there were some tumble-down ruins on some terraced areas above the river. I couldn't say as to what they are the remains of from that one visit, but they were extensive enough to indicate that something of significance had once stood on the hill. There are a number of possibilities: a Dutch or Portuguese fort; a citadel from the period of Sumatran domination of Malaya; or something even older such as a Buddhist temple built by Indian missionaries before the birth of Christ. Perhaps the ruins will be none of these, but I'm here to attempt to find out what they are.'

195

'How fascinating!' said Maeve. 'I had absolutely no idea so many possibilities could exist. I suppose I see Bukit Klang at least once a week when I'm out and about in the motor car and never would I have entertained the thought that it could have been so historical.'

'Well, of course, running through the possibilities is one thing, but sometimes things turn out to be less exciting than one would have hoped. If it is a Dutch fort up there and nothing else, the history goes back only three hundred years.'

'But that seems even positively ancient when you think that we British have only been in Selangor for fifty years. Have you started your dig already?'

'Next week. I only arrived at Margaret and Henry's last Monday and since then I've been organizing a team of workers and arranging accommodation adjacent to the site: generally getting the whole thing set up so that work can start smoothly. If the ruins are up to expectation I'll be here for four months.'

'Will visitors be allowed?' asked Maeve. 'I for one would love to see a genuine archaeological site. At the Empire Exhibition at Wembley years ago I visited the replica of Tutankhamen's tomb which I found very interesting. But to see history in the making as you uncover these ruins, that would be even more interesting.'

'Oh yes, visitors are welcome. Feel free to pop over once I get things started.'

'Tell me, Mr Manconi,' chimed in Carol Beatie, 'how does one get a job as an archaeologist? Do you work for the museum in Kuala Lumpur?'

'No. I'm employed by Rajah Brooke. I'm his general factotum I suppose, when it comes to history, archaeology and other bookish pursuits. Sir Vyner is a keen historian and amateur scientist. I've been his librarian for about three years but the position actually encompasses a great deal more than just managing his library at Kuching. For a couple of months each year I will carry out some archaeological fieldwork, at other times some archival

196

research, it depends on numerous priorities; I'm not restricted to Sarawak because of course you can't package history into neat contemporary parcels. Sarawak might be ruled by the Brooke family now, but centuries ago it was part of someone else's kingdom and consequently clues to Sarawak's past are all over Malaya and the Dutch East Indies. That's why I'm in Selangor this year. On Bukit Klang I might find some evidence of an old empire which could link together sites from here to Sumatra to British Borneo.'

'You must know Rajah Brooke well,' commented Carol. 'How wonderful! From what one hears, he sounds a fascinating man; such a glamorous lifestyle he and his Ranee live.'

'I suppose so,' replied Nick. 'Depends what you hear. I certainly enjoy working for him. He is a generous employer in terms of allowing me to pursue projects such as this and he can be a stimulating conversationalist. He's up with the play on all sorts of academic endeavour in British Malaya and the Dutch East Indies and, because of this, attracts all sorts of interesting people to visit the palace at Kuching.'

Carol was not to be put off by Nick's extolling of Rajah Brooke's intellectual curiosity at the expense of hearing about his social life, and continued to pump him for more details about the intimacies of the Brookes. Nick did his best to provide details of how the palace was decorated, how the Rajah and Ranee spent their days with their yachts, Rolls Royces and other paraphernalia of the fabulously wealthy, and what international society lions had been recently entertained at Kuching. Maeve could see that he was trying to be diplomatically discreet and answer Carol's questions but at the same time she was sure that, like herself, he was becoming increasingly irritated at Carol's name-dropping and persistence in sticking with the one topic of conversation. He obviously wasn't comfortable discussing his employer in this way. For a moment the music from the gramophone impinged on the conversation and Nick took advantage of it.

'Margaret, would you care to dance?'

'Love to.'

They got up and disappeared into the crowd.

'That's what I call an interesting man,' said Carol, speaking to Maeve. 'Such sensitive, dark eyes, oodles of mystery about him. And a friend of Sir Vyner Brooke too. I must make sure I see more of him while he's in Selangor. I don't imagine he knows many people over here. In fact,' she decided, 'he can't otherwise he wouldn't be staying with the Amburys. Not the most scintillating of couples I feel.'

Maeve liked the Amburys and for an instant felt like jumping to their defence. But why bother, she reflected, Carol Beatie would probably describe her and Kenneth to others in exactly the same way. The only way to combat such nastiness was to pretend to have heard it in a more charitable way than it was in fact meant.

'I don't think I'd say that,' she said by way of reply. 'They seem to be quite old friends.' The conversation dribbled off. Carol Beatie didn't make a habit of speaking to women if there were men close at hand and turned her attention to a noisy fellow with a bobbing adam's apple who had been hovering near her for a while.

'Teddy,' she shrieked theatrically, 'where have you been, you naughty boy? You promised me a dance earlier.' Teddy gallantly extended a hairy, knuckled hand and took her away from the group. Maeve caught Nancy's eye.

'Now you know,' said Nancy with a laugh.

The evening was still young by Malayan precedents and the party was still strident and swinging at 3 a.m. Among Maeve's dance partners was Nick and they chatted some more about his work as they weaved about the crowded floor. He was pleasantly unassuming about his novelty value among the planter community and Maeve enjoyed hearing him talk about his plans for the next four months. The awful Carol Beatie continued her role as vamp off and on throughout the evening, her crassness sometimes becoming amusing to Maeve's group, but more often just annoying. Nick Manconi had become the focus of her attention and if Maeve, Margaret or another woman was speaking to him, Carol generally made an attempt to insinuate herself into the conversation. Such a silly woman, thought Maeve as yet again the New Jersey accent cut through the gay repartee like a blunt saw on hard timber. She turned to say something to Kenneth when suddenly there was a scream, followed by some quiet apologies. Margaret Ambury had knocked over her pink gin. It had flowed across the table in a fast little stream and cascaded down on to Carol's lap.

'Oh, I'm so sorry, Carol! I do hope it isn't stained! I don't know what to say. I'm very sorry!'

Carol, who had uttered the scream, glared at her and then tried to soak up the alcohol from her silk dress. She grabbed some serviettes from the table and began blotting the fabric, only to let out another shriek when she inspected the results. One of the serviettes had the remains of a curried canapé lodged in its crumpled-up folds and Carol, in her haste to minimize the wetting, had pressed the mess into her dress. The result was disastrous. Across her lap were watery, yellow-brown blotches which looked as if their removal would require some cleaning solvents not on hand at the Bangi Club.

'It's ruined! You, you . . .!' she glared at Margaret.

Nick stepped in. 'An accident, you know. Such a nuisance, I know, and jolly bad luck. It will clean up though, so your dress isn't ruined. I saw just the same sort of thing happen only a couple of months ago at the Istana at Kuching, at tiffin. Her Highness the Ranee splashed some mulligatawny soup on her raw silk day dress. The result was worse than this but I saw her in the same dress a day or two later and you wouldn't have known what had happened to it.'

Carol looked at Nick suspiciously; was he teasing her? He looked genuinely concerned and she decided to ignore the shadows of amusement on the faces of the women about her which had appeared as Nick spoke of the accident at Rajah Brooke's table, and take him at face value.

'You may be right,' she conceded, 'but it's finished my evening. I can't stay, looking like this. It really is too bad! Where is Mervin?'

Her lugubrious husband materialized at her side.

'Mervin, take me home please,' and with a few 'goodnights' to the favoured of the party, Margaret of course being snubbed, the Beaties swept out of the Club. Maeve, cheered at their departure, couldn't help but think that Margaret's clumsiness had happened a little too pat to be the accident it was passed off as, and gave her a smile. In return she received a conspiratorial wink, which took in Nick as well as herself.

He too smiled at his friend and said, 'Really Margaret, that was too bad.'

With the Beaties' exit there was a discernible relaxing of the mood of the people around the table and, without a single word uttered in regret of their departure, the party continued.

There wasn't much for Kenneth to do on the estate these days. Instead of moping about the bungalow day in and day out, he took to visiting Ali more regularly than he had in the past. The Rajah of Sungei Kemudi too had been affected by the rubber slump, not only from the cessation of latex from his own estates but also from revenue losses connected with his control of the labour market. With no one requiring coolies anymore, his rake-off from controlling quotas dried up to nothing very quickly.

To a superficial observer this diminishing of the Rajah's income would have seemed immaterial to his well-being. Rajah Ibrahim was famous for his wealth and he was ostentatious in displaying it when it came to expensive motor cars and flashy arrivals at important social and political occasions. However the Rajah had a number of overheads which required a constant influx of cash into the palace coffers, and consequently the continuing slump of 1929 was a matter of grave concern to him as well as to the British planter community.

The most pressing at the moment was a gambling debt

of 28,000 Straits dollars which he had recklessly accrued in a single evening's card playing at the Sultan of Johore's Istana in the new year. But beyond that was the need for a regular supply of cash every couple of months to keep two blackmailers – neither knew of the other's existence – at a healthy distance from the police. Both were too prominent in the Malay community to be unobtrusively murdered; and anyway the Rajah assumed they would have drawn up incriminating documents to be opened in precisely the circumstances which would indicate an unnatural demise, so he had come to a satisfactory arrangement with each of them.

Their secrets – one concerning the procurement of pubescent boys, some of whom hadn't been seen since the party the Rajah required them for; the other about the death of a young man who had ended up at the Port Swettenham Infirmary a decade earlier – were safe as long as the money flowed into the royal treasury. But it wasn't, and as March 1929 rolled by it was becoming worryingly apparent that prosperous times were a long way off. However Ali still had time for his usual pursuits and that included Kenneth's regular appearances to play their games of billiards.

'Off your game a bit, old man,' chivvied Ali as Kenneth bungled an easy cushion shot. 'Got something on your mind?' Kenneth had already lost three games in a row since he had arrived at the Istana at 3.00 p.m.

'Nothing more than usual. Staring poverty in the face seems to have made me more reflective than I used to be, I suppose. Damn poor show when it affects a man's game of billiards though. I'll try to do better; I can't stand to see you win by my default.'

Ali responded to the joke. 'Kenneth my friend, you'd lose anyway. My eye has never been better!' and to emphasize his remark he sent the ball into the centre right pocket with a dexterous cannon shot. He continued, 'The slump is hurting the British badly isn't it. How about you personally?'

'Life certainly isn't what it used to be. Given what is happening to some planters though, I mustn't complain. For a start Maeve and I don't have a family so we can tighten our belts to a degree that those with children can't. It's tough for those who have to send their wives and kids back home so they can remain on their estate living on the smell of an oily rag without the added misery of watching their dependants also having to do it. Maeve and I are having, to be honest, a bit of a rough patch at the moment but, goodness, I couldn't bear to see her have to return to London along with the others.'

'Yes, it would be a hard decision to be forced to make, husband and wife separating to opposite sides of the planet,' said Ali, nodding in sympathy. He took his turn at the table and the two friends played in silence, save for the click of billiard balls, for a couple of minutes before Ali again spoke.

'Got any contingency plans, old man, if your estate is closed down completely? Are there other fields open to you here, or would you go back to Britain?'

'I hardly dare think about that sort of situation. There's already a pool of ex-planters canvassing the government to find them work and I hear that they've had damn-all luck. As for the estate closing up shop completely, well I'm counting on that not happening. I'm running it on a shoestring budget anyway. These days I have precisely ten coolies working and they are on reduced wages. My salary is right back where it was when I started out as a cadet in 1920. My company are hardly putting a cent into the place, and I think their plan is to keep Kuala Tanah just ticking over, not operational but ready to be so immediately rubber prices rise again.'

'That salary reduction must be tough to live with. How on earth do you manage?'

Kenneth laughed. 'With difficulty. Maeve has a kitchen garden and I've taken up hunting. Basically we get by; eat cheap meals and try to drink less.' He went on in a more serious tone. 'It is an awkward life though, as I have a lot of time on my hands and no spare cash to help while away the extra hours. I can't stand hanging around the estate with no work to do but to go to the Club means spending money I don't really have. I've dipped into the books Maeve gets from a lending library in Kuala Lumpur, but I'm no reader when it comes down to it, and trying to become one just made me more irritated and bored than I was before I picked them up. I like doing things! Sitting around with my nose in a book seems a waste of time.'

'I can see it must be very frustrating being unable to do your job properly,' sympathized Ali. 'Let's make this the last game. I have a business proposal I've been mulling over lately in which you could perhaps have a place. Would you be interested in hearing about it?'

'Yes, I would.'

Kenneth watched Ali expertly line up the shots to win the match and put his cue in the rack.

'Your lucky day, Ali. I think my newly acquired diet of flying fox and rice sweepings is affecting my game. Otherwise you'd never have cleaned me up in this way. Four straight matches! I'm disgusted with myself!'

'Ha, experience always wins out in the end,' replied Ali. 'Come on, let's go on to the verandah for some refreshments. I'll tell you my proposal when we're comfortable.'

'Kenneth, do you know how the government of Selangor raises half of its budget requirements each year?' inquired the Rajah as they stretched out in their cane chairs sipping Persian tea and nibbling on pisang cakes. Kenneth shook his head, his mouth too full at that exact moment to answer politely.

'Opium taxes. So much opium enters the country that the revenue raised from it eclipses any other tax or duty you care to name. Opium is the mainstay of the economy.'

'I didn't know that.'

'There's more money made from selling opium to the Chinese tin miners than there is from the tin ore they extract. Since we have all been affected by the rubber slump . . .' Kenneth gave him an inquiring look, 'yes, me also, my friend. Even my fortunes have suffered since last August. The slump has prompted me to look at this interesting business of importing opium into my country. Without a doubt the government does extremely well out of it. Opium can be purchased for a pittance in Bengal. It is shipped across from Calcutta at no great cost either. However once it is locked up in the bond warehouses at Port Swettenham, Penang and elsewhere it suddenly becomes an expensive commodity. Also a vital one. Unlike you and me and other sophisticated users of the drug, most opium smokers are addicts through prolonged over-indulgence.

'Those wretched tin miners will pay any amount to ensure their opium is on hand and the Selangor government has, in its wisdom, set the duty payable at a level high enough to make a great deal of revenue for itself but, at the same time, keep it just reasonable enough so as not to provoke mass uprisings and riots among the tin workers. There is enough leeway between the duty payable at the bond stores and the sale price in the tin mining towns for middlemen – distributors and smoke-house proprietors – to make a living. Further to these insights, I also recognized that what profit can be extracted from this business by private individuals is gathered at the beginning by Bengalese shipowners, and, here in Selangor, by Chinese traders and shopkeepers.'

Ali poured himself another glass of tea and continued. 'At this point it crossed my mind that perhaps Malays should have a part in this business. In these troubled times it seems wrong that the one really profitable enterprise in Selangor should be entirely in the hands of migrants. I started to think that local businessmen like myself should have a hand in it too.'

'A sound idea I agree,' said Kenneth.

'I did perceive a problem immediately however.'

'What was that?'

'Not enough profit. A man in my position cannot become a common trader of merchandise. It is inconceivable that a Rajah of Sungei Kemudi could become a purveyor of opium, tendering along with a rabble of Chinese for a government licence to distribute opium and setting up shop in a dump like Kuang.'

'Couldn't you get a middleman?'

'It's not just the prestige considerations. There is also that limited profit margin to be looked at. It seems to me that there is room for another importer in the business. I thought to myself, why don't I buy the opium in Calcutta and have it shipped into Selangor in a way that circumvents the point where it acquires its duty, and sell it, through brokers, directly to the Chinese community? One could sell it at a handsome profit, and at a price much more agreeable to the Chinese than that at which the government markets it.'

'That sounds awfully like smuggling to me,' commented Kenneth with a smile. 'There must be some pretty fierce penalties against it. Otherwise others would be doing it.'

'Oh, I'm certain others are doing it, but only on a small scale; a brick or two of compressed opium hidden in the floor of the hold of a small ship, stuff on that level only. I envisage an undertaking on a larger and more professional scale that would not only reap respectable returns for the risk involved but also, because it's well organized, impossible to detect.'

'Hmmm, sounds a very dodgy proposition. The little I know of them, the Straits Settlements Customs and Excise lads are no fools. Wouldn't you be up against a clever organization with a lot more experience in these things than yourself?' As he spoke he remembered that he, in fact, knew very little about Ali's activities, and the gossip he had heard over the years would suggest that Ali was, on the contrary, quite au fait with combating government law enforcement departments such as the Customs and Excise.

In reply Ali just tapped the side of his nose knowingly with a pudgy forefinger.

Kenneth continued. 'Why are you telling me this anyway? I couldn't help you, for as you know, I haven't a bean to my name.'

'Before I answer your question,' replied Ali, 'I have one

to ask you. What do you think of the idea, assuming for the moment the importation side of the proposal operates without problems?'

'Well, naturally the profits you describe are tempting, but it's not really money for nothing, is it? If you get caught I imagine it's prison, if not for you, at least for the smaller fish in the organization. The money I like; the risk I'm not sure justifies the gains.'

Ali rubbed his bottom lip pensively. 'The profits are substantial, a lot more than I think you realize. But first: how can you help me? You can, a great deal. Needless to say what I'm about to tell you is in the strictest confidence. I'm sure I can trust you.

'I propose to avoid the opium duty by shipping the stuff, at night, into the Kemudi river. Once up-river it can be transported by road and rail all over Selangor and Negri Sembilan. Now that will take time. No vessel can get in and out of the Kemudi, and leave a cargo well inland, within the hours of darkness. I see the opium being off-loaded downstream of here during night number one and, an evening later, shipped up to another go-down which would be close to road transportation. From there, at an unhurried rate, it can be taken to Bangi and dispatched to the distributors. I see my part of the business ceasing at Bangi. Chinese businessmen can take over from there.

'Now, go-down number one will be hidden in the mangrove forests where the Kemudi is still tidal. There's a maze of winding tributaries and streams there so it will be no problem putting the opium safely away from curious eyes. Go-down number two is more problematical. It can't be near here for several reasons. For a start there's only a single road out of this part of the river and consequently any increase of traffic can be easily monitored. Secondly, my rival for ruling Sungei Kemudi, Idris Hussein, is just nearby at Bukit Klang. Too close for comfort when one is involved in a secret enterprise like this. He would be to the authorities in a flash if he suspected something out of the ordinary. So ideally this area should be passed by and the go-down be erected further upstream.

'That idea naturally brought you into my plans. Kuala Tanah Estate is ideally located for the second go-down. Among those whom I trust only your estate has both access to the Kemudi, via the Tanah stream, and to the roads. From your place there are several roads to get to Bangi, all of them well used, so the opium shipments wouldn't attract any interest at all. The Tanah can be easily reached during the night from where I think the go-down number one will be, and because you are my friend, cargo will be safe. Your coolies are not working so no one has any reason to be out and about on your estate except yourself. It would be foolproof.'

'Christ, I don't know, Ali. I doubt if I'm cut out to be a smuggler. Perhaps if I was alone I might be tempted but there's my wife, you know. I'm not sure a married man should be listening to this scheme. If things went amiss, she would suffer too.'

'I am certain they won't go amiss. It's a clean, straight-forward plan involving only a few specially selected men I can count on utterly. The more difficult part, that of distribution, is not my concern at all. My Chinese contact will receive the opium, pay my agent, and immediately all contact between me, the shipper, and he, as distributor, is broken off. Your part, absolutely vital as it will be, is very small and, of all the parts making up the enterprise, the most hidden away. We are talking about a shed hidden among the trees and bamboo near the Tanah and Kemudi confluence which, once the cargo is deposited there, will require a visit or two by motor lorry, to remove it to Bangi. I'm not sure how many shipments I will under-take, maybe one every four to six weeks, so activities will be rare and unobtrusive at the far corner of your estate. Your share of the profits will of course reflect the value with which I regard your assistance. I was thinking of 10,000 Straits dollars a month while we are in business. Once the slump is over, well, the government can take back its monopoly.'

Kenneth was flabbergasted! Ten thousand Straits dol-lars a month! Good grief! That was eight times what he had been earning before the slump! In these terrible times, the sum represented almost untold wealth. Christ, he thought to himself, a couple of years as a smuggler's accomplice and I could buy my own estate. He started to laugh.

'Ali, you do have a way of making a dubious proposition suddenly seem quite attractive. It does seem a devilishly risky business however, so I'd like to think it over first before giving you an answer.'

'I wouldn't have expected otherwise with you, old man. Never rush into things, a sound principle I say. I tell you what, why don't you come back next week and we can actually go over the territory and discuss the idea at the same time. I'll have my launch on hand so you can see just what the transshipping involves.'

Kenneth agreed, and the conversation returned to the more abstract aspects of the plan. When Kenneth said his goodbye an hour later he had concluded that, by and large, the scheme was a good one.

Chapter 14

Bukit Klang, 1929

'Kenneth, why don't we motor over to Bukit Klang tomorrow and visit Mr Manconi? I'd love to see the archaeological site.'

Maeve and Kenneth were reclining out on the verandah with an after-dinner drink, enjoying the velvety blackness of the evening. About them, but not bothersome, the air was full of flying insects homing blindly in on the softly hissing pressure lamp Kenneth had hung on a nail at the eave some way down from where they sat. From that distance it cast a faint but companionable orange light which didn't intrude on the mood of the night.

'He should be settled in by now as it's nearly four weeks since we met him at Antonia's farewell.'

Kenneth didn't reply immediately. Ali's proposition had been going round and round in his mind and, although he had almost decided to help, he hadn't gone back to Ali to talk about it. Maeve's idea of visiting Bukit Klang would provide that opportunity. While Maeve had a look at the dig and whatever else was going on at the hill, he could see Ali and take the launch trip.

'Yes, all right,' he answered. 'I tell you what though. I'm not all that interested in archaeology. Why don't you look at the site while I nip over to Ali's Istana? Last time I was there he wanted to show me some of his plantations and land from the river and I could take him up on the offer while you're with Mr Manconi. Kill two birds with one stone, so to speak.'

'Certainly, but how about time? I don't want to be guilty of trespassing on Mr Manconi's time all afternoon. How long will you be with the Rajah?'

'Oh, about three hours at the most, I imagine. Look, I'll come up to the site and see how you're placed, and then see Ali. I won't go on his launch if Manconi looks very busy.'

It turned out that an afternoon's tour of the archaeological site was in no way imposing on Nick Manconi's time.

Maeve and Kenneth motored out to the village of Bukit Klang in the early afternoon. Parking the Ford under the shade of a huge peepul tree, Kenneth asked directions from a villager who came out to enquire their business, and he and Maeve were sent along a track which quickly began to wind its way up the hill through dense kamunting and kadadu scrub. They must have climbed 600 feet before the track began to level off. Malay voices, chatting and laughing, indicated that, not far off, was the archaeology dig.

Huffing and panting with the exertion of the climb through the hot still air, they walked on to a broad terrace which showed every sign that it had been recently stripped of its vegetation. A dozen or more Malay labourers were digging into the ground under the shade of canvas awnings stretched across parts of terrace on bamboo poles and, talking to a Malay who had the air of a supervisor rather than that of a coolie, was Nick Manconi. He looked up and saw Maeve and Kenneth approaching him.

'Good afternoon!' he called. He exchanged a few more words with the man and then crossed to where Maeve and Kenneth were standing. 'Kenneth and Maeve Clouston isn't it?' he said, shaking their hands. 'Delighted to see you here, you're my first British visitors to Bukit Klang. Come to see the place I hope?'

'Yes please,' replied Maeve. 'Ever since you offered the invitation at the Bangi Club I've been meaning to take you up on it. And here we are!'

'Excellent. There's quite a lot to see; at least there is if you don't mind a bit of scrub bashing. Most of the site is still covered with secondary growth but I've had tracks cut in various places and it is possible, with some pushing, to get about. We can start here though,' he gestured to the workers about him, 'where things are positively civilized.'

'Actually I can't stay,' interrupted Kenneth before Nick got launched on his explanations. 'I've some business with Rajah Ibrahim just nearby and, much as I'd like to see what you're up to, I'd better see His Excellency. What would be a good time to return?' He pulled out his pocket watch. 'Half two. Ideally I'd like to be away until sixish, but Maeve and I wouldn't like to take up an unreasonable amount of your time, so what would suit you?'

'Make it six if you like, seven if it's more convenient. I've been working like a coolie up here for the past twenty days and there's nothing I'd like better than an afternoon off to show my first visitor the hill. It will take hours to see it properly anyway, so don't rush back. Once it is twilight we will be at my quarters at the kampong. Simply meet us there if you're later than you anticipated. Anyone will tell you where I am at the village.'

'That's very good of you. Well, cheerio Maeve, Mr Manconi, I'll see you later.' Kenneth turned and went back down the track.

'Well, where do we start, Mr Manconi?' said Maeve surveying the activity before them.

'Please call me Nick. I'd feel more comfortable if you did.'

'Certainly. No "Mrs Clouston" either, Maeve is what my friends call me.'

'Right. Now where to begin? It's been a hectic time and I've developed a case of tunnel vision when it comes to looking at this place. Each discovery has been so interesting that I haven't really tried to join them up into a proper story that would make sense to a visitor like you. Today will be a good opportunity to do just that. Let's stand in the shade.' They walked to where some trees cast a shadow across the terrace and then he began.

'The hill has signs of long history. Bukit Klang, as you know, is generally very steep. The south and east sides are cliffs rising straight out of the river; there's creepers and trees clinging to the sides so the steepness isn't quite as apparent as it really is. You've just climbed the west side and that is not the gentlest of slopes. The north side of the hill is the least precipitous. All this adds up to the place being an excellent natural fort. The only problem preventing this is the fact that there is no flat land on the upper part of the hill upon which would-be inhabitants could live. That was solved by making terraces such as the one we're standing on now. The hill is excavated away there,' he pointed to the uphill side of the space, 'and flung over the edge,' he swung his arm across to the southern side of the terrace.

'Eventually you end up with a flat building area half dug into the hill and half built up. I don't know when this process began yet, but I've found enough artefacts and ruins to indicate that Bukit Klang was a Malay stronghold some time in the past. They flattened the summit and three or four areas below it to the south and east. Below these terraces are the cliffs. To the relatively gently sloping north they erected a stone wall which seems to have run from the river in an arc right round to near here. There's only bits of it left but enough to show that it must have been substantial.

'Some time later, and I'm proposing centuries, the Portuguese came. It has to be after 1511 because that is the date Alfonso d'Albuquerque defeated Malacca. I think it could only be a few years afterwards, maybe a decade or so, that Bukit Klang also became Portuguese. We are not far by sea from Malacca and consequently a Malay stronghold in this part of the Straits of Malacca would be a threat to the trade monopoly the Portuguese were trying to impose on the region. The Portuguese garrison appears to have enlarged one of the Malay terraces on the hill, one just below us, and made another on more or less the same level around on the east side.

'Now, you've got to imagine this place without thick vegetation, because, bare, Bukit Klang commands all of the Kemudi River. There would have been cannon on the lower terraces and not a vessel of any description would have got past without the Portuguese knowing about it.

They did this again and again and, in the end, controlled all this part of the Malayan coast. No Malay Sultans or Rajahs could do business without the Portuguese acting as the middlemen.' Nick paused. 'As for the end of Bukit Klang's time as a fort, that I don't yet know. It's a question the answer to which I expect to find in the digging, along with a lot of other information about its history.'

'Why the need for forts in the first place?' asked Maeve. 'I thought Malaya was nothing but a jungle before the British came. What was worth fighting for here, or should I say, worth defending? The river must have been lined with impenetrable forest, the way it still is in the highlands. I should have thought it a rather inhospitable place to have eked out an existence.'

Nick nodded. 'You are half right. There probably wasn't enough jungle wealth up the Kemudi to warrant building a fort on the scale this one seems to be. Nevertheless, rhinoceros horn, spices and a few other exotic things would have regularly passed here. But I imagine this fort would have been a headquarters for the orang laut of the Kemudi and the coast for miles north and south.'

'Orang laut? Who are they?'

'Boat people, pirates really. These river kingdoms were largely made up of floating citizens whose loyalty lay mainly with the Rajah rather than with a particular area they felt was home. There's still a lot of them about in boat communities all over Malaya and Sarawak and they are very loyal to their headman or their rajah, if they have one. Being maritime folk they could range all along the coasts of Malaya and Sumatra and the hundreds of islands between, and, as well as poaching cargoes in other Rajahs' areas, they could force traders to call in to places like the one we're standing on right now to pay duties and taxes. This part of the world has been at the crossroads of trade for millennia so there has always been competition for a piece of whatever merchandise happens to be passing. Did you know for instance that Roman statuary, coins and pottery have been excavated from the ruins of an ancient seaport in French Cochin China?'

'I had no idea!'

'Ptolemy, a Greek living in Egypt 130 years after the birth of Christ, mentions this part of the world in a Geography he wrote. As well as Malaya he mentions a trade emporium called Sabana which is probably where old Sir Stamford Raffles decided, 1,700 years later, to build Singapore. Shipping, trade and merchant cities – it's all happened in the South China Sea many times over.'

'Well, this is an absolute eye-opener to me,' said Maeve. 'I've been in Selangor a year and never heard any of this before. It's all so interesting. I wonder if anyone else here knows about all this history right before their faces?'

'Hmmmm, I doubt it. Interest doesn't seem terribly great to me. As I said when you and your husband arrived, you two are the first British visitors I've had the pleasure to show around in three weeks' work.' Nick started to laugh. 'And I lost half that audience within five minutes of their arrival.'

'You mean Kenneth?' said Maeve. 'You'll have to excuse him. He is a dear, but he is not much interested in history and such things. But I'm certain he would have stayed if he hadn't had business to attend to with the Rajah. By the way, have you met the Rajah? I know he lives very near here. Kenneth seems quite thick with him, they are old friends, but I'm never invited. White women apparently aren't especially welcome at his Excellency's Palace.'

'That doesn't surprise me. Malay rulers are generally pretty strict Muslims which means women have a very set place in the social hierarchy. However I wouldn't automatically feel slighted because you haven't been invited to the Istana with your husband. The Rajah is a bachelor and he probably doesn't know what he would do with you if you turned up.'

'I'd come to that conclusion too,' replied Maeve. 'It's a pity though as it's probably my only chance even to get close to a Rajah and his palace. Kenneth's there a lot.'

'I haven't been there either so you are in good company.'

'I'm surprised to hear that. I would have thought you would be of interest to him, particularly as you're digging on an old Malayan fort.'

'Well that's just it actually. The fort is on the land of his traditional adversary, Idris Hussein, so he won't come over. The two families have been at each other's throats for centuries – on and off – and although I believe there's a stand-off at present it probably wouldn't take much to start a local war. The Idris family stronghold is the village of Bukit Klang where you would have parked your motor car. I'm their guest.'

'Does that mean that this hill would once have been their fort?'

'It's theirs in deed of title, but in terms of tradition, heir to the reputation of the old warlord who originally carved it out of the hill and all that, well, at the moment, that is impossible to say. On the north side you have Rajah Ibrahim's palace, so in a way he is laying claim to the hill; while on the west side is the Idris village looking very much at home with this place as its neighbour. I'm not even sure if there's much prestige to be got from possessing the fort. Until I came along the place was left alone. But that question aside, the Bukit Klang villagers have got interested in what I'm doing.'

He chuckled. 'Money helped a little. I managed to hire a dozen labourers to do the spade work and they have actually become quite interested in what artefacts have so far come to light. Often, towards the end of the afternoon their friends wander up to see what is new. I find their interest quite gratifying. But enough standing around. Let me show you what I've found.'

Nick led Maeve out of the shade and across the terrace to a shallow, extremely neat sided hole in the ground. A straight, vertical-walled trench cut through one side of the pit and went clean across the terrace. Six Malay coolies were carefully digging into the floor of their hole with trowels, scooping the dirt into shallow iron pans of a type commonly found in the tin fields. When full, they were carried off and emptied through a wire mesh above a spoil mound in order to retain any artefacts the workers may have missed collecting while scraping and digging. The exposed walls of the pit showed a network of different coloured strata while, on the floor, the most obvious feature was a half-circle of squared stones. The curve they delineated disappeared into the wall of the pit.

'What are those?' asked Maeve.

'Bases of pillars. Once they would have supported columns made of bricks. We've found a few to confirm the idea. I'm guessing the curve we see here continues into a full circle which would make the classic plan of a place of worship, known traditionally as a candi. Originally there would have been a roof overhead sheltering a shrine of some sort.'

Under another shaded area was a makeshift table and some buckets of water. A workman was washing sherds of pottery and other odds and ends, some of them shapeless to Maeve's eye, and laying them out on the bench top. Nick bent and picked a fragment of a pot up and handed it to Maeve. She turned it about in her hands. It was the bottom of a bowl, porcelain with a beautiful transparent green glaze, under which was incised a design of two small fish.

'How pretty! Is there a story to go with it?'

Nick pointed to a dozen other similarly coloured fragments. 'It's all porcelain from southern China. It looks typically thirteenth-century Sung, and of reasonable quality. The presence of porcelain tells me that after 1200 to 1300 this citadel was quite a prosperous place and that it dates back to about this period in history. Of course it's not just the porcelain telling me this, most of this rubbish helps build up a picture and a period to set it in. This, for instance.' He picked up a strange-shaped piece of terracotta. 'This is an eavesboard tile from a roof. These tiles are the first to go on a tiled roof and are found all over this part of Asia. There're more of them over there, and that there,' he pointed to an L-shaped fragment, 'is a ridge-capping tile. Tiled roofs indicate substantial architecture and as they were excavated at the same level as the porcelain one can assume they date to more or less the same period. Together another piece of the picture can be completed.'

'It's like a puzzle, isn't it?' enthused Maeve.

'Exactly. And it's surprising how much a few artefacts can tell you sometimes. Between them, and the signs in the ground itself, quite a lot of history can be gleaned.'

They moved on around the terrace and Nick led Maeve to a short path made virtually into a shady tunnel by the vegetation arching over from either side, and out on to a much larger terrace. This, like the first, had been cleared of trees and scrub, and a large area had further been skimmed of its top soil. An expanse of red and brown mottled dirt showed where the labourers had been at work recently. Now they were at the far end, digging at another marked-off area.

'Here,' said Nick when they reached the edge of the stripped away area, 'I've found the remains of an audience hall or balai.'

Maeve looked hard at the ground. 'Where?' she asked. For the life of her she couldn't see anything suggesting a building.

Nick laughed. 'See that discoloured circular spot there, the dark brown spot in the reddish soil about the size of a dinner plate?'

'Yes.'

'Okay, now look to its left, about five feet away, see another? Good, now go the same distance again and you'll find another, and another, and so on. Got it?'

'Yes, it's a row of patches.'

'Now look across to the other side of the square and you'll find another row parallel to this one. These are the remains of two lines of wooden pillars, long rotted off at ground level, but nevertheless showing where a large building once stood. The ground among the pillars is packed down. These factors, plus some finds such as more tiles, tell that this was once where a roofed hall with open sides once stood. A ground plan such as this is typical of a balai. Now, from its presence here I can deduce, with a fair amount of certainty, that the royal apartments will be found on the area above here because customarily that is the usual siting of a palace in relation to the audience hall.'

'My goodness,' said Maeve, 'I can feel the hill coming alive, being populated again even as you talk!'

She pointed to where the workmen were toiling. 'What's there?'

'Another candi, I think. More shaped foundation stones have been found arranged on a circular plan.'

'And here?' She pointed at a large mound about twelve feet high which jutted out from the hill for a third of the way across the terrace.

'It's a landslip, I think, rather than anything more exciting. I had a scratch about it a couple of weeks ago and found most of it is a huge boulder embedded in the ground. Rolled from further up, I imagine, and too heavy to warrant pushing it out of the way.'

The tour continued. Nick guided Maeve through some barely adequate tracks in a long looping climb which eventually brought them to the summit of the hill some eight hundred feet above the Selangor coastal plain.

'All over here were the royal apartments. I've found enough remains to know they're under all this.' He gestured at the rampant undergrowth. 'Once the view would have been magnificent. No big trees as there are now, but rather ornamental gardens and orchards sloping down to the north to end against the palace wall. I bet it was absolutely lovely.'

'They must have been fit,' panted Maeve. 'All in all it's quite a climb.'

'Probably never went down very often,' remarked Nick. 'Servants and slaves would have done all that sort of thing.' He sat down in the shade of a very ancient pomegranate, a self-sown descendant of the long-gone garden, and relaxed. Maeve joined him and they chatted away.

They must have talked for at least an hour before Nick suggested he complete the tour of the hill.

'Would you like to see the rest of what I've discovered? There's a couple of terraces down along the south and east sides which date to the Portuguese era. We've got to go near them anyway so, if you'd like to take a look, I'd be glad to show them to you.'

'Yes I would,' said Maeve, getting to her feet and smoothing her dress out. 'I find everything you've shown me very interesting. I'd like to see anything you care to point out.'

They set off down the path they had walked up earlier, but branched off on to a very rudimentary track before they reached the terrace with the balai and candi. This descended quite steeply and branches and vines scraped and whipped against Maeve as she clambered down behind Nick. I wish I had worn jodhpurs, she thought to herself as her skirt snagged yet again on some small thorned climbing vine she brushed against. As she unhooked it she noticed dozens of burrs clinging to the right shoulder of her cotton blouse, and picked those off too.

'Nearly there,' called up Nick. 'Careful at this point, the surface is rather crumbly.' She heard a scraping sound followed by a pitter-patter of rolling pebbles as Nick momentarily skidded on the friable track.

Five minutes later level ground was reached. The terrace had been cleared of much of its vegetation, this time right to the edge. Nick took Maeve over and showed her the precipitous drop beyond the terrace.

'I'll have this cut down completely later on in the season,' he said, indicating the bushes and ferns still growing across the site. 'But I thought it wise to clear this edge completely so that none of my workmen could inadvertently fall off it. Up above where they are now' — he pointed over his left shoulder where, above them, Maeve could distantly hear the workmen talking among themselves — 'they can't come to much danger, but here it's a different story. Just look at the drop.'

Maeve stood as close to the edge as she dared and peered over. The hill fell away vertically to the waters of the Kemudi. Thick vines and leafy shrubs clung to the cliff but apart from these there was little to impede the view down to the river.

'I don't think I like hanging over drops like this,' she said, stepping back. 'My goodness! How far are we above the river?'

'About five hundred feet, I'd estimate. The cliffs extend all along here for a couple of hundred yards. They make up the inward bend of the river; it flows right around it from the north out to the west. This terrace was built, I'm sure, by the Portuguese. There's another, just through there to the south-west, at the same level.'

'How can you tell?'

'No Malayan artefacts have been found here for a start. Then there's a very characteristic Portuguese-type castellated wall, at least the remains of one, along this edge. Look there and you'll see what I mean.'

Maeve walked over to a stack of hewn stone blocks which were patinated with black lichen, green velvety mosses, and the marks of old vine and creeper adhesion pads. They looked ancient.

Nick went on. 'Once the wall stretched across here, just high enough to protect the artillery-men who would have manned the cannon from bombardments from the river. And over here is more evidence.' He walked to a mound about fifty yards away. As they drew close, Maeve saw that it was a heap of tumbled masonry. 'Look at this.'

Maeve studied the block of sandstone Nick pointed to. It was part of what had obviously been a large relief decoration. A man lay across the bottom, dressed in a flowing robe and with a crown-like thing on his head. What she could make of the figure's expression looked very doleful. Another figure was standing on the man. The upper part of his torso was missing as it was on another piece of sandstone, but what was present clearly showed a military figure with sword in hand.

'What does this mean?' she asked.

'The subjugation of a king. This is part of a larger tableau showing one ruler being humiliated by his victor. You can see the symbol of kingship in the form of a crown on the prone figure. I've seen a very similar relief carving in Goa, the Portuguese colony in India, and it's clear that the standing figure here is a Portuguese conquistador. The one in Goa is on the arch of the gateway over the road leading from the port to the Old City, and this too may have originally been a sort of triumphal arch or gateway where Malayan aristocrats would have to have passed to do business with the Portuguese here. It's not the most subtle way of saying who runs the show, is it, but I dare say it made its point clearly to the locals.'

'When are you going to excavate here?'

'Towards the end of the season – October, perhaps. First I want to sort out what's happening above on the terraces where there's all the Malayan history to be uncovered.'

Maeve ambled about the terrace and eventually ended up at the cliff edge again in order to admire the view. The broad, coffee-coloured Kemudi stretched before her as it flowed from the north. In the late afternoon light it was beginning to take on a burnished copper appearance. About a mile upstream it turned to the right and disappeared among the rubber plantations which filled most of the middle distance. Below the hill there weren't rubber plantations but instead the usual landscape of palms, mango and durian trees, and other cultivated vegetation which characterized Malayan settlements. A short jetty poked its way into the Kemudi but there was no village.

'Is that part of Bukit Klang village down there?'

'No. That's the end of Rajah Ibrahim's garden. His Istana is several hundred yards back from the river. You can't see it from here though. Possibly you could from where we were earlier if I get the summit cleared of tall trees. I've seen it from a couple of vantage points in my exploratory surveys about the fort, it's a fine-looking place in its own way – sort of neo-Gothic-cum-Islamic architecture.'

As they stood looking, the sound of a running engine became apparent. Then, below them, a low, long motor launch came into view, its sharp bow cutting a perfect V into the smooth surface of the Kemudi, the gentle bow waves fanning out either side to emphasize the arrow-like passage of the vessel. The launch was painted white and a varnished interior was visible where the low cabin gave way to an expanse of deck lined either side with bolster-padded benches and chairs. A green flag with some sort of black-and-white emblem in its centre fluttered from the short jack-staff at the rounded stern. Maeve could make out a couple of white-suited figures sitting towards the back. Could that be Kenneth? she wondered. The launch glided alongside the jetty and a bevy of uniformed sailors busied themselves with making it fast to the land. The figures in white stood up and Maeve immediately recognized Kenneth.

'Look, there's Kenneth,' she said to Nick. 'That other man must be the Rajah. He's bigger than I would have imagined, quite portly really. I wonder if they can see us?'

She waved but Kenneth was talking to his companion, and although looking towards the hill, didn't appear to notice. She shouted, 'Kenneth!' but again there was no response.

'We're too far away I think,' said Nick, also looking down at the jetty.

As they watched the larger man clapped Kenneth on the shoulder and the two of them began to walk away from the water and quickly disappeared from view.

'We should make tracks too, I suppose,' said Nick. 'How about a cup of tea, Maeve? After all the climbing you've been doing, you deserve it.'

'I'd love a cup.'

Nick led the way back to the terrace they had started from three hours ago. It turned out to be not much higher up the hill than the one they had been standing upon, just further over to the west. The labourers had departed, their tools laid out on a couple of old sacks alongside the pit in preparation for the next morning's digging. Maeve stopped and had another look at their efforts.

'You know, I've enjoyed this afternoon more than I think you'd ever realize. It's been so stimulating listening to the story of this place. I know I'm being presumptuous, but would you need any help? I'd jump at the opportunity to work on a real archaeological dig and this is a wonderful place. Voluntary of course.'

'Well,' said Nick, 'perhaps you can. How are you at drawing?'

'Nick, I was a school teacher for three years, drawing is one of my many accomplishments,' Maeve replied with a smile. 'What sort of drawing?'

'First of all, plans and sections of the squares. All this information has to be drawn on to plans before we dig it up to go deeper in the site. Then there's the artefacts to be measured and drawn. The finds have to be drawn as I can't lug all the actual objects back to Kuching. I'll keep the most interesting but sketches of the greater majority will have to suffice for much of our finds. What do you say?'

'I'd love it! It would be such a thrill to help. I can't make it here every day of course, but would three or four days a week be a reasonable commitment?'

'It would be fine. Let's go and have that tea and while we take it easy I'll show you what drawings I've done so far so that you can see what I require. Come on, the track down to the village is over here.'

Chapter 15

Sungei Kemudi, 1929

Because of an early-morning telephone call from Kenneth the Rajah was waiting for the Englishman's arrival that afternoon. As Kenneth ran up the grand entrance stairs Ali strode into view from the shadows of the opulent verandah.

'Good of you to come Kenneth, old man,' he said, shaking Kenneth's hand in welcome. 'We won't hang about here. My launch is waiting for us, so let's get on board. Come this way.'

He led Kenneth into the high-ceilinged hall and then out along a marble corridor to a door on the eastern side of the palace from which Kenneth could see the park and the river. A servant in slippers and dressed in tight concertinaed trousers and long silk coat buttoned to the throat, pale-pink turban upon his head, pushed up a parasol as the Rajah stepped into the blazing sunlight and kept pace with Ali as the two friends walked along the shell-grit path to the jetty. Kenneth provided his own shade with his solar topee placed firmly on his head.

'What a beautiful boat,' commented Kenneth as they arrived at the river.

'Elegant lines hasn't she? I'm very pleased with it. Only had it a month. Sayyid brought it up from the shipyard in Singapore as soon as the monsoon ceased.'

Sayyid, Kenneth surmised, was the unfriendly looking captain standing at the head of the gangway awaiting their arrival.

'Selamat djalan, Tuan,' said the man respectfully to Ali, bringing the palm of his right hand up and touching his forehead with his fingertips.

Ali acknowledged him and, taking Kenneth by the arm, led him along the narrow deck beside the spacious cabin with its large windows towards the stern. Here, two steps down, was an open deck which encompassed the beam of the vessel. Along both sides and across the stern, cushioned benches and two cane chairs provided seating. A canvas awning across the forepart of this space provided the ever-necessary shade from the equatorial sun and it was under it that Ali and Kenneth seated themselves. The captain gave the order to cast off and a crew of four or five uncouth-looking Malays untied the hawsers and shoved the launch away from the little wharf. Kenneth didn't like the look of them at all. A bunch of cut-throats, he thought to himself.

'Minta maaf, Tuan. Handa ka mana, Tuan?' asked Sayyid. 'Where would you like to go?'

'Upstream first, I think,' replied Ali. 'As far up as the Tanah.' He turned to Kenneth. 'I want to show you two things concerning my scheme. First, the river route to convince you that prying eyes will be few and far between, even today, let alone in the small hours of moonless nights. Then, second, to view the two places I feel are perfect for a discreet go-down in which to store our merchandise during its journey to market. The tide is still a little low for our purpose near the mouth of the Kemudi so we'll ignore the proper sequence of things and visit the site number two now. It will only take an hour in this and by then the estuarine places we're interested in will be navigable – the tide is on its way in. Sit back and enjoy the ride.'

As he finished speaking the launch surged forward and began to motor swiftly upstream. The river was about a hundred yards wide here and fringed with jungle on both banks. The sight was deceptive however, for only one or two hundred yards behind the wall of wild, rampant foliage, rubber plantations began their seriated acreages. This part of the river Kenneth vaguely knew from his two journeys on Straits Company steamers. Soon, on the starboard side, Tangga Gajah came into view. Moored to its tall piers was a rusty bulk-petrol barge, its contents being pumped up into wharf storage tanks; from Ali's launch Kenneth could hear the putt-puttering of the two-stroke pump at work. In the vaporous mid-afternoon heat the river port looked a rundown, sorry-looking place, the heat haze shimmering off its weathered corrugated-iron- clad buildings giving the collection an aura which sympathetically softened the utilitarian shapes of the settlement.

The launch quickly left Tangga Gajah behind as it continued its journey. The banks began to draw closer together and the Kemudi narrowed to about thirty yards in width. The forest looked lifeless as the miles passed.

'Nearly there, I would say,' said Ali as yet another bend sailed by them. 'I was up here only a fortnight ago. A large dead tree on the water's edge is the landmark for the mouth of the Tanah. Ah, there it is!' He pointed forward and over to the right.

A huge white and grey tree arched over all its neighbours, completely leafless and dry and bleached-looking as old bones. Strange fruit-like things were, however, hanging off its highest branches in their scores. Kenneth couldn't make out what they were until the launch was directly opposite them. It was a colony of flying foxes; dangling head-down by their feet, they were oblivious to the launch observing them as they slept the day through. Only when twilight fell would they stir themselves and prepare for another night of foraging in the forest.

The wall of jungle gave way for a stream some fifteen or so yards wide to flow into the Kemudi. The Tanah. Only a mile up it and Kenneth would be at the south-eastern boundary of Kuala Tanah Estate. The novelty of arriving at his estate from this unfamiliar direction captured his interest and he paid close attention as the launch, at diminished speed, made its way up the tributary. They disturbed a group of monkeys sitting on branches almost overhanging the water who had been nonchalantly stuffing leaves and flowers into their mouths until the launch startled them. They eyed the boat warily, the most cautious retreating into the deeper vegetation in preparation for flight if it should be necessary.

It wasn't. The launch continued on its course, and the jungle began to thin out to swamp, the banks starting to resemble the Tanah as Kenneth knew it from the estate – bamboos, palms, cyclads and wet-land rushes and sedges.

'This stretch of river is your estate, though I'll wager you've never been here,' said Ali, pointing to the right hand side of the stream. He called out a command and the launch slowed and made for the bank. 'It's here where I think you could contribute to our little scheme.'

The launch came to rest against a high part of the bank which was naturally clear of bush for three yards back from the river. Along with Ali and Kenneth some of the crew, armed with broad, razor-edged parangs, jumped on to the land and awaited further orders. Unlike the stretch of Tanah he was familiar with, Kenneth found the ground firm underfoot. He noticed that it could provide a reasonable foundation for a go-down. He looked around.

'I can see it's a suitable place in terms of access from the river, Ali,' he said, 'but what about from the other side; from my estate? I haven't a clue where we are though I can guess we're in the rough, south-east area which has never been developed into plantation. How do you propose to shift the stuff from here on to a track?'

'We're closer to your plantation areas than you think. Some of my fellows did a little reconnaisance when we discovered this eminently suitable bank two weeks ago. I hope you don't mind, but it was trespassing with your interests in mind I assure you.'

Kenneth laughed. 'You've got it all worked out, haven't you. Come on, show me.'

Ali gave a brief command to the men standing by and as they moved into the bush and scrub Ali said to Kenneth, 'Follow them, I'll wait here; you'll be back in ten minutes.'

Dodging around the palms and more substantial clumps of bamboo, the men dexterously hacked a trail with their parangs, Kenneth following behind. The land dipped a couple of feet and immediately became swampy. They squelched through this for several hundred yards, acquiring a couple of leeches apiece on their ankles before the land started to rise very gently again.

Kenneth realized that the piece of solid ground Ali's launch was tied against must become an island at times of flooding. The shallow slope tilted for several hundred yards before levelling off and was of a high enough elevation for Kenneth to get some bearings. They were standing on a ridge, really more an ancient muddy dune than anything more geologically significant, which sloped down into another boggy depression exactly like the one they had just traversed. Beyond that was another slope, this time with a scatter of rubber trees across it.

Ah ha, now I know where we are! he thought to himself. A driveable laterite track was in among the furthest trees. Ali had been correct in identifying this area as a usable route for the transshipment of the opium, and a very discreet one too. No one came down here; he himself visited this part of the estate rarely as it hadn't been tapped for years. Of course, with the slump, not a soul had any interest in this part of the estate. Nevertheless there was a track and, although he hadn't actually driven over it for at least a year, Kenneth guessed that it wouldn't take much to make it serviceable.

He turned to the men and said, 'Okay. We'll go back now,' and gestured in the direction from which they had come. In five minutes they were back at the launch.

'What do you think?' asked Ali who was seated in the stern of the launch. He rose and joined Kenneth on the bank.

'Very convenient for an enterprise of such a secret nature,' said Kenneth.

'First class, I'd say,' said Ali. 'Close to transport yet completely out of the way.'

'Tell me about the go-down you would erect here,' went on Kenneth.

'It wouldn't be very big; perhaps a shed ten by five yards in plan; panel walls, tin roof, with an atap covering to hide

228

it. Inside it will need shelving but the floor could remain dirt. While you were absent on your walk Sayyid and I looked for a suitable site and I think back from here some twenty or thirty yards would do. That would leave a thick screen of vegetation between it and the river.'

'Yes, it would fit there,' said Kenneth. 'Well, show me the other site, the one for the first go-down, I won't commit myself until I've seen everything, if you don't mind.'

'Of course not, dear boy, of course not. You've got a businesslike approach to the scheme which I appreciate.'

The trip downstream with the current was rapid. In half the time it took the launch to make its way up to the Tanah they were opposite Bukit Klang. The steep hill was beginning to cast a giant shadow across the Kemudi as the sun began its descent to the west. From low in the water its cliff-girt flanks looked impregnable.

'Been up to meet Manconi, the archaeologist?' asked Kenneth, scanning the ramparts.

'No,' replied Ali off-handedly. 'I've decided that this archaeology business isn't my concern, problems of protocol and all that really.'

'What do you mean?'

'Bukit Klang is on my neighbour's property and his and my family don't see eye to eye. I can't see Idris Hussein inviting me up to see the excavation, and I'm not going to express any great interest in it just so he can reap some satisfaction from thwarting my curiosity. Actually, to be honest, I'm not especially thrilled about ruins anyway. There's hundreds across Malaya so I don't know what's special about this one.' He turned to look back at the hill, now receding into the distance as the launch sped on. 'I suppose it has a rather gloomy and forbidding presence when viewed from the river however. Could that justify a dig I wonder?' He looked vaguely pensive for a moment, and then he went on. 'What is he like, this Manconi fellow?'

'I've really only met him briefly,' answered Kenneth, 'but he seems a decent-enough chap. I can't imagine I'd

have much in common with him, what with his being
a librarian and archaeologist, and me being a planter.
My wife Maeve finds him interesting because he's very
knowledgable about history and she likes that sort of
thing.'

'Is he to be at Bukit Klang for long?'

'I think until August or September.'

'In that case I'm bound to run across him. If it wasn't
for the fact that he is quartered at Bukit Klang village I'd
ask him over to the Istana for tiffin.'

The landscape was changing as they talked. The river
became greyer in colour and its banks were now several
hundred yards apart and, other than the odd coconut or
nipah palm, covered with mangrove forest. Occasionally
an iron pole with flaking paint advertising its presence
stood out from the water, navigation signals for the steamers, but unnecessary, with the tide well on its way in, for
a vessel with as shallow a draught as Ali's launch. The
sand bars they marked were well below the twin screws
of the boat.

About half an hour down from Bukit Klang the launch
angled in towards the northern bank. It had no real form
but rather was just a muddy slope creeping out from the
water. It looped in and out, here a miniature bay, there
a tiny headland, all supporting the ubiquitous mangrove.
Sometimes the Kemudi delved quite deeply into the low
forest and it was impossible for Kenneth to make out
whether it was a tributary he was looking at, or the
beginning of the Kemudi delta with its dozens of islands.
He didn't like the look of the mangroves. Their spindly
aerial roots linking branches directly to the mud and their
sombre foliage gave them a predatory, unnatural air. The
mood they conjured up wasn't helped when, before his
eyes, a log lying on the mud beneath the trees suddenly
metamorphosed into an eight-foot crocodile which moved
with surprising swiftness into the river and disappeared
beneath its murky surface.

'Did you see that! Christ, it gave me a fright!' he
exclaimed to Ali.

'One of our guardians, old man. The crocodiles are perfect protectors of our opium go-down. Who in their right mind would ever come snooping down here, eh?' He laughed. 'There's hundreds of them. That one was a youngster, some are twice as big; revolting brutes aren't they?'

The launch turned into one of the off-shoots of the river, a branch which was about twenty yards wide and meandered towards the north west. After navigating half a dozen loops the launch drifted to a halt in mid-stream, its motor idling. Kenneth estimated that the main channel must be only a couple of hundred yards away to their left. He couldn't see any permanently dry land anywhere about them; tide lines on the trunks of the mangroves indicated that at high tide even the highest mud banks would be under a foot of water.

'This is where the first go-down will be,' said Ali. 'I'm not going to build one but, instead, float one in, and ground it under the mangroves. That grove over there looks as good a camouflage as any.' He pointed to a place where the trees cantilevered over an indent in the mud bank. 'There's literally a hundred miles of these waterways' at the mouth of the Kemudi. Even if someone suspected something nefarious was going on, they wouldn't find it among all the possible hiding places. Another point too, the place will only be accessible about the time of high tide. Try finding this spot at low tide and the mud will prevent you from getting within fifty yards of it.'

'That I can believe,' said Kenneth, referring to Ali's first claim, 'but how do you find it again yourself, or the captain making the drop in the first place?'

'I rely on Sayyid. He knows how to navigate to here day or night. As to the incoming shipments, Sayyid will always rendezvous with them. They will simply come up river on a suitable nighttime tide – we're not far from the Straits here so navigation, although tricky, won't be problematical this close to deep water – and when they see some specially arranged lights, the code to be

231

arranged along with shipping deals weeks earlier, they stop. Immediately Sayyid and his assistants will off-load the cargo and while the steamer returns to the open sea, he will bring the stuff up to here. All very neat and tidy. It can sit here for as long as it likes. If any of us feel uneasy, well, we wait until such a feeling passes, and then Sayyid can move it up to the Tanah. Again, it can be stored until we know that it is safe to shift once again.

'The procedure is fool-proof, Kenneth. I've shown you the lie of the land today to set your mind at rest but you need never return here again. Your part of the business will be to oversee the security of the number two go-down and that means, really, that you just go about your affairs in a normal way on your estate and make sure no one starts trespassing on its more remote corners. Once a month perhaps you will have to direct a few lorries along your back roads to pick up the parcels, and that's it. All very neat and tidy, I'm sure you'll agree.'

'Yes, it does seem well thought out,' agreed Kenneth.

Ali gave Sayyid an order and the launch began its return trip up the river. The two men sat quietly, each seemingly occupied with his own thoughts. Ali, in fact, was watching his friend surreptitiously, monitoring his expression to see whether a few more words would be necessary to allay Kenneth's qualms. He decided not to break Kenneth's silence. Bukit Klang came into view and the launch glided under the precipitous cliffs towards the jetty.

'Well, what do you say, old man? Want to become a rich man?'

Kenneth didn't reply until he was standing on the wharf. He turned to Ali who had stepped alongside of him. 'I'll do it, Ali. It's bloody madness, but they're mad times so I'll do it.'

Ali clapped him on the shoulder. 'Jolly good, old man! I knew I could rely on you. Thanks for joining the show; we'll do well, just you wait and see! Come on, let's have tea at the Istana.'

Chapter 16

Selangor, 1929

Ali moved faster than Kenneth had expected. By the end of April the go-down at the distant edge of the estate had been built. One day Kenneth received a telephone call from Ali informing him of the presence of the shed, and Kenneth motored through the estate to have a look. It took him a good hour to establish just where along the Tanah boundary he was to cease driving and start walking, but eventually he felt sure enough of the topography to stop the Ford and stride off towards a vaguely familiar mound. He had guessed correctly. At the top of it he found the track which Ali's men had cut on that first waterborne visit and soon he came to the go-down. It was as Ali had planned it, a rough but completely functional shed. The door was not locked so Kenneth poked his head in to see the interior.

Windowless, it was dim but he could see sturdy shelves arranged along each wall, three to a side, the highest being about five feet above the pounded-earth floor. He walked along a zig-zag track to the river bank and looked back. Not a sign of a building could be seen, nor of the path leading to it, its entrance being cunningly located behind a small profusely foliaged tree which appeared to be in among all the other plants rather than actually in front of most of them. Kenneth was impressed with the care Ali's men had taken.

Since he had thrown in his hand with his friend's scheme he had suffered a few sleepless nights about his involvement. God knew he needed the money; everybody who had a rubber estate did these days. Maeve and he were living virtually hand to mouth. But so much money? He

233

had never got involved in anything shady in his life until now and, suddenly, here he was on the verge of becoming a big-time smuggler.

Not exactly small beer he pondered to himself anxiously. An old English adage came to mind which made him feel a little calmer: better to be hung for a sheep as a lamb. Yes, if he was going to break the law, it made sense to be bold and reap a decent profit for the risk rather than be timid; the consequences, after all, would be the same if he were caught. Which, he always decided when these thoughts bothered him, was extremely unlikely.

Kenneth, however, was not well cut out for a life of crime. One morning Ali telephoned and asked him over to the Istana to assist in organizing the first shipment of opium. Kenneth's heart sank at the news, and he immediately became agitated and depressed. Maeve, unaware as to the nature of the call, noticed only his unhappy mood. Thinking it was the old problem of the slump and their poverty, she had tried to comfort him.

'Don't get down in the dumps, dear,' she said. 'We're managing very well, I think. Is it the coolies' problems again?'

Out at the coolie lines the signs of quite serious hardship had become apparent. Pneumonia had struck a couple of families and some undernourished children had succumbed. Kenneth had taken their deaths badly even though it was beyond his means to alleviate any of their problems. They were all more or less in the same boat with each family, whether they be Indian or British, having to fend for themselves.

'No, no,' he said distractedly, 'it's nothing like that. I've just a few things on my mind that's all.' He paused, lost in his thoughts and then went on. 'Look, I need the car soon. Today's not one of your days you're helping Manconi, is it?'

'Yes. I was going over before lunch to complete some drawings. I thought today was one of the days you try to do some office work.'

'It can wait. Ali has got some agricultural co-operative

234

scheme he wants to talk to me about, so I really must get over there.'

'If it's the Rajah's you're going to, let's go together and I'll meet you at the dig when you've finished your business.'

'I don't want to hang around Bukit Klang waiting for you,' he said irritably. 'For all I know I may only be at Ali's for an hour. What will I do for the rest of the afternoon while you're drawing?'

'Come and keep me company,' she joked, but the flippancy in her voice drew no cheerful response from her husband. 'Cheer up, Kenneth. Look, complete your business, and as soon as you turn up at the dig, we'll leave. I don't have to stay all afternoon. I only do so because there's nothing especially pressing for me here until the evening meal needs preparing. I'll simply do as much as I can at the excavation, Nick doesn't expect me to work any more than I care to, so there's no problem.'

'Oh all right,' agreed Kenneth grumpily and stalked off to get ready.

His anxieties about the scheme were not diminished when he was shown into the Rajah's study by a footman. Ali was not alone. With him were Sayyid, whom Kenneth remembered from the launch trip three weeks ago, and a slender Chinese man whose small pox-scarred face and mean, pinched line of mouth made Kenneth inwardly shrivel. Sayyid looked like the pirate he undoubtedly was but this man looked even more malevolent.

'Kenneth, my good fellow,' called Ali, rising to his feet. 'I'd like to introduce you to Ha Hek, our man in Bangi. Sayyid you've already met.'

Ha Hek simply nodded at Kenneth. Sayyid touched his forehead and muttered, 'Selamat pagi – peace on the morning,' with a gravelly voice which sounded distinctly lacking in warmth. Kenneth nodded in return and sat down in the only vacant seat.

'Tea?' Ali inquired. On a large silver tray on a table next to him was the usual paraphernalia of tea things.

'Yes please.'

A servant came soundlessly forward, poured a cup, and handed it to Kenneth.

'I thought it appropriate that we four should meet at least once,' said Ali, addressing the group. 'It's a serious undertaking we are about to proceed with and I feel each of us can gain confidence in its being a successful enterprise by taking measure of each other here today. Ha Hek, Kenneth, is the purchaser of our shipments. It is he who will be totally responsible for taking the opium from the Tanah go-down to wherever it is consigned. My part of the business effectively ends when Sayyid and his men deposit the stuff in the go-down. Ha Hek, upon my receipt of the purchase money, will liaise with you and arrange a convenient time to pick the shipment up and it's your job to see the stuff off your property. Once it's on the open road, on its way to Bangi or whatever, it has nothing to do with us. It's all very simple and straightforward, as I think you'll all agree.'

Kenneth nodded, and then asked, 'The way it is planned, I won't actually know when there is opium in the go-down until Mr Ha contacts me, that's correct isn't it?'

'Yes,' replied Ali. 'Unless you pop in occasionally to check security; things like that. It would probably be a good idea to have a look every now and then just to make sure no one has been snooping around. But, in terms of procedure, you can put the whole business out of your mind until you hear from Ha Hek every month or so. Then you simply have to ensure that they can get quietly and unobtrusively into the estate to carry out their business.' He laughed. 'You know, make sure Ha Hek's lorries don't trundle past on the night you are holding a garden party, that sort of thing.'

Kenneth looked over to Ha Hek and inquired, 'How will you contact me?'

'I will telephone you, there is no other way,' the man replied in good English. Kenneth was surprised at the relatively unaccented intonation. 'Once I have been

236

informed that the opium is on your estate, I shall get in touch with you and arrange a meeting place at a safe time so that you can guide me and my men to the go-down. I perhaps will not always come, so on each shipment you must act as guide from the road to the go-down and return. That is all I require. The rest is, as his Excellency says, all my responsibility.'

'Good show, what,' interjected Ali. 'It will go as smoothly as clockwork. Now, you will be pleased to know that the first shipment is due very soon. I won't say when, not because I don't trust any of you gentlemen I earnestly assure you, but simply because I believe that the principle of not letting the left hand know what the right hand is doing is a sound one. Each of us has a vital role to play in making the venture a successful one and I feel, now that you have all met each other, that you can each go about your particular part of it confident that the others are doing their bit just as professionally as you yourself.'

The meeting broke up shortly afterwards and as Kenneth motored the short distance to Bukit Klang kampong where he would park the Ford and meet Maeve, he pondered the situation. Apart from Ali, he certainly didn't care for his partners in crime. The way things were organized he knew he would never see Sayyid again, but he had an on-going commitment with Ha Hek which he didn't relish at all. Night-time rendezvous and secret telephone calls with that sinister fellow and his hirelings weren't his idea of an evening out at all.

He drove into the village, somnolent in the early-afternoon heat, and left the motor car in the same place as he had on that first visit a month earlier. His arrival roused a couple of half-starved curs from their scavenging on a nearby refuse pit into a baying chorus which ceased instantly when half a coconut shell, flung by an unseen hand, whanged into the dirt next to one of them. Hairless tails between their scrawny haunches, the dogs slunk off. Kenneth made his way through the village and up the hill track to the archaeological site.

The place had changed considerably since his brief, earlier visit. Much of the top soil had been stripped from the terrace revealing a jumble of stone alignments and patches of various red, brown and ochre-coloured clays, all marked out within lines of cord pegged this way and that across the ground. He spotted Maeve at the far end under a palm-leaf lean-to shelter, bent over a folding table, sketching something on to a sheet of paper. Of Manconi there was no sign. In some of the work squares labourers were digging and scraping away. Maeve was so absorbed in her work that she was unaware of Kenneth's presence until he said hello right next to her.

'Oh, hello! You almost gave me a start,' she said.

She put her pencil down and stretched. Kenneth saw that she had been sketching decorative patterns from a collection of pottery sherds lying on the table.

'How was your meeting?'

'All right.'

'Is it time to go? I'll just go and tell Nick you're here – he's just over on the next terrace – and I'll pack up.'

Kenneth suddenly didn't feel in a great rush to return to Kuala Tanah. His mind kept turning over the morning's discussion and, more than anything else, he wanted to collect his thoughts. Here would be as good a place as any, he decided.

'No, don't,' he answered Maeve. 'I can see you are in the middle of a drawing. Why don't I have a look about, I shan't bother you or Manconi, and we can leave a little later. There's nothing at home to hurry back to.'

'Oh, thanks. I would like to do some more. Look,' she showed him her drawings, 'can you believe that these pots were made and decorated eight hundred years ago? Just think of all that history; of their manufacture in China; of being shipped out in great junks to the emporiums of Malaya and Sumatra and Java; of the hands that once touched these before they came into mine; it's almost eerie to actually become a part of this history too.'

Kenneth looked down at her, wide-eyed and excited with what she was involved in, and briefly felt a pang of envy at the pleasure Maeve was able to extract from some old broken bowls and dishes. They meant nothing to him and, despite Maeve's explanation, still looked nothing more than rubbish. He smiled at her affectionately.

'Where do you suggest I wander? A view would be nice to sit and look at while you work on. Is there a good spot with a shady tree conveniently at hand?'

'Just below us. Go through there,' she said pointing to the track connecting the two terraces at this level, 'and you'll find Nick. Ask him to show you the track to the Portuguese terrace. It has a great view upriver.'

'Okay, see you soon.'

Kenneth had a brief chat with Nick who was supervising operations on the audience hall site and then went down the steep path to the cliff-top terrace. He sat down under a huge-leafed pluang tree, and resting his back against the rough bark of its trunk, gazed out across the landscape. It was the vantage point from which Maeve and Nick had seen the launch and Kenneth too looked down at the vessel moored to its jetty, and, beyond, to the Kemudi flowing towards him out from the hazy backdrop of plantations. It was a good place to let his mind wander.

Although he had reconciled himself to the inherent dangers of the smuggling operation, today's meeting with the Chinese element of the project had unnerved him. Ha Hek was not a man he could ever feel comfortable with, everything about him suggested a hard-bitten criminal who, Kenneth was certain, would be utterly ruthless in protecting himself and his interests. Okay, so Kenneth himself was now moving in the same secretive environment by virtue of joining Ali's scheme to deprive the Selangor Government of a proportion of its taxes, but he hadn't anticipated having to deal with such thuggish characters.

As he sat there, he thought of the stories he had heard over the years about the Chinese vendettas waged in the densely settled tin-mining communities; of the bloody feuds that had periodically erupted between the secret societies set up by the different Chinese groups that found themselves living shoulder to shoulder on the Malay tin fields. There had been terrible murders and police acquaintances had, on occasion, described some horrific scenes they had investigated.

He remembered a story told over at Kelang by a police commissioner about an outbreak of violence near Kuala Lumpur back during the War. It ceased as swiftly as it had emerged, and when the police visited the lodge of one of the secret societies alleged to have been involved in the placement of a number of corpses about the landscape they found, on a table, the decapitated heads of all the society's officers, some nine or ten of them, with their dismembered hands neatly placed before each face. Of the rest of them – the bodies and limbs – they were never located, as also the perpetrators of the gruesome crime. Now he was involved with such people! The thought troubled him greatly.

He pondered about Ali's organisation of things. The Rajah, he began to realize, had removed himself from the immediacy of the smuggling by paying others to face the day-to-day risks. Of course, at the bottom line, he was as much involved as anyone, but he could sleep easily in his bed while Sayyid and his men off-loaded the opium in the crocodile-infested darkness of the Kemudi delta, and dream on as Kenneth led Ha Hek and his cut-throats through plantation and swamp at some godforsaken hour near midnight. Middlemen took those chances, which could for a number of reasons – accident, betrayal, stupidity – lead to being shot at by the Customs and Excise Department, or cut up by a parang-wielding thug who would think no more of killing Kenneth than he would an animal.

I need a middleman, thought Kenneth. If I can find someone to guide the Chinese across the plantation, someone I could completely trust, then my life is going to be easier.

He knew he could afford to pay someone, what with the amount Ali was going to give him as his share of the venture; the problem was, who?

Suddenly it came to him: Sue! His Chinese mistress of three years back before he married Maeve. Of course! Viewed simplistically it was the perfect solution. She was the one Chinese he could trust, and she was still living on the estate.

This latter point was in fact one that had weighed now and then on Kenneth's conscience since he had returned with Maeve. With their arrangement at an end Sue had quietly moved back to the little hidden bungalow she and Lalee shared along with several dependent relatives. Kenneth had discreetly visited her not long after he had returned from Britain to see what was happening at this unofficial household and to hear what plans Sue had for her future. She had none, being content to stay on where she was. She had a good roof over her head and she and Lalee had found ways to grow and barter enough of life's necessities to get by. There didn't, to Kenneth's mind, seem any reason why she should leave the estate: he was very fond of Sue and things would have continued between them had not his need for a wife sent him back home in 1927.

In the present economic slump the bungalow the Chinese women lived in would never be needed by Kuala Tanah Estate to accommodate staff so, all things being equal, they could stay on. And they did so. As to the matter of his conscience, Kenneth did feel somewhat uneasy having his ex-mistress living a quarter of a mile away from his and his wife's home; Maeve, he felt sure, would not like to know that the only other woman he had felt close to was still living on the estate. Maeve, of course, had no idea that such a person had been in Kenneth's past, and Kenneth, although he had occasionally run into Sue, had never been intimate with her since becoming the married manager. He felt he owed Sue at least the security of the home she had made for herself, and the situation, what with its combination of casual secrecy and happy ignorance, was a satisfactory one.

The more Kenneth thought about employing Sue to act as his intermediary, the more he liked the idea. For the first time in eighteen months he would pay her a visit, this evening, before sundown if he could arrange it without arousing Maeve's curiosity.

Suddenly he felt more at peace with himself than he had ever since Ali had proposed the smuggling enterprise. He had been tempted, and had fallen, really, against his better judgement. But now, he felt less of a pawn in the enterprise – an extremely well rewarded one, he conceded – and was taking charge of his part of the scheme of things. He refocused his attention on the landscape before him and enjoyed the view for another half hour before returning to the dig.

Maeve was still at her drawings when he stepped on to the terrace. Next to her, also seated on a folding camp stool, was Nick, talking to her while turning a sherd of porcelain over in his hands.

'Hello there,' Kenneth called as he approached.

'Hello. Enjoy the view?' replied Maeve.

'Quite spectacular. It's interesting to see the area from above for once.'

Maeve put down her pencil. 'Is it time to be going back to the estate?'

'When you're ready. How much do you have to do?' Kenneth looked at the page of drawings. They were beautifully done, cross-hatched and shaded carefully to bring out the particular details required by Nick – an imprint on the underside of the base of a bowl; a decorative motif around a jar lip; some distinctive geometric design work painted on an edge fragment of a plate.

'By jove, you're very good at this, old thing!' he exclaimed. 'I had no idea you could draw.'

'Very good, aren't they,' enjoined Nick. 'Absolutely first class for my study purposes. I don't know what I would have done without Maeve, my drawings are much sketchier.'

Maeve looked at her husband and at her friend with a happy smile on her face. 'Such compliments from the pair of you. I'm quite taken aback.'

Nick pulled out his pocket watch and looked at the time.

'Look, you two, don't rush off. Come and have tiffin with me. It's nearly four o'clock. We can go down to the kampong now. The food fare will be modest I'm afraid, Bukit Klang isn't exactly a gourmet's paradise but a decent cup of tea can be guaranteed. What do you say?'

Maeve looked at Kenneth; it was he, after all, who had originally not wanted to stay.

'It's very nice of you to offer,' he said to Nick. 'I could do with a cup and I'm sure Maeve will be delighted to linger a little longer near the dig. It's all I hear these days,' he joked. 'What is new at the dig, what wonderful new finds, and who might have left them. The way she goes on I'll end up being an expert myself without even wanting to.'

'Kenneth, you do exaggerate,' Maeve laughed in her own defence. 'An occasional word here or there perhaps, but I thought I was being very disciplined about trying not to bore you.'

'It doesn't bore me, dear. I think it's wonderful you've found an interest here.' He looked at Nick. 'You're not married, are you?'

Nick shook his head, and Kenneth continued: 'Well, it's very hard for the wives to feel at home in Selangor, or anywhere in the East I suppose. We men have our work to preoccupy us but it can be tough on the womenfolk, at home so much of the time. Maeve has done really well to make something of the place. Archaeology really isn't my cup of tea but I think it's good that it's Maeve's.'

'I do agree,' said Nick. 'Especially as I'm getting these excellent drawings because of her interest in Bukit Klang. And, talking of cups of tea, let's go and have ours. I'm beginning to feel quite parched.'

They made their way down to the village. It was now beginning to show a little more life than it had when Kenneth had driven into it a couple of hours earlier. Nick took them to his lodgings which was an odd-looking structure, half traditional kampong house, and half PWD

243

hut. The Public Works Department part of the building had been acquired on the completion of the wharf construction at Tangga Gajah more than thirty years earlier. Surplus to Government requirements it had been moved to the kampong where it had been elevated on to stilts and had added to it two extra rooms made of bamboo and atap fronds. Its incongruous appearance had mellowed over the years but its still singular presence had always made it stand out and, without anyone ever making a conscious decision about its status, it had become the guest house where visitors could be put up. When Nick had approached the chief, Idris Hussein, about living in Bukit Klang, the place was immediately where everyone thought he could live.

'It's a queer house,' said Nick to Kenneth as they approached – Maeve had, naturally, been there numerous times since she had started her voluntary work a month ago – 'but very comfortable. Come on up to the verandah and make yourselves comfortable. I'll get Mubin to bring out cool drinks for starters. Just excuse me for five minutes while I change.'

Maeve and Kenneth plonked themselves down in the ubiquitous cane chairs found on every white man's verandah in the East and idly gazed out across the village while they waited for Nick to return. A small boy, stark naked, crossed in front of where they sat, guiding with a long cane a flock of snow-white ducks who waddled purposefully towards a bamboo corral in among some low bushes out to their left. The houses were widely spaced apart and Nick's nearest neighbours were a good thirty yards away.

On the porches of a couple of homes people were sitting around gossiping, smoking fat banana-leaf cigarettes, and enjoying the antics of a baby in a mother's arms. The scent of wood smoke became noticeable as the evening cooking fires began to be lit. Nick's servant softly padded up to Maeve and Kenneth and placed a tall glass of lemon squash for each of them on the low table that stood between them. A few minutes later Nick joined them, dressed in loose-fitting flannels and a white, open- neck shirt.

'Tea will be here soon,' he said as he sat down in a vacant chair. 'Please excuse the absence of gin in your drinks, but by living here I have to observe Muslim custom and that means no alcohol. To be honest, it's not much of a sacrifice to have to make. Also it makes visits to Bangi Club and to planter friends' places all the more special, for it really is the excuse for a drink from my point of view.'

'God, I'd die without my daily whisky,' said Kenneth.

'Kenneth, a day or two's abstinence could only do you a world of good,' countered Maeve with a laugh. 'Really, I think if the white tuans of Malaya quit drinking for a week, half the distilleries in Scotland would go broke.'

As she spoke the verandah began to shake, at first fairly gently but then quite violently. Both she and Kenneth started and looked mutely at Nick, who wasn't at all perturbed at the motion, for an explanation.

'Blasted swine,' he said, getting to his feet. 'Hang on a tick, all will be peaceful again in a moment.' He ran down the steps and, picking up a length of bamboo, began prodding at something under the verandah. Disgruntled squeaks and snorts registered someone's displeasure at this attention. The rocking stopped as two massive, bristly, black pigs with bellies that sagged to the ground lurched out from beneath the house and ambled off with discontented grumbles to another set of building foundations. Nick threw down the stick and looked up at Maeve and Kenneth.

'The brutes use the piles of the house to scratch their bottoms. The first time it happened it was at night and I thought it was an earthquake. I flew out of the house in my sarong and inadvertently gave them about as big a fright as they had given me. The event made me an overnight sensation; I think it took about a week to live it down. It was really quite funny once I calmed down! The pigs must have thought so too because they keep coming back.' He ducked down to look under the house. 'Damned if I know what it is about this set of piles that they find so

245

satisfactory though. They come by at least once a night and give the place a thorough shaking.'

'What revolting-looking specimens of pig,' commented Maeve. 'However, when you compare them to the dogs, one would have to admit they are almost elegant. I've never seen such ill-cared-for dogs until I came to Selangor.' Out before them a couple of virtually hairless and scab-encrusted dogs sloped across the village grounds, on cue almost, to illustrate her point.

'I don't think the villagers see them as neglected. They're simply dogs who live in the village, no one owns them, no one likes them, they simply get by as best they can,' said Nick. 'Actually the horrible things do provide a service as far as the locals are concerned. Although everyone here is Muslim, there is still a strong undercurrent of the older religion within their present beliefs. Everyone believes in ghosts and demons still, and are convinced that they roam through the village at night seeking to invade the households and possess their sleeping occupants. One thing apparently prevents them from doing that and it's the incessant howling these brutes give voice to every night – and all night I might add. No evil spirit will come near the place because of the din, so the theory goes. For the first week I feel I hardly slept; they carry on all over the place until the cocks take over at dawn.'

He bent down and picked up his stick to warn an emaciated bitch with thin flapping teats which was nosing around. 'Manconi's patented pig and dog stick,' he joked as he swung the bamboo through the air to emphasize to the dog that it wasn't welcome. 'If I lose my job as archaeologist-archivist I'll market these instead.'

Amid laughter he rejoined Maeve and Kenneth on the verandah. Tiffin arrived shortly and the Cloustons enjoyed the impromptu social occasion greatly. Kenneth, Maeve quietly observed to herself, was enjoying himself. Over the past months he had remained moody and had not regained his old easy-going self. Although he had perhaps become a little less irritable, this morning's sulk notwithstanding, there were times where he would withdraw from Maeve and keep whatever was preoccupying him bottled up. Solicitous attempts to get him to talk about his problems only made him snap at her and Maeve, expecting the strain between them to disappear when things on the estate again became more economically viable, left him to his thoughts these days. Tonight was like old times, she thought to herself. Kenneth was light-hearted as they listened to Nick's tales of airforce life in the Middle East, and of some of the amusing stories that circulated about his employer, Sir Vyner Brooke and his penchant for the favours of the wives of his staff. However all too soon night had fallen and the frogs, cicadas and unnumbered night-time creatures sounded up their chorus. It was time Maeve and Kenneth departed.

'Cheerio,' called Nick after he had swung the crank handle for Kenneth and the Ford had puttered into life.

'Goodbye, thanks for tiffin,' replied Kenneth.

'Goodbye, I'll be back tomorrow,' said Maeve.

As they bounced along the track towards the main road Kenneth commented to Maeve, 'He seems a decent sort. Some of those stories were very funny, weren't they?' and he started laughing to himself at the memory of them.

'Yes, he's a nice man,' said Maeve. She put out her hand and lightly clasped her husband's arm and they motored home in companionable silence through the balmy Malayan night.

Chapter 17

Selangor, 1929

Kenneth didn't waste any time in seeing Sue. The next morning, on the pretext of visiting the coolie lines, he cut across the plantation to her and Lalee's bungalow. She was sitting on the steps sewing a hem of a skirt when he emerged from among the rubber trees and she was surprised to see him.

'Kenneth, why are you here? Is it bad news about the house, am I to leave?'

'No, no,' he reassured her, sitting near her but being circumspect about being too close to her, 'nothing like that. I have a business proposition which may in fact be good news. First though, is Lalee around?'

'No. Lalee moved to Seremban in the New Year. She has a new man to look after. A red-faced Tuan with lots of money but no wife.'

'Good, for what I have to tell you is for your ears only.' He went on to explain the part of the operation he was involved in, at the same time being careful to omit any mention of Ali and any of the circumstances that brought the opium to Kuala Tanah. Sue listened without interrupting him, nodding now and then to indicate that she understood what was involved. Her face remained impassive until he mentioned the sum of money he would pay her. A flash of interest suddenly lit up her eyes. Kenneth guessed that Ali had probably seen the same glint in his eyes when he had launched the idea to him two months ago.

'Well, what do you think?' he asked.

'I will do it for you, Kenneth, and I will do it for the one thousand dollars a month. I think it must

248

be dangerous for you to be offering me this amount however.'

'Not dangerous, just risky, like any high-earning business enterprise. It is illegal, I've explained all that, but other than crossing the Government, there is no physical harm you or I can come to. I want your help because I can rely on you. I need a trustworthy friend to deal with the Chinese businessmen involved in the scheme.'

He arranged that he would next see her when the transshipment was planned and left.

He hadn't been in his office for more than half an hour when the telephone jangled on the wall next to his desk. It was Ali.

'Can you come over right away, old chap? I've something important for you.'

'Yes, all right,' Kenneth looked at the clock on the wall. 9.15 a.m. 'I'll be there round about ten o'clock.'

He put the earpiece back in its cradle and rummaging for the car key in the desk drawer, wondered what it could be that Ali was impatient about.

At the Istana a servant took Kenneth into the study. Ali rose from where he had been seated at his mahogany roll-top desk and greeted Kenneth.

'This won't take a minute but I'm sure you'll feel the journey was worth making.' He pointed to a side table and said, 'This is yours, my friend.'

Kenneth looked and then did such a double-take at what he saw that Ali quietly laughed at the Englishman's response. There, in five neat stacks on the polished table top, were 10,000 dollars in Straits currency. Kenneth looked in stunned silence: it was more cash than he had ever before seen in one heap.

'Ten thousand dollars a month was our agreement. Ha Hek just paid me for the first shipment and here is your share of our profits. I had the sum made up in one hundred dollar notes in case the one thousand dollar bills were a bit conspicuous for a rubber planter to be paying his bar chits with; I hope it's all right with you.'

'Oh yes, very considerate of you,' mumbled Kenneth.

Christ! he thought to himself, what would he do with so much money? He could hardly open a bank account. He was going to have to get a safe or something which could be easily hidden in his office. Another thought occurred to him. If the money was here, so too must be the opium.

'I must say you move fast, Ali. At yesterday's meeting I assumed the first shipment must be a month away at least. Good grief, you must have had the stuff at Kuala Tanah Estate even as we talked.'

'Half of it was,' said Ali. 'Sayyid organized the rest of it last night. Ha Hek will pick it up this coming night. This being the first shipment he is anxious to recoup his outlay, this being some of it' – he pointed again to the piles of banknotes – 'as soon as possible. Possibly next time things may be a little slower. Personally I'd like it off my hands as rapidly as possible. As of this morning, it's yours and Ha Hek's responsibility. Tomorrow it will be just his. Also, just this once, he asked me to tell you that he will be expecting you at eleven o'clock this evening. He will be five hundred yards south of your estate driveway with transport ready. With future shipments he will deal with you directly. Your money can always be picked up here; I think that's best. You've been a visitor for so many years now that no one would ever think that you'll be leaving here with thousands of dollars in your jacket pocket every now and then.'

Kenneth stacked the bank notes up and Ali gave him a long banker's envelope in which to put them.

'I'd better get back, Ali, my wife expects to use the Ford later in the day. I suppose I'll get used to this double existence soon enough; smuggler once a month, under-employed planter for every other day; it's all rather strange right now.'

'You'll adjust, old chap, mark my words if you don't. When in doubt, count your savings. It always works! How about a game of billiards next week? After all this business scheming it really is time we got back to the important things in life.'

Kenneth had to laugh; good old Ali, he seemed every time to get things into a proper perspective.

'Good idea. See you later then.'

As he motored home Kenneth was constantly aware of the bulky envelope in his pocket. Ten thousand dollars for a couple of hours' work. He was ecstatic! He passed through Salak, briefly stopping to purchase a heavy duty tin box and a large padlock at the Chinese general store.

Back at the bungalow he helped Maeve fix a brunch. He was starving.

'Ali has invited me over for a billiards tournament this evening, Maeve. It's to be a late game so I won't leave until ten-ish. Don't wait up for me.'

Maeve looked at him over the rim of the teacup she was holding in two hands, elbows on the table. 'I wish some of your friends would come to terms with the fact that you're no longer a bachelor. I don't like spending my evenings alone.'

'You won't be alone. I'm not leaving till late.'

'It's the same thing. I have to go to bed alone, that's what I'm talking about too.'

'Well, look, I'm sorry. I hadn't realized it would annoy you, otherwise I would never have accepted the invitation. But I can't get out of it now, he is expecting me.'

Maeve pulled a face to show that although she was cross she did accept his apology.

'Well, you tell his Excellency that your wife also expects the pleasure of your company, especially in the middle of the night.'

When he had finished eating Kenneth made a quick excursion over to Sue's bungalow to arrange to meet her shortly after ten. She was to walk over to the driveway and wait for Kenneth, out of view of the bungalow, when he motored out to the main road.

She was there, as were Ha Hek and three cronies in a shabby three-ton Dodge truck at the roadside where they said they would be. Ha Hek came out of the shadows as Kenneth pulled up in front of the truck but immediately retreated when he saw Kenneth was not alone.

'Stay where you are, Clouston,' he said in a voice menacing in its tonelessness. 'Who is your friend?'

'It's okay,' replied Kenneth hoarsely. He was frightened at his reception. He explained Sue's presence and the trust he had in her. Soon the Chinaman cut him short and began to speak directly to Sue in Cantonese. Whatever passed between them appeared to satisfy him and, after some consultation between all the Chinese, Ha Hek reverted to English.

'Okay, we are to go now. Would you please lead the way. I shall follow without headlights.'

Kenneth and Sue didn't speak as they bumped through the plantation. He could sense the tension within her but could think of no words that would be appropriate to break the silence between them. As they drew closer to the river a light ground mist began to filter through the plantation, turning the expedition into a more unsettling, nerve-wracking experience than perhaps it would otherwise have been; its presence accentuating the mysterious nature of the journey. At last Kenneth reached the slope overlooking the route to the go-down. Here the mist was thicker, obscuring the nature of the terrain to about three feet above the ground.

It reminded Kenneth of a dry-ice effect he had seen at a pantomime in London half a lifetime ago, establishing in his imagination a weird sense of *déjà vu* which made him none the more comfortable about his present movements. Quickly he led the Chinese through the dew-dripping vegetation and ooze of the swamp to the go-down, each of the contingent having an electric torch to help guide their steps. Sue stayed up at the vehicles. Ha Hek produced a key for the large padlock, which hadn't been there when Kenneth paid his earlier visit, and unlocked the door.

Inside were about fifty square packages, wrapped in oiled paper and securely tied with coarse sisal rope. All were the same dimensions, about two feet along each measurement. Without further ado the men grabbed a package each and departed for the truck. Kenneth followed suit and also carried one back. In the dark the walk took longer than in daylight and by the time Kenneth reached the Dodge the weight of the opium was hurting his arms and hands. He pushed the package on to the deck of the truck and joined Sue in the Ford. It wasn't his job to manhandle this stuff, he thought to himself. He would simply wait until they were ready to leave and then complete his role as guide.

In the dim light he could see that Sue looked miserable.

'Cheer up, they won't be long. Twelve trips back and forth and the job is done,' he said gallantly and put a comforting arm around her shoulders. She leaned against him and seemed to relax a little. With his free hand Kenneth lit up a cigarette and prepared for a wait.

It took nearly three hours to load the truck. At 2.40 a.m. Ha Hek came over the Ford. Kenneth could smell the rank sweat of the man's exertions from several yards away. 'Show me the way out of here,' he demanded.

When they reached the main road Kenneth pulled over and the Dodge did the same. Ha Hek hopped out and without acknowledging Kenneth, had a conversation with Sue. By its flow Kenneth guessed it concerned future instructions for Sue whereby she could be contacted in ways which would leave him out. Sue kept nodding her head and making noises of affirmation as Ha Hek went on.

They left, still without headlights, and Kenneth drove Sue home.

At her steps he meant to pay her the one thousand dollars and say goodnight but when he pulled up she turned to him and said, 'Please stay a short while. I'm frightened.'

He knew she was, so he escorted her up the stairs and into the house. Sue lit a candle and motioned him to sit on a low bed against the wall, it being the main piece of furniture in the room. She sat next to him, and, letting out a deep sigh, rested her head against his shoulder.

'Kenneth, these are bad men. They are Triad — Thit Kuan, "Iron Society" — very bad to do business with them.'

'Look, before you say anything more, here's what you earned tonight, here!' He pulled out the ten 100 dollar notes that were hers and laid them on her lap. It was twelve times more than he had paid her to be his mistress. 'I know it's dangerous but look at the money! That's what you get for taking a risk.'

She started to cry quietly, releasing the bottled-up tension that had been welling up in her since the adventure had begun five hours earlier. Kenneth put his arms around her and held her to him, her tears wetting his shirt. Thoughts about Sue, memories he had thought he had long suppressed, pushed their way out of goodness knows where and into his consciousness. Sexual stirrings of an intensity that had evaded him for months with Maeve began to course through his veins. I must go, he thought to himself unconvincingly, I shouldn't be here.

'I want more than this,' Sue said, moving the money to the floor. She had felt his ambivalence and acted accordingly. She quickly unbuttoned her shirt and flung it away and, bare-breasted, hugged him close. Kenneth continued to hold her, his desire to leave melting as he touched her smooth skin. Sue slipped her hand in under his shirt and began to stroke his stomach. He sighed, and Sue withdrew her hand, only to place it lower down on his trousers. She could feel through the duck cotton that he was hard, and she began to squeeze him softly and rhythmically until he fell back on the bed, pulling her with him. Lust welled up in his body in a way it hadn't for a long time, and Sue, equally transformed, responded fiercely.

Kenneth didn't get home until nearly five o'clock. He didn't join Maeve in their bedroom but instead bunked down on the spare bed. He felt he needed to be alone after a night of such climactic events. Already it was beginning to resemble a sequence of dreams rather than fact and it was only the smell of Sue lingering on him and the tactile memories of her soft body that made it all unarguably real after all. Before he fell asleep he wondered why Sue could produce such a response in him when Maeve couldn't. He loved Maeve, he was sure of that: she was physically attractive, and enjoyed making love. In fact in their conjugal bed she enjoyed it more than he did. For months now she had initiated the cuddles and fooling about that led to sex; he personally would have been happy to pass on many of the nights.

But Sue tonight had brought all the excitement of making love, of indulging in the dark, warm pleasures of satisfying a lover. Perhaps, he concluded, Malaya had got under his skin far deeper than he had ever realized; that in the final analysis he preferred an Asian lover who encapsulated all the mystery and heat of the East in her very being, to an Englishwoman, fresh from a totally different environment. He would have to decide what to do about this new turn of events, but not right now.

The affair with Sue only complicated things for Kenneth. Already living a lie about his business dealings with Ali – he had invented a story about a joint horticultural venture between him and the Rajah in which they were experimenting with the growing and marketing of some new crops in order to justify his greater number of visits to the Istana, and to explain the presence of more cash around the house – he compounded his unease at being dishonest with Maeve by being unable to relinquish Sue. Despite his best intentions, he called at least once a week upon her and, to their mutual pleasure, consummated his yearnings.

Three weeks after the first shipment, a second cargo of opium was ready to be picked up at the go-down. The afternoon prior to Ha Hek's nocturnal visit, Kenneth went over the route from the main road to the go-down location with Sue until she had memorized it. When at last she could direct him to the spot where the vehicles parked without any prompting, Kenneth felt reassured that the night journey would go smoothly. He paid her in advance and stayed at home all evening.

In mid June there was a third load, and then another in the second week of July. Kenneth's secret cash box was beginning to resemble a scene from a train-robbery movie he and Maeve had watched one evening over at the Club, a stock Hollywood strongbox filled with stacks of high-denomination bank notes. Sometimes he looked at its contents and the sight filled him with dread; the stacks may have represented freedom from the constraints of the slump, but, more than that, they were a recurrent reminder of the danger he was in; money such as this was big trouble if not managed extremely carefully. It worried him constantly, and Maeve suffered accordingly.

Once evening she again broached the subject of Kenneth's apparent lack of interest in her.

'I'm sorry, old thing,' he replied, thinking fast but trying not to show it. 'It isn't personal. I still feel the same as I did two years ago when I first met you. I just can't shake off the damn slump feelings; they bother me all the time. You know, being the manager of nothing, receiving the pay of a junior office boy; pointless stupid stuff like that.'

'I thought I would have provided a pleasant distraction in that case,' complained Maeve. 'I'd like you to get your mind off what you have no control over and turn it on to us just sometimes. The world hasn't ended because of the slump, we've got to go on.'

'I am trying,' he replied. 'Perhaps there's something wrong with me, physically I mean. I'm a bit spiritless. Maybe a visit to the quack is in order.'

'Here's some spirit for you,' Maeve said. She got up from her chair and plonked herself down on his lap. 'Come on!' She playfully put her arms around his neck in a headlock and hugged him close. He returned the embrace but made no attempt to extend the intimacies even though Maeve's cleavage, four inches from his face, was the open invitation she intended it to be.

'Kenneth, you're a difficult case, no two ways about it,' she joked, finally releasing him. 'What is it?' she

256

continued, suddenly serious. 'It can't just be the slump, it has been going on so long our changed circumstances are normal now. And as regards money, since you've been working with the Rajah we've a little more, certainly enough to indulge in the occasional luxury again. Have you something on your mind about us? You used to be so ardent but nowadays I can't seem to stir you.'

Kenneth gave her a squeeze. 'I still love you,' and kissed her on the cheek. 'I suppose the slump has triggered off a number of things in my mind that never used to worry me – age, prospects, a future in Malaya, things like that. I'll get over it. Please try to put up with my moods. I know it's a lot to ask but I'm sure I'll be my old self again before too long.'

Maeve didn't think much of that explanation but let matters lie. There was no point, she decided, in trying to cajole him into a friendlier, more intimate frame of mind if he was going to keep balking at her suggestions for a more regular love-life. Try to let him be; she was certain that whatever was weighing him down, it must eventually pass.

The months passed, though the situation didn't alter for the better and, although she and Kenneth were company to each other, Maeve was sure her expectations for more attention were not unreasonable. It annoyed her to be preoccupied in such a way and she tried to entertain her thoughts with more uplifting topics. However one evening in August she witnessed something that made her focus even more on the subject of her husband's lacklustre marital efforts.

Kenneth was out somewhere in the Ford. The sun had set about an hour ago and Maeve was preparing the evening dinner to be ready upon his return. A green salad would be a nice side-plate she decided and, taking a torch she climbed down the back stairs of the bungalow to visit the small kitchen garden she had started back over near the acacia trees where it could get some shade. Here she had grown a small range of vegetables and herbs to complement what she could buy at the market at Salak.

Despite a couple of failures, such as tomatoes which blight got to every time, the garden had been productive and, also, fun to nurture.

The night was cloudless, and a near full moon rising over the rubber trees cast enough light to see by. Maeve felt it was a pity to spoil the atmosphere it created and switched off her torch. The warm air sang with cicadas and an intermittent clunky, bell-like sound indicated that some night-feeding birds were about. Maeve had never been able to discover the name of the birds but their curious song was part of the distinctive evening sounds that she had grown to associate with Kuala Tanah Estate. She walked slowly towards the garden, enjoying the time of evening, past some sheds and a little potting house used by the gardener. Off the path, over to her right some twenty yards away, was the cook's humble house where Pravan and Indra lived.

She was opposite their house when she heard a gasp followed by a low cry coming from the doorway which was open to the night. Maeve stopped. Again she heard it: a quiet indrawing of air from someone and then a moaning, crying sort of sound as if the person – and it sounded like a woman's voice – was in pain. She moved towards the door to see what was the matter; already she could make out Indra lying on the floor, her hands clasping her lower abdomen. She must be ill, thought Maeve. She hurried towards the entrance and, only a few yards away, was about to call out when belatedly she could finally see what was happening in the softly lit room. The shock of the scene froze her voice and she could only stare in stupefaction. Her feet seemed glued to the earth. Something in her prevented her from turning around and walking away.

It was Indra lying on the floor and she was not crying out in pain, but in pleasure. She lay there, her long black hair in sweeping disarray about her, eyes shut, lips apart. Maeve, now this close, could see that Indra's bodice was unbuttoned and her breasts spilled out, their large nipples black against the darkness of her shiny skin. Her sari was

258

bunched up about her waist and to Maeve's amazed sight it was not her belly she was clutching, but Pravan's head. Maeve was transfixed. Indra's legs were raised and apart; Pravan's shoulders butted up against the underside of her knees and thighs, his face up against her sex.

She held him by the back of his head, rocking it in a rhythm that elicited cries from her each time he did something down there with his tongue. The gasps came at quicker intervals, the two participants responding in mutual excitement as Indra became more and more frantic with passion. Suddenly Maeve saw her tighten her hold on her husband's head and push her pelvis forcefully against him, moaning briefly and uncontrollably as her thighs tightened and clamped around Pravan's ears. Pravan grasped her around her waist until the paroxysms faded and she went limp.

Go! Go! Maeve said to herself. They can't see you but they will if they get up. Go on, walk away! With half a mind she began to tiptoe backwards, carefully and silently moving away. Indra reached down and ruffled up Pravan's hair as he lay there, still prone, between her thighs. He pushed himself up and moved over Indra. Get out! a voice inside Maeve's mind ordered. But she stopped and continued to gape, half guilt-stricken at being a Peeping Tom but half fascinated with what she had witnessed. Indra directed her husband over her.

Maeve saw him in silhouette, her attention drawn to his tumid member large and potent against the yellow light of the room. He crouched over her and Indra wiggled along the floor to get completely beneath him. She took his penis between her fingertips and, as Pravan leaned forward, guided it into her mouth. Letting go, she lay there as Pravan made love between her lips.

Maeve felt weak at the knees; the scene was unprecedented in her imagination. Pravan moved faster then, as she goggled, Indra lifted a hand and grasped his testicles. He gasped, involuntarily arched his back and a series of shudders wracked his taut body. Maeve could see Indra's lips sealed around him and her throat gulping as she swallowed his seed. The voice in her head was imperative: go away! Yes she must. The lovers lay at each other's side; one or other must get up soon, perhaps to close the door they had inadvertently left open, though in normal circumstances no one would have seen them, for no one walked this way at night except for themselves. Go on, go! Maeve felt completely drained. All thoughts of the salad were forgotten. She dragged herself back to the bungalow and lay down on the bed, her senses on fire.

She had had no idea people made love in that manner. It was unbelievable! It was also stimulating. She knew from an all-too-familiar ache in her belly and breasts that some part of her being had been erotically moved by the embraces of the unsuspecting lovers. Her mind was in a turmoil of conflicting responses which ranged from disgust to titillation, all overlaid with a contempt for her own naivety in the ways of the world. The passion the two had expended amazed her; the pleasure and care each took in accommodating the other made her jealous.

It suddenly made her feel that her small predicament with Kenneth had taken on larger implications. Had Kenneth ever made her feel as Indra seemed to feel with Pravan ministering to her? She decided no, but that was only part of it; had she ever made herself feel that way; given rein totally to the erotic moments of her love life and allowed them to take her where they would? The answer, she knew, was no. The little difficulty of Kenneth's flagging interest suddenly seemed more complex than it had before and the evening suddenly seemed depressing. Everything in her experience told her that what she had witnessed was unnatural, yet the pleasure they generated for themselves contradicted such a conclusion. She hadn't thought to achieve such an abandonment to her passions until this evening.

As she lay there the same images of the dark bodies of Indra and Pravan returned again and again. How could she want him that way? This and other questions were pointless and rhetorical, and could not be answered because she had no experience in such things. This is no good, she said to herself, stupid thoughts going round and round and doing my mood no help at all. She felt grubby from her role as voyeur and decided to bathe before Kenneth returned. He shouldn't be long now, she thought, glancing at the bedside clock. Half an hour after he said he would be home, that's about usual. She took off her clothes and wrapping a sarong around herself, went to the bathroom.

Try as she might, during the ensuing weeks after she had seen Indra and Pravan, Maeve could not rid her mind of the images of the pair lost in their passion. Memories of Indra's expression as she had lain there while her husband performed haunted Maeve's ruminations about the past year in Selangor. Indra, it seemed to her, had been transported with pleasure by the entire act Maeve had covertly watched. That state of erotic bliss, she argued to herself, should be hers also: she had a husband and, even if she was uncertain what it was she wanted, for the wantonness of Indra simultaneously excited and horrified her, she knew she was missing out on something Kenneth could help her attain.

Except he wasn't interested, and she didn't know why.

Although he did his best to be solicitous to her, Maeve knew his lovemaking to be less than rapturous on the rare nights she managed to provoke some response out of him. His kisses were almost perfunctory and nowadays limited to her lips; her shoulders, breasts, hips, all wanting caresses, squeezes and lingering attentions of a willing mouth and gentle hands, were ignored as he fulfilled the basic requirements of the act. Too often as Maeve lay at his side fantasising on being taken as Indra had been taken by Pravan, wishing Kenneth to take her so passionately that she would be unable to resist whatever he wanted, her hints at lovemaking would be brushed aside by 'not really in the mood dear' or 'don't feel up to it' remarks.

Kenneth's rebuffs only heightened her frustration, and she made a determined effort to suppress them and get on with enjoying the other facets of her life. The archaeological dig particularly provided her with stimulation which, even if it wasn't of the sort that she daydreamed about so regularly with Kenneth in mind, was very enjoyable.

The unfolding of Bukit Klang's history had quietly continued during the months Maeve helped Nick. The shallow excavation pits of March were now four feet deep as layer after layer of the hill's ancient occupation were peeled back. A couple of squares had been abandoned of late as Nick moved part of his workforce down to the Portuguese-period terrace. It was now September and the dig had only a few more weeks to run before Nick would have to pack operations in. Maeve cheerfully whiled away her days with her drawings of pit cross-sections, floor plans, and representations of artefacts. Once in a while she changed jobs to pick up a trowel and help Nick excavate. It was work she enjoyed for it gave her the opportunity to get a bit of dirt under her fingernails and to feel the satisfaction of manual labour in her limbs.

It was in just this sort of state of mind that she worked away with Nick one afternoon, her hair tied back with a headscarf, cotton shirt sticking to her back, jodhpurs soiled at the knees and across the bottom from the brown soil at which they scraped. She was cleaning around a row of dressed stones which, judging by the shallow geometric frieze incised into them, looked to be the lower coursework of an interior wall of a building.

'Could you pass me that brush please, Nick?' She needed to sweep up a shovelful of crumbly clay. He gave no answer, and she looked up to see him so engrossed in his work that he hadn't heard her. He was on his knees several yards away, working on a similar section of wall. She refrained for a moment from repeating her request and instead quietly watched him. They were working in partial shade so he was hatless and without a shirt. He did his work swiftly and carefully, and Maeve could see the concentration he put into the task at hand in his eyes and expression. He stretched forward to reach for a trowel from a collection of tools lying scattered near him.

It must have been something in the way he moved for suddenly Maeve's heart gave a lurch, and a warm, undeniable ache of arousal spread out from the pit of her stomach to embrace her being. In that moment she suddenly had the memory of Pravan stretching over his wife slip into her thoughts. She looked at Nick's strong muscular arm reaching for the thing he needed, the stance emphasizing the lean fitness of his torso with its softly contoured bands of muscles making ridges across his chest and up around to his shoulder blades as he leaned forward on his knees, his stomach flat where it disappeared into the waistband of his trousers. Against her will, Maeve's imagination took over completely and for a few seconds her consciousness was monopolized by the picture of that strong body over her, his bare, hard stomach hovering, filling her field of vision as she took him in the way Indra had her man.

The vividness of the scene was astonishing and evaporated as instantly as it had materialized when Nick found what he was looking for and rocked back on to his haunches to begin work again. Maeve was amazed at herself and began to blush. She busied herself at the stone wall in order to distract herself, scratching away with her trowel and trying to think coherently about a totally different subject. But neither the forthcoming week's evening menus, nor reflections on Nick's lunchtime conversation about Portuguese imperial history did much to distract her from the erotic yearnings within her. She stood up to give her knees a break and discovered her knickers were damp with lust. Good grief, she though, this is embarrassing!

'Having a break?' inquired Nick.

'Just for a minute,' Maeve replied. She gazed at him as he looked up at her, thinking – but hoping no sign of such thoughts showed on her face – how attractive he was with his eyes warm and friendly, and with that slightly crooked smile on his lips which made the corners of his eyes crinkle in such an endearing way. Her heart began to pound again and she felt another gush of wetness. 'I'm just going to stretch my legs,' and she walked away.

Maeve was determined not to let these extraordinary sentiments alter her relationship with Nick. Although the die was cast as concerned her own emotions, and there probably wasn't a day on the dig when she didn't fantasise about being close to him, she had too much common sense to think there were any realistic implications in her daydreams. For a start she was married, and even if she and Kenneth were having rocky times right now, they would pass when life returned to normal in Selangor. Then there was the fact that she and Nick had become good friends over the past five months. During all this time spent working together there had never been the slightest intimation of an affair being possible. Nick had made it clear that he found her skills invaluable at the dig and that he found her amusing and intelligent. Now and then, he had sought advice from her – all, in sum, showing that he found her a good friend and colleague whom he greatly respected.

Concealing her newly acquired tenderness towards him Maeve continued to work at Bukit Klang as before. In her heart though, she was sad to think that the dig was soon to finish and Nick would return to Kuching. Daydreams aside, he had become a very dear person to her and his departure from Selangor would leave a large hole in her life.

Chapter 18

Bukit Klang, 1929

The excavation at Bukit Klang had only a fortnight to run when an important discovery was made. Maeve arrived one morning at the site to find an animated Nick shifting operations from the lower eastern terrace back up to one of the two terraces where he had first begun the excavation in May. No one had been working there for at least six or eight weeks and suddenly here was a team of labourers setting up a new square.

'Hello,' Maeve called as she approached her friend. 'What's all the activity about?'

'Hello Maeve. Something quite exceptional may have turned up. Come and have a look.'

She walked over to where he and the labourers were by the large mound of earth and rock which jutted out from the hillside and on to the terrace.

'Look at this.'

Maeve looked at where Nick was pointing. In among the general debris of the mound was a smooth-faced piece of rock. Peering closely she could see lettering of some form chiselled into it.

'When I first surveyed the hill I had a look at this place,' said Nick. 'I think I told you about it. Under this is a very large boulder. I scratched away at the earth in several places around its perimeter but only found featureless granite. The easiest explanation at the time was that it, along with all the smaller rocks, dirt and clay here, rolled down from above, but in last night's rain there was a little landslide and this morning a face of the boulder was washed clean of its covering. This is what we found. Very exciting! You can see that the line of script is pretty well parallel to the terrace so I think it's something to do with everything else on this level. It couldn't have rolled down the hill and ended up so precisely this way, I'm sure.'

'Do you know what it means?' asked Maeve excitedly. This sort of discovery was the very stuff of archaeology.

'Not a clue. There looks to be more of it either side of what the rain cleared and I had an exploratory scratch about first thing this morning, and there's at least another line below this. I've taken this crew' – he gestured at the workmen hammering in pegs and tying cords to grid up the area – 'off the terrace below in the hope of finding out about it all before the end of next week. It's somewhat frustrating to come across this when we have so little time left but I mustn't complain as it was fortuitous to find it at all.'

Maeve spent much of the afternoon watching progress. Uncovering the writing was proving to be very difficult. Other large stones lay against it and the clay and soil were hard-packed between and around these. In the heat of the middle hours of the day the workers grew more and more torpid. Finally Nick stopped the proceedings. He and Maeve sat in the shade nearby while Nick pondered his next move.

'First I'm going to have to erect some sort of shelter over it so that we can get at least some relief from the sun. Then I'm going to have to carefully consider a plan of action. If today is anything to go by I'm going to be lucky to get to the base of the thing before I leave.'

'Can't you extend your stay?' asked Maeve casually but with more than archaeological discoveries in her motives for enquiring.

'No such hope. I'm afraid I have to be back in Kuching by the first of October. Even with Rajah Brooke there's a limit to how much fieldwork I can take. I'm cutting it fine as it is for once I've stopped digging, all the stuff has to be packed up and moved to Tangga Gajah to catch the steamer. If I'm to get back in time, everything has to be on the wharf by the 20th.' He looked pensive. 'I think I should come back next year. The place deserves a second

266

season. Whether I can justify it to the Rajah is another matter however. My instincts tell me that inscription is too important just to walk away from and I'll impress that point on Sir Vyner.'

'Have such things been found before?'

'Extremely rarely, to the best of my memory,' replied Nick. 'There was an interesting Hindu shrine located eight years ago at Sungei Batu in Kedah which may have similarities to this, for the script here looks vaguely Sanskrit-like. Up there I think it was pretty conclusive that the site was an Indian trading station whereas here we've found nothing that doesn't fit with an early Islamic kingdom.' He thought for a moment and went on. 'There's the famous Singapore Rock, of course, perhaps this one is similar to that.'

'What is the Singapore Rock?'

'In the 1840s an inscribed boulder was uncovered on the foreshore of the harbour at the mouth of the Singapore River. Not far from where the Post Office is today. It was about the size of this one and covered with lines of words. Unbelievably, some army engineers of the time blew it to smithereens and only a couple of fragments survived and these are, I believe, now in the Calcutta Museum. It was never deciphered before its destruction and of course now only a little remains. These bits indicate that it was a proclamation of who ruled Singapore, what his antecedents were, and who were in vassalage to him. No date survives so it's a small tantalizing bit of history floating in time. The complete text would have been a very important piece of information. Such pointless stupid destruction.

'But to get back to the present; if this boulder here has the same sort of information on it, it's a major discovery. That's why I think, come what may, it must be excavated and the writing translated.'

The uncovering of the inscription moved slowly. At the end of the week Nick had ascertained that the words extended for six feet around the boulder and there were at least five lines.

'You know,' he said to Maeve one day, 'I'm beginning

to think this isn't an accidental burying of the writing. This debris is just too resistant to our efforts to have accumulated naturally. I haven't come across any other strata on the site which are anything like this. If we're looking at a deliberate attempt to hide the writing from view then I'm sure we're on to something very intriguing.'

'You'll be sorry to see Manconi leave next week, I imagine,' said Kenneth one evening. 'You've put in a lot of time up at the dig these past six months, you must almost be an archaeologist in your own right by now.'

'Yes, I will miss the interest of Bukit Klang; it's been a lot of fun,' said Maeve. 'As well as having been a fascinating experience helping on a dig, working over there has made me feel much more at home living in Malaya. Do you know what I mean? Instead of just being a settler on an alien landscape I feel a part of the life here now that I know something of its history. It's been a wonderful opportunity working with Nick.'

'I've thought you've settled in very well,' said Kenneth. 'Some of the new mems take forever to adjust to life here. They have my sympathy of course, it is a tough place in many ways, but I think it's wonderful the way you've found things to occupy you and made things happen. I haven't seen anyone else do it as well as you. How is the dig going by the way?'

Maeve told him about the discovery of a rock and its inscription.

'Nick says he may come back next year to uncover it completely. At the moment he doesn't know what it says, but it looks like an important find.'

'I must say it sounds more interesting than the broken plates,' said Kenneth, 'more like proper archaeology. Perhaps it says "take ten paces north, three skips to the east, and dig down six feet" whereupon you will find untold wealth in buried treasure.'

Maeve laughed. 'It would be marvellous, but I wouldn't count on it leading to an Aladdin's Cave. Nick thinks it may say who was the ruler of Bukit Klang. Not only that, but perhaps the first ruler; the writing is very unusual he says and is possibly early Islamic. It could be a commemorative stone, something which is a cross between an English foundation stone and a memorial for some important occasion, you know, like Nelson's Column.'

The opium business took Kenneth to Ali's the next day, so he drove over with Maeve to Bukit Klang. His friend was in a congenial frame of mind and after the usual transaction of funds had taken place in Ali's study, the Rajah suggested they have a game of billiards.

'Love to,' said Kenneth, feeling carefree with yet another weighty packet of Straits dollars in his jacket pocket. 'My wife is at the archaeological site and I know she would like to spend the afternoon there rather than have me drag her away.'

'You English are a strange breed at times,' mused Ali. 'Does it not trouble you that your wife is alone with another man, for what seems, or so I have surmised from our conversations, to be day after day? Are you not concerned that this archaeologist will take advantage of your wife in these circumstances?'

'Not with Nick Manconi,' said Kenneth. 'He is a good chap and very dedicated to his work. I've seen them together and believe me it is a mutual interest in the old rubbish strewn about that hill that gets them going. There's some fellows I wouldn't trust in a similar situation, but Manconi, he's an archaeologist, not a womaniser. I know the latter when I see one, I can tell you.'

Ali smiled and said no more.

As the game proceeded, Kenneth passed on to the Rajah what he had heard about the dig. When he started to tell of the boulder Maeve had been chatting about, Ali's noises of polite acknowledgement, indicating that he had been listening while playing his shots, ceased, and he looked over at Kenneth, sharp interest suddenly showing in his eyes.

'Tell me about this boulder again, I missed some of the details.'

Kenneth repeated what little he knew.

'Hmmmm, very interesting,' said Ali, bending down to pot a ball. 'You say this Manconi fellow is leaving soon.'

'Yes, next week.'

The game, and then another, continued. Kenneth, on a winning run, hadn't noticed the sombre, thoughtful mood that had slipped over his friend, but Ali very definitely had something on his mind. As soon as Kenneth had left, the Rajah rang for his secretary. Soon a stooped and elderly, scholarly man entered his study. Abang had been the personal secretary of Ali's father and, because of his prodigious knowledge of family matters and local politics, Ali had retained him after he had succeeded to the position of Rajah on his father's death. He had a great respect for the old man.

'Abang, I've just heard some news which may be ominous. An English friend of mine has told me about an inscribed boulder uncovered by the archaeologist up on the hill. Years ago I half recall you and Father discussing our ancestors' manoeuvres to maintain our paramountcy here in Sungei Kemudi. I've never troubled myself to find out the details of my illustrious forebears' conniving and scheming to keep what we have; for I too have had my own problems to solve on this score. I have succeeded but what is this inscription on the stone? Do you have any ideas? It sounds old and therefore steeped in tradition; could it be a threat to my position of Rajah? That is what I am wondering?'

Abang thought for a while, and then shook his head. 'I know nothing of this stone, but I think you show wisdom in being concerned about it. Perhaps if I could see it I would be able to tell you something.'

'Yes. The difficulty is that it is imperative I show not the slightest interest in it. I haven't visited Bukit Klang and to do so now would advertise to everyone that, at last, there's something up there worth seeing. It's the last thing I want to do.'

'You say the words are cut into the rock?' asked Abang.

'Apparently,' replied Ali.

'This evening as soon as the evening star shows itself send two of your servants up there with rice paper and charcoal and get them to make a rubbing of the inscription. That way I can study it safely when they return. If you send them to me now, I will show them exactly how to go about it.'

That evening Ali and Abang pored over a length of smudged paper that stretched across the study floor. Against the black streaks of the charcoal stood white rough-edged letters. Abang had glued the separate sheets together with starch paste to make a sequence of the lines so far uncovered. Both men looked serious.

'This is a very old script, your Excellency, dating right back to the very first of your royal forebears. I can only understand pieces of what is here and all indications are that the words extol the governing qualities, not, I'm afraid, of your royal line, but of another family's.'

'Whose?' asked Ali. 'Is it Idris Hussein's?'

'I think it very likely, your Excellency,' replied Abang quietly.

'Well, well, after all these centuries, this turns up,' mused Ali. 'It won't be a problem for long. I'll deal with it, and the Husseins will have to wait at least another six hundred years for some evidence or other to assert their claim.'

It was easier said than done however. At this time it would be disastrous to set an explosive off under the rock, this, decided Ali, being the only manageable way of dealing with the thing. Such an event would bring a police investigation to Bukit Klang, for explosives could only be used under licence and were generally restricted to the tin fields. A shipment of opium was due in a couple of days' time and the last thing he wanted was police on Bukit Klang and on the Kemudi river. Somehow, something very much more subtle would have to be done.

Then it occurred to him, do nothing! The dig had to

271

finish in two or three days' time and it was apparent from the fragment of inscription that Manconi was a long way from uncovering the rest. The man would leave and the inscription would stay. There was no urgency after all. He had only to keep calm and wait. After all no one else viewed the words as anything but curious and, perhaps, potentially interesting. Thanks to Abang's almost esoteric knowledge of such matters, only he and his secretary knew what a genuine threat a translation could be to his position. Wait; be patient; and deal with the boulder when it would be convenient to do so.

To be certain of his facts he telephoned Kenneth and casually asked when Nick Manconi was leaving Bukit Klang.

'Hold on, I'll ask Maeve.' A moment later he was back on the line. 'Are you there? Next Thursday.'

Ali hung the receiver up and felt things were under control. Next Thursday was less than a week away. All digging must stop very soon. He was right.

The following Monday saw the end of the excavation; the last days were to be devoted to packing. Maeve came over for a final day's work, which was, as it turned out, to take the same rubbings as Ali had surreptitiously acquired himself a few evenings earlier. Nick spent his time photographing the site.

Maeve was just taking a look at the boulder after completing her task when she heard Nick call her name. She turned around to see him snap her picture.

'The artist at work,' he said, winding on the film. 'That was for the record, now one for my album. Smile.'

She did, despite preferring not to smile on cue.

'Can I take one of you – for the record?'

'Sure.' He handed her the Rolleiflex and walked over to the boulder so as to include the discovery in the shot.

'Ready?' said Maeve, peering into the viewfinder. Oh, I'm going to miss you! she thought to herself. He stood there against the background of rock and tangled vegetation, eyes and lips smiling in an affectionate way at

272

her, the warm wind ruffling his hair as he waited for her to compose the picture. 'I'm taking it,' she continued, pressing the shutter lever as she uttered the word 'it'.

'Cheer up, Maeve, you're looking a bit down in the dumps,' he said as she handed back the camera.

'I've so enjoyed being an assistant to an archaeologist,' she said with a wistful smile. 'I can't help feel sad that it's over.'

'Perverse as it may sound, I'm glad you feel this way. It tells me you've enjoyed the dig as much as I have. I speak from experience when I say that there are always regrets when it comes to packing up a successful archaeological dig – the more successful the more melancholy you feel when it's over for the season. Don't get too down, Maeve, there will be more excavations in store for you. With your talents there will always be a place for you.

'I'll keep you in touch as to what is going to happen here. I'd like to think I'll be back next April and, all things being square with Sir Vyner, I will be.' He turned and looked around. 'Well, no use hanging round here. Bring your stuff and we'll begin packing it.'

Nick left after the usual boisterous send-off at the Bangi Club. In the six months he had been in the neighbourhood he had made many friends so the farewell social was well attended. In a short obligatory speech he thanked one and all for their kind invitations to their homes; he thanked the Club president for allowing him to become a temporary member of such an eminent establishment; and he particularly thanked Mrs Maeve Clouston for the invaluable help she had given on his archaeological site. When the clapping had subsided and the general conversation again rose to a raucous babble, Nick asked Kenneth if he minded if he asked Maeve for a dance.

'Of course you may ask,' interjected Maeve, giving Kenneth a nudge on the arm intended for all to see. 'I'd love to!' Kenneth laughed, happy to see Maeve enjoying herself and, turning back to the general conversation, didn't give her another thought until it was time to leave. Maeve, similarly preoccupied, but with entirely different thoughts, danced with Nick for the rest of the evening.

Chapter 19

Kuching, Sarawak, 1930

A deep rumbling detonation rolled across the river and reverberated through the town opposite. Nick half awoke from his sleep at the blast. He wasn't startled, for the same thing woke him every morning in Kuching. The noise was the time gun at Fort Margherita some four hundreds away from Nick's bungalow on the left bank of the Sarawak River. At 5.00 each morning it fired its charge into the dark new day and again at 8.00 every evening. Nick cocked an ear to assess the weather. Sure enough, the rain was drumming down on the split wooden shingles which roofed his home. He had fallen asleep to its sound the night before. As he lay there, only just awake, there was a rustle of the bed sheets and his lissome Dyak companion of the night slipped away and out from under the mosquito net to get dressed. The gun was allegedly fired at this particular hour to rouse the sleeping capital of Sarawak to another day's activity.

At five o'clock in the morning though, there was hardly a surge of activity in the dark streets on the other side of the river in response to the boom. Nick had commented years ago that in fact the time gun was only to remind the mistresses of the sleeping tuans across Kuching that daylight was coming and that it was the hour they should discreetly retire, under the cover of darkness, to their own homes. There was a faint click of the screen door to the verandah closing shut as his own concubine – a sixteen-year-old beauty with a copper skin and long, straight, jet-black hair – responded to the summons and went out.

Nick lay in bed dozing for another two hours. There

was no hurry to get up. It was in the middle of the north-east monsoon season and the long spell of rain each day slowed business to fit into the dry periods when one could get about without being drenched in seconds flat. When he finally roused himself it had stopped raining. He had breakfast on the verandah of his house, a small bungalow high on stilts built at the eastern edge of the royal grounds more or less half way between Rajah Brooke's Istana and Fort Margherita.

The former was a splendid colonial edifice of white concrete, colonnaded and decked with broad verandahs, and with a grey stone neo-Gothic tower in front. Fort Margherita was a small bastion with very unwarlike Tudor windows in its thick walls giving it a certain odd charm. Between the two symbols of royal power were sprinkled a number of small offices and bungalows across the manicured lawns, prettily hidden by large shady trees and shrubs. These were the homes and bureaux of the score or so of officials who were required to be close at hand to the Istana.

Nick looked down the sodden lawn to the river a hundred yards away as he sipped his third cup of tea. The river was brown-coloured and turgid from six weeks of monsoonal deluges. The bottom steps of the landing opposite were now five feet below its surface. If the sky stayed free of rain for another fifteen minutes he decided, he would cross over and pay a call on Edward Smith, the Curator at the Museum. Despite the rain-pregnant grey clouds just overhead which hid the surrounding hill tops and dragged ragged skeins of mist though their lower slopes he might be lucky and stay dry.

The clouds seemed to have lifted slightly as he set off for the landing, stout boots on his feet and a large black umbrella under his arm. In his right hand he held his brief-case. A tambang, rowed by a wizened Chinese ferryman, took him across the river to Kuching town. Striding through the river-bank bazaar he walked up the main street past the Courthouse, Post Office and St Thomas's Anglican Cathedral to the cheerfully disordered public gardens wherein stood the Sarawak Museum. The town's business was well underway and the streets were crowded with Malays, Chinese and Dyaks going about their various concerns. Kuching was a small place but cosmopolitan for all that.

'Morning, Manconi,' called an acquaintance about to enter the Post Office. Nick waved with his umbrella a greeting in return. As he passed the moss-encrusted stone wall to the grounds of St Thomas he noticed, seated in among the headstones, an artist, a European of about forty, sketching the Cathedral. He had to be a visitor as Nick knew, either by name or face, the sixty-odd white men who made up the European community in Kuching.

He breezed into the Museum and knocked on Edward Smith's office door, and in response to a distracted 'come in', entered.

The curator was studying a quantity of Iban artefacts spread out over a large table. The shelves lining the walls were weighed down with similar objects as well as various natural history specimens, either stuffed into a halfway animated state, or floating, prenatal-like, in jars of alcohol.

'Hello, Nick, how are you?' said the curator. 'Take a seat.' He removed a small stack of *Journals of the Royal Asiatic Society* from an aged leather-upholstered chair so that Nick could sit down.

They gossiped for a few moments about the Museum and of mutual colleagues and then got down to business, namely a discussion about Nick's finds at Bukit Klang. The drawings and artefacts had been at the Museum since late November and Nick, having made some preliminary conclusions about them to himself, was keen to hear what Smith had to say.

'It's a good range of artefacts you unearthed. They definitely indicate that Bukit Klang was quite an important Malay bastion. I've seen some of these decorative motifs before, you will be interested to hear.' Smith flipped through a number of foolscap sheets of cartridge paper until he found the designs he was talking about.

'These ones. They are fifteenth-century Ming. There's a bit of it around on some sites in Java and Dr van Callenfels – you know him? Works for the Nederlands East Indies Archaeological Service in Batavia – has traced it to some Chinese cargo manifestoes which date to 1415 or thereabouts. It's very good quality porcelain so only the wealthiest rulers of the period would have acquired sets of it. Nice for you that it has turned up in southern Selangor. It looks as if you have an important site on your hands. These are jolly good drawings by the way. Very clear.'

'I can't take the credit for them I'm afraid,' said Nick. 'My stuff is not that good. I had good luck in that the wife of one of the local planters was interested in archaeology and offered to help. She was very useful in lots of ways but it's her drawing talents that became indispensable.'

'That must have been a bit of a novelty, having a woman on the site. I hope,' he joked, 'that you always behaved like a gentleman.'

'To be honest, if she hadn't been married, I might not have. She was fun as well as useful to have on site, and rather nice looking into the bargain. Rest assured, however, I maintained a stiff upper lip of the best Rajah Brooke tradition when faced with such temptation.'

Edward Smith laughed. 'And when did a Rajah Brooke ever present a stiff upper lip at the sight of a pretty woman? Certainly old Sir Charles, and now Sir Vyner, have reputations for something going stiff in such circumstances but I believe it was never anything attached to their faces.'

They both chuckled at the joke. Edward then unrolled the rubbings of the writing on the boulder that Nick had to leave, excavation unfinished.

'Now this is very interesting. I've had a good search for anything like it in the literature and have come up with a few things. What success have you had at deciphering it?'

'It's too incomplete to make much sense of the thing, but at least I think I have the writing identified. It's a variant of Sanskrit which is found on monuments in some coastal archaeological sites in east Sumatra and, a bit more often, in west Java.'

'Yes, I'd come to that conclusion too,' said Edward.

'Right. Well, with assistance from some weighty Dutch tomes on ancient Javanese kingdoms I've translated what we have here on paper. It is a declaration of authority, by whom I still don't know because these lines are all his titles: "Lord of the Three Worlds", "direct descendant of Iskandar", you can imagine the sort of accolades – Master of all You Survey, Look and Tremble in his Shadow type of thing. I don't know if I told you, but the boulder stands near the audience hall I excavated which of course, now that I know something about the text, would be the appropriate place for it.

'I can just see it: while delegations of chiefs, ambassadors, traders, and suchlike hang around waiting for their moment with the King the only thing to read is this verbose declaration reminding them of his importance. The name of the King is presumably on the section of rock under the earth. The fact that the lettering is West Javan means the proclamation dates back to the very earliest converts to Islam in the region. Something in the vicinity of seven centuries old, that's what I'd say.'

He tapped the rubbing enthusiastically. 'I've simply got to have another season at the site. This stuff is too exciting to be left sitting in the ground.'

'Yes, I think you should. How will the Rajah take the suggestion? I know he likes to have you round Kuching to liven up his dinner parties now and then when they seem to be flagging, and I recently heard the Ranee lamenting about your prolonged absence last year.'

'Ah, to be indispensable in the social whirlwind of Kuching society! I'm flattered to hear I'm so valued,' said Nick. 'Seriously, though, I don't think the Rajah will mind. I think he will be as intrigued as we are about this inscription and will insist on the mystery being unravelled.'

The two men talked on for another hour or so about their respective fieldwork plans for the year. Edward was spending half the year, once the monsoon floods had subsided, up on the Balui River, living and studying the tribespeople of this remote region. The morning passed. Eventually Nick pulled out his watch and looked at the time.

'I must make tracks to the library. Look, why don't you call over for a drink later in the week? We could continue this conversation then.'

'Actually we may be able to do so sooner than that. Isn't tonight your usual night to be dining with the Rajah and Ranee?'

'Yes, each Tuesday while they're in residence. Why?'

'I and my house guest have received invitations to dinner this evening at the Istana. We'll all be at table together.'

'Good show. Who is your visitor by the way? Anyone I know?'

'A chap called Barton, Cranleigh Barton. He's an artist in watercolours. I met him in Singapore last August and since then he has been up the peninsula into Siam and French Indochina on a painting expedition. I gave him my card though I never really expected him to make it to Sarawak. He has, however. Interesting fellow, been to a lot of places and is very knowledgeable about history.'

'I think I passed him at work outside St Thomas's. There was a chap with a sketchbook there.'

'Bound to be Cranleigh. He was out on the town as soon as it stopped raining this morning.'

Nick stood up and stacked the drawings he had left with Edward into his briefcase. 'Well, old man, see you this evening,' and left the Museum.

The drawing room of the Istana was a jolly scene when Nick arrived. Not only were Edward and his guest there, but also the elderly Commissioner of Harbour Dues and Customs, his wife and a woman in her twenties whom he introduced as his niece, Cecilia. The six of them made small-talk over dry sherries, waiting for the inevitable boom of the time gun at 8.00 p.m. whereupon, with regal punctuality, the Brookes would join their guests. When they did, the diminutive Ranee came on the arm of a British Naval officer in tropical dress uniform (he must be on leave from Singapore, thought Nick to himself, for there were no warships at Kuching), and his Excellency the Rajah escorted a willowy young platinum blonde Nick had never seen before. Edward Smith caught Nick's eye. The Ranee and Rajah both had reputations for having flings with youthful members of the opposite sex and being none too discreet about it either. The Ranee was in her mid-forties, Sir Vyner at least a decade older.

Discarding their partners at the drinks table the royal couple did the rounds of their guests and, by the time the pleasantries were complete and everybody made to feel relaxed, the gong tinkled at the doorway to announce dinner.

It was an entertaining enough affair. Nick found he was placed at one end of the table opposite the naval officer. The Ranee sat between them and at his right was seated the Commissioner's niece, Cecilia. As the officer directed most of his attention to the Ranee, Nick found conversation more interesting with Cecilia and with Edward Smith and Cranleigh Barton who were at the centre opposite. They discovered that between the four of them they formed a widely travelled group, and the talk flowed readily and amusingly about various cities and countries they had visited. Now and then the Ranee and the officer joined in the general repartee and the Ranee told some stories about her father-in-law, Sir Charles Brooke, the somewhat eccentric Rajah who had ruled Sarawak for sixty years before her husband.

'He had some odd habits you know, which one was expected to accept as completely normal. You won't believe this but it's true, I assure you. When he held parties here, grim affairs I can tell you, he would, when nature called, relieve himself over the balcony rather than take the trouble to walk to the lavatory. Of course, everyone pretended it wasn't happening but then I put my foot in it one night. Oh dear!' She started to laugh. 'When I heard this sound of water falling on the flowers below I said in my ignorance, "listen, it's begun to rain!" You could have heard a pin drop in the ensuing silence, such general embarrassment! Didn't worry the old man though; he finished, buttoned himself up and, with a steely glare from that one eye of his to all and sundry, rejoined the group he was with. Extraordinary!'

When the women rose and left the men to their cigars and brandy, Nick had a chance to bring up the topic of a second archaeological dig at Bukit Klang. The Rajah was in a congenial mood, fuelled in part no doubt, thought Nick to himself, with anticipatory thoughts of the forthcoming romp with the platinum blonde.

'Certainly, Manconi,' he jovially agreed. 'You can have the field leave for something this important. Pleased to let you have it. I hear our Museum is beginning to make a name for itself in scholarly circles and discoveries of this sort will continue to enhance our reputation. So, go to it.'

They talked a little more about the dig and then the Rajah moved on to other topics. 'Barton.'

The artist turned to the Rajah.

'I want some pictures from you. Sylvia' – Sylvia was the Ranee – 'tells me you turn out a jolly fine watercolour. Now, I want some pictures of the Istana from the front lawn, of the Court House, the Museum and . . .'

Nick's attention drifted away from the Rajah's talk. His mind was still on the subject of Bukit Klang and as he thought about it he found his mind conjuring up images of Maeve. He mused over memories of her soft smiles and unselfconscious enthusiasm which were his lasting impressions of her. A good-natured soul, he thought to himself. He missed her conversation and insights more than he cared to reflect upon. He decided, now that he had permission to return to Selangor, to write to her and ask if she would lend a hand this time round too. His thoughts were interrupted by the Rajah.

'Time we joined the ladies.'

As events turned out, there was more to this statement

than at first met Nick's eye. Several hours later, after many glasses of champagne and some lively dancing to the royal gramophone, Nick found himself in bed at his own bungalow with Cecilia, the Commissioner's niece.

They lay entwined in a confusion of bed linen and pillows, Cecilia applying lascivious kisses to his lips as her arms held his head close. They had made love wholeheartedly, she ardently and furiously, Nick equally so until, despite her continued passion, he began to feel he had had enough. She detached one of her arms from around his neck and reached down to caress him. Slowly she managed to coax his flagging member into doing its duty and, rolling on top of Nick, fitted him into her. In the dim light of the lamp Nick watched her happy face, absorbed with inward pleasure as she quietly squirmed on him, and let her do as she pleased.

Although Cecilia bore little resemblance to Maeve, Nick's thoughts shifted to his friend back in Selangor. It was probably the similarity in their build that triggered off the thoughts again. Nick had now and then assessed Maeve's charms when she wasn't aware of his glances. He was after all flesh and blood, and she, he had concluded very early on, was an attractive woman. There had been times when he had quite envied Kenneth Clouston. Cecilia had nice breasts and though not, Nick thought, as large as Maeve's must be, big enough to put the memories of Maeve into an erotic reverie for the first time. He reached up and, with Maeve in mind, gently cupped them in his hands and lightly squeezed them.

'Oh, that's better!' sighed Cecilia. Nick's passion had returned with the contact and she felt him enlarge inside her. 'You like these do you?' she whispered, more to herself really than to Nick, and moved her shoulders so that her breasts rolled between his hands. 'That's perfect! Keep touching me, keep doing that.' He did, and continued to do so until finally she flopped down on him, satisfied and worn out. When she recovered she propped herself up on her elbows and looked down at him.

'That was lovely, darling. I must go, it must be ever so late.'

She put her dress on but left her shoes off. Her underthings she crumpled into a tight ball and stuffed in her evening bag.

'I'll see you across to your house,' said Nick pulling on his trousers and grabbing a shirt from the back of a chair. The Commissioner lived half a mile away in a large bungalow up behind the Istana. They could walk across the lawns to it.

'Thank you.'

With a torch to light their way they walked barefoot across the lawn, their steps leaving dark, flattened patches on the damp grass. A few lights shone from across the river but all else was a velvety black. Nick followed his own footsteps back five minutes later. The evening with Cecilia had been fun but Nick felt a little out of sorts with himself; something didn't feel good within but he was having difficulty in pinning his discontent down to a particular cause. He wasn't sleepy, so he lit some lamps in the bungalow and rummaged through the papers and letters on his desk until he found a packet of photographs. 'Bukit Klang' was pencilled in large letters across the flap. He quickly sorted through them until he found what he was looking for.

The photograph was of Maeve, smiling warmly and bright-eyed at him. In the background, slightly out of focus, was the boulder with its inscription. He looked at the picture. She looked so pretty with her hair brushed back from her forehead, her dark, arching eyebrows defining her features and, as he had remembered so clearly earlier on, her sweet friendly smile. Yes, he thought to himself, she is a lovely person.

Taking the photograph with him, he walked over and put a record on the gramophone and sat down in a cane armchair to study it further. The record was from a boxed collection of Mozart opera arias. As Nick sat there in the dark early morning of Kuching he let the music wash over him, Maeve's picture before him. The music was soft and poignant, haunting oboes and clarinets complementing Caruso's controlled, beautiful tenor as he sang of Tamino's love for Pamina. Nick knew the opera; it was *The Magic Flute*. Tamino would be gazing at the enchanted picture of his love, placed in his hands by the Queen of the Night as he sang from his soul. The voice of Caruso filled Nick's mind.

> Dies Bildnis ist bezaubernd schön,
> Wie noch kein Auge je geseh'n!
> Ich fühl'es, ich fuhl'es,
> Wie dies Götterbild mein Herz mit
> neuer Regung füllt.
> Dies Etwas kann ich zwar nicht nennen
> doch fühl ichs hier wie Feuer brennen.

It fitted his mood perfectly.

Chapter 20

Selangor, 1930

'Clouston,' called a voice from a table near the verandah of the Selangor Club. 'Come over here, old man, and join us!'

Kenneth looked to where the voice came from but as the group were back-lit by the blazing white sun of the afternoon shining on the cricket pitch beyond them, he couldn't at first identify who was greeting him. He walked towards them and at last recognized him.

'Reggie Wynd! Well, I'll be damned! How are you, old man!' He wrung the man's hand. 'I haven't seen you for ages, how are you?'

'In the pink, old boy. Might have put on a bit round the middle,' he patted his drinker's paunch, 'but that's an occupational hazard, the White Man's Burden eh, what! My goodness, you're looking well, hardly seem a day older than the last time I saw you which must be at least a couple of years ago. It must be that new wife of yours, eh. Now a drink for you. You will join us, won't you?'

'Delighted.'

Kenneth sat down. Reggie was with two other men. Kenneth was introduced to them.

'Gentlemen, this is Kenneth Clouston, a friend of mine from the old days in Seremban when he and I were younger and less wise than we are today. This is Cedric Clarke' – Kenneth shook hands with an unfriendly, hatchet-faced man and hair brushed fiercely back – 'and Bruce Elleslie.' Kenneth leaned over and shook the damp hand of an overweight, pasty-faced man with a ginger moustache.

'Kenneth is a planter down on the Kemudi,' Reggie

went on by way of explanation to his friends, 'and Clarke and Elleslie are in the police force, inspectors both of 'em.'

'How interesting,' said Kenneth. 'Ah, thank you.' His whisky had arrived.

'What brings you to Kuala Lumpur, old man?' asked Reggie after they had raised their glasses to each other's health.

'A bit of post-monsoon fun I suppose. My wife wanted to do some shopping, have a gay time at the theatre and that sort of thing, and I thought I could look up some friends. Didn't think I'd run into you though. I'd completely forgotten you'd been transferred.'

'How are things with you? I hear there's virtually no rubber business these days. Quite a number of the old crowd at Seremban have moved on; not a bean in rubber they said.'

'It's pretty bad all right,' replied Kenneth. 'I've still got my estate, the company wound down production and things are just ticking over. The plan made sense back at the beginning of the slump in 1928 but I'm now wondering if the industry will ever get back on its feet what with that share market crash in New York last October. Now everything seems to be crumbling and businesses are being forced to cut back. A world-wide depression is what it's about I'm told.'

'Yes,' said Clarke. 'I think the only growth industry in Selangor in 1930 is crime.'

'Really?' asked Reggie. 'You and your lads are busy these days then?'

'Worst I've known in twenty years of police work,' said Clarke. 'When hard economic times come that's when society starts to crack at the seams.'

The two police inspectors warmed to their subject and, fortified with a few more stengahs, began to tell of the breadth and the scale of crime in Kuala Lumpur. They were not the sort of stories Kenneth heard down at Bangi so he listened with great interest to the tales of robbery, assault, misappropriation and murder the officers described.

'Now domestic violence is a new problem that's coming to the attention of the police,' went on Elleslie. 'Now that money is hard to come by people are being forced to stay home instead of going out. Hanging around the house, the husband and the wife get on each other's nerves and quite often one will take a swing at the other. We've had a few mems charging their husbands with assault this year, and one gentleman who had his head stoved in with a bedside lamp wanted to book his wife but decided not to when a couple of lads started smirking as he started to go into details. Decided he'd look even more of a fool once it made trial.'

Kenneth bought the next round. 'Fascinating stories. What is the biggest crime you've had to handle?'

'Hmmmm. Difficult one to answer. A couple of years ago there was some sort of religious conflict among the Tamils in northern Selangor which manifested itself in the shape of some rather nasty murders as each faction got stuck into the other. After we finally isolated the ringleaders and hanged three of them things quietened down.' Elleslie took a swig from his drink and searched his memory for other great challenges to the peace and order of Selangor. 'There's a major investigation underway at the moment. Nothing gruesome about it, at least not so far, but it's a tough nut to crack.'

'What is it about?' asked Reggie.

'Keep it to yourselves, we're not supposed to discuss cases we're working on, but you're white men. Some enterprising gang have been depriving the Customs Department of millions of dollars of duty on opium. The opium revenue dropped by a quarter last year, a big loss by anyone's calculations. As a quarter of the Chinese miners didn't suddenly drop dead, or, as our investigations revealed, stop smoking the stuff, the obvious conclusion was that they must be buying smuggled opium. If offered at a lower price than the government-approved shops can sell it they would naturally buy elsewhere. And they have. Through Chinese informers we've managed to purchase some blocks of the stuff and, sure enough, it's without government stamps. The word is out from the Commissioner of Customs and the Resident's Secretary himself that we've got to stop the flow. Easier said than done though. We've got more men on this than we've allocated for a single case in years and there hasn't been much joy so far.'

Listening to this story Kenneth's pulse rate quickened and he felt sick. Jesus, what have I got myself into? he wondered. By the amount of money Elleslie had mentioned as being involved, Kenneth knew that the dent in the duty collected by the Selangor Customs and Excise Department couldn't be because of their little enterprise. It was the seriousness with which the police inspector viewed the crime of smuggling that made him inwardly agitated.

He made an effort to get his nerves under control and asked, 'How come it is so difficult to tackle?'

'The business caught us by surprise so we weren't geared up to combat it. Up until May last year opium smuggling simply wasn't a big problem in Selangor. The customs lads at Port Swettenham, Port Dickson, Penang, and so forth would find the odd block of the stuff but nothing suggesting organized crime. Then, out of the blue last May, there were hundreds and hundreds of pounds of the stuff around and the flow hasn't dried up since. We've organized ourselves quite a bit since, and now have good security at the ports. All that has shown, however, is that the stuff isn't coming into Selangor in the conventional way. We're going to have to look elsewhere.'

'So you say there was no opium smuggling before May 1929?' asked Kenneth. This can't be right, he said to himself, May is when we started and our shipments aren't worth millions. Or are they? He felt very sick at the implications of this last thought.

'That's right. Now my theory is that we're dealing with an international gang with a lot of experience and a lot of connections. We don't have to look far for the distribution network within Selangor, any one of a score of secret societies could do it, but damned if we can put our finger on the outside agents.' Elleslie took another drink from his glass and emptied it. 'We will get to the bottom of it, always do, but it's a bit of a job.'

Kenneth distractedly ordered more whiskies all round. He was horrified and angry at what he had just learned. It was their opium the police inspector was talking about and there were no two ways about it, he was in serious trouble. And all for 10,000 dollars a month! Suddenly that enormous sum paled into insignificance against the millions Ali was making. The bastard! The rotten, conniving bastard! I've been played for a fool, right from the outset! He vowed then and there that he would see Ali tomorrow and have it out with him. His part in the enterprise was over and he would tell Ali so in no certain terms.

The four men continued to sit around telling stories and discussing things. Kenneth would have liked to have left but as he had arranged to meet Maeve here he would have to stay put. Yet another round of drinks were ordered and Kenneth felt woozy in the head. At last he heard Maeve call hello to him and, swivelling in his chair, he saw her approaching.

The four men stood as she arrived at the table and Kenneth did the introductions.

'Like a drink, dear?' Kenneth asked when they had all sat again.

'Just a lemon soda, please, no gin.'

Kenneth signalled to the drinks waiter nearby and gave the order, adding to it four more stengahs.

'Oh, it's good to get off my feet! I've had a lovely time in Java Street' – this was the principal shopping street in Kuala Lumpur – 'and bought some super things.' Kenneth noticed that she was in an outfit she had ordered to be made yesterday at a tailor's in Petalling Street. It suited her well.   'Have you been doing the shops, Mrs Clouston?' asked Reggie,

She smiled. 'One doesn't come to Kuala Lumpur not to shop. This is only my third visit in two and a half years so I make sure I enjoy it.'

'Clouston,' continued Reggie. 'I thought it was desperate times in rubber. Seeing you next to your charming wife you look positively prosperous.'

Kenneth tried to maintain what was obviously meant to be a joke. 'It all goes to Maeve, old man. Anything to keep a woman happy, you know.'

'Oh Kenneth, you do exaggerate!' replied Maeve. 'They are terrible times, but Kenneth is involved in a horticultural project with Rajah Ibrahim u'd-din and we're making ends meet again.'

'That's showing some initiative, old boy,' said Reggie. 'It's good to hear that you're not taking the slump lying down. British pluck and enterprise, eh. Good for you.'

Maeve looked at her wristwatch. 'Kenneth, we should get going. I've got tickets at the Hippodrome for tonight's show so I'd like to have a rest at the hotel before we go out for dinner.'

They left.

'Rather a lot of money for a destitute planter, don't you think?' remarked Inspector Elleslie laconically to his colleague when Reggie Wynd was not listening.

'Just what I was thinking,' murmured Clarke.

For the rest of their stay in Kuala Lumpur Kenneth was withdrawn and untalkative. Eventually on their journey south to the estate Maeve lost all patience with her husband.

'I'm sick of your moods, Kenneth, I really am!' she expostulated angrily. 'What is it that's eating you? You've been going steadily downhill for over a year now and I'm fed up. Anyway, it's not just you going downhill, you're taking me with you.' He remained silent. 'Come on, I want to have a serious talk with you.'

'If you must know,' he burst forth, 'I'm sick of this bloody country, with its climate, and with the people in it! I want to leave, never see Selangor again in my life. But I can't, can I? I'm trapped here by the slump and the depression. I'm utterly sick of it all!'

'That includes me too, does it?'

He looked at her and then softened. 'No, Maeve, it doesn't include you. I'm sorry you have to live with me in this state.'

'So am I,' she retorted emphatically. 'The Kenneth Clouston I married back in 1927 is becoming a faded memory. You're changing and it's not into someone finer than that person I married back in London. If it's Malaya that's doing this to you, then by all means let's get out. With the Kenneth of old I could be happy anywhere.

'We could go to lots of places. You could make a go of it elsewhere, just like you have here. As your friend Reggie said at the Club, you've managed to find something with your friend the Rajah when many others felt they had no alternative but to pack up and leave. Well, with that sort of initiative you could find a niche in another country which didn't get you so depressed as Selangor does.

'But do buck up, Kenneth. I've really had enough of you being moody and no fun at all. We used to have a lot of good times. Nowadays, just when I think it's like the earlier times and we're enjoying each other, crash! Into one of your moods you suddenly descend. It's awful! I feel lonely and unwanted, and wonder why I'm here at all!'

Kenneth looked miserable as he continued to drive. What could he say? Maeve knew nothing of the real events behind his misery. The lies he had woven to protect her from discovering the truth were becoming more and more sordid as the months passed and, rather than keeping things simple and straightforward, had in fact compounded his problems. Christ, the way things were heading Maeve might leave him. He hadn't planned it this way at all.

'Look,' he said desperately, 'I'll make a real effort to pull myself together, I promise.'

'Starting now.'

'Phew, that's a tall order. But okay, starting now.'

They found a mutually interesting topic and began chatting. The miles rolled by and Kenneth found his spirits rising as he listened to Maeve talking away. Tomorrow, he decided, he would visit Ali and withdraw from the enterprise. In his secret strongbox he had something like 150,000 Straits dollars, a fortune in these troubled times, and that was reward enough for the year of risks.

The next day in the Rajah's study at the Istana Kenneth informed Ali of his decision.

'I'm afraid you can't pull out just like that, old man,' said Ali, smiling at Kenneth.

'I have to, Ali. The whole thing is too nerve-racking for me. I'm cracking up and it's noticeable. My wife, who doesn't know a thing about what we're into, is very worried about the state I'm in. We're having a rough patch because of it all. I can't tell her what's on my mind, and she can't see anything so terrible in my life that could warrant the mess I'm in. She thinks it might be her not being wanted, stuff like that, and, all in all, things are getting bad for me. If I get out of the smuggling business, my problems will disappear.'

'No, it's out of the question. There're the others in the enterprise you must consider. You, my friend, are a link in a chain. To break it means it is, from that time forward, useless.'

'I was in Kuala Lumpur these past few days and heard from a couple of police acquaintances that there's a major investigation underway to nab the smugglers. This business of yours has got under the skin of some very important people up there. From what I could glean from our discussion they are not mucking around; they sounded confident that they would eventually arrest those involved. Far too deep water for me to want to stay around, Ali, I want to get out as of today.'

'Kenneth, it's been deep water from the moment you agreed to join us. And as for the police, why it's their job to appear confident when talking of the curbing of crime. I am certain, absolutely certain, that they haven't a clue as to who is behind the opium smuggling. I repeat again, you cannot leave our little conspiracy at this time. I really think we should talk about something else.' Ali's smile was becoming somewhat fixed as he said this.

'Damn it! Who are you to tell me I can't pull out? I came over here to tell you, not ask!' Kenneth lost his temper. 'I don't want the strain of the whole secret business in my life any more, and that's an end to it.' He paused, red-faced, and then got launched again. 'Besides, I also learned in Kuala Lumpur that what I thought was a gentlemen's arrangement between us, is not so pukka sahib after all.'

'What on earth are you babbling about, old man?'

'I'm babbling on about the fact that for every 10,000 dollars I earn you receive a million, that's what I'm talking about!'

'Your sums are a little exaggerated but that is beside the point. It is absolutely none of your business as to what I extract from the enterprise. I recall clearly the delight with which you accepted 10,000 dollars as your part of every shipment. I would advise you to remain delighted and to immediately cease taking an interest in others' affairs.'

'I'll burn the bloody go-down to the ground on my estate. That will put a spike in the works. I'm out and that's that.'

The Rajah sat himself at his desk and unlocked a slender drawer, removing from it a brown envelope. He tossed it to Kenneth.

'You can keep these, I have more.' Kenneth looked at him questioningly. 'Go on, open the envelope.'

To his mortification, inside were half a dozen very clear photographs of himself and Sue cavorting nude on the ground. There was no mistaking who were pictured, or what was being done.

'You bastard!' he said venomously to Ali.

He remembered the day. He and Sue had gone to the go-down at Sue's request. She had felt unsure of some of the twists and turns of the route that first time she had led Ha Hek there without Kenneth's assistance, and had asked him to go over it again the next day. Once in the vicinity of the place she had become amorous – Kenneth recalled being surprised at the time – and had been so sexily insistent that he had submitted to her attentions then and there. Some of the more interesting of their couplings he was now confronted with in these pictures. He looked at Ali.

'Insurance policy. Ha Hek and I don't like any loose ends.'

'You mean she works for Ha Hek?'

'No, she is frightened of Ha Hek. He asked her to set this up and naturally she agreed. Ha Hek doesn't like his suggestions refused – he has a rather awful reputation about dealing with people who disagree with him. The pictures, though somewhat artless, have a function. You will not burn the go-down will you? And you will continue to assist in our enterprise, yes?'

He walked over to Kenneth and, smiling, gave him what would have looked to an innocent observer a friendly slap on the cheek. It stung. He then held Kenneth's jaw in his hand and swivelled the Englishman's head so that he looked directly into his eyes. The Rajah's grip was placed so that his fingers clinched his left cheekbone with so much pressure that Kenneth winced. Ali's eyes were frightening in their deadliness, his smile a nasty grimace.

'We do understand one another don't we, Kenneth?' He didn't need an answer. He released his grip, gave Kenneth another 'friendly' slap on the other cheek, and returned to his desk. 'Even if you hadn't come by today I was going to call you. There's another payment due to you. Here,' he tossed an envelope to Kenneth, 'it's all correct.'

Kenneth knew by its weight that it was another 10,000 dollars.

'That's taken care of business. Tea on the verandah is in order.'

Kenneth got to his feet and, feeling like the whipped dog that he was, followed the Rajah out of the study.

Chapter 21

Selangor, 1930

A few days after this sorry episode Kenneth handed Maeve an envelope from the mail with a Sarawak stamp affixed to its upper corner and a Kuching postmark on top.

'It must be from Nick,' said Maeve excitedly. She slit the top edge and pulled out a three-page letter. She read it with a smile on her face. 'He is coming back to Bukit Klang for a second season. Wonderful! He asks if I could help again, and this time he can even offer me a small stipend. What do you think, Kenneth? Do you mind if I work on the dig again?'

'No, of course not,' he replied. In truth he was quite pleased the opportunity had again arisen. With Maeve occupied elsewhere he felt less guilty about his concealments. It did him no good seeing her about the bungalow day after day with his secrets bottled up inside himself.

Nick turned up in April with all the paraphernalia required for a six-month dig boxed up in several large wooden crates. He established himself back in the Bukit Klang kampong guesthouse, acquired a new pig-stick to deal with annoying individuals of the local livestock, hired a team of labourers, distributed small gifts to the children, and generally made himself at home.

Maeve motored over to the village after he had settled in. They had already remade their friendship at a couple of functions organized by the British community to welcome him back — a curry dinner at the Amburys' and a cocktail evening at the Bangi Club — and so today she was to hear and see Nick's plan of action for the coming months.

'The main reason for this second season,' said Nick as

they walked up the track to the site, 'is to get to grips with the boulder and its significance. I want to get all the inscription and then take a look at the ruins above the audience hall terrace. That's where the royal apartments would have stood. I need to see how extensive they are. Who knows, we might even find some genuine treasure. Only in 1926 they found a small cache of gold jewellery in a similar context up on Fort Canning Hill in Singapore. Perhaps we shall too. If there's time I will have a poke around again on the Portuguese levels. It's the other part of the history of the hill and it would be nice to leave in September with the whole story of the place explained.'

They reached the first terrace and crossed over it to the little connecting path which brought them to the audience hall terrace. The boulder was buried under a small mud slip and nothing of it was visible.

'The hill has taken a bit of a beating in this year's monsoon hasn't it,' commented Nick, looking at the slide and some others near it, all tumbling down from the slope above. 'I suppose my scrub clearing last year wouldn't have helped matters much as it would have opened up the ground to the weather more than it has been for years. Still, no real damage done. We'll have this cleaned up within a few days.'

Work began and Maeve and Nick quickly fell back into the routine established the year before. Maeve felt herself blossoming. Being around Nick with his insatiable curiosity in all the finds his workmen brought to light provided the intellectual stimulation she had missed while he was away in Kuching. 1930, she decided, could be a good year despite Kenneth's nameless worries and anxieties back at the estate.

It was more than a fortnight before Rajah Ibrahim learned that the archaeologist had returned to Bukit Klang. The news was unwelcome. Despite every intention to destroy the inscription up at the archaeological site, he had in fact forgotten to do anything about it once the dig had packed up.

It would have been so easy, he thought to himself testily, to have rolled the thing into the river one night. He could have had an army of workers up there to do the job last December and no one would have been any the wiser. How could he have been so careless? The reason was simple. His mind had been preoccupied with interests closer to his heart than ancient rock engravings. He had spent much of the first months of the monsoon season away from Selangor at a secluded retreat in the north, spending large sums of his recently acquired wealth on procuring pubescent boys for his peculiar gratifications. It had been a splendid if somewhat expensive holiday, and it annoyed him to have let such a little thing as dealing with the Bukit Klang boulder slip his memory because of it. Now that the English archaeologist was back on site, it became a much trickier problem than it should have been. It would have to be dealt with delicately, and although he couldn't immediately think of the appropriate method, he was confident he would soon find a solution to the existence of the inscription.

Three weeks into the season, in early May, Nick and his team arrived at the site at 6.30 to commence another day's work to find a small disaster across the audience hall terrace. In the night the place had been completely vandalized. The spoil buckets were squashed and their bottoms kicked out, the sieving screens torn and their frames twisted, trowels had blades snapped in half, shovels their handles wrenched off. The carefully measured and marked-out excavation squares had had their cord perimeters torn up and the sides of the holes, usually straight and precise, trampled down. A table of pottery sherds laid out the afternoon before had been up-ended and the finds strewn across the ground. A dog, its scrawny throat cut, lay in among the porcelain and terra-cotta sherds in its own congealed blood.

The men looked in dismay at the mess, completely speechless. Then with anxious eyes they turned to look at Nick to see his response. He was ashen. Who would do this? Locating Daan, his supervisor for the season, in among the cluster of workers, he called him over and together they surveyed the damage at close quarters.

'Who would do this, Daan? Who in the village would act like this?' he asked the quiet Malay.

'Surely no one, Tuan,' he replied. 'I know of nobody who would want to do this.' He called over to one of the labourers who ran off at Daan's instruction to the kampong. 'I have told him to fetch Idris Hussein. He has to know of this outrage to our village honour.'

They continued to look at the wreckage of the site. Fifteen minutes passed and a middle-aged Malay of dignified appearance arrived on the terrace. Idris Hussein and Nick greeted each other, 'Selamat pagi' – peace on the morning – which seemed for once not quite suitable for the occasion. The chief looked at the site with a serious expression on his face.

'I'm very sorry to see this, Manconi. It is very distressing to see such careful work wantonly ruined. I do not know who could have done this except to say that it was no one from Bukit Klang. The excavation has been naturally much talked about but no one has any malicious intentions towards you. My people like you. For some you have provided work, and for the rest, entertainment.'

'So you haven't any idea of who would take the trouble to do this?'

Idris Hussein slowly shook his head.

'What about the dog? Why add it to the general mess?'

They looked at the small repulsive creature spread out across the ground. Again the chief shook his head from side to side and said, 'Apart from adding to the distastefulness of the crime I can see little importance to it. Perhaps a very superstitious person would see something ominous in its presence, retribution from evil spirits it and its companions may have warded away from the innocent during its life, something in that category maybe. But no Moslem would feel concerned, apart from a very natural desire to not have to clean it up.'

There was nothing to be done but to set to work

and re-establish the dig. Nick, not as convinced as the chief as to the unsullied purity of the labourers' faith in the message of Mohammed, dealt with the dog himself. Taking care not to touch its flea-infested carcass, he wrapped it in an old sack and, dragging it down to the cliff edge, hurled it over. Carried by the Kemudi it would, by evening, be out at sea. He chose, too, to deal with the bloody sherds, and leaving the workers under Daan's direction, took them down to the village in two of the least damaged buckets. At the bottom of the hill he met Maeve just arriving for a morning's work.

'Good morning,' she said cheerfully. One look at Nick's face, however, told her that things weren't well with him. Quietly he told her what had happened as she accompanied him to the river bank where he proposed to wash the bits and pieces of pottery. Maeve squatted down beside him and helped.

'This is awful!' she said when he completed the tale. 'What a pointless, stupid thing to do!'

'Yes it is. I can't think of a single reason for anyone to bother. There was nothing worthwhile to steal, and a look around would have shown anyone that. No, for some obscure reason someone wants to make the point that I shouldn't be there. It's the only explanation I can come up with that makes any sense, except I don't know anyone who would feel that way. Idris Hussein is emphatic that no one from here resents the work I'm doing. It's an utter mystery.'

'It's so unfair, all that work ruined.'

'To look on the bright side, the mess the actual dig is in can be remedied. There's still some equipment unbroken – it's at my house – so work can continue. I'll just have to buy some more to replace what's broken. It's very unsettling however. I'm sure the workers are unnerved by it too.'

He stopped talking and in silence they completed the washing and carried the pottery sherds to his bungalow.

'From now on I'll bring each day's finds down here. I

don't think it's safe any more leaving them up on the site. As for the equipment, it will have to stay. Otherwise it will be a sizeable chunk out of each day just lugging the stuff up and down at the start and finish of work. Come on, let's go and see how Daan is getting on.'

It took the better part of two days to tidy up the shambles. The mood at the site was, for the first time since Nick had set foot on the place, sombre. However, once the damage was rectified and new work commenced, spirits again rose. Nick maintained a small team at the boulder and had eight men on the flattened summit of the hill forty feet above and to the north-west of the terrace. Another line of text was emerging on the face of the rock as the men laboriously unearthed the debris covering it. They were now down two feet into the terrace and five lines of the inscription had been exposed. Nick was pleased with progress.

Exactly a week after the night of vandalism another incident occurred, this time much more menacing than simply destructive. Seven black fowls had been slaughtered and their blood sprayed around the place. Three were near the boulder and four up at the palace excavations. Further scouting around discovered a disembowelled dog, its entrails draped about on the religious structure near the audience hall which had been excavated last year. To Daan, Nick, and Idris Hussein, who had again called at the site, the spectacle was senseless. However about one-third of the workers were badly rattled by the slaughter, attributing it to evil spirits living among the ruins.

'Great,' said Nick sarcastically. 'This is just what I need, the scaring of my workers to the point that they are too frightened to come up here.'

It took most of the morning for Daan to convince them that humans had created the sight that had greeted them and work again commenced after lie-down that afternoon.

'This is serious,' said Nick to Maeve later that day. 'I'm

301

going to be lucky to get everyone working here after this incident, I can tell you. Daan has done the trick now, but once they start discussing it over some palm wine I can see it being attributed to spirits and demons again. The more Moslem of them won't worry themselves as to whether this is the result of the supernatural, but as for others, that I'm not very confident about. Beyond that problem, though, suddenly this site isn't a nice place to work at. How can any of us concentrate on the job when we know that someone has got it in for us? I think about it constantly – who have I made an enemy of without even knowing it? It's an unpleasant feeling to say the least.'

'I know,' said Maeve. 'It has to affect everyone here. Now that it's happened twice I'm sure everybody is going to be on edge just wondering what on earth is going to happen next. Somebody is obviously trying to frighten the dig to a standstill. Much more of this unpleasantness and they may succeed. Ugh,' she involuntarily shivered. 'It's awful to see these dead chickens and the dog. The smell is enough to put one off, let alone the malicious implications behind the deed. What can be done?'

'Nothing that I can think of. It's out of the question to consider putting a watchman up there. No one from Bukit Klang would do it, and I can't. I suppose all I can do is hope that whoever is behind it has had their amusement and will leave us in peace from now on.'

The next day the labour force was short of three workers. Daan explained to Nick that the men weren't prepared to return to the site. It was, he said in his low voice, all too clear to them and their families that the ghosts of the old people who had once lived up on the hill were warning Nick to stop his excavations of their former palace. The dig had disturbed their rest of centuries and only worse things would happen if Nick disregarded the warnings.

Nick shrugged his shoulders and said, 'I'm sorry they've left, Daan, they were good workers. How do you feel about the dig?'

'It's not ghosts, Tuan, I know that as well as you do.

302

We could lose some other men however if anything else happens. It's a bad business and everyone is concerned.'

A day later and Nick's plans were in complete disarray.

The attack came at the end of the day's work. As Nick and Maeve were packing the day's finds into a couple of wooden boxes to carry down to the village they heard some panic-stricken shouts in the distance. The calls came from the direction the workers had straggled off in only minutes earlier. The terraces were in shadow, the sun, behind the hill, tracking towards sunset as Nick and Maeve ran across the dig and down the path which led to the kampong. Only a hundred yards down it they came to a group of the villagers gathered around two very shaken men.

'What happened?' puffed Nick as he ran to them. He looked at the two men who were the centre of attention. They were pale and fear showed clearly in their eyes. Both had bleeding scratches on their bare skin, some quite nasty-looking.

A babble broke out as ten people tried to explain. Nick looked around for Daan. As he did the supervisor emerged from the surrounding scrub.

'What happened?' Nick asked a second time.

'These two men, Tuan, say they were attacked by ghosts. Just back there.' Daan pointed back up the path where it made a sharp turn back on itself to avoid a rock outcrop. 'They were ambling down the track when two figures in grey robes from head to foot came from nowhere and pushed them down the slope. They went crashing down there in among the trees. I was maybe thirty yards in front of them and I didn't see or hear a thing until the sound of them tumbling down, and their shouts.'

'They weren't struck or beaten? Only pushed?'

'That's right. Once we had all gathered here and found they were not badly harmed I went back up to see if there was any sign of their assailants. I found nothing. There are however rough tracks up there which could have been used to sneak along up to here and to flee over afterwards.'

Nick looked again at the bleeding and shaken workers.

'Why do they say they were ghosts and not men?'

'They were not dressed as men, they say. They were not there, then suddenly they were, right next to them. And neither can remember any impact or pressure against them as they were propelled off the path. At this time of day, Tuan, it is easy for simple men to believe in ghosts and spirits.'

Daan was right. With the hillside in shadow the bush did take on a some what eerie atmosphere. Whole areas under the leafiest part of the canopy were quite dark in the late afternoon light, and it didn't need a vivid imagination to people it with sentient beings.

Everyone made off down the hill in a bunch. Nick was about to join them when he remembered the finds sitting in the boxes back at the dig.

'Maeve, I'm going back to get the boxes.'

'You'll need some help. I'll come too.'

As they walked back up to the terraces they talked about the attack. It was impossible to conceive of why anyone would be doing these things. It was, however, imperative that Nick get to the bottom of it, otherwise he would have no excavation. Still talking, he and Maeve walked back on to the terrace where the boulder stood. Twilight was not far off and the whole terrace was suffused in a grey-green light. Nick stopped dead in his tracks and grabbed Maeve's arm. There, standing at the far end of the terrace over a hundred yards away, was a grey, shrouded form. They stood there, transfixed with shock. Who the hell was it? wondered Nick.

'Stay here,' he whispered to Maeve.

He began to approach the figure stealthily. About half-way across the open space it moved, turning slightly and lifting its head so as to look at Nick. Where a face should be Nick could see nothing, the shadows cast by the robes concealed any human details. Nick felt the hair on his arms rise and, despite the heat, he felt chilled. I don't like this at all, he thought to himself as he forced his feet to keep stepping in the direction of the thing standing there.

Suddenly, only thirty or forty yards from the apparition, he tripped on a pegged-out length of cord marking the perimeter of a square. He didn't fall, stumbling instead for a pace before he recovered his balance, but in that instance the figure had vanished. He turned wildly round but it was out of sight.

'Did you see where it went?' he called to Maeve.

She ran up. 'No! When you tripped I watched you, I was so worried! Nick, none of this makes any sense to me, it's frightening!'

'I know. It spooked me as well. If to scare me off Bukit Klang is the intention, then someone is doing a good job.'

They gathered the boxes and left the site.

'You know,' said Nick as they carried the stuff through the kampong, 'I'm going to be damn lucky to get any workers up there tomorrow. Tonight might well have been the last straw for all of them. No one needs this sort of trouble in their lives, least of all the villagers who have been peacefully living alongside Bukit Klang citadel for generations.'

Nick's fears were half-realized. That night as he sat brooding at the guest-house the men of the village had a meeting which lasted long into the night. Next morning he went over to the chief's house to hear from Idris Hussein what the future was to be for the excavation. When he returned, Maeve was waiting for him on his verandah. He sat down next to her and told her of the meeting.

'I'm not going to be closed down. The dig can continue. Idris Hussein said that there was no way he and his people were going to be bullied or frightened into sending me away. He regards the incidents as an affront to his and Bukit Klang's reputation. He said that if they hadn't wanted me here he would have said so last year. He has no more belief in the existence of ghosts than you or I.'

'After yesterday evening I'm not so certain any more,' interrupted Maeve. 'That figure looked unearthly.'

'I know what you mean,' replied Nick. 'Anyway Idris

Hussein is as interested as I am to find out who is up to these silly stunts. His reasons are to do with funny business on his land rather than for my sake, but our interests are in common. And, of course, the bottom line is that the excavation can continue. I don't mind saying, now that it's over, that I was worried that they'd tell me to pack my bags today.'

'How about the workers? Will they come back?'

'Half won't. Idris Hussein may have his feet planted firmly on the ground but I'm afraid at least eight of the team have refused to go back.'

'That's terrible, Nick. How will you manage without them?'

'I talked with Idris Hussein about that also. He doesn't mind if I bring in five or six workers from outside the village. He wants to see the work done properly as he feels the nonsense reflects badly on his village. What I'm going to do is go up to Kuala Lumpur tomorrow and see if the Museum can let me have some of their trained archaeological staff for a couple of months. I know the curator there and feel, as long as the Museum itself doesn't have a project underway, that I'll be able to get them seconded to here. With technicians like that I should be able to get by just as well with half what I had before.'

The plans did work out as Nick had hoped, and a week later the dig recommenced with renewed vigour from its team of workers.

Nick had managed to borrow five technicians from the Museum. All were residents of Kuala Lumpur and a rather urbane lot when seen alongside the kampong people. They were lodged in a couple of empty huts not far from Nick's bungalow and within a few days their novelty value had lured many of the villagers to their quarters each evening after which the sounds of drinking, laughing and singing were heard till a late hour. Inspecting the rather sorry-looking bunch of workers at the first morning's dig after the friendships had been cemented – they were all suffering from hangovers – Nick wondered if he had

306

done Idris Hussein much of a favour bringing this bunch of city sophisticates into his once-peaceful backwater of Selangor.

The weeks passed busily. By mid-June the foundations of a sizeable part of the royal apartments had been exposed and Nick was able to start making some suppositions about the buildings and their architectural features. On the terrace below, nearly all the rocks had been prised away from the inscription and it was now clear that the original ground level which the boulder rested upon was about three feet below the present-day surface. A sixth line of script had been uncovered and nothing since. It was beginning to look as if Nick had, at last, uncovered all there was to read.

Since the 'ghosts', all had been unmolested up at the dig, and the three incidents had been almost forgotten. Then, in late June, things looked as if they were going to repeat themselves, for one morning Dann and Nick found that all the equipment had vanished and the various excavation squares wrecked. Hunting the site for clues, Nick found that the shovels, trowels, brushes, tape measures, and everything else required for a scientific dig had been pitched over the cliff into the Kemudi – a couple of tools hanging in the vines on the cliff face indicated where the rest had gone. Work stopped again for a couple of days while everything was replaced.

'The only conceivable reason for all this destruction is that we must be close to uncovering something that somebody doesn't want us to find,' said Nick to Maeve one afternoon over a cup of tea. 'I've talked to Idris Hussein about it and although he has wracked his brains, he has no memory of stories about buried treasure or anything that could be of value.'

'It didn't happen last year so presumably it has something to do with where you are digging this season,' said Maeve. 'That can only be the royal apartments. The boulder was uncovered at the end of last year.'

'Hmmm, I think you're right,' agreed Nick. 'Dashed if I can think of any feature up there that suggests we're about to find buried wealth though. Following such a theory through to its logical conclusion, however, it tends to endorse the suspicion that we're close to doing just that. Why else would this week's vandalism have taken place? After all, the best way to stop an archaeological dig is to throw all the equipment away.' He paused to finish his drink of tea. 'And if we're that close, blowed if I'm going to give up now. They won't get a chance to chuck the tools away again for a start. From now on, each man brings his trowel and spade home with him each evening.'

One night at the end of the month, Nick decided to take a night-time walk up to the site. All day he had been feeling uneasy within himself. He hadn't been able to locate the source of his mood other than sense that it had something to do with the dig. The odd sensation continued to nag at him as the evening passed. Finally, putting aside the notes of the day's activities which he was in the practice of writing up each evening, he went to look at the citadel before turning in. He hopped down from the verandah. It was late and life in the village was at an ebb as household after household fell asleep. Nick walked through the quiet village, his presence setting up the familiar baying and howling of the dogs as he strode towards the hill. Preoccupied with his thoughts he was oblivious to the racket. He also failed to notice a dark figure flitting among the houses shadowing his moves; following him.

The track in among the bush was pitch-black as he walked up the hillside, an electric torch guiding his steps, but once on the terraces a fat sickle moon cast enough light for him to make out the features of the excavation. He shielded the beam of the torch so that his eyes could adjust to the darkness. Nothing seemed amiss but his unease was now even more manifest. Something wasn't in order, of that he was sure. He walked to the next terrace, the one with the boulder. Nothing wrong here either, he noted. He walked to the far end where, with recent clearing, one could now see a stretch of the Kemudi. It was silver and as still as a pond in the moonlight. It all looked so peaceful.

Nick walked down to the narrow Portuguese terrace where the view was more expansive. He must have stood there for five minutes, contemplating the scene. Suddenly he heard a rustling of shrubbery and a crushing of dead leaves on the ground. Someone was approaching! He turned to find himself confronted with a figure. The person's face was masked but Nick had time to see the surprise in the eyes that stared back at him. He opened his mouth to demand the figure's business but the man reacted even more promptly. With a blow that knocked the wind out of him Nick just had time to register that he had been hit with a blunt weapon of some sort. He failed to feel the second, for the world exploded into a galaxy of slow-moving lights and shooting stars and he felt as if he were floating in the dark night as the cudgel struck him a glancing blow on his skull. He passed into unconsciousness.

He was unaware of anything; that he was on his knees, or that the mysterious visitor put a sandalled foot to his chest and pushed him backwards over the cliff. Certainly he was unaware, only seconds after he had come to rest up against a tree a few yards below where he had been standing, of a grunt of pain above, and the sound of a heavy object plummeting through the frail vegetation close by him. Of the splash his attacker made when he hit the surface of the Kemudi five hundred feet below, Nick heard not a sound.

Chapter 22

Bukit Klang, 1930

Nick came to with shafts of bright sunlight stabbing into his eyes. The world rocked about him. Lying on his back, branches and trees and palm fronds swung into view and then out. He had a splitting headache. Voices could be heard, Malay voices sounding anxious and worried. Where was he?

A face appeared above him, it was Daan's, looking extremely concerned. He was on a crude, hastily constructed litter made from hacked-up branches and vines, and his workmen were carrying him down the hill. He must have had an accident, he decided. He could not recall it, and judging from the pain in his head it must have been something that laid him out. Even pondering the cause made his head ache even more, so he abandoned thought and just lay there as the procession brought him to his bungalow.

When he next surfaced he was in his bed and Maeve was sitting at its side. His head pounded, but at least it was dim and shadowed in the house and this time he could keep his eyes open. He looked at Maeve and she smiled. From her eyes he could see that she had been crying.

'Hello, Nick, welcome to the land of the living,' she said, giving his hand a squeeze.

He tried to say something but his lips were too dry and parched to shape the words, Maeve helped him into a reclining position and held a glass of water to his mouth. He sipped it until it was empty.

'What happened? I can't remember anything since last night.'

'Daan and the workers found you this morning. Some-one attacked you and threw you over the cliff up at the dig. Oh, Nick,' she started to cry, 'you were so close to falling. Daan said one of the few substantial trees growing out from the cliff stopped you. No one knows how long you had been there but you were found at 7.00 this morning.' She pulled out a handkerchief from her skirt pocket and wiped her nose. 'Do you remember anything? Were you up on the site early this morning?'

A few memories came back.

'No, last night. I went up last night to check things. It must have been near eleven o'clock. How did they find me?'

'During the morning scout about, one of the boys found a lot of blood at the edge of the cliff. He peered over and saw you jammed in the tree. They made a quick stretcher and brought you down here immediately. When I turned up for work you were here, wound bathed and bandaged and looking like death. I'm so glad to see you awake!'

'My head tells me that's where I was hit. Any other damage?'

'Daan says no. You have a big shallow gash above your right ear he says. Headache stuff but not serious. He said he expected something worse because of all the blood, but there's not. Talking with him earlier, he was wondering if you had fought with your attacker and stabbed him or something. He's certain it's not your head wound that left the puddle.'

'I don't remember any fight at all,' answered Nick. 'Someone was there, that I do recall; then, absolutely nothing until the trip down this morning.'

Maeve looked at him with concerned eyes. 'You're coming home with me to be looked after, and, with some European comforts about you, you'll be on your feet in short order.'

'That's kind of you, Maeve,' Nick replied.

'As soon as you feel well enough to get up and be moved to the motor car, we will leave. You needn't worry about bringing anything, you can wear Kenneth's stuff. I'll just move the Ford to your front stairs so that you don't have to be carried far.' She left and when she returned, only minutes later, she found Nick adrift in a restless sleep.

Later that day she drove him carefully to Kuala Tanah and Kenneth and Pravan, the cook, lifted him into the spare room.

'It's a bad business,' said Kenneth when he and Maeve were in the living room. 'I don't like to see a man like that laid out, and in such a cowardly way. I wouldn't have thought an archaeological dig would bother anyone, let alone drive them to attempt murder.'

Ali's intimidation of Kenneth had soured the friendship of nearly a decade and for a while Kenneth ceased visiting the Istana except to collect his money. Ali however maintained his welcome for the Englishman and by May the billiard tournaments had again become a part of Kenneth's social life. He couldn't forget about the collection of photographs Ali held over his head but, in the final analysis, there was nothing he could do about retrieving them and, as time passed, they became less of an issue. So, too, the fear he had felt when he had learned of the police investigation into the opium smuggling. As the months passed and nothing seemed to interfere with the regular shipments up the Kemudi, the consequences of being caught by the authorities seemed remote.

After Nick had been installed in the spare room Kenneth decided to drive to Ali's to tell him of the attack upon the archaeologist. Every now and then the Rajah had made a few off-hand enquiries about progress up on the hill and Kenneth, if he could, would oblige him with whatever gossip Maeve had passed on. Also, he felt in the mood for a game of billiards.

He discovered that Ali, for once, was not overly enthusiastic about enjoying a match. His mind seemed elsewhere until Kenneth brought up the morning's business at Bukit Klang.

'Kenneth, this is preposterous! You can't be serious telling me that someone tried to murder Manconi. I've

312

never heard of such a thing! Archaeology is a gentleman's pursuit, old man. People don't go around murdering archaeologists.'

'At Bukit Klang someone wants to. No doubt about it. He's at our place recovering from a hell of a crack on his head and from being pushed off the cliff overhanging the river. A tree stopped him going any great distance, thank goodness.'

Ali shook his head in mock amazement. 'It seems inconceivable. Surely it's just as possible that he simply fell off? After all, didn't you say that it happened when he was up on the site last night?'

'Yes. I wondered that too. There's more to the story however. Someone, and it's not Manconi, apparently bled like a stuck pig up there. Either they had a fight and Manconi got something into his attacker before he went over the cliff, or,' he hesitated, '. . . or, I don't really know. I suppose Manconi must have stabbed the person; he just doesn't remember.'

'Perhaps the police will find out,' said Ali casually. 'I suppose they have been informed.'

'No, I don't believe so. Manconi certainly hasn't telephoned them, nor have Maeve or myself. From what Manconi was saying I think Idris Hussein feels it's his problem as it's his land the dig is on. I imagine he will deal with it – if, of course, he ever finds out who did the deed.'

'Well, this is all very curious and not at all typical of our peaceful part of the world. Give Manconi my sympathy when you return home, I really am most sorry to hear of his, um, "accident" last night.'

They played on. When Kenneth had departed Ali rang for his syce. When the driver arrived the Rajah addressed him angrily.

'Where's Mubin?'

'I don't know, your Excellency.'

Ali hit him; hard enough to make the man's nose bleed.

'Where is he? I know you two sleep together so if anyone knows where he is, you do!'

'I don't know, believe me, Excellency. He went out last night to carry out your instructions up on the fort at Bukit Klang and has not returned. He never came back.'

Ali gave the man a vicious clout across the head and, cursing him, dismissed him. Where was Mubin? He was as loyal as they came, there was no way he would have cleared out. Perhaps he had panicked, for at no time was he instructed to attack and maim people. To frighten, yes, that had been part of the brief Ali had given him, but to try and kill Manconi? It was inexplicable.

In the Rajah's mind there seemed to be only two possibilities for his servant's disappearance: either Manconi had killed him and his body lay up there in among the dense bush; or Idris Hussein had captured him, probably wounded by the sounds of the mess up there, and would no doubt extract a confession from him. This would do him, the Rajah of Sungei Kemudi, no good at all.

For the first time since the combined businesses of opium smuggling and archaeological site destruction had entered his machinations, the Rajah felt a shadow of uncertainty creep over him. With Mubin's unaccountable absence perhaps the unravelling of his carefully woven scheme of things had begun. He didn't like loose ends.

The Rajah probably would have felt less threatened had he been able to know that, at the precise moment these thoughts were occupying his attention, Mubin's body was being torn to pieces by a large crocodile in the esturine waters at the mouth of the Kemudi, not far, as it happened, from his secret go-down.

Nick recovered quickly from his wound and in six days felt he had rested enough to be able to return to Bukit Klang. Apart from his wish to get stuck back into the dig now that the season was over halfway through, he was also looking forward to his solitude back in the kampong. Being a guest of Maeve and Kenneth had brought its own small problems, if problems they could indeed even be described.

At Bukit Klang he found it easy to maintain a warm,

shared interest in archaeology with Maeve which never drifted into anything remotely more than platonic. Being a guest, and a semi-invalid at that, altered their relationship in a way that Nick felt could be problematical if he stayed too long, for he enjoyed being nursed by Maeve and having her company from the time he woke till bedtime. Once he caught himself thinking of her in the way that he had back in Kuching six months ago, pondering her pretty face and attractive figure as she moved the lunch things from beside his sickbed. It was, he decided, time to leave.

While he grew to appreciate her company more than he knew he had any right to, he also decided that Kenneth Clouston was a man with a lot of things on his mind. Kenneth was friendly enough, but always a little distracted when about the bungalow; jingling keys or turning over loose coins in his trouser pockets; flicking rapidly, but with no real interest, through the newspaper: impatient mannerisms which suggested some deep underlying anxiety.

He seemed to be waiting for something, but Nick could not hazard a guess as to what it could be, except to decide that it never came while he was at Kuala Tanah. Kenneth would also come and go erratically. 'Off to the coolie lines,' 'off to Ali's'; 'off to Salak'; and Nick, a few minutes later, would hear the Ford cough into life and putter away. Kenneth looked a troubled and unhappy soul and Nick wondered what it could be.

Maeve drove him over to Bukit Klang on the Monday and he again took up residence in his old quarters. The dig had progressed well under the guidance of Daan. Maeve had kept an eye on things as well and Nick was pleased with what he saw.

'I think we're finished here,' he said, looking at the boulder with its inscription now completely exposed. 'Take a couple of rubbings of the lettering and I'll photograph it too. I'll send the whole thing back to Kuching where my friend, the Curator of the Sarawak Museum, will decipher it.' He looked up the slope.

'For the next four weeks I'll concentrate our resources on the royal apartments. That will leave about a month up my sleeve for any special things that crop up.'

The silly row with Kenneth one July morning was about an issue Maeve couldn't see any grounds over which to even argue. Kenneth needed the Ford to motor over and see Ali, and Maeve proposed they share the trip as they had often done in the preceding months, and meet up later over at Bukit Klang. But, for some unexplained reason, on this occasion it wasn't good enough. Kenneth ranted and raved for a good half hour before Maeve could get a word in edgeways.

'For heaven's sake, Kenneth! There's no reason why you can't drop me off at the village and pick me up when you've done your business with the Rajah.'

'I'm sick of hanging around the dig. Plodding up that steep hill to find you, and the rest of it.'

'Look, you don't have to even come up. Send one of the kampong boys. For twenty cents they'd run a mile for you.'

As usual, behind Kenneth's peevishness was the ever-present anxiety about the smuggling. It was only a fort-night since he had picked up his most recent payment but Sue had told him yesterday, after they had made love in the afternoon, that in the evening another shipment was being taken off the estate. The frequency of the cargoes was increasing and that meant, as far as Kenneth was concerned, additional risks of his being caught out. He had drunk too much in the evening and now he was cross with himself and sick at heart.

'Kenneth, don't be unreasonable. Why make things difficult. You know I don't mind leaving Bukit Klang early if it fits in with your plans. Come on, we'll go together. There's no reason for me to have to stay here.'

In the end he conceded the point and, in ill-humour, motored over to the village after lunch.

Nick and Maeve were having an exploratory scratch about among the Portuguese ruins on the lower terrace. Some carved blocks of stone all piled up in a heap of dirt and other rocks, and interlaced with creepers, scrub and ferns, had caught Nick's interest. As they peered into the shadowy recesses and nooks of the rubble heap, events were conspiring to make this day one which would alter the paths of their lives forever. Like many such days, it seemed to hold nothing especially significant at the time, and only later would the players in the drama of their larger life be able to pinpoint that afternoon as the pivotal one for much of what was to happen afterwards.

Nick was inspecting the pile about three yards away from Maeve when he heard her call his name quietly but urgently.

'Nick! Nick!' She almost whispered it.

He turned to hear and said, 'What is it?' But as he spoke he saw she need not answer. There, crawling across her blouse was a chestnut-brown centipede as long as a man's hand. Nick knew immediately the danger she was in. The insect was extremely venomous and, if threatened, would bite; of that he was certain.

He walked quietly and slowly over to her. The revolting-looking creature was climbing gradually up Maeve's cotton blouse. Right now it was clinging to the material just below her left breast out of Maeve's line of sight beneath her bust. Nick waited a few seconds until it began to climb out on to her bosom and, when it was there, gently tugged the blouse from each side, his intention being, with the insect hanging upside down, that it would lose its grip and fall to the ground.

It didn't. It did however react to the unstable nature of the textile beneath its myriad feet. Lifting its polished head, it began to weave about in an attempt to find more congenial surroundings. Nick didn't like the look of the situation at all. He would have to brush it off, and quickly. The insect made its way over the curve of Maeve's bust and stopped once it was on the upper side where the blouse was taut against her breasts. Maeve could feel it through the material and dared not glance down, concentrating instead on Nick's face in front of her. To Nick, the half-coiled insect looked like a monstrous brooch.

'I'll get it off now; just breathe quietly and don't be startled.' Nick had a twig in his right hand.

Maeve felt his left hand cup her left breast. He lifted it, pushing gently at the same time so that it swelled up and out with the pressure. Suddenly the centipede was on a prominent mound, right at its highest point, making an easy target. Checking that there was no chance of its landing on another part of Maeve, Nick swept it off with the stick and it went flying into the rocks.

Maeve let out a sob of relief and leaned against Nick as all her strength drained away from her body. Nick put his arms around her and patted her back, holding her tight to prevent her toppling to the ground.

'It's all right. You showed great presence of mind, it's all right.' He continued to hold her and Maeve's strength slowly returned.

'Oh, that was awful. I've never been so scared.' She released her arms from around his waist where, with no conscious memory of having done so, she had flung them. She looked at him, his kindly face only inches away from hers. Her breast was warm with a sensuous ache from his clasp; with the centipede gone, the memory of his touch dominated all her senses. 'I need a seat. What a shock!'

On the terrace above, Kenneth turned on his heel and, red with rage, stormed back across the dig and down to the motor car. He had not witnessed the whole incident with the centipede unfortunately, but only the last seconds; also the ensuing embrace. He saw that swine Manconi mauling his wife and Maeve swoon into his arms in response. So that's what the bloody dig has been about. They've probably been having it off for months.

Right, what was he going to do about it?

He sat in the Ford. His first impulse, to drive off and leave them, seemed pointless now that the first waves of fury had left him. The other side of the coin, namely to confront them, didn't seem a particularly wise idea either. He was in a turmoil of conflicting emotions which ripped him apart. He must talk to someone.

Although he had only left the Istana an hour earlier Kenneth decided to talk to Ali. The Rajah, although surprised to see his friend return, cordially welcomed him in.

Kenneth looked haggard and unwell.

'What disaster has befallen you since you left, old man? You look simply dreadful.'

Kenneth told him.

'You say you don't know what to do,' said Ali solicitously. 'Here, in Malaya of the Malays, I would kill him. He is taking what is yours, something that is precious to any man.'

'God, Ali! I can't just go and shoot him or something. I'd get hung for a deed like that, British justice being what it is.'

'Accidents happen, dear boy, even to the charming Manconi. Scorpions in the bed, faulty brakes on a motor car, a villager running amok. If you want it, something can happen.'

Ali sounded persuasive. To Kenneth's brain, reeling with irrational thoughts brought on by a year of tension, guilt and excessive drinking, the idea sounded feasible. Manconi wouldn't get away with screwing his wife. He'd settle the swine in a way that would look to the world like an accident, yet achieve his needs at the same time.

The Rajah looked at his almost crazed friend with an expression of benign satisfaction. He himself could gain a great deal from the demise of the archaeologist. If Kenneth was prepared to race off and do just that, well, that would be the end of his worries concerning the inscribed stone. The loose ends may yet be neatly retied, he thought to himself cheerfully.

Chapter 23

Bukit Klang, 1930

'I've got to spend a couple of days away from here,' said Nick one morning. 'I have to go to Singapore on business for Rajah Brooke. I'll be back on Thursday with a surprise.'

'What sort of surprise?' asked Maeve, bent over a sketching pad doing a drawing of a brick wall within one of the work squares up on top of the site. A large umbrella shaded her from the sun.

'If I told you, it wouldn't be a surprise. You wait, it's going to be something quite remarkable.'

It was.

Four days later Maeve was again sketching among the ruins of the ancient palace when she heard a distant roar of a combustion engine. She looked up from her work. It had to be a motor car or a boat engine, except it was unusually loud. Its resonance suggested it was some distance away but approaching rapidly. Most odd, she thought to herself. Then, against the pale yellow sky she saw it, an aeroplane, the first she had seen in Malaya. It was coming up from the south, directly towards Bukit Klang. As it drew closer all the workers leapt to their feet, yelling excitedly and pointing at the aircraft as it sped towards them. There was a deafening roar and the thing barrelled overhead, clearing the summit by not more than fifty feet. Everyone spun round to watch it depart.

The aeroplane banked slowly to the right, the cloud-filtered sun lighting up the top planes of its wings as it lazily continued to turn, eventually completing a circle. The second time it passed the summit the aeroplane came in lower and somewhat to the side so that it was almost level with the flattened top with its cluster of workers jumping up and down and waving. It was a flying boat, and behind its rakish windscreen Maeve could see the pilot, clad in a leather flying helmet and goggles, looking at them. He smiled and waved. Maeve recognized the man immediately despite the speed with which he was moving, it was Nick!

Suddenly she was jumping up and down with the rest of the workers, shouting and laughing.

'It's Nick!' she yelled. Everyone looked at her questioningly. 'It's Tuan, Tuan Manconi!'

Looks of amazement followed the plane. It headed due north, losing altitude all the time. At the point where it was little more than a dot just above the green horizon, a flash of sunlight indicated that Nick had banked the aeroplane again. Back it came, low and directly above the Kemudi, dropping all the time until it seemed to be just skimming the surface of the river. Moments before it disappeared from view behind the shoulder of the hill, a sharp white line shot across the water as the flying boat's keel cut into the river.

'He's landing! He's coming to the kampong,' called Maeve. At the word 'kampong' there was a stampede off the site as the workers and Maeve ran helter-skelter down the paths to the village. When they got there the entire human population of the place was on the canoe and boat landing at the river's side. Beyond, off-shore six yards, floating like a piece of duck's down on a pond, was a flying boat, its engine silent. Nick was surrounded by a crowd on the bank, directing some men to tie a rope which tethered the craft to a conveniently placed coconut palm.

'Hello,' Maeve said breathlessly. 'That was quite a surprise!'

'Thought it would be,' laughed Nick in return. 'It's Rajah Brooke's newest acquisition. I'm to get it across to Kuching next week before he returns from Great Britain. He's letting me use it in the meantime for a spot of aerial surveying, so I thought I'd bring it up here for a couple of days' exploration. From the air I might be able to locate another Bukit Klang, who knows.'

'It looks beautiful,' Maeve said admiringly.

The hull of the flying boat was plywood with a varnish finish like glass. Without wings it would have been easy to have imagined the craft as a fast, streamlined motor boat, low and sleek with a racy windowshield and small sidepanes curving away each side of the cockpit. At the rear of the hull, however, it became distinctly less boat-like for the beam of about four feet tapered away to nothing but a support for the large upright rudder and its tail planes.

Behind the cockpit, flush with the upper surface of the fuselage, was a large wing of stretched canvas over a wooden framework. Directly overhead was an even more expansive wing supported on twelve long struts, each tensioned by a pattern of wires. The pusher engine sat under this wing, large square radiator to the front, wooden propeller at the rear behind the black mass of the motor. The wings and rudder were a stark white with a large green 'B' painted on the latter. Across the bow, in flowing lettering, was written 'Sylvia'.

'Yes, it's a beauty. It's an American Curtiss Seagull,' replied Nick.

'I didn't know you could pilot a flying boat,' said Maeve. 'I thought you flew in the deserts of the Middle East when you were in the RAF.'

'I hadn't until I worked for Rajah Brooke. He has another plane, an old Short two-two-five seaplane which the Ranee flies on occasion. I use it now and then. This craft is to replace it though.' He stretched. 'Right now I could do with a cup of tea, care to join me?'

'Love to.'

They returned half an hour later to the river bank. The crowd had diminished as the heat of the afternoon drove them back to their shady homes and only some children were still about, splashing and playing in the river. Nick pulled on the rope and slowly drew the flying boat towards the bank until it grounded on the soft mud only a yard or two from where they were standing.

'I've got a little bit of fine tuning to do on the engine. I won't come up to the site just yet. What are you going to do?'

'Kenneth is coming soon to pick me up. It's too hot to sit here; if you don't mind I'll just sit on your verandah and wait for him. I won't say goodbye as he will want to see the flying boat. I'll bring him here when he arrives.'

'Okay. See you later.'

Kenneth drove up fifteen minutes later. Maeve took him down to the aeroplane and they both chatted with Nick as he tinkered with the engine.

'Nearly done,' Nick said. 'Maeve, feel like doing me a favour? I need the roll of insulation tape we have with the archaeological equipment. It's in that Shell Oil box with all the measuring tapes back at the bungalow. At least it should be, unless you took it up the hill today.'

'No, I didn't. I'll go and fetch it for you.'

'Thanks.'

She walked briskly away. Kenneth looked with great interest at the machine, wading into the river to look at the cockpit controls, and to inspect its ailerons and other bits and pieces. He had never been close to an aeroplane before and he found its complex construction very interesting. He was peering into the cockpit for a second time when he heard Manconi mutter a curse and clamber down from the engine.

'I've just remembered. I used the tape to mend something just before I went to Singapore. It's not where I told Maeve; she'll never find it. I'll be back in a tick.'

Kenneth looked at him somewhat bleakly, but made an attempt to seem friendly. Since that afternoon on the site he had nursed black thoughts against the man and had not relinquished the idea of harming him. As he stood there, alone with the aeroplane, a plan, so simple yet utterly brilliant, materialized in his imagination.

He looked in the cockpit at the fuel gauge. It was, as he had thought, a gravity feed system and the gauge showed the amount of petrol in the tank by means of a glass tube containing a petrol level. This could be gauged just as one would mercury in a thermometer − 'full' at the top, a series of gradations underneath, and a red line near the bottom labelled 'empty'. Right now it showed 'quarter'. Looking around for a suitable tool to carry out his plan, Kenneth found a pair of pointed pliers on the fuselage along with an oily rag and a couple of screwdrivers.

Leaning into the cockpit he crimped the copper tubing that led to and from the petrol gauge. The children gambolling in the water took not the slightest notice of his actions. Now it would show 'quarter' forever, no matter how much fuel was actually on board. The sabotage took but a moment and, replacing the pliers where he had found them, he returned to the bank.

That would fix Manconi! The man would fly with a false security in his petrol reserves only to run out of fuel in mid-air, and crash who know where. Ingenious, thought Kenneth to himself; that will teach him to seduce his, Kenneth Clouston's, wife and expect to get away scot-free.

Only a few minutes passed and Maeve and Nick returned. He completed his task and, putting the tools away, said, 'Maeve. I'll take you for a spin. Ever been in an aeroplane?' He held out his hand to help her clamber into the second seat in the cockpit. It was beside the pilot's so that he and a passenger sat shoulder to shoulder.

'Maeve,' called Kenneth in an agitated way. 'You can't go! We've got to go home!' He leapt to his feet. 'Sorry old man, we really must get on our way.'

'Kenneth, you're not making sense. We're in no hurry. I've always wondered what it must be like to fly,' said Maeve.

Kenneth was pale and speechless. All he eventually managed to say was a lame 'don't go'.

'It will be all right, Kenneth,' Nick reassured him. 'Flying is as safe as houses these days, you needn't feel anxious for Maeve's safety. I'll give her a twenty-minute spin and then do the same for you. It will be fun.'

Kenneth watched, appalled at his own stupidity as Nick moved the flying boat out to mid-stream. Nick passed Maeve a leather helmet like his own and they both put them on. The motor roared and the Curtiss moved with ever increasing speed until it lifted off like a delicate bird from the river and swung to the north. Then it was out of Kenneth's sight.

Nick took the flying boat in a wide arc across the coastal lowlands of Selangor in towards the hills. Maeve was overwhelmed at the experience. Below her were the plantations she knew so well; the roads she had driven over countless times. They flew out along the foothills of the highlands, over Bangi and along the railway line towards Seremban. Another swing and they headed for the coast south of Port Dickson, the red cliffs of that town stark in the diffuse sunlight. In the Straits of Malacca low, dark-green islands began to appear and Nick swooped towards them. They were small but signs of habitation were visible in the way of one or two buildings. No one came out to watch as they thundered overhead. To the west the ragged swamp coastline of Sumatra loomed.

It was too noisy to talk comfortably. As further islands passed under the wing Nick gave a twirling motion with his forefinger, meaning he was turning to head back to Bukit Klang. The flying boat banked once more when, suddenly, there was silence. Nick looked over his shoulder. The propeller was idly windmilling, clearly without power yet the gauge showed plenty of fuel. He straightened up the plane and headed towards the nearest island.

Maeve's hearing, long deafened by the motor, began to recover and, as she watched the hills of Malaya sink lower and lower below the horizon, she could hear the wind whistling in the rigging of the wings and making a buffeting sound against the windscreen. She glanced at Nick, wondering if they were in serious trouble, but the look on his face reassured her that he was in control of the situation.

Unpowered, Nick skilfully guided the aeroplane towards a suitable-looking beach on an island to his right. The trick would be to bring her down close enough to the sand to be able to push the plane to land, but not so close as to run it up on to the beach and rip its bottom out. The third situation was too awful to contemplate, namely falling short and stopping in deep water. The Straits were too shark-infested to indulge in a swimming-towing exercise and if he misjudged it, they would be adrift. He was confident that a blockage had caused the problem: it would be easily fixed provided he put her down correctly.

His judgement was as sound as it had ever been in his former RAF days and the Seagull rocked to a halt only twenty yards off-shore. Quickly Nick baled out, rope in hand, and, waist deep in the tepid sea, pulled the flying boat to shore.

'An unexpected landing but nothing to worry about, I'll have it going soon. Here,' he put out his arms to lift Maeve, 'let me carry you ashore. Enjoy the island while we're here, there may be something interesting to see.'

She watched him investigate the problem from under the shade of a palm. It didn't take long, and from his expression as he waded to the beach, the results appeared to be worrying.

'I am out of petrol. I'm afraid we're stuck here until someone rescues us.'

Maeve went pale. 'How could that have happened?'

'That's the really bad news in the whole story. The gauge has been tampered with so as to show that there's fuel in the tank when in fact there isn't. I'd been flying on the assumption that there was still plenty of petrol and the gauge still tells me even now there's a safe margin left. But there isn't. There isn't a drop. The deeply troubling thing is the fact that the sabotage had to have been done at Bukit Klang. The gauge was in perfect working order on the flight up.'

'Oh Nick! Who could do a thing like that? Who was there? Only me, the villagers, Kenneth, and the workmen from the site.'

'The conclusion is rather awful,' said Nick looking tense. 'If I go through that list,' he counted off on his fingers, 'you didn't do it; I don't think the villagers could have had the know-how to do it, and anyway none of them touched the cockpit area; the workers from the dig fall into the same category; which leaves only Kenneth I'm afraid.'

'Surely not!'

'Whoever did it knew what they were doing, the damage is quite cunning and would require an extensive understanding of engines. Then there's the fact that I never saw anyone get into the cockpit while I was working on the machine. I only left it for those seven or eight minutes when I followed you back to the bungalow, and that was when Kenneth was alone at the plane.'

He shook his head in disbelief as he contemplated their situation.

'If he did do it, no wonder he was so anxious for you not to take a flight with me. He was expecting me to run out of petrol, presumably to crash. If we'd been over land instead of the sea when the juice ran out we would have been in big trouble.'

'My God,' said Maeve, 'I think Kenneth has gone mad. I can't think why he would want to do this to you. No reason at all. He likes you!'

'It's beyond me too. He wanted to kill me, that's a terrible thing to discover about someone I thought I knew.' Nick searched his mind. 'The only thing I can recall is that for the last month he has been somewhat unfriendly towards me. It seemed uncharacteristic of him but, knowing he has had something on his mind recently, I didn't think too much about it. Can you think of anything?'

'He's been moody and preoccupied for ages, but it has been worse recently. I think he's going mad. Oh dear!' Maeve started to cry. Huge sobs wracked her body as she sat there, face in her hands. Nick looked on dumbly, unable to think of anything that could make her feel less miserable.

He checked the time. Just past four. In a couple of hours

it would get dark. Better make the flying boat secure and find a camp, he thought to himself. Once the plane was tethered and anchored so that it couldn't float into danger, Nick unloaded his travelling kit which, luckily, he hadn't taken off back at Bukit Klang, and the emergency equipment the aircraft carried. Dumping it on the beach he set out to explore the island.

Maeve joined him. At the north end of the beach were a couple of dilapidated houses up on stilts, seasonal homes of orang laut, or sea people, who, Nick surmised, must use the place for fishing. The atap cladding was missing from one but the other would be serviceable once some patching had been done on the floor and roof.

'Come and help me fetch all the equipment,' said Nick as Maeve continued to look around in dismay. 'Try to put the circumstances of our unexpected stay here out of mind, it's not going to help brooding over it. I don't expect we'll be here more than a day.'

'I find it so hard to believe,' said Maeve as they trudged up the beach with their arms loaded with stuff. 'My husband trying to kill you. What did he think he was doing?'

Kenneth waited an hour by the river, ears tuned to hear the smallest growl of an aero engine. The little flying boat, however, did not return.

With heart of lead, his bowels twisted with fear, he walked to the motor car and drove slowly home. His mind worked sufficiently to make the journey safely but beyond that, it was a void. He felt incapable of any action, of any rational thought at all. A stiff whisky settled his stomach a little. He reached for the telephone and asked the operator for the Police Department in Bangi.

In a faltering voice he told the Inspector, a friend of sorts from the Club, that Nick's flying boat, with Maeve as passenger, had failed to return from a short flight.

'Don't worry, old man,' said a brisk voice in reply to the details Kenneth gave out. 'We'll find them and they'll be safe, of that I'm sure. Leave it to me.'

Kenneth felt exhausted and ill. He patted his pockets

for his cigarette case and came across a fat envelope –
yet another of Ali's. He pulled it out and spun it on the
desk with such force that the unsealed flap folded back
and the banknotes fanned out across the desktop. He
looked at them grimly: they, and the hundreds accumulated in the strongbox, seemed to be at the root of all
his troubles. What a mess! he thought to himself; what
a bloody disaster.

'You are very well equipped for such events,' commented
Maeve, scanning the camp Nick had pulled together about
the fisherman's house. There was tinned and desiccated
food, a parang for cutting things, a collapsible bucket for
collecting drinking water, and all sorts of items to make
survival possible in inhospitable places. There was also
Nick's suitcase with his sleeping things and a couple of
changes of clothes.

'All aeroplanes have an emergency kit. With a downed
flying boat, a couple of fish-hooks and some twine can
make the difference between life and death. That sort
of equipment is essential in case the exceptional should
happen. We'll get by all right.' He hesitated and then went
on, 'I'm sorry about the mosquito net. There's only one,
which means we'll have to share it. It's awkward but I
think it's unwise to do without it. Things are spartan
enough without providing an unexpected treat for a thousand marauding mosquitoes. Do you agree?'

'It's the sensible thing to do, of course I don't mind.'

'Well, I'm going for a swim before twilight arrives.
Won't be long.'

He grabbed a sarong and a clean shirt and went back
along the beach towards the flying boat. From a distance
of fifty yards Maeve covertly watched him strip off and
stride naked into the sea. Maeve felt herself flush at the
sight.

It was worse later when, under a star-blazing sky, she
crawled beneath the mosquito net and lay next to Nick.
She too had gone swimming and wore another of Nick's
sarongs from his suitcase. She decorously maintained a

foot of space between herself and him, the most the single-bed netting would allow without her touching it. Nick lay there, bare-chested with his sarong knotted around his waist, breathing evenly. They had earlier talked for hours around the camp fire he had lit, and now there seemed little more to say.

'Goodnight,' she said.

'Goodnight,' came a sleepy voice in reply.

Rest for Maeve did not come easily. As she lay there, Nick's presence imposed itself on her consciousness more and more. Her thoughts kept returning to times when she had felt desire for him, of the sensation his strong arms gave her when he carried her to land this afternoon, of his smile and of her daydreams involving him. She also thought of Indra's and Pavan's passion that night a year ago, a vision which had never left her imagination.

Suddenly she felt angry at Kenneth for denying her such abandonment. Already outraged by the events that placed her on this island, now she felt a hot fury that, because of his insane act, she was now in an even worse predicament, marooned with a man with whom she had been trying to deny her lust during every week she worked alongside him. She was married, good grief, and her foolish husband had managed to do this to her! She lay there quietly but a fierce battle of principles and desires raged within her. She thought of Indra taking everything she wanted from her husband and compared it with Kenneth's indifference; she thought of their marriage vows and Kenneth's commitment to them. Then she rolled over and reached for Nick.

Chapter 24

The Island, 1930

He took her hand in his; perhaps, she wondered, he
hadn't been asleep either, and she snuggled up next to
him, resting her head on his chest. A wave of desire swept
through her from head to toes; it was as if the floodgate
of a dam had opened after an age closed tight, and she
allowed herself to be swept along with the emotion. She
slipped her hand under Nick's sarong and caressed his
manhood until it filled her palm, then, getting to her
knees, she bent over Nick's supine body and kissed his
chest and belly. As she moved lower her soft cheek began
to be nuzzled by his hard member. Twisting her head her
lips kissed its smooth contoured tip and then, parting
them, she took it into her mouth.

Momentarily uncertain what to do she rolled her tongue
around its crown and drew him in deeper. The effect was
as if a charge of electricity had coursed between her and
Nick, an almost palpable vibration which made her lust
even more overpowering. She felt Nick untie her sarong
and, as it fell free from her body, touch her breasts. They
were the gentlest of caresses. His palms brushed her nipples and his fingertips pressed the surrounding roundness
so delicately and tantalizingly that she thought she might
faint with pleasure.

Languidly she sucked and licked him, taking him in as
far as she could and then withdrawing to the tip again.
She could feel the tension within him as she moved her
head up and down, he straining to keep as much of himself inside her as possible each time she almost let him
slip from her lips. And while her mouth absorbed erotic
sensations of an intensity she had never before perceived,

beneath her Nick created further delights as he gently kneaded her breasts as they swung voluptuously above him. They produced such a yearning and abandonment throughout her body. She wanted his lips around their points but at the same time could not relinquish what she had already. Voracious with lust, she took him deeply.

At that instant her mouth was filled with a gush, then another, and another, of Nick's semen. She hadn't known what to expect. It had a power of its own as it kept coming: his very essence seemed to flow with it and she swallowed it avidly, sucking until no more came. His orgasm heralded a dream, and later she could only recall parts of the night, so overwhelming became her passion.

Nick rolled over on top of her and did extraordinary things to her breasts. He kissed her salty lips and every conceivable part of her. Every piece seemed sensitive to his touch. He pushed his loins against hers and entered her, the fullness of the penetration taking her breath away. He could have stayed there forever, she decided, as he pushed gently against her, at the same time licking and sucking one nipple, then the other, as he moved within her. Then he shifted his position. Maeve lay there eyes closed, half focused on what his hands were doing to her breasts, and half in excited anticipation as to what else might happen.

She felt his cheek brush her thigh and suddenly her sex was absorbed by a soft, wet sensation. She reached down and stroked his head, his tongue lapping at her like the littlest of ripples against a beach. The sensation was too much. In a sudden surge, a wave of ecstasy rolled through her body and, apart from the awesome pleasure her body released in spasm after spasm, all was beyond her consciousness.

They lay in each other's arms as the night wind whistled though the palms above them. Nick finally broke the silence.

'I think I've died and gone to heaven.'

Maeve hugged him. She felt she was overflowing with happiness. She could think of nothing to say, words simply didn't seem adequate to describe the tumult of emotions that coursed through her, so she hugged him again and held him close. The night felt timeless, its starry darkness cocooned them in a space far from ordinary life and Maeve marvelled at it all.

Nick began stroking the outline of one of her breasts with his fingertips. His touch felt so lovely, she thought, and she lay there quietly tingling as he traced his fingers down to her waist and up along her rounded hip. He squeezed her haunch gently and retraced his route. He makes me feel so good, Maeve thought, every bit of me feels wonderful. She could sense his returning passion and responded with her own, taking him once again in her mouth to fulfil both him and herself.

By dawn she had lost track of the ways and frequency of their lovemaking for it seemed, as the lightening sky revealed a horizon, that such a night could only have been a distorted fantasy. But it hadn't, for beside her, asleep, lay Nick. She crept away, dragging her crumpled-up sarong along with her, and once outside ran into the sea to bathe. It was ridiculous, she told herself, as she dived again and again under the surface like a seal, I'm marooned on a deserted island and instead of being a disaster, it's wonderful!

There wasn't much to do while they waited to be rescued except fish for their food, gather firewood, collect coconuts, and enjoy each other's company. They must have ended up under the mosquito net in a passionate embrace three or four times a day.

'I think I must be making up for lost time,' laughed Nick one morning as he lay on his side, stroking Maeve's bare back.

'Are you suggesting that you had been considering me in this way for some time then?' teased Maeve, her head resting on her arms as she lay there on her front luxuriating in his touch.

'No,' protested Nick. 'You were a married woman, I would never have entertained such ideas.' He laughed and

333

then conceded, 'Well, not very often. But, to be honest, the occasional carnal thought did flit across my mind. You are very lovely, you know. Anyway, what about you? Did you ever envisage this?' He gave her bottom a contemplative squeeze.

'I have to say yes,' Maeve replied, opening her eyes and smiling at him. 'Dreadful as it is to confess to such moral lapses, yes I did think of us as lovers quite often at the dig.' He gave her an amused, quizzical look and she went on. 'I had to think of something up there, after all. I realize now though, that I got nowhere close to imagining the real thing. I've been in seventh heaven here, my darling: I didn't know love could be like this.'

She closed her eyes again and, after some more caresses, Nick stretched himself over her, his chest to her back, and slowly made love as she lay there, passive in her pleasure.

The ninth night passed and still not a sign of a search party.

'I don't know whether to sound optimistic or pessimistic,' said Nick, 'but I don't think we are going to be rescued in a hurry. I expect there's people looking all over for us and someone should have been in this direction. They haven't, so I think we'd better resign ourselves to a bit of a wait.'

'I have no complaints about the company,' Maeve joked. 'But the diet is getting a bit limited.' She was referring to the emergency rations.

'Don't complain,' scolded Nick. 'There's only a couple more tins of bully beef left. After that it's fish, fish, and nothing but fish. These past days, my dear, have been the halycon days of our food fare. You must savour the noble bully beef while it's still on the menu, not comment on its culinary inadequacies.'

'It's all right for you, five years in the Air Force and bully beef seems normal. But for us with more refined palates, it's grim stuff.'

'Oh, you liar!' he laughed, lunging at her. 'I'm sure I

had flying-fox stew at your place last year. Now that's on a par with bully beef and don't deny it!'

'All right, all right!' she shrieked as Nick wrestled with her. 'I love bully beef! I weep at the mere mention of the stuff! I can't live without it!' She looked up at him and became more serious. 'I can't live without you.'

'Me and canned beef, what a duo,' Nick said, persisting in the joke. He bent and kissed her on the lips. 'Well, I can do without the bully, but I'm getting grave doubts as to whether I will manage without you.'

Five days later and the signalling bonfire still lay unlit on the beach. Neither Maeve nor Nick had sighted a single vessel.

'I'm beginning to think we'll be here forever,' said Maeve cheerfully.

'The Straits of Malacca are the busiest shipping lane in the world, I'd have thought something would have sailed by. These islands must be right off the route,' speculated Nick in reply. 'Oh well, something will turn up eventually. What are you going to do once we get off here?'

'I've tried not to think about that. I won't go back to Kuala Tanah immediately. I know I'll have to confront Kenneth eventually but I need to consider what I have to say. I think he must have been slowly going mad this last year. It's the only explanation I can think of to account for his behaviour.

'Because of what he tried to do to you, and after what you and I have been through, I'm not sure if I'll be able to bear being in the same room as him. I simply don't know what my feelings towards him will be when I see him again. He's got a lot of explaining to do.'

'I'll have to get back to the dig,' said Nick. 'I'm determined to complete the excavation and get to the bottom of what is going on up there. But what about us? What are we going to do? I love you, Maeve, and I very much doubt I can go back to our old relationship of just being good friends.'

'I know,' she replied tenderly. 'I'll sort myself out, Nick, you can count on that. I think my marriage is finished but I have to see him face to face, that I know, and talk it through.' She looked thoughtful, then said, 'Come here and give me a cuddle.' She leaned over from where she was sitting on the ground and tugged his hand. 'I don't want to think too much about the future right now; it seems fraught with problems we don't need to consider here.'

Maeve bestowed some wet kisses on Nick's face and he gave her an affectionate hug.

'Let's go to the hut, it's softer on the bed,' she murmured to him.

Nick lay on his back in the relative coolness of the fisherman's house, Maeve sitting astride his hips. He loved looking at her from this position, her soft belly and round hips rising up from his torso, and her arms stretched out either side of his head so that her breasts hung before his eyes. He reached out and held her about her waist and gave her body the gentlest of shakes. The large breasts swung heavily and tremulously from her shoulders and he raised his face, trying to catch one or other of the broad points as they brushed across his lips. Maeve wriggled appreciatively and took up the swaying herself, luxuriating in the sensation of their fulsome weight and Nick's attention to their nipples. She bent forward and stifled him between them as she fitted his potent member into her and then returned to her sitting position, taking him in one glorious slide right within her.

'You have the most beautiful breasts,' said Nick, fondling them. He took one between his hands and bestowed a kiss on it before returning his attentions to both. 'Magnificent.'

Maeve almost purred at the sensation he produced.

'I used to feel slightly self-conscious about their size, women's fashions being what they are, everyone trying to look like a boy and so on. However they do seem to have come into their own with your attention. They seem just right when you touch them.' She cast a glance down at them. 'They do have a nice shape about them, don't they,' and she flexed her shoulders so that they jiggled in his palms. 'Hhmmm, I like you holding me like that!' she sighed, and continued the business at hand.

Maeve and Nick were lolling about in the shade on the twentieth day when Maeve thought she heard a sound unlike the noises she had grown used to on the island. She hushed Nick and listened intently.

'Can you hear?'

Nick cocked his head but couldn't hear anything out of the ordinary.

'No.'

'I'm sure it's a motor! Concentrate.'

They stood up and searched the horizon. Maeve was right. Way out on the sea two praus were moving across the water, the sound of their putt-puttering engines now audible to both of them.

'Light the fire!' they yelled at each other and ran along the beach to the bonfire, Nick grabbing as he went the package of twigs and paper they kept under the house where it was always dry. Thrusting it under the laid sticks he put a match to it and quickly a plume of smoke rose up from the beach.

'Put some leaves on it to make more smoke,' he called to Maeve as he fanned it into a blaze.

The praus, half a mile out, turned and made for the beach. Nick looked at Maeve and said, 'Like it or not, we're about to be rescued! Which reminds me. For the sake of decorum perhaps you'd better start wearing my sarong under your armpits again, I'm not sure Malays are ready for a mem with a bare top.'

She laughed and unwrapped the sarong from her waist to retie it about her upper body. 'Civilization, here we come!'

The crews of the two fishing praus were amazed at their discovery. After showing them the flying boat and discussing the lack of petrol the Malay captains siphoned off two gallons of petrol from their tanks and into the aeroplane. Neither would accept payment, insisting that it was the least mariners could do for fellow beings in distress. They waited to make sure the aero engine would fire up. Maeve and Nick scurried off to change into their clothes of three weeks ago and throw together what remained of the emergency kit.

With a cough and some splutters, the engine burst into raucous life. Nick guided the Curtiss seaward. It aquaplaned into the air, the roar of its engine drowning out the cheers and shouts of the rough Malay fishermen standing on the beach. Nick took the plane in a circle and zoomed along the beach over their heads in farewell. Maeve watched the tiny islet diminish into a small blot on the pale brown sea as Nick headed for Malacca on the already visible coast of Malaya.

'Mrs Clouston, Mr Manconi, I am amazed and delighted to see you!' said a surprised Straits Settlements customs official. 'Just about all hope had been abandoned for your survival.'

They were sitting in his dockside office and the little town of Malacca lay behind half hidden among its trees. The official continued:

'Yes, this is absolutely first class, we were all dreadfully worried as the search failed day after day to find hide nor hair of you. Um. . .' he hesitated. 'You no doubt will want to return home immediately, Mrs Clouston. There is, however . . . um . . . a bit of bad news I have to give you. It has to be confidential. Your husband is in gaol in Kuala Lumpur. He was arrested four days ago on opium-smuggling charges.'

338

Chapter 25

Kenneth caught sight of himself in the mirror on Maeve's dressing table as he staggered to the bed. He had just vomited over the balcony at the side of the bungalow. Even with his indifference to his appearance these days, he was taken aback at the face that peered back at him from the glass. He looked awful; every bit as awful as he felt. Maeve had been missing for over two weeks now and the remorse of every hour had eaten into his soul. Deep lines were etched down his cheeks, a bristly beard emphasizing the haggardness of his face; bloodshot, stony, staring eyes indicative of a deranged being glared back at him. His hair was greasy and lank.

The shock of the sight quickly passed. He was past caring about most things these days, spending his conscious hours dulling his screaming guilt with whisky and gin. The bungalow, once a tidy, cheerful place, had become more and more unkempt, like its occupant, as the search for Maeve and Nick continued day after day. People had reported hearing an aeroplane that afternoon over Bangi and so the search had concentrated on the foothills of the Negri Sembilan Highlands for the first week. Then other reports had come in saying an aircraft had been seen over the coast north of Bukit Klang; another said south, near Port Dickson, and the search had spread out to explore the coast. So far neither land nor sea searches had turned up any wreckage.

Pravan put a meal on the table twice a day but invariably Kenneth ignored it, seeking solace instead in alcohol. Ten empty whisky bottles and three empty gin bottles were strewn about the living room and bedroom. The last mail he had picked up lay unopened on his desk. A parcel of books for Maeve from the lending library in Kuala Lumpur sat on an occasional table, a constant reminder to Kenneth that she was meant to be here. Drunk enough to be ill but not enough to let sleep slide into his tortured brain, he collapsed on to the bed. The mosquito net was twisted up and over to the far side. He hadn't meant to dispense with it, but the insects didn't seem to care for him any more anyway; possibly they found the alcohol content as damaging to them as it was to Kenneth's own body.

There was loud knocking at the front door. Odd, thought Kenneth dimly, who could that be? Visitors, bearing sympathy and some of the now empty bottles, had come fairly frequently during the first days of Maeve's disappearance but when Kenneth's understandable depression deteriorated into several unpleasant irrational outbursts with overtones of violence, his friends decided it was wiser to stay away until he quietened down. This night-time knock announced the first callers for seven days. He shuffled across the living room and into the hall to open the door. Standing in front of him were four police officers, three European and one Chinese. Kenneth vaguely recognized one as Inspector Elleslie whom he had met in Kuala Lumpur at the beginning of the year.

'Mr Clouston, we'd like to speak to you,' said Elleslie in an official sort of way.

'Is it Maeve? Have you found the flying boat?' Hope suddenly surged in his heart.

'No, I am afraid it's not. I'm sorry about your wife's disappearance. We would like to come in please.'

Kenneth stepped aside and let the four police officers tramp in, their heavy boots echoing on the bare teak floor.

'Clouston, we're here to arrest you on opium-smuggling charges,' intoned Elleslie. 'I could give you an official warning about your legal rights at this point but we'd rather have a friendly chat with you first. It would be in your interests to co-operate.'

Kenneth looked frantically round for the closest chair.

He was going to fall to the floor if he didn't find a seat immediately. Adrenalin rushed through him and he felt he was going to throw up. Christ almighty! This was not supposed to happen – ever!

'I don't want any bullshit from you,' said Elleslie. 'We know you're up to your neck in this smuggling racket with your friend Rajah Ibrahim and with the Triads in Bangi. We've been watching you lot for months and we've decided we've had enough.'

'I don't know what you're talking about,' said Kenneth sullenly.

Elleslie looked skyward in mock disbelief. 'Ganes,' he said, glancing at one of the officers, 'have a look around this pigsty while I impress upon Clouston the seriousness of his predicament.'

The man went into Kenneth's office.

'What I want from you, Clouston,' continued Elleslie, 'are directions to where you are keeping the stuff. We've been watching a truck trundle off your property, two days after the river activity, time and time again. Really, we could set our clocks by it. Now, it didn't take much detective work to decide that the opium is being landed on your estate. Neither did it take much more to realize that you were involved.'

Ganes emerged from the office, as if on cue, with Ali's last payment in his hands. Kenneth had never locked it away and for the past fortnight it had been sitting on the desktop. The officer handed the 10,000 dollars to Elleslie.

'It takes me a year to earn this sort of money, Clouston, and, as I have to buy things, I don't leave it lying around unspent.' He turned to his officer. 'Where was this?'

'Just lying on the desk, sir.'

'Keep looking, there's got to be more. Pull the place apart if necessary.'

Elleslie turned to Kenneth. 'Would you explain how you came by this?'

Kenneth said nothing.

'You're a white man, Clouston, so I'll make it easy for

you. Take us to where you store the stuff and I'll see that you get extremely considerate treatment from the police. There's a variety of charges I can lay against you. Some could see you in prison for the rest of your miserable life. But, with some co-operation from you, perhaps it will just be a rap over the knuckles and your Club memberships terminated. I don't want to see an Englishman in a Malayan gaol but I do want to tidy up this mess you and your friends have made. Make up your mind and quickly. You're nabbed anyway. The truck is coming tonight, we know that. If you don't show me the store we'll stop it and cart its occupants away with you. But take us to where I want to go, and tell me things I need to find out in order to stop further shipments, and perhaps you'll fare better than you deserve to.'

Kenneth held his head in his hands and looked at his feet. He was trapped, he knew; there was a bit of instinctive fight in him which told him to stonewall them and be damned, but it was just bravado. Although he conceded that he hadn't much to live for with Maeve gone, the only realistic thing to do was to co-operate.

'All right. I'll help.'

Ganes returned with the strongbox that had been stashed away in the office.

'Care to unlock this?' enquired Elleslie in a voice that brooked no contradiction to the statement.

Kenneth did and for the last time in his life, looked upon a fortune. Nearly 200,000 Straits dollars packed the metal box. Elleslie let out a low whistle.

'You have been busy, haven't you,' was his comment.

They all went outside into the night. Kenneth discovered two vans out in his driveway full of armed constables, as well as the bull-nosed Morris the officers had arrived in. He was bundled into the back of the motor car.

'Now, be clever and take us to the landing place by a route that won't be used by the Triad's vehicle. I don't want to run into them before they reach the store.'

There was no sign of any activity when Kenneth finally brought the group to the far end of his estate. Elleslie stationed one lot of constables among the rubber trees where Kenneth said the truck would load up, and located the others in the scrub around the go-down. Everybody settled down to wait.

Ages seemed to pass until, finally, some voices were heard approaching. A group of men walked into the cleared space in front of the go-down's door and a metal-on-metal sound told Kenneth that the padlock was being unlatched. Elleslie switched on his powerful electric torch and six Chinese men were starkly illuminated against the wall of the shed. The Chinese police officer barked out a command. The men looked confused and, after some brief milling about, three of them scattered for the cover of the vegetation. A shot rang out, followed by shouts and cries, and the men stood still. Kenneth was relieved to see that Sue was not with them. She must be at the truck and hopefully might escape.

The police handcuffed five men to each other and they were led away in a line. The shot had killed the sixth with a bullet through his chest. Two constables lugged him back between them. Kenneth followed along dumbly, but sufficiently aware of things to stay well back from the Triad captives. Brief as his glance had been at the whole affair from his hiding spot well back from the go-down, he was pretty sure Ha Hek was among the men. If he was, then Elleslie had caught a big fish in the first cast of his net.

Kenneth continued to hover in the background when the Chinese truck driver was added to the group. No Sue. At least that was a consolation, he thought; he couldn't have stood seeing her handcuffed with the rest while he stood back like a Judas. This bunch he couldn't have cared less about, but he would have felt bad about Sue.

Back at the bungalow Elleslie heard everything Kenneth could tell him about the organisation of the scheme.

'Right. Clouston, I'm not going to take you off with the rest,' announced Elleslie. 'Tomorrow you will go over to Rajah Ibrahim's and collect your money as usual. He

343

mustn't suspect anything. You are going to have a couple of police boarders with you from now on; you won't be tempted to do anything silly like trying to run away then. I'm going to work up a plan to nail your friend. I expect you're going to have to be around to help hatch it.'

Kenneth did as he was told and stayed at Kuala Tanah for a few more days. Then, without warning, two police officers arrived and took him to Kuala Lumpur where Elleslie formally charged him with evading Selangor's Customs and Excise laws. Kenneth, locked in an isolated group of cells reserved for special prisoners within the forbidding-looking walls of Kuala Lumpur's gaol, felt prospects were looking decidedly poor for his future.

Inspector Elleslie had come up against an unanticipated problem: it was extremely difficult, both legally and politically, to arrest a member of Selangor's royalty. The plan the police formulated to break the smuggling ring centred on the next shipment of opium upriver. Kenneth's inability to show them the location of go-down number one – a secret trip on a police launch had become hopelessly lost among the serpentine maze of the Kemudi river mouth when Kenneth tried to find it – decided the police to intercept the shipment at Bukit Klang. Such a place would give them the advantage of some high ground and also, with the Istana so close, an opportunity to confront the Rajah Ibrahim and his henchmen red-handed with the contraband opium.

It was at this point Inspector Elleslie and his colleagues discovered that to arrest the Rajah at the same time as his boatmen would be such an outrageous breach of protocol that politically it wasn't on. In vain Elleslie pointed out to the Resident's Secretary that if they didn't, most of the point of the exercise would be lost. It was clear that the Rajah was bankrolling the scheme. To pick off his confederates, whether they be Chinese secret society, Kenneth Clouston, or these unidentified boatmen, would not affect the flow of opium for long while the mastermind of the whole enterprise was still free. However no matter how persuasive the arguments, the Rajah was to remain unmolested.

'Look at it this way,' said the Secretary. 'Selangor is not a British colony. We're here as advisors, not rulers, at the invitation of the Sultan of Selangor and his Rajahs. They rule the place. I know in practice it's more complex than that, but we're talking of principles. And the fundamental principle here is that we work for the rulers; we enforce their laws. Consequently we can't arrest the Rajah for breaking his own laws. He, even if he didn't personally make them, certainly inherited them: he made them so he can break them.'

'But these are the Customs Department laws, not traditional laws of Sungei Kemudi or Selangor,' protested Elleslie. His Commissioner agreed.

'The Resident is not going to argue the matter. It's only fifty years ago British civil servants were being murdered here for, from a Malay point of view, taking too great an interest in Malay affairs. "Meddling" is the word they used then and will again no doubt if we British stray into questioning royal authority. By all means stop the smuggling on the Kemudi but don't get involved with Rajah Ibrahim.'

He looked at the two policemen seated on the other side of his expansive desk and concluded, 'I know, and you know, the Rajah Ibrahim all too well. The Residency has a secret dossier on the man half an inch thick. I imagine your department has a copy, and more, on him as well. He's a swine whose criminal activities include murder and bribery: this smuggling just adds a few more pages to the stack. But he is untouchable. He is a Rajah, a prince of the realm which we have the job of helping to govern. Include him in your list of detainees and we lose our jobs long before he loses his. And that's an end to it.'

As the two police officers were driven back to their headquarters down in the town they continued to analyse the situation.

'We've got two or three weeks before the next shipment will turn up on the river. Let's see what we can dig up in the meantime which might help us get our man,' suggested Elleslie.

'Do it quietly and keep the Secretary's advice in your mind at all times,' said the Commissioner. 'I like my job and I'm not about to lose it because of an inspector's misguided enthusiasm to close the case of the decade. No mistakes!'

Although neither official could possibly have known it, help was to appear from a surprising source.

Maeve and Nick booked into a Chinese hotel Nick knew about, just off Heeren Street, for their first night back in civilisation. It was a clean establishment with the atmosphere of old Malacca and Maeve liked it immediately. It also had a reputation for providing an excellent table.

Dinner that night lived up to both their expectations and after a repast that avoided any taint of fish or coconut, they planned the immediate future over glasses of port.

'First thing tomorrow morning it's essential I fly the aeroplane to Kuching. Rajah Brooke will have returned by now and will be anxious to hear that I, and his new aeroplane, are safe. I suppose I'll be away two or three weeks. What will you do?'

'I've decided I shall stay here and think about everything that's happened over the past year. Hearing of Kenneth's activities has been a bombshell but it certainly explains why he has been the way he has. He's not a man who works well under stress. I remember for instance, he found it hard dismissing his coolies and assistants back in 1928 when the rubber slump hit. From what the Customs Officer told us about the business, Kenneth has been dealing with some very nasty characters, so no wonder he was so nervy these past eighteen months. I wonder how he got involved? I've never heard him refer to any Chinese friends or associates ever.'

'Why would he do it when he so obviously wasn't cut out for it?' pondered Nick. 'He must have been sweating it out every time he dealt with the stuff. All the time I've known him he always looked troubled and preoccupied;

now I know why. He must have known that he'd be in for the high jump when he got caught; phew, what a weight to have on one's shoulders. I could almost feel sorry for him except for the fact that he tried to kill me.'

'I'm now certain he is deranged,' went on Maeve. 'The strain of keeping such a secret must have been incredible. Somehow, perhaps he thought you knew something about his activities and therefore he had to kill you. Something you said that he misinterpreted. Only someone in the throes of madness could have sabotaged the flying boat, it wasn't an act of the Kenneth I first knew.' She sipped her wine. 'To think,' she mused, 'I believed our increased income came from his business partnership with his Rajah friend when all along it was from smuggling opium.'

'Is that how he explained the additional money?' asked Nick.

'Yes. He said this horticultural experimentation of his and the Rajah's was doing well. We had a decent income again despite the slump and the depression.'

'Is that why he was always over at the Rajah's?'

'Yes,' she replied. 'Now that I think of it, though — just what was he doing over there so often if this horticultural thing was non-existent? My goodness, do you think the Rajah of Sungei Kemudi could be involved too?'

'Surely not,' replied Nick, 'he's royalty. Out here that usually means they have vaults full of cash. He wouldn't need to become a smuggler, I would say.'

The waiter hovered.

'Coffee?' asked Nick of Maeve.

'To be honest,' replied Maeve in a low voice, 'I'd like to get upstairs and see what sex with you is like in a real bed with linen and pillows.'

Nick started to laugh. 'I think I'll pass on the coffee too.' He dismissed the waiter and they stood and left the dining room arm in arm.

Nick half woke Maeve, just as the day was breaking, with a kiss.

'I'm off. See you in a fortnight. Don't get blue.' He

kissed her again and was gone. Maeve lay there dozing in the soft bed. Its mattress felt like a cloud after three weeks of lying on a bed of dried leaves thinly covered with sarongs and clothing. Soon she heard the roar of the Curtiss engine out in the harbour, at first loud but then diminishing as the flying boat tore out across the water and into the western sky.

Nick swung the aeroplane around and headed for Singapore 130 miles to the southeast where he had to refuel before the 400 mile flight due east across the South China Sea.

It was mid-afternoon before he was over Kuching. He felt tired and half deaf from the motor noise. Better announce my arrival, he decided. The nose of the flying boat dropped towards the little town cradled between green hills and the river, and he piloted it slowly and gracefully across the river and over the Istana. Below, on the manicured lawn, he saw the aeroplane's shadow race towards the palace, up its front wall and across its shingled roof before being fragmented among the treetops of the wood behind. He banked and returned from the opposite direction, this time winging over the town before swinging to the left into a turn which would place him nose forward into the Sarawak's slow current.

Sir Vyner and the Ranee were at the landing steps of the Royal Compound to greet him. On the opposite bank hundreds of townsfolk crowded the riverside bazaar to see the flying boat.

'My boy, I thought I'd seen the last of you,' said the Rajah shaking his hand. 'We've all been very worried about your disappearance. Come up to the Istana and tell us about it.'

Nick told them about his rescue the day before and about something of the preceding three weeks. He had decided earlier to omit the details concerning Kenneth Clouston's part in the whole affair, and instead attributed the faulty petrol gauge to a leaky valve and a bubble of air.

'Three weeks, eh,' chuckled the Rajah. 'Sylvia and I

have only been back from England a week. No one told us you had already been missing a fortnight – just missing, that's all. I hope your companion in misfortune was congenial company, eh what.'

'That aspect made the forced landing a bit awkward, I must say,' replied Nick. 'We muddled along though and made the best of the situation until we were rescued.' That's the understatement of the year, he thought to himself, as Sir Vyner continued to talk.

Tired as he was, Nick crossed the river that evening to visit his friend Edward Smith for it had been to Edward he had sent a copy of the full text of the inscription on Bukit Klang more than a month earlier. Smith was delighted to see him.

'I saw you this afternoon overhead,' said Edward as they walked from his front door to the living room, 'and I was extremely relieved I might add. Everyone has been concerned. Nothing extravagantly morbid but, you know, we were all worried.'

Nick repeated the tale he had told the Brookes that afternoon and then got down to business.

'It's as we suspected,' said Edward, rolling the rubbing out along the floor and dumping some books at either end to prevent it curling up. 'It's a royal proclamation, impressing upon anyone who reads it, just who rules the roost in the neighbourhood.'

'A name, that's what I'd like to see,' said Nick. 'I'd completed the excavation before I ended up a castaway and it's clear that the boulder sits on the same cultural level as a pile of porcelain sherds which I can date back to the late fourteenth century. Somewhere round the 1370s to 80s, that's where I'd place this writing in history.'

'Oh, there's a name,' Edward ran his finger along the second to bottom line. He stopped at a group of letters. 'Here – Idris.'

'Idris!' Nick exclaimed. 'Are you certain?'

'Absolutely.'

'My God,' murmured Nick. 'What a surprise!' He shook his head. 'Talk about a find! This inscription can change the world over in the little universe of Sungei Kemudi. It's a bombshell.'

'Come on, then, let me in on it,' demanded Edward. 'What's so amazing about finding out that the Rajah of this place, 550 years ago, was called Idris?'

'The chief at Bukit Klang today is an Idris. His family and the Rajah Ibrahim's have been at each other's throats for centuries, contesting as to which of the families is the traditional ruler of Sungei Kemudi. The Ibrahims have always been able to produce the evidence to retain the loyalty of the river people but the Idris have always insisted that the real truth had been buried by the Ibrahims. I've heard the story several times and always assumed Idris Hussein meant that a few vital pages had been torn out of a palm-leaf book centuries ago, something like that.

'But the evidence really was buried! It took us months to unearth this writing as it was virtually cemented in with laterite and stones. Someone, and there's no doubt in my mind that it was an Ibrahim, deliberately walled this up five hundred years ago, thus removing from sight the one thing that proclaimed the legitimacy of the Idris to the throne of southern Selangor. My God! This is really going to put the cat among the pigeons! With this the Idris can, on traditional grounds, claim back Sungei Kemudi. It won't be Rajah Ibrahim once this gets out, but Rajah Idris, the first for five hundred-odd years!'

'Good heavens,' commented Edward. 'What an extraordinary consequence for an archaeologist to set in motion. Knowing a little about Malay politics I'd say we're about to witness a blood-letting along the Kemudi River. You may be in great danger if you return, Nick. I can hardly see you as the favourite person in the Ibrahim family's list of friends.'

Nick suddenly felt as if he had been struck, so devastating was the next revelation that burst in upon his thoughts.

'The vandalism, the destruction of the site, the attempt on my life, I now know who is behind it. Rajah Ibrahim!

He's the one man who had everything to lose if the dig continued. My God! So that's what it was all about.' He shook his head in amazement. 'Somehow he must have got wind of the inscription and checked it out. He was way ahead of me and tried to get me off the hill before I uncovered the crucial letters. But how did he know? He never came to the site.' He sat there pondering, trying to recall who among the visitors to the hill would have passed on such seemingly uninteresting news to the Rajah Ibrahim. After all, until this moment the inscription had no great significance to a casual visitor. Suddenly he knew. Kenneth Clouston.

This is verging on the fantastic, he thought to himself. Was Kenneth Clouston Rajah Ibrahim's hired assassin? Did Clouston sabotage the flying boat on the Rajah's instructions? He realized he couldn't have done so directly, as Kenneth only fortuitously visited the aircraft. There was no way anyone could have heard that he, Nick, was going to fly into Bukit Klang that afternoon. Clouston must have acted on an impulse when an opportunity presented itself, under some broad brief from Rajah Ibrahim that he was to do away with him if a suitable situation presented itself.

Nick followed the thought to its logical conclusion. If Kenneth was working for Rajah Ibrahim in this matter, then he was likely to be working for him elsewhere – such as smuggling opium. That's why Kenneth was always over at the Rajah's, they were organizing the opium shipments! He almost reeled at these conclusions.

'I can't mind-read,' interrupted Edward good-humouredly. 'Who told the Rajah about the inscription? I can see from your expression that you've put your finger on someone.'

'It's amazing. I've just realized that while I've been cheerfully and naively running an archaeological dig, all around me there's been intrigue and crime. My site – Bukit Klang – is smack in the middle of a huge trade in illicit opium and I never heard a whisper. And now it's going to be the centre of the biggest political shake-up

351

for generations.' All he could do was shake his head in wonderment. Nick was, in fact, wrong about some of his conclusions, but in his final deduction he was on target: Kenneth and Rajah Ibrahim were partners when it came to smuggling.

'I must return to Selangor immediately! I can't sit on this information. Idris Hussein must see the inscription and your translation, and I must talk to the police investigating the smuggling racket.'

'Hang on,' said Edward, 'you've only just got here.'

'No, I must go as soon as possible. You wouldn't by any chance know when the next streamer calls, would you?'

'Tomorrow,' laughed Edward. 'The *Kelantan* arrives in the early hours and leaves before dark. I'm taking it, so you can share a cabin if you like.'

'Marvellous. You can tell me all about your trip upriver while we're making the crossing. I'd really like to hear about it.'

It took Nick five days to get to Kuala Lumpur. In the police station he told Inspector Elleslie of his observations and theories concerning Bukit Klang.

'A very interesting story, Mr Manconi,' he said when Nick finished. 'I appreciate you coming here to tell it. First, I'd like to know if you intend laying a charge against Clouston over tampering with your aeroplane?'

'No. It didn't turn out how he meant it to, and it would only bring more grief to Maeve. Anyway, it sounds as if he's in enough trouble as it is.'

'Fair enough. Well, you may be surprised to hear that we have known about Clouston's relationship with Rajah Ibrahim since February this year. It was the amount of money he appeared to have on him that first aroused our curiosity. He spent too freely to fit my idea of a rubber planter in dire straits, so we watched him.' The inspector smiled. 'We also kept an eye on the Kemudi River – from Bukit Klang.'

'What!'

'One of your workers from the Selangor Museum wasn't quite what he seemed, I'm afraid. Liam Chun is one of our undercover men. He's kept a nightly watch on the Kemudi ever since May, recording river traffic, things that skulk through the dark, anything suspicious.'

'My goodness! I never would have known. He is a useful assistant to have on a dig.'

'He's a better policeman. As a matter of fact he was responsible for dealing with your assailant that night you were up there. In line of duty he followed you up to the dig and happened to witness the attack. He intervened but too late for you to have avoided injury. Your attacker went over the cliff, we never did find out who he was. Expect you're right though, in assuming it was one of Rajah Ibrahim's men.'

'I'm simply amazed at what I'm hearing,' said Nick.

Elleslie went on. 'I am very interested in this business of the inscription. There's no doubt about it, is there?'

'None at all. Edward Smith is a first-rate scholar.'

'Then we'll nail the bugger yet!' said Elleslie gleefully. 'You say you're going to Bukit Klang tomorrow? Well, get this news to Idris Hussein as soon as you can. I'm running out of time. If there's a chance that Ibrahim isn't deposed by the end of the week, I want it to happen as soon as possible. I'm sure another shipment is due then, and if he has lost his authority, well, he's answerable to the law just as any other citizen of Selangor.'

Maeve missed Nick, but his absence in Kuching gave her the opportunity to think without any outside distractions. Also, Malacca was a charming little place in which to do just that. For a long time the town had been a backwater of the Colony of Straits Settlements and it had that special ambience of a once-important town which had gracefully declined into a delightful, dilapidated seediness as other cities such as Penang and Singapore took its place in the scheme of things. The pace of life in Malacca pottered along. It suited Maeve's contemplative mood perfectly.

Her life with Kenneth, realistically, seemed finished, she

353

told herself. Not only had he destroyed so much of the gaiety that had originally sparkled between them during this past year and a half, but he had cast a deep shadow over her trust and belief in him. As for the attempt to make Nick lose his life in an aeroplane crash, she decided for reasons she didn't bother to rationalize, that of all the damage Kenneth had done to their relationship, this was the least to resent. The experiences his stupidity had set in motion had been so wonderful, so exquisite, that the reason for them taking place at all paled into insignificance.

But Kenneth was her husband and she had not undertaken her marriage vows lightly. It was more than this though. She alone could understand the pressures and torments he had put himself through and, in that understanding, felt compassion. He had always had a vulnerable side to him and it was a part of him she had warmed to early on, and admired when she saw him with his planter colleagues. He lacked that thick skin so many of them had grown – and pickled in alcohol she mentally added – to cope with life in Malaya. She remembered how the responsibility of dismissing the coolies had weighed upon him in the early months of the slump and of how he had genuinely cared for their futures when, all about, other planters dealt with the same difficulties ruthlessly. True, they didn't crack up as Kenneth had, but they had never had the sensitive qualities Kenneth possessed and which had made him her husband.

She thought of the other planters who had gone under because of the rubber slump. There had been one who had hung himself from a tree in his own plantation, another who had blown his brains out, both in southern Selangor; and several had had nervous breakdowns and had been put away. Kenneth's madness was just another response to the appalling pressures of being impoverished in mid-career, after years of work in a hard climate among hard men, to discover it had been all for nothing. This she could understand, perhaps when no one else would be able to, and it mitigated against ending her marriage to Kenneth.

That was sympathy; but there was also love to be considered. Did she still love Kenneth? She didn't think so. Nick was who she loved, of that she was certain. To her very marrow she wanted him with her. He lived within her every minute of the day: when she sat idly reading in the warm shaded verandah of the hotel; when she went for her ambles about the town looking at the little shops in the quaint narrow streets; and when she lay on the broad bed in her nightie and listened for the night sounds to lull her to sleep. Oh, how she loved him and longed for his return.

But Kenneth was her husband and she had once vowed to stick by him in joys or in sorrow. Well it was certainly the latter right now. Was she about to fail the first real test of her marriage? Because Kenneth had been unable to fulfil his obligations as well as he might have, did that give her the excuse to opt out herself, and withdraw the support she knew her husband must so desparately need right now? Again she didn't know: duty or love, that appeared to be the equation she must work on.

On Wednesday, as she returned from a stroll about the ruins on St Paul's Hill and the Studthuys on the south bank of the Malacca River, she found a letter from Kenneth waiting for her at the hotel's reception desk. It had been sent to the Customs Department to be forwarded to her; obviously the Office in Malacca had informed him that she was alive and lodging in the town.

She opened the envelope with trepidation and sat on the bed to read it.

The letter was an outpouring of apologies and self-condemnation. Kenneth begged that she visit so that he could explain everything more completely, and begged that she not dismiss him from her life. He explained that he hadn't known what he had been doing, and that he was utterly remorseful about the misery he had brought upon her. It was, she thought, surprisingly eloquent for Kenneth and it touched her deeply. She decided she would visit him but not immediately. She still had a lot of thinking to do.

In the post that day was a letter from Nick, like Kenneth's postmarked Kuala Lumpur. It was a rushed scrawl to tell her he was on his way to Bukit Klang and would see her in Malacca that weekend, Saturday morning most likely. Wonderful! she thought to herself.

The translation of the Bukit Klang inscription was the bombshell Nick had thought it would be when he showed it to Idris Hussein. After gathering together several of the senior men, and issuing orders to the others, Idris Hussein commandeered Nick's borrowed car and and had him drive him and his advisers to the railway station at Bangi. The delegation was to visit the Sultan of Selangor in Kuala Lumpur.

By the time Nick had motored back to Bukit Klang the atmosphere of the village was electric with tension. All the men were armed with parangs and spears, some even had army-issue Lee-Enfield .303s which, thought Nick, must have been come by illegally. Bamboo barricades were being thrown up around the perimeter; all in all the once-sleepy village now had the appearance of an armed redoubt. He strode up to the dig where Daan was still loyally directing the workers.

'Hello, Tuan,' they called as he walked up to him. 'We are very pleased to see you are alive and well.'

'Thanks to Allah, yes I am.'

'Allah be praised.'

Daan showed the progress. Nick was deeply touched that his foreman had continued work throughout the weeks he and Maeve were posted missing. The foundations of the royal apartments were not yet completely uncovered but the ground plans were clear. Daan had even instigated some work in an area which looked as if it might have been a formally arranged garden, and had located some piping which led to the remains of a fountain.

'Well done,' complimented Nick. 'I think today might be our last day up here Daan, the hill is about to become a battlefield judging from the activity in the village. Would you get everyone to pack up everything and abandon the site please.'

'Certainly, Tuan,' said the supervisor and went off to organize the workers.

'Liam Chun,' called Nick to the man working away in a square by himself.

'Tuan?' He walked over to Kenneth.

'Inspector Elleslie told me I owe my life to you. Thank you.'

The man smiled. 'All in the line of duty, sir. I was to keep an eye on all visitors to the area and, long-term guest that you are in the village, you fell into the category. I was glad I was up there to help.'

'Well, thanks again anyway.'

Events at Bukit Klang began to move fast. Nick stayed on to photograph the areas excavated during the five weeks he had been absent from the site, and to map the foundations and so forth that had been unearthed.

The next day a contingent of police arrived in the village. The Lee-Enfields vanished from sight immediately but the villagers maintained their armed vigilance while the police lugged a large searchlight, operated by battery, up on to the dig, and another to the river bank. Elleslie was commanding the operation.

'What's going on?' asked Nick.

'Last night a shipment went upstream. On every occasion in the past a second one has gone up the following evening. That's tonight and it's going to be the final one. We're going to stop it all right here.'

'I passed the translation over to Idris Hussein yesterday,' said Nick. 'He went off to see the Sultan on the afternoon up-train so I suppose we'll hear about that particular issue soon.'

'Soon!' laughed Elleslie. 'There's a political crisis raging as we speak, Kuala Lumpur is ringing with gossip about it. Apparently the Sultan summoned a Council of Rajahs last night to discuss the inscription. A small army of Moslem scholars arrived at his Istana along with all the

Rajahs of Selangor shortly after nightfall and the meeting is still continuing. The pundits are saying Ibrahim will have to give way on the matter. However I'm sure the man will extract at least some compromises out of it all.'

'You still hope to arrest him?'

'Oh, yes, but perhaps not tonight after all. It would have been very satisfying to me to have marched up to his door in the early hours of tomorrow and charged him, but he's not here. Anyway the meeting has to run its course before we act with him. We'll get him though.'

Nick, too curious to stay in his bungalow, joined the watchers on the river bank that night.

Towards midnight the faint sound of oars could be heard out across the water. There was a brief whispered conference between Elleslie and Liam Chun and then the searchlight was switched on.

A bright cone of light stabbed across the smooth surface of the river and transfixed a laden boat in its centre. The operator swung it slightly left, then right, and illuminated a second small vessel, equally full of cargo. The boats turned. The other searchlight beamed down from the hill above, trapping one of the boats in its beam while the river-side light concentrated on the other. Three canoes with armed police on board raced out from the bank near Nick and headed for the smugglers. They had been so quiet Nick had been completely unaware of their presence.

Shots rang out. The orang laut were aiming for the searchlights and Nick dived to the ground as a ragged volley of bullets homed in on the river bank. The police returned the fire and, for what must have been only a few seconds but seemed like an eternity, bullets whined back and forth across the river. The cargo boats, still illuminated in the white light, floated slowly downstream, no one now at the oars. Two or three bodies lay sprawled across the bundles of opium, half a dozen others floated alongside the boats.

Elleslie turned to Nick.

'Unless I'm mistaken, we've just heard the opening

shots of a small war here. This village isn't under arms for nothing. There will be some fun and games between the Idris and the Ibrahim as of today, and you, Manconi, just have to be enemy number one to one of the factions. For your own safety I would strongly advise you to leave tomorrow.'

Nick took the Inspector at his word and left for good the next afternoon.

'Nick! You're two days early, this is wonderful! Wonderful!' exclaimed Maeve as she answered a tap at her door at nine o'clock that night. 'Ohh, how nice to hold you again.' She pressed herself against him, her arms holding him tight. Nick could feel her warm breasts against his chest as he returned the embrace.

'I was just going to go to bed with a book,' she said as she closed the door.

'Well, you can throw away the book,' Nick joked as he drew her to him again. 'It's lovely to see you again, my love. You look rested and happy.'

They piled into bed, and made love unhurriedly. Then Nick told her all the news: of the translation; of the conversation with Elleslie; and of last night's events.

'You must be exhausted,' said Maeve. 'You've been on the go non-stop for a week by the sound of it.'

'I suppose I have. But I'm staying here for a fortnight and not going anywhere. I have to be back in Kuching at the beginning of October so I've got two weeks to spend with you and to write up the dig. It's going to be bliss!'

'I think so too,' replied Maeve, snuggling up to him. 'It's so good to have you back.' She stroked his body and could feel him revel in her touch, and she laughed with happiness at her contentment.

While Nick was with her, Maeve put off any further analysis of her predicament with the two men in her life. She was so totally happy with Nick at her side that the days slipped past without her even noticing. They went for a walk each morning before the day warmed up into its usual enervating equatorial steam bath, and the middle hours were spent writing up the excavation. A photographer just round the corner, next to the Hong Kong and Shanghai Bank, processed the films Nick had snapped on those last two days at Bukit Klang, and Maeve helped index them into the reports. Evenings were just as lazily filled with dinner and a stroll afterwards before retiring to their room.

One morning, Maeve didn't know what day it was, they were having a cup of tea in a small Indian teashop diagonally opposite the Church of St Francis of Xavier, when a newspaper headline on a paper seller's stall caught Nick's eye.

'Hang on,' he said, putting his cup down and rising to his feet. 'I'll just buy the *Times*.'

In a minute he was back with a copy of the *Straits Times*. The lettering across the top of the front page was heavy and black, 'New Rajah', it read and under it in smaller typeface, 'Political upheaval in Sungei Kemudi'. Nick scanned the page while Maeve craned over to read it also.

'My goodness,' she said. 'You really started something, didn't you? Is it safe for you to return to Bukit Klang now that Idris Hussein is Rajah of Sungei Kemudi?'

'I doubt it. Did you read the paragraph about the violence along the river? There's several dead and a score wounded so far, it claims. I think it will take months for the new order to impose its authority on the more recalcitrant of the Ibrahim supporters. You can be sure Ibrahim is not the only big loser in this, there'll be a bunch of them fighting a rearguard action to hang on to what they can of their former privileges. No, I think southern Selangor will be an unhealthy place for me for quite some time.'

Finally came the last day of Nick's stay in Malacca. Despite her efforts to make it as happy as the others, Maeve found her mood tinged with sadness the whole time. That night as they lay in each other's arms they talked about the future.

'I won't ask you to divorce Kenneth so that we can

get married,' said Nick. 'All I'll offer, if you do decide to leave him, is myself as friend, husband, whatever. I know you have a lot to work out, so don't feel there's any pressure from me for you to come to a decision. The only irrevocable thing is that I love you. I can't imagine ever not loving you.'

'I know, Nick.' She lay with her head on his shoulder, her right arm flopped across his chest. 'I've decided I'll leave tomorrow also. I'll go up and see Kenneth and get whatever has to be tackled over and done with. The four weeks here have been like a balm to my anxieties. I'm pretty sure I'll sensibly deal with seeing him. I know I couldn't have at the beginning of the month.'

She stirred and rolled on top of him. The night became a dreamlike pleasure world of erotic and sexual delights as they loved each other as if for the last time.

At the railway station the next morning Nick saw Maeve to her train. He was leaving a little later in the day on a Straits Steamship Company ship for Singapore.

'I'll be staying at the Europa Hotel, write to me there,' she said tearfully. 'I'll be there for weeks, I imagine.'

'And you write to me at Kuching,' he replied, holding her hand.

The whistle on the locomotive tooted. It was time to leave.

'Goodbye darling, see you soon,' she said, reaching up and kissing him.

'Goodbye. I'll write as soon as I reach Kuching.' He hugged her tight and released her. 'Goodbye.'

The next day, in the afternoon, Maeve was led across a quadrangle of flagstones to a small wing of white-washed cells within Kuala Lumpur Gaol. The unremitting security of its high walls and barred and steel-shuttered windows depressed her spirits and she began to dread seeing Kenneth. The officer marched briskly to a steel door, and, producing a ring of keys from a trouser pocket, proceeded to unlock it. Beyond was a reception room containing a wooden table with a straight-backed chair either side of it

361

and another chair over against the wall. Maeve was asked to sit at the table and the warder disappeared through another door. From the echo his hobnail boots made on the floor, Maeve guessed it was a corridor he was walking along. The steps stopped. Silence. Then a distant clanging of steel doors, and the steps became louder as he approached. Kenneth stepped through the door.

'Hello Maeve, thanks for coming.' He didn't try to touch her but just sat down in the seat opposite and smiled shyly at her.

Maeve was surprised at the change in him. Kenneth looked healthy and clear-eyed; years had dropped from his face.

'Hello, Kenneth,' she replied. Now that she was in front of him she didn't know where to start.

'You look awfully well for a convict,' she began.

'It's the lack of alcohol for a month, plus three meals a day again. I'm surprised at the change myself. I don't think I'll drink again if I get out of here, I actually enjoy not drinking I discover.'

'Kenneth, why did you sabotage Nick's flying boat? It's the one thing in this whole mess you've got yourself into that I don't understand. He was never anything to you but a friend. What madness came over you? You must explain if we're ever to get anywhere as of today.'

'I was insane, that I now know, Maeve. At the time though, I couldn't bear the idea of you two having an affair. Ever since I saw you together up on the dig, I was obsessed by it. When the opportunity came to pay him back, I did so unthinkingly. And oh so stupidly.'

'What are you talking about? What affair are you talking about?'

'Yours and Manconi's,' said Kenneth miserably. 'One day when I came to pick you up I saw him with his hand on your bosom and you in his arms. I just saw red. I know it was a pathetic response but, given everything else happening, I couldn't see anything in proportion.'

Maeve looked puzzled for a moment. Then she realized what Kenneth must have witnessed.

362

'You prize clot!' she yelled at him. 'He had probably just saved my life. A giant centipede had crawled on to my blouse. I was petrified but Nick got it off. If he hadn't held me I would have been on the ground in a dead faint. Oh, Kenneth, you idiot! Why on earth didn't you say something right then and there?' She stared at him, then as the irony of the whole situation dawned on her, started a chuckle, which grew into a laugh. 'My goodness, you sabotaged Nick's aeroplane because you thought we were having an affair.'

Kenneth looked nonplussed and awkward. 'I don't know what to say. I'm a complete ass. Really Maeve, I'm incredibly sorry to have done it. If I knew how to make it up to you and to Manconi, I would. It must have been hell stuck on an uninhabited island wondering if you were ever to be rescued.'

'Why did you get so angry anyway? Given the attention you've bestowed on me these last eighteen months I would have thought I would have been justified in having an affair. I'm surprised you felt jealous.'

'Maeve, I've always loved you. You know the whole awful truth about what I was involved in so you now know why I was such a bastard all that time. I'm not offering excuses,' he hastily added. 'What I've done to our marriage is inexcusable. I'm just explaining. If I could set the clock back eighteen months I would. But that's impossible. I do love you, Maeve. One of my fears all along, as I wrestled with my panic over what I'd got myself into, was that I would lose you. When I saw you that afternoon I thought I had. I think I still have but it's because of my own stupid actions. I am really very sorry, Maeve. I've been a total cad to you whom I've needed and loved more than anything else in this world.'

To Maeve's dismay he started to weep quietly into his hands.

'Kenneth, nothing is over yet. You're still my husband. I have to think a lot about everything you tell me. Here, use my hanky.' She rummaged in her bag and produced a white linen handkerchief and handed it to him.

'Cheer up. You've got more problems than just us on your shoulders so let's just take them one at a time. I'm not leaving Kuala Lumpur until I know exactly what I want to do. I can see you every day if that's allowed.'

'That would be marvellous, really marvellous, Maeve,' replied Kenneth gratefully.

They talked for another hour and a half and then the warder asked Maeve to leave. She stood up, hesitated, and then came around the table and gave Kenneth's shoulders a comforting hug as he sat there.

'You know, you should have quit drinking long ago, I can see the Kenneth Clouston I knew in London, now that you've stopped.'

Maeve returned the next day. Soon there wasn't anything more to say about Kenneth's past activities, they had talked themselves dry of the topic and they began to talk about other things: the dig, Ali's demise, the news in the morning's paper. The future was avoided by both of them. Kenneth had visibly responded to Maeve's first visit and looked cheerful now that he had unburdened himself. Perhaps there was hope for them after all, thought Maeve as she walked back to the Europa. But of course there wasn't, she immediately reasoned; Kenneth would be lucky to be out of prison in ten years' time. It was silly to entertain any thoughts that they could be husband and wife again with the criminal charges he was facing.

It didn't however turn out that way. The next morning Kenneth was taken to the prison governor's office. There, along with prison officials, was a magistrate and Inspector Elleslie. The Inspector was in charge of the formalities.

'Clouston, you are about to make history, albeit of a rather shabby kind. First, you are part of a great white-wash arranged by the Sultan of Selangor and the British Resident.'

Kenneth looked blankly at him.

'Oh yes, your miserable name has been bandied about at the highest levels. The upshot of it all is that the ex-Rajah Ibrahim is not to be charged with drug smuggling so as not to embarrass the Malay aristocracy; and you are not to be charged with drug smuggling, therefore sparing us, the British community, any embarrassment. Congratulations,' he added caustically.

'Your erstwhile royal friend is going on an extended holiday to the Seychelles Islands where it will take him many years to obtain a passage back to Selangor. You make the history books again. Clouston, you are to be deported from British Malaya, the first Briton to be so treated for more than twenty years. Well done.'

Kenneth was dumbstruck. Free! He was free to go!

'Don't look so delighted. There are some conditions. One, you never speak to anyone about this, with the exception of your wife, and two, you make your exit extremely discreetly. You have a month to tidy up your affairs and to get out. To the best of my knowledge little word has come out about this sordid business so you may even leave without being totally disgraced. Remember though, leave you will, and go quietly about it.' Elleslie reached for some documents. 'Sign these.'

Kenneth did so and they were witnessed by the magistrate and the prison governor.

'That's that,' said Elleslie. 'Clouston, I'm not having you hanging about the streets of Kuala Lumpur giving the place a bad name. Is your wife coming this afternoon?'

Kenneth nodded.

'Well, you stay here until she does and you can leave with her.' He looked at the warder by the door. 'Put him in the main reception area until Mrs Clouston makes her daily visit. He's free to leave then.'

'They've dropped all charges?' said Maeve, incredulous at the news. 'Everything?'

'Yes, with certain conditions attached, the first being that I leave with you.'

'Let's go before they change their minds,' she said, jumping to her feet. Minutes later they were out in the busy street.

'Maeve, there's a million things we have to talk about,'

said Kenneth, his voice edged with uncertainty. 'Can I come back to the hotel and try to sort things out?'

She looked at him with a soft smile on her lips and said, 'Of course. I was going to suggest it myself.'

Up in her room, they talked of things that they had to discuss, earnestly and seriously, and the hours turned from afternoon to night. Maeve had dinner brought up to the room and they continued until late in the evening.

'I can't stay awake any longer, Maeve. I'll sleep on the settee so as not to intrude on you if that's all right.'

'Sleep in the bed you silly thing,' she said. 'I'll join you later.' Perhaps, she wistfully thought to herself. 'I've still got a few things on my mind.'

He fell asleep and Maeve moved to a cane chair at the open french doors in order to look at the night sky, letting her thoughts freewheel among the scattered constellations within her view. What a tumultuous time it had been! The sky took her mind back to the night skies of her voyage out to Malaya three years ago. Such a time that had been, she sighed to herself. She and Kenneth had been so suited to each other it had seemed then. He was amusing and romantic in her eyes, and a home in the East had appeared perfect in those innocent days. What if the slump had never occurred? she wondered.

She cast her mind back not quite so far, to her first twelve months in Selangor when rubber was a profitable, established industry. The parties, picnics, and socials: they too had been fun. The bubble that was hers and Kenneth's domestic happiness had only burst when those rubber prices went through the floor.

She turned to look at him sleeping there. In the dim light he again looked the handsome young planter she had known on the balcony of that dance hall in Hammersmith in September 1927 when he had haltingly proposed to her, sleep having softened the worry lines from his brow and cheeks. He looked vulnerable and in need of care. She had liked his lack of brashness then, and now she saw that same look on his face as he rested on the bed.

Nick. She would never have met Nick unless she had

married Kenneth and come to Selangor with him. She might never have worked with him if Kenneth hadn't surrendered sole possession of the Ford and taught her to drive so that, as it turned out, she could motor over to the archaeological site as much as she liked.

The thoughts followed wills of their own across her imagination and, as the night passed its zenith, settled down into a conclusion Maeve accepted.

She undressed in the bathroom and slipped into her nightie. Tiptoeing across the room she clambered into bed beside her husband and was soon asleep.

It was on the edge of day when something woke her. The room was barely light and the air cool and refreshing. She turned her head to see what had disturbed her. Kenneth sat on the side of the bed looking out to the french doors where she had sat earlier. By the sag of his shoulders she guessed he was lonely and sorrowful and she instinctively put out her arm and, taking him around his chest, pulled him back into bed alongside her. He rolled towards her and buried his face in her shoulder. Her skin felt wet immediately. He was crying.

'It's all right, Kenneth,' she said, wrapping both arms around him. 'It's all right. We're together. It's been a long bad dream and now it's finished.'

She hugged him comfortingly and kissed his hair again and again to sooth him. He moved his face at last and she kissed his cheek and his eyes softly. Somehow, imperceptibly, the kisses became more lingering, and then, finally, her lips met his. It felt good and she bestowed another on his mouth. A warm glow spread through her body. Perhaps, she distantly thought as her desire mounted, this will tell me what I should do. And with that last lucid thought she let her passion take her where it wanted.

Kenneth responded more gently and imaginatively than she had known him to do for nearly two years, touching her where suddenly it mattered, and rising with her urges no matter what they were. With a thrust he entered her but withdrew as she guided him on to his back so she could sit astride him and tease herself by letting her breasts swing, one, then the other, into his open mouth. She repeated the motion, exciting herself ever more intensely as she continued. She wriggled her bottom so that Kenneth re-entered her, and, in a climactic thrust, felt his semen surge deep within as her own orgasm came.

Towards the end of that week she wrote to Nick to tell him of the extraordinary events, such that she knew of them, that had led to Kenneth's unexpected release. She also told him of their mended marriage and the hope she had for it holding together. There were, she wrote, many things they would have to work through to re-establish the trust it had once held for her. And she wrote of her love for him, and that he would always be her special friend. She dropped it in the mail-box in the wall of the Post Office, confident Nick would understand and continue to love her.

The next day a letter arrived from Kuching; hers and this one had crossed in the mail. She sat down in one of the dozen armchairs in the foyer of the Europa and opened the envelope.

Nick was leaving Kuching. Not forever, but at least for five months. The Rajah was returning to Europe in November and Nick, as his librarian, was to accompany him in order to attend some book auctions in which the Rajah was interested. It would be, Nick wrote, an interesting experience visiting some of the famous private libraries in Great Britain and Europe. He went on in his characteristically enthusiastic way about the impending journey and, two pages later, endorsed his love and friendship for her.

Maeve laid the letter on her lap and smiled at the image of Nick that was her mind's picture at that moment. She loved him for his zest for life and for his concern for those around him. She loved him so much, but life could possibly be such a whirl of adventures that lesser mortals such as herself would never keep up with him. Love him she always would; she loved Kenneth too, though without that edge of excitement Nick had conjured out of her; and it was Kenneth she would stay with.

On 1 November, on the eve of their departure to Sydney, Australia, Maeve was told by Dr Nesbit, a general practitioner with rooms in Watling Street, that she was pregnant. If any doubt had lingered in her mind during that October about the rightness of that decision, it did no longer.

Epilogue

The telling of the tale had taken several hours.

'I could do with a cup of tea, how about you?' Maeve asked Leila, getting to her feet.

'You stay there, I'll make it,' said her daughter. She put the electric kettle on in the kitchen and returned to the lounge. 'It's amazing to hear about Dad's misspent youth. My goodness, what a racket he was involved in!'

'He wasn't a youth, dear. He was in his early thirties and should have been old enough to know better. He couldn't have though. The rubber slump of 1928, and the great Depression that followed were unprecedented experiences, times that made many people do things that in a less traumatic period they would have steered a mile clear of.'

'You know, I find it hard to believe that you spent three weeks on a desert island in the company of what sounds like a most delightful man, and that nothing happened,' said Leila teasingly.

'Really, Leila!' replied Maeve with mock shock. 'I was a married woman. In those times gentlemen had a respect for women that I think is almost extinct in this day and age. Of course nothing "happened" as you insist on putting it. The archaeologist was a thoroughly decent man; he respected all my wishes.'

Leila went out to make the tea and returned a couple of minutes later with everything on a tray.

'What happened to your archaeologist friend?'

'We corresponded all through the thirties and remained good friends. He stayed with Rajah Brooke for a long time and travelled extensively. Then he was working for the

Singapore Museum. On 8 December 1941 a bomb during a Japanese air-raid landed on the building where the staff were sheltering. It was in the Sydney papers that everyone was killed. I never heard from Nick again.'

'Oh dear, that's very sad.'

'It was indeed. Kenneth and I were both very upset when we realized Nick was among the casualties. He was a fine man.'

The mother and daughter sipped their tea companionably.

'I'm really glad you told me about Malaya, Mum. I had no idea you and Dad had lived such adventurous lives.'

'I suppose it is an adventure now that it's twenty-odd years ago. But the business deeply troubled your father, I'm sure it frightened him more than he ever let on, and so we never talked about it. I knew he didn't like to be reminded of what he regarded as the most foolish period of his life, and I never did.'

Leila yawned. 'Lectures first thing tomorrow. I'm off to bed. 'Night.' She kissed her mother and left the room.

The night was balmy so Maeve stepped outside on to the lawn where she had been sitting in the afternoon. Scent from the spindly trunked angels' trumpets assailed her senses. A few steps further and the frangipani blooms asserted themselves. The garden smelled so special on summer nights, she thought to herself. A flood of memories had spilled out with the telling of that small piece of family history to Leila.

As she stood there, looking out towards the harbour, Nick's face came before her mind's eye: large as life with that lovely crooked smile and his warm eyes grinning at her. He had been such a great friend and she had, as she had vowed all those years ago in Malaya, never stopped loving him. Kenneth took his place for a moment, not as he had appeared at the end of his life when he was in his fifties, but young as he had been along with Nick. She started to weep softly for their deaths, for each in his own way had been a loved friend.

She pondered over what she had told Leila, and what

she hadn't, for there were parts about that period of her life she knew she would never tell anyone. However, one small but important detail of those days — the result of that incredible time with Nick put her in a quandary. Should she, she wondered, tell Leila that Nick Manconi had been her father? Tonight as she had looked at Leila while relating the tale she saw flashes of his looks and mannerisms show again and again in her daughter's personality. There was a lot of him in her, she smiled to herself.

Sydney, 5 April 1953

'Come on, Leila, do hurry up or we'll be late,' called Maeve from the lounge. 'I've telephoned for a taxi and it will be here soon.'

'I'm ready, I'm just trying to get used to it. This isn't what I would have chosen to wear you know,' replied Leila from her bedroom.

'I know that. That's why I chose it. You would have turned up in your usual student rags. I paid for the tickets so I reserve the right to be seen with a suitable partner.'

Maeve and Leila were off to a night at the opera. *The Magic Flute* was being presented in the Sydney Town Hall by the Sadler's Wells Opera Company under Norman Tucker. It had been difficult to procure tickets but Maeve had nevertheless obtained two. Leila, who was desperate to go, could only attend if she wore what Maeve borrowed from her shop for the night. It was this selection she was now being rather coy about. At last she emerged from her room.

'I say you look smashing!' she said as soon as she set eyes on her mother. 'Very chic.'

Maeve blushingly agreed with her. She was dressed in an evening gown that complemented her middle-aged figure perfectly. It was dark-blue spun silk; a long full skirt dropped to the floor, the slim-fitting straight-topped bodice emphasized by a wide band at her waist. Slender straps held it up. Together with the choker of pearls around her throat, and the long evening gloves on her arms, her bare shoulders looked classically elegant. The stole to complete the outfit lay draped over an armchair next to her.

'You look very lovely too. I told you I'd get something absolutely right for you,' Maeve said, returning the compliment. 'I do know clothes, you know.'

Maeve's exasperation with her daughter's dress sense had been a standing joke for years. She was right, Leila looked beautiful. Maeve had borrowed from her shop window a calf-length evening dress in white with a strapless bodice. Across its wide skirt ran horizontal bands of large flower designs, 'bayadere', which was the latest thing in Sydney. She too wore gloves with a bracelet over one. Her other jewellery was restricted to pendant earrings.

'What was all the fuss? You look like a fashion plate.'

'This takes a bit of getting used to,' Leila said, tugging at her low décolletage.

'It's the fashion,' Maeve replied, thinking her daughter's figure had never looked better. 'It looks good on you.'

Leila glanced down at her lightly tanned chest and cleavage and decided that perhaps her mother knew best after all.

A car tooted from the street.

'That's the taxi. Let's go,' said Maeve.

The various foyers of the Sydney Town Hall were a milling throng of elegantly dressed men and women. The Clouston women couldn't see a soul they knew and eventually made their way to the stalls. Maeve's seats were good ones, only eight rows back from the orchestra pit and five seats in from the left side aisle; not quite centre stage but close enough. They sat back while the theatre filled. The orchestra tuned their instruments . . .

One row in front and half a dozen seats to the right of Maeve and Leila, midway between them and the right side aisle, was seated a distinguished-looking, middle-aged man whose senses were absorbed with the music pouring from the orchestra and singers. The opera was well into Act One and Papageno was about to be muzzled by the handmaidens of the Queen of the Night. The most famous of all Mozart's arias was about to follow; Tamino's song of love, inspired by the tiny portrait of Pamina in his hand. The familiar music washed over the audience and Tamino began to sing:

> Is she the dream to which I waken,
> The pursuit where I am overtaken,
> Body and mind and heart and soul?
> She is! To love her is my goal.

Nick Manconi let the beautiful aria lift his spirits and carry them away. He had heard this music countless times. Tonight, for what reason he never knew, it took his thoughts high and away and, for a moment, out of time to a bungalow in a wet Kuching night twenty-three years ago. As his imagination wandered something made him break his reverie. He glanced over his left shoulder to the line of faces in the row behind lit softly by the reflected stage lighting, and his heart nearly stopped.

It can't be her! His brain became almost dizzy as his pounding heart pumped adrenalin through his body. He looked back at the stage. Tamino sang of his need for Pamina. But those finely arched eyebrows and full lips – he had once known them so intimately, he had never forgotten the lines and shapes of that face he had loved so dearly. It had to be her. The atmosphere of the theatre changed as the Queen of the Night made her majestic entrance. Nick turned to sneak another glance.

It was her! He knew in his heart it was Maeve. Discreet as he had been, his second glance had attracted her attention. As he turned away she looked at him. For an instant their eyes met, hers at that first millisecond of contact just curious, then she started and stared as if a dagger had pierced her bosom. Utterly confused and with heart racing, he attempted to return his attention to the performance in front of him.

Maeve was devastated. This cannot be, she repeated to herself as her mind tumbled with confusion. He had been gone eleven years! I've lived half my adult life knowing my dear Nick was numbered among the war dead! Her heart bumped alarmingly: Nick is alive. Something began to melt within her and a curious emotional mixture of fear and delight took over and slowly, gradually, she calmed down. She stole a look at him. Even though he was now grey-haired and with the less precise jawline of the middle-aged she could see that it was him but she wondered whether, if she hadn't seen his eyes, she would have recognized him.

After an eternity the curtain fell on Act One and it was the interval. Leila and Maeve exited by the left aisle but Nick was forced to take the other on the far side of the theatre. As she turned to walk out Maeve glanced across the crowd of seats and caught the man's eye for a moment. He looked dumbstruck and she wondered if she looked the same from over where he stood. She must find him out in the foyer.

Nick pushed his way through the crowd trying to find Maeve. It was an absolute crush of people, he couldn't see her anywhere. To make it more difficult she wasn't the tallest of people either, he thought to himself as he anxiously looked this way and that. He heard his name called.

'Professor Manson, Professor Manson.'

He turned and saw one of his graduate students, Leila Clouston, at his side.

'Hello Leila. Enjoying the performance? It's a wonderful production isn't it.' He did his best to be congenial while all the time distracted with trying to find Maeve.

A woman stepped next to Leila and Nick could only gape.

'Professor Manson, this is my mother. Mother, this is Professor Nicholas Manson, the lecturer I've told you about at university.'

Their response astonished Leila.

Professor Manson took her mother's hand and said hoarsely, 'I thought I'd never see you again.'

'I thought you died in the war,' replied Maeve faintly.

They continued to hold each other's hand, speechless.

'You two look as if you've seen ghosts,' said Leila. 'You know each other from somewhere?'

'Leila, this is Nick Manconi, the archaeologist I was telling you about a couple of months ago.'

'My goodness,' said Leila, momentarily rendered speechless herself. The bells rang the warning that Act Two would begin in five minutes.

'You two will have a lot to catch up on. Mum,' she looked at Maeve, 'I'm going back in. I don't imagine you'll be wishing to see the rest of the opera.'

'I'll meet you here when it finishes. I need to talk to Nick.'

The crowded foyer emptied and, from within, the orchestra could be heard. Nick led Maeve to a sofa between some potted palms over near the grand stairway and they sat down.

'I don't know what to say. You along with all the Singapore Museum staff were reported dead back in the first days of the Japanese war,' said Maeve. 'I never heard from you again.'

'But I wrote, several times,' explained Nick. 'I wasn't at the Museum the day it was hit, but I'm not surprised I was mentioned among the casualties, Singapore was chaotic in those last weeks. I got out through Sumatra and eventually ended up in Ceylon. I wrote to you from there as soon as I could. I suppose it must have been mid-1942 that I did so.'

'To the usual address?'

'Of course.'

'We moved to northern New South Wales in early 1942. Kenneth was involved in some war work up there. Your letters never reached me. We didn't come back to Sydney until 1945 and then it was to a different home.'

'My God,' said Nick, 'this is overwhelming. I never thought I'd see you again! Living overseas, there was no

376

way I could trace you. I've only been living in Australia six months and I'd long ago decided it would be impossible to find you, so I didn't even attempt to. For all I knew you might have gone back to Great Britain. But you're here!'

'And you teaching Leila,' marvelled Maeve. 'What an extraordinary coincidence.'

'Oh, I don't know,' said Nick. 'You were a good archaeology assistant, it's probably in her blood.'

They continued to hold hands and talk. Maeve told Nick of Kenneth's death a year ago.

'Why did you change your name?' asked Maeve. 'If Leila had been chatting on about Professor Manconi instead of Manson I would have been over to the university like a shot. Manson just didn't ring any bells.'

'Because of the war. After Mussolini entered the war in 1940 Italian names weren't terribly fashionable things to have in British Malaya. There was talk of interning enemy aliens, meaning German- and Italian-named people, so I changed it by deed poll to Manson. Made life a lot easier.'

'My goodness, my dear Nick next to me again,' murmured Maeve. 'If I'd been given a pound note for every time I've thought of you these twenty-two years I'd be a wealthy woman.'

'It's wonderful to see you again,' replied Nick, squeezing her hand.

Applause filtered through into the foyer and ten minutes later the happy throng poured forth from the theatre. Leila found them chatting on the sofa.

'Nick is coming home for a cocktail,' announced Maeve and, on his arm, they walked to the taxi rank.

Leila made everyone a drink and sat, sipping hers in bemusement as she watched her mother and her professor laughing and talking away about people and events she had never heard of before. She couldn't get a word in edgeways. She finished her drink.

'Goodnight. I'm off to bed,' she called and retired to her room.

Finally, very late, Maeve and Nick ran out of things

that had to be said. They sat there silently, each thinking their own thoughts within the cocoon of the other's companionship.

'Nick,' said Maeve in a soft voice, breaking the silence of minutes, 'let's go to bed. You can't go home.'

Wordlessly he followed her. She turned off the lights and took him to her room.

'Let's leave the light off,' she said. He heard the rustle of her clothes as they fell to the floor, then the touch of her hand as she led him to the bed. With a sigh of profound contentment she wrapped her arms about his bare body and held him. This time she wasn't letting go of him.

She and Nick were having a late leisurely breakfast in the sunlit kitchen when Leila slopped in. It was Sunday and she didn't rise until at least mid-morning on the weekends. She was in a dressing gown and too-large slippers which flip-flopped on the floor as she walked, Maeve and Nick could hear her approaching the kitchen long before she reached the door. Nick glanced at Maeve and she smiled reassuringly back at him. The sound of the slippers stopped.

'Oh,' said a surprised Leila. She recovered quickly. 'Good morning, one and all.' She caught her mother's eye and began laughing.

'Mother, I knew there was more to that desert-island story than you were letting on!'

'Have a seat and join us,' replied Maeve, smiling in affection at her daughter. 'There's actually more to the story than that. Sit down and I'll tell you the rest.'

THE END

SHAKE DOWN THE STARS
by Frances Donnelly

There were three of them, three bright pretty girls – though Beattie was beautiful rather than merely pretty – who all came from the same village and who couldn't wait to throw themselves into the golden future.

Virginia was shrewish, bitchy, and biting. Even though the family estates were mortgaged up to the hilt she was still the squire's daughter and she didn't let anyone forget it. She just knew that when she 'came out' and turned into a real London debutante, everything was going to be O.K.

Beattie was only the gardener's daughter – and Virginia didn't let Beattie forget that either – but as well as being beautiful, Beattie was bright. Beattie had won a place in a teacher-training college and nothing was going to stop her putting the village and everything in it right behind her.

Lucy was – well – just thoroughly nice. Used by everyone – and especially by Virginia – all she really wanted was to marry nice middle-class Hugh, with whom she was wildly in love, and carry on living a nice middle-class life.

What none of them had reckoned with was that it was 1939. The three pretty girls were about to be thrown headlong into the turmoil of the war.

'I warmed to *Shake Down the Stars* and I think it will be tremendously successful'
Susan Hill

0 552 12887 2

A MULTITUDE OF SINS
by Margaret Pemberton

Since she was ten Elizabeth had been forced to give way to the men in her life. First her father, a lonely, selfish widower who needed his daughter as his companion, then Adam, her middle-aged husband, who carried her off to the brittle world of Hong Kong society, ignoring the burning musical talent that she constantly had to repress.

And then she met Raefe Elliot, womaniser, soldier of fortune, who repeatedly rocked Hong Kong with his scandals, and between the two of them flared a wild release of love that exploded into the most shocking scandal of all.

As the Japanese prepared to invade Hong Kong, as the old world was about to be forever destroyed, Elizabeth at last found happiness – in her love, and in her progress as a musician.

And then the thunder of a savage and terrifying battle broke over her life, and she and Raefe became fugitives in a wartorn world.

0 552 13092 3

SPRING IMPERIAL
by Evelyn Hart

Cara Thornton was shy, strictly reared – by her elderly Briga-
dier father – and twenty years old when she fell wildly in love
with Lance Gardner. She had never met anyone like him in
the whole of her conventional, middle-class life. For Lance,
devastatingly handsome and heir to a crumbling palace in
the Ganges Basin, was Anglo-Indian – great-grandson of a
British officer and a Moghul princess.

Against the wishes of her family, in spite of his poverty and
her inexperience, they made their plans. He would return to
Calcutta to prepare a home for her. She would follow in a
year's time - in September 1939. And in the meantime they
would write, and Cara would stand firm against the pressures of her family.

Thus began their lifetime story of love, of separation, of
betrayal, of danger in war and constancy in peace.

0 552 13438 4

LUSTRE
by John Maccabee

Abandoning his family in New York, Tom Aspinall signed onto the Medusa, sailing for Tahiti. Escaping the flames of a sinking ship, castaway on a Pacific island, he was a man without a country, without a past, destined for a fate that beggared an emperor's dreams. As Tom Street, he plundered the seas for their voluptuous jewels, lost his heart to a magnificent beauty – and battled a relentless enemy determined to destroy his empire and the woman they both desired. In his wake he left a trail of blood and treachery, as Tom Street became legend, the man who conquered a kingdom in pearls – and swore vengeance in the name of love.

0 552 12871 6

YANGTZE
by Alan Fisher

It had taken seventeen days for the ship to arrive in Shanghai, and during that time Reed had taken a violent dislike to Linda Bishop. He was an ex-flyer, a soldier-of-fortune, no longer young, who had seen most things and been to most places. She was a journalist, young, cool, aggressive, daughter of a missionary, and she had no time for Reed, who didn't always shave and knew too much about China.

They had neither of them reckoned with the Japanese armies sitting outside the gates of the city. A war was about to erupt and not only Linda wanted to get out.

It was Reed, a man who drank too much, a hero, a cynic, who found himself in a rotting junk sailing up the Yangtze with a group of mixed refugees. And amongst them was Linda Bishop, whose ideas began to change as the Japanese armies moved closer.

0 552 13298 5

A SELECTED LIST OF FINE TITLES
AVAILABLE FROM CORGI BOOKS.